THROUGH
CLOUD
AND
SUNSHINE

THROUGH
CLOUD
AND
SUNSHINE

COME TO ZION

VOLUME 2

DEAN HUGHES

**DESERET
BOOK**

SALT LAKE CITY, UTAH

Library of Congress Cataloging-in-Publication Data

Hughes, Dean, 1943– author.
  Through cloud and sunshine / Dean Hughes.
    pages cm — (Come to Zion ; book 2)
  Sequel to: The winds and the waves.
  Includes bibliographical references.
  Summary: Will and Liz struggle to deal with their new life in Nauvoo, Illinois as they witness important events in the history of the Church of Jesus Christ of Latter-day Saints. Meanwhile Jeff and Abby, living in 21st century Nauvoo, face their own challenges as they learn about Jeff's ancestors.
  ISBN 978-1-60907-525-5 (hardbound : alk. paper)
  1. Mormon converts—Fiction. 2. Mormon pioneers—Fiction. 3. Religious fiction. I. Title. II. Series: Hughes, Dean, 1943– Come to Zion ; volume 2.
  PS3558.U36T48 2013
  813'.54—dc23   2013009217

Printed in the United States of America
Edwards Brothers Malloy, Ann Arbor, MI

10 9 8 7 6 5 4 3 2 1

For my grandson,
Robert Taliesin "Tal" Hughes

And for all the missionaries and dear friends
we came to love in Nauvoo

PREFACE

I often hear a complaint about novels that are published as a series. "By the time the second book comes out," readers say, "I can't remember what happened in the first one." I understand the problem, so let me provide some brief reminders of characters and plot elements, merely to get you started on this second volume.

The story in *The Winds and the Waves*, volume 1 of *Come to Zion*, starts with a portrayal of Will Lewis, the first son in a family of tenant farmers. He lives near Ledbury in Herefordshire, England. He longs to improve himself and escape his life of poverty at least in part because he's in love with Elizabeth (Liz) Duncan, a solicitor's daughter who attends the same church he does. Both families are part of the United Brethren who, in actual history, were converted in the late 1830s by Wilford Woodruff.

Will eventually finds his way to the LDS Church, marries Liz, and immigrates to Nauvoo, Illinois. The two experience some harsh realities, but they develop deeper faith as they travel on a sailing ship and then on a Mississippi riverboat. Liz struggles to leave her parents and her beloved sister Mary Ann, and realizes that in Nauvoo her life will be much more demanding, but she and Will have hopes for a satisfying future in Zion.

A contemporary story about a second Lewis family is interlaced with the first. Jeff Lewis, who is the fifth great-grandchild of Will Lewis, has lost his job in California. He is still in his first year of marriage to the former Abby Ramsey, originally from New Jersey. Jeff and Abby are offered an opportunity for free rent if they re-model a house in Nauvoo. As a young couple starting a life together, they struggle to know what their futures should be, but they like liv-ing in the historic city where Jeff's forebears once lived. When they learn that their unborn baby may have a heart defect, they pray and hope for the Lord's help.

Actually, I hope the stories are much more exciting than this summary would make them sound, but I hate to give away "every-thing" to readers who pick this book up first and still plan to go back and read the first volume.

The characters in the two Lewis families are fictional, but I have researched the era and tried to portray the setting and history as ac-curately as I can. If I have done my job, you should be able to "feel" and understand the conditions in England during the apostolic mis-sions and gain a deeper sense of the struggle to establish Zion in Nauvoo.

History is tricky. We tend to filter everything we learn about the past through the perceptions of our own time. Perhaps there's no way around that. But the Church of Jesus Christ of Latter-day Saints, in this early period, was in a process of growth, with doc-trines and policies continuing to be revealed. Modern Mormons are naturally surprised that practices and attitudes that have long been clarified were developing at the time, not set. As you read *Through Cloud and Sunshine,* try to comprehend the conditions of the time and the mindset of the early Saints.

The lists of commodities recommended by organizers of the pioneer migrations across the plains to the Great Basin invariably included coffee and tea. Not only did people in Nauvoo commonly use such hot drinks, but they sometimes drank wine or used tobacco. Contemporary Latter-day Saints must remember that the admonitions of the Word of Wisdom (see Doctrine and Covenants 89) were not given "by way of commandment," and were not considered binding for temple attendance until the early twentieth century.

When Patty Sessions visits the home of Liz Lewis in the novel that you are about to read, she places her hands on Liz's head and gives her a blessing. That may surprise modern readers. Such blessings by women were not uncommon in Nauvoo, and they were given through the power of prayer. When asked about this practice, Joseph Smith said, during a meeting of the Female Relief Society of Nauvoo on April 28, 1842, that "there could be no devils in it if God gave his sanction by healing" the people who were blessed in this way (Sheri Dew and Virginia H. Pearce, *The Beginning of Better Days* [2012], 104). It was always clear to Joseph Smith and other Church leaders that such blessings were performed by faith, and were not priesthood blessings. Latter-day Saints are now directed that only those who hold the priesthood should use the "laying on of hands," but many of the women of Nauvoo had great faith, and their prayers were certainly heard and answered, as Joseph Smith knew.

In 1843, in Ramus, Illinois, Orson Hyde preached a sermon in which he said that God and Jesus Christ could dwell in a person's heart. After the meeting, Joseph Smith told Apostle Hyde that he would correct some doctrinal mistakes from Hyde's morning speech. In Doctrine and Covenants 130, which contains Joseph's response, we learn that the idea that God and Christ could dwell in a man's heart is "an old sectarian notion, and is false" (v. 3).

Now, think about that. Our Primary children wouldn't make the same mistake. The Church had been organized thirteen years earlier and the First Vision had happened ten years before that. How could an Apostle not understand such a simple concept? If God and Jesus are separate and both have bodies, how could they "dwell" in anyone's heart? The only answer I know is that certain "sectarian notions" had long persisted among the Saints. The idea of the Holy Trinity was taught by Christians, both then and now, as a mystery. We see indications of three beings all through the scriptures, but in A.D. 325, at the Council of Nicaea, a decision was reached by vote that the three beings were miraculously one. That idea, along with the doctrine that God was a spiritual being, was certainly believed by most people who joined The Church of Jesus Christ of Latter-day Saints, and many must have clung to that way of thinking about the Godhead.

Confusion over the nature of God plays a part in this novel. When Joseph Smith delivered the King Follett Discourse in the spring of 1844, some members considered the sermon blasphemous. It was actually, as Joseph argued in the last sermon of his life a few weeks later, only a further extension of what he had long taught about the nature of God. For those who were still dubious about a God with a body, the idea that God had once been a man was entirely too much to accept. The doctrine was considered by some dissenters not only false but proof that Joseph was a fallen prophet.

Those who left the Church at that time, however, were especially opposed to the practice of plural marriage. To understand that, simply ask yourself how you would feel if you were now asked to live "the principle." The early Saints were often descendants of Puritans, and they lived in a world of Victorian morality. Most who heard of plural marriage for the first time were immediately shocked and often offended. Brigham Young, known widely for having many wives later on, recorded his response when he first heard the doctrine: "It was the first time in my life that I had desired the grave, and I could hardly get over it for a long time. And when I saw a funeral I felt to envy the corpse its situation, and to regret that I was not in the coffin" (quoted in Robert L Millet, Camille Fronk Olson, Andrew C. Skinner, and Brent L. Top, *LDS Beliefs* [2011], 494).

So don't be surprised when my characters find nothing but distaste for the practice when they learn of it. What you also may not realize is that in the beginning, plural marriage was taught privately to individuals, not publicly to the general Church membership. The first recorded revelation about the "new and everlasting covenant" of marriage, and about plural marriage, is contained in Doctrine and Covenants, section 132, written down in 1843, but Joseph had, according to his report, received revelations on the subject much earlier. He had been taught that monogamy was normally the will of the Lord, but that in certain eras, when commanded by God, individuals had been sanctioned to marry more than one wife—as we see in the scriptures (see 2 Samuel 12:7–8; Jacob 2:27, 30). Joseph Smith certainly knew what critics would say—and do—should this new Church announce such a doctrine, and so he followed God's direction and for a time taught it only to a small circle of Church leaders. It would not be publicly announced until 1852 by Brigham Young, then in the safety of the mountain west.

Rumors, of course, would spread in a town the size of Nauvoo, which meant that most people learned of plural marriage second hand, and needless to say, misunderstanding led to controversy. One man who fueled that controversy was John C. Bennett. Bennett had become both the mayor of Nauvoo and a member of the First Presidency of the Church, but his history, unknown to Joseph Smith, was that of a scoundrel. When it was discovered that he had been using a distorted version of the doctrine to seduce women, not to marry them, he was brought before the high council, where he begged for forgiveness. When it was learned, however, that he hadn't changed his ways, he was excommunicated, and that set him off on a campaign of lecturing and writing newspaper articles and a book, all "exposing" Joseph Smith and the Saints. He claimed that Joseph practiced "spiritual wifery," which was his name for his own seductive, illicit behavior.

The problem for Joseph Smith was that these accusations were untrue. He did not use the Lord's doctrine of plural marriage (Doctrine and Covenants 132) to commit illicit sexual acts. He had to deny Bennett's accusations, but that appeared to be a denial of plural marriage. The doctrine of the "true and everlasting covenant of marriage" was holy to him, sacred, and he was not sanctioned to announce plural marriage to the world. When evidence of such relationships among leaders of the Church mounted, however, dissenters and enemies used plural marriage as one of their justifications not only for murdering Joseph and Hyrum Smith, but for pressuring the Mormons to leave Illinois.

Joseph Smith wrote an essay on "Happiness" that was printed in his *History of the Church.* B. H. Roberts made corrections and added notes to the history and republished the seven volumes from 1902 to 1912. Roberts said that it was not known exactly when the essay was written, but he believed that it had reference to the practice of eternal and plural marriage. The following is a section from that essay:

> That which is wrong under one circumstance, may be, and often is, right under another. God said, "Thou shalt not kill"; at another time He said, "Thou shalt utterly destroy." This is the principle on which the government of heaven is conducted—by revelation adapted to the circumstances in which the children of the kingdom are placed. Whatever God requires is right, no matter what it is, although we may

not see the reason thereof till long after the events transpire. (Joseph Smith, *History of the Church*, 7 vols., ed. B. H. Roberts [1932–51], 5:135)

You will notice similar language in my fictionalized account of a conversation between my character Will Lewis and Joseph Smith. When I portray Joseph Smith or other Church leaders expressing specific doctrines or opinions, especially in meetings where notes were taken, I use their own words, or paraphrases of those words. These particular words explain the problem Joseph was up against. He knew the world would see plural marriage as wrong, but he also knew what he had been commanded to do. He was caught in the dilemma of having to keep plural marriage private and sacred at a time when rumors were making the practice seem lascivious.

So, in reading this novel, try to understand the time, the atmosphere, and the attitudes of the early members. See this story through their lenses, not strictly your own. We sometimes wish our history had no "difficulties," but we should all hope that when our own descendants try to understand us, they will be generous in their interpretation of our motivations and desires to do what is right.

CHAPTER 1

Will Lewis pulled off his cap and used a bandanna to wipe his face. Nauvoo was steamy this time of year—hotter than anything he had ever experienced in England. He had been sick with cholera back in May when he and his wife, Liz, had limped off a Mississippi riverboat, and he was still not back to his full strength. He got up early every morning and worked hard, but by afternoon he could feel himself wearing down. It was August now, 1842, and he had had some months to get used to such weather, but today was worse than usual.

Nauvoo was overgrown with corn, the stalks reaching much higher than Will's head and filling almost every patch of open ground. Will had been forced to plant his garden rather late, but his own corn was coming on strong. He had missed the chance to plant spring vegetables—peas and cabbage and the like—but his potato plants were now producing. His root crops—carrots, beets, parsnips, turnips, onions—were also surviving so far. Weeds were thriving too, and even though he had put in a hard morning plowing deep-rooted grass out on the prairie, he still needed to catch up on his hoeing in town.

Will stretched his back and was about to start hoeing again, but as he glanced past the house he saw a family—a man and woman and three small children—open the gate out front and walk into the yard. John Griggs, a neighbor, was with them, carrying a large travel trunk on his shoulder. He stopped near the house, grunted as he lowered the trunk to the ground, and then walked on toward Will. "What's this, Brother Lewis?" he called. "I'd heered you'd moved from this place."

Will took some careful steps as he worked his way out of the garden row. "We *have* moved, Brother Griggs," he said, shaking John's hand. "We're staying in our new place now, but I thought I'd keep this garden going and see what I could harvest from it—if everything doesn't burn up in the heat."

Brother Griggs laughed. "That's what I thought last year when we first come, but some plants like the heat. I never seen corn grow like it does here."

Will had never seen this kind of "corn" grow at all. What he had called corn in England was called wheat here, and this American "maize" wasn't anything he'd ever tried to raise. But Will's attention was drawn to the family standing behind John. "Are these folks planning to move into this old cabin?" he asked.

"We was thinkin' so. What's yer 'pinion? Will the roof hold out the weather one more winter?"

By then the man of the family had stepped up alongside Brother Griggs. He was a stubby fellow dressed in homespun trousers and a worn linen shirt that was stained yellow around the neck. He was maybe thirty years old and was built strong, with thick legs and arms. He had a heavy growth of whiskers. "Lewis, is it?" he asked.

"Aye. Will Lewis."

"Then ye're Welsh, the same as us."

"Back in time, we were. But I was raised in Herefordshire, in England, along the border of Wales."

"Johns is my name. Daniel Johns. And Welsh through and through, from Merthyr Tydfil."

"Are you only just come off the boat?"

"No. Not at all. We been here half a hour, maybe more." He grinned.

Will laughed and then shook hands with Sister Johns and greeted the children. "My wife and I lived in this shack when we first got here," he told Brother and Sister Johns. "The family that owns the lot would be happy to sell it—so if you find it a good place to put down roots, you could purchase the land and build a better house right here."

"But you chose not to do that yerself?"

"No. We picked out a lot up this hill to the east, on top of the bluffs."

"I cannot say what we might do in time," Brother Johns said. "For now, we need someplace to lay our heads for the winter."

"You can get by in this old cabin for a time. But before snow flies, there's plenty to 'fix up,' as people say here. If you can purchase yourself a lot and start felling trees—or buy timber—folks will help you raise a good log house. That's what they did for us."

"It's that 'purchase' part I cannot manage just yet," Brother Johns said. "This shanty will have to do until I find work and can save some money."

Will nodded. He was still holding the brim of his cap in one hand. He wiped his face again. "I'll tell you what. If you want to help me tend to this garden, we can share what comes of it. That will help you get through the winter. And Sister Johns, if you can learn to make cornbread—and even more, if you can learn to eat

4 · DEAN HUGHES

the stuff—I'll turn this stand of maize over to you. I'm raising a fair crop at the Big Field outside town. I'll have enough to grind for our own needs."

Sister Johns nodded, but she looked so weary, Will wondered whether she had heard what he had said.

"I wish we'd ha' come when you come," Brother Johns said. "Brother Griggs was tellin' me 'bout that farm. He says ever'one can plant there, if they like. But I know nothin' 'bout farmin' at all. I been a coal miner since I was a lad, nine years old."

"I can help a little, Brother Johns. I can plow some ground for you out there so it will be ready to plant next year."

Brother Griggs said, "Will bought hisself four yoke o' oxen. He plows ground for people who wants to open up them prairie lands."

"Six teams, now," Will said. "I had to buy two more. That heavy grass wears down oxen faster than I ever would ha' thought. I plow with three teams and change off, or sometimes use six yoke, all together."

"How much do you charge for that, Brother Lewis?" Brother Johns asked.

"Well . . . two dollars an acre. But if you don't have it, you can pay me later. We all try to help new folks get started."

"Thank you, Brother Lewis," Sister Johns said. "Those is the most hopeful words we've heard so far."

Sister Johns was short, like her husband, but she was pale and thin, the skin of her face drawn tight over her cheekbones. She had some missing teeth in front, and the teeth that were left were mostly brown and broken. She was probably around the age of her husband, but she looked older. She was holding a baby who was just as thin.

"Did you have a hard crossing?" Will asked.

"I cannot think how we ever come through alive," she said. "Li'l

Peter and me, we was the worst, but all of us puked up more'n we ever held down." A little boy, about four, was standing close to Sister Johns on one side, and a younger girl on the other. Both of them looked too weary to stand up much longer.

"Do you have bedding and dishes and—"

"We do," Brother Johns said. "We ain't quite so bad off as we look just now. An' I can labor twelve hours a day. If someone will give me a chance, I'll prove myself."

Will didn't want to tell Brother Johns how few jobs were available in Nauvoo. It was a matter of everyone scratching out a living however they could. But Will said, "For now, get some rest. It won't be long 'til you can start cutting this corn. My wife and I don't have much ourselves just yet, but we can spare a little food to help you get by—and Brother Griggs and I will let your neighbors know that you need help until you—"

"I don't want a handout," Brother Johns said. "I on'y need work."

Will wondered whether he should offer Brother Johns a job. He had his farm at the Big Field to look after, and he plowed for other men, and he had begun to cut roads. He had used the skills he had learned grading railroad beds in England to make a man a good road. That job had led to an offer from a Hancock County official. Will was now cutting eight miles of new public road, with more roads promised him as soon as he could get to them. So he actually needed some help. The problem was, he was trying to get money ahead for the brick house he hoped to build next season, and he also wanted to buy a farm of his own.

Will had his dreams. He wanted that farm, but also a fine house in town, and he wanted Liz to have rugs on the floor, fancy furniture, even a pianoforte—everything she had once had in Ledbury. But getting started had been more expensive than he had expected.

He had bought a building lot in timbered land on the bluff, so he hadn't had to buy logs, but he had purchased window sashes and doors, and shingles for the roof. He had also had to buy a strong plow with an iron share—to turn the prairie sod—and he had needed tools. There had been a well to dig and to outfit, and the groundwater was so full of lime, he already knew he needed a cistern to collect and store rainwater. He had bought a cow and had penned it in with a makeshift fence, but he needed to build a cowshed and a good corral. The cow—along with a churn and butter molds—had all cost money, and so had a pregnant Berkshire sow and a flock of chickens. The money Liz's father had given her was gone now, spent on the oxen, and most of his own savings were spent besides.

He certainly could have used a hired man, but paying Brother Johns would cut into Will's profit, and he knew only one way to get ahead. He needed to use his own strong back to earn and save every dollar he could. The roadwork had been helpful because the pay was in cash—a rare thing in Hancock County—but the plowing for farmers usually paid out in a few bags of grain, or maybe some chickens. People starting out were like Brother Johns. They needed to prepare land for farming, but they had no cash and sometimes nothing to trade. They all intended to pay him in time, but Will wondered how he could ever accomplish his plans if he didn't get something in his hand more often—and more quickly—for the work he had already done.

So Will didn't offer work to Brother Johns. It was Brother Griggs who said, "Let me do some askin' about. The Law brothers is openin' up a gristmill and a sawmill, and they might be lookin' to hire some men."

"And I'll help you repair that roof," Will said.

"Just show me what needs to be done and I'll take it on myself."

Will nodded. He wiped his face again, and then he handed the hoe to Brother Johns. "I'll let you take over this garden," he said. "But I'd recommend you not hoe until morning. Get out of this heat until then."

"Is it always this hot?" Sister Johns asked. She used her sleeve to wipe sweat from her face.

"No," Brother Griggs said. "In winter, it's so cold your nose freezes shut when you take a deep breath." He laughed. "So just take an average, summer and winter, and it all evens out."

Brother Johns did laugh a little, but Sister Johns looked down at her baby as if to say, "I'm sorry, little one, that I brought you into this."

"Sister Johns," Will said, "it's Zion. It's more work than I ever imagined, but it's worth it. In ten years it will be the finest place in the world to live."

"I know. It's what we keep sayin'. But I didn't know what it was like to cross a ocean."

Will patted her on the shoulder. "I know," he said. "But it's behind us now. We have to look ahead, not back."

She was nodding, and so was Brother Johns, but Will knew it would take them a while before they stopped wondering whether they should have stayed in Wales. And there were harder things to deal with than the weather and the poverty. Will wondered whether anyone had told them that Joseph Smith was hiding out these days and they may not see him for a time. Lilburn Boggs, the former governor of Missouri, had survived a pistol wound in May, and he had accused Joseph Smith of ordering Orrin Porter Rockwell, a fellow Mormon, to pull the trigger. Governor Carlin of Illinois had agreed to an extradition order, and Joseph had been arrested. Only a judgment in Joseph's favor in the Nauvoo Municipal Court had delayed his being hauled back to Missouri. But he was being sought again, and the fact was, Joseph didn't dare allow himself to be taken. He knew that he would be murdered in Missouri.

There were also other problems that worried Will just as much. John C. Bennett, who had served as a counselor in the First Presidency to Joseph Smith and also as mayor of Nauvoo, had been accused of immoral behavior and had been excommunicated from the Church. But since then he had been writing letters to newspapers "exposing" Joseph Smith as the "King of Impostors."

Will believed that all of Bennett's claims were outright lies, but he knew the effect the man's accusations were having on people across the country, especially in Hancock County. He had seen plenty of animosity as he dealt with local citizens. There were now around five thousand Mormons in Nauvoo, and the influx of immigrants was shifting the balance of power. Such rapid change was both angering and frightening to those who had lived in the county before the Saints had begun to settle in the area.

Will wasn't happy with the attitude of some of the Saints, either. There were always rumors being passed around the city, and some of them were critical of Joseph Smith. Life was hard here, and some people were doubting that they had been wise in coming.

Will did want a house and a farm. But more than that, he wanted to live with a people who followed Jesus Christ. He told himself every day not to listen to rumors, not to worry what John Bennett and a few others had to say, but to keep his eyes on the reason he had brought Liz to live in Zion. She was expecting a baby in October, and he wanted their child—and all the children they would have—to be raised among the Saints.

"Brother Griggs tells us there's been a good deal of sickness here," Sister Johns said. She looked at her baby again, and Will knew what she was thinking.

Will tried to think what to do. He had his dreams, but he also wanted this new family to feel what Zion could be. He hoped they wouldn't be too disappointed by some of the difficulties they would face. Some Saints had already moved away, disillusioned. He hesitated, wondering whether he would regret his words, but then said, "Brother Johns, I could use some help some days. It's hard to plow with so many oxen—keep the rows straight and scour the blade as I go. If you can't find any better work, I could pay you a dollar a day to labor with me. I'm thinking I could get more acres finished in a day and come out just as well."

"That would be fine indeed, Brother Lewis," Brother Johns said. "And I'd learn somethin' about farmin' at the same time."

"Aye. No question."

But Will was watching Sister Johns, whose eyes had filled with tears. "Thank you. Oh, thank you," she was saying. What Will couldn't push away entirely, however, was his concern that the wages he paid someone else might actually set his own plans back. The house he wanted to build was already seeming less of a possibility for the coming year.

• • •

Liz Lewis had walked out to "get a little air," but she hadn't lasted long. The temperature in the house was oppressive, but the outside air was worse. There was not even a breeze to stir the leaves on the trees. Her baby was squirming inside her, as though too hot itself, and that made her wonder how she could hold out for two more months. She was not sleeping well. In England temperatures always cooled at night, and she could snuggle down in her bed. But the heat in Nauvoo persisted all night, and her body seemed a furnace. She had tried to find good positions for sleeping, but she simply never felt comfortable. She knew she kept Will awake with all her turning and shifting. The truth was, she resented him a little when he did sleep, no matter how hard he worked every day. But all that was part of the crossness she was feeling lately.

Liz sat on one of the straight-backed chairs Will had brought home that summer. They were someone's castoffs, but of pretty good quality, and Will had repaired the broken rungs. He kept saying he wanted to buy better furniture now that they were in their new cabin, but Liz knew it bothered him to spend anything right now. He had promised her father that she wouldn't have to live in a log cabin very long. Sometimes she thought Will worried more about that promise than he worried about her—and was much too stubborn for his own good. She tried to remind herself that he was never lazy, that he would always work hard to provide for her, but she still wished he would work fewer hours and come home to her more often.

Liz actually knew that she should be pleased that she and Will had come as far as they had in such a short time. Will had prepared a few logs even when he was still weak, but then their neighbor, Warren Baugh, had gathered a group of Church brothers and they had finished felling a good number of white oaks. A week later, some of the same men had returned and raised the cabin in a single day. It was a "block house," made of hewn logs, squared to give the outside of the house a flat surface. Will hadn't plastered the house yet, but it was one of the things he soon planned to do—or at least he kept saying that he would. What he had done was put down split-log puncheon floors so that Liz wasn't walking on dirt. The thick walls were well chinked, and Will had bought and installed sashes with glass windows. The house had two rooms: a large living area, sixteen by sixteen feet, with a fireplace and a dry sink, and also a separate bedroom. That was more than most newcomers had, but then, the builders had followed Will's plan.

The house was not as hot as the badly chinked shack they had lived in on Partridge Street, but that was hard to remember on a day like this when the humid air seemed to penetrate the walls. It didn't help that Liz was carrying an extra layer of fat. When she had first arrived in Nauvoo, she had talked to Patty Sessions, a midwife, who had told her she was too thin—and that wasn't good for the baby. Liz had made up for that since then, but she felt ugly when she looked in her little mirror and saw her rounded cheeks. She had always been told how pretty she was, with her dark hair and pale green eyes. She knew it was vain to worry about her looks, but in truth, she hated to think that her beauty would wear out here amid all her work, and with the birth of more children.

Liz had been telling herself that she would soon have to cook something for dinner, but she kept putting off building a fire. And then, to her surprise, Will walked into the house. She had expected him to work in the garden much longer. He had left very early that morning, but he had returned to the house not long after noon and said that his oxen simply couldn't keep working in the heat. He had decided to let them rest in the shade at the farm where he boarded them while he caught up on his garden.

"Too hot for oxen, but not for you?" Liz had asked him.

But he had responded the way he always did. "I can't just sit here all afternoon. There's too much to do."

That wouldn't have been so bad if he hadn't stepped through the door just when she was sitting down. She stood now and said, "I was just going to start a fire. But you don't want to eat already, do you?"

"No. I'm leaving again. Brother Lancaster promised to pay me for the plowing I did for him last month. I need to walk out to his place and see what I can get from him."

"Walk out there in this heat?"

"Not to the farm. Just to his place on the east edge of town."

"Couldn't you rest a little, just once, and—"

"Certainly. And I will one of these days." He smiled at her. "But I've wanted to get that money for the last fortnight and I haven't found time to call on him."

Liz gave up. Will would rest someday, all right—when he was in his grave. She worried sometimes that he would reach that grave way too early. "When should I plan to have supper ready?"

"There's no hurry. Don't even think about starting a fire in the house. If we need to cook something, I'll build a fire outside when I get back."

Now she was a little ashamed for the resentment she had been feeling. He was such a gentle, good man—and he was looking very handsome with his good-hearted smile and his face so browned from the sun.

"Why cook anything?" Will asked. "Don't we have some bread and butter we can eat? That's all I need—that and a gallon of cold water."

"Did you bring anything fresh-picked from the garden?"

"I should have pulled a few carrots and parsnips, but there's a new family down there, and they need the food more than we do." She watched him look down at the floor. She could always guess when he thought he'd let her down. "A Welsh family named Johns are going to stay in that old shack. They look like ghosts, all of them, worn down about as bad as anyone I've seen get off the boat."

"Other than you, you mean?"

"Maybe. But I didn't look at me."

"I did."

Will nodded. "I told Brother Johns he could keep up the garden and I would help him, and then we'd share the pickings. I know you were expecting to have a root crop to store for the winter, but I don't know how I can haul everything back here right in front of their noses—when they hardly have anything to get by on."

Liz understood that. She would have done the same thing, she was sure, and she was glad Will thought that way. "That's fine," she said. "But we need to think about winter. We have pigs to slaughter, but we can't live on pork and cornbread."

"I know. I thought about that when I was walking up here. That's why I'm calling on Lancaster. If he'll pay me, I can buy enough beans and wheat flour to get us through."

She nodded. She was well aware that many people had less than she did. But she didn't like cornbread, and Will hadn't planted wheat this season. If Brother Lancaster didn't pay them, and they couldn't buy wheat flour, she hated to think how long the winter would drag on.

"Lie down for a while, Liz. You look tired."

Liz didn't need to be told how awful she looked. "I'll lie down when you do," she said, hearing the crossness return to her voice. She even saw Will cringe, as if to say, "Uh-oh. I just said the wrong thing." And then he cleared out.

Liz was sorry. She told herself that when he came back she needed to tell him that she appreciated his hard work. But for now, she could only think of what she had just lost. She had helped Will sow that garden, and she had hoed weeds when she was in no condition for such work. Now everything was probably gone—or at least split in half. She had counted on having those potatoes for the winter.

• • •

Will was worried about Liz. She *didn't* look well, and she was hard to please lately. Though his own mother had gone through lots of pregnancies, Will didn't remember her ever being quite so peevish. That only led him to his most pervasive thought: he had taken Liz away from a life of luxury and ease, and she was holding up surprisingly well. She was working hard, and she never complained about the load she carried. His solution was always the same. He needed to earn more money. He needed to buy bricks. He needed to build a house with thick walls. In time, he wanted to hire a young woman to do some of the cooking and housecleaning. He knew that he was cheating Liz every time he plowed a man's field and then let him off without paying. This was their business venture—the one Joseph Smith had recommended to him—but it wasn't a business at all if he ended up wearing out his oxen and receiving nothing for his work.

Will walked out Mulholland Street to the east end of town. This was the main thoroughfare of the upper part of Nauvoo, but today no wagons were passing through. There were not even any children playing outside the log houses. He turned north and passed Hyrum Smith's farm, and he did glimpse, in a pond at the bottom of a gully, a little band of naked boys splashing in the water.

He had been to Marcus Lancaster's house once before to ask about the money, but Brother Lancaster had said at the time that he didn't have any cash, that he would try to pay Will next month. Well, it was "next month" now, and Will wasn't leaving until he received at least partial payment—if not in cash, in something Will could use for barter.

Brother Lancaster worked with leather. He and his sons did some tanning and some harness repair—that sort of thing—in a log shed out back of his house. When Will reached the Lancaster place, he walked to the shed, but he found no one there, so he came back around the house and knocked on the front door. When the door opened, Brother Lancaster was standing in front of him in his shirt-sleeves. "Oh, Brother Lewis," he said. Will heard the uneasiness in his voice.

"I was just wondering," Will said, "if I could get what you owe me today. I need at least some of it."

Brother Lancaster stepped outside and shut the door behind him. He was a tall man, big in the chest, but he had a face like a bookkeeper—thoughtful and serious. "Shor is hot," he said. "You ever seen it this hot before?"

"This is my first summer here, but no, I don't think so. I guess yesterday was about as bad."

"I think it's even worse today."

Will hadn't come to talk about the weather, and he could pretty well guess what all this was leading to. But he had been preparing his arguments all the way out here. "You said last month you could pay me by now. I'm trying get some supplies put away before winter, and I need some ready cash."

"Who do you know who pays ready cash?" Brother Lancaster asked. His voice sounded tight now, as though he were annoyed that Will would suggest such a thing.

Will drew in some breath and said calmly, "You hired me for two dollars an acre, Brother Lancaster, and I plowed twenty acres for you. That's forty dollars you owe me. I can't carry that much on credit. If I do that for everyone, I'll be broke and my oxen will be dead."

"Then I'll tell you what. Go around to all the men in town who owe money to me, and get a few dollars from each one of 'em. I'm up against the same problem. I've done a lot of work this year—and how much do I have to show for it?"

Will looked down at his own worn boots, and noticed at the same time that Lancaster's boots looked new. He had also caught a glimpse inside the house and seen that Sister Lancaster had nice furniture: a set of overstuffed chairs and an oak cabinet. He suspected that Brother Lancaster hadn't invited him in for exactly that reason—that he didn't want Will to see how well he lived. "But Marcus," Will persisted, "I didn't do 'a few dollars' worth' of work for you. I was out there the better part of a month, and I was pushing my oxen just as many hours as they could take. You agreed to the price. You never said once that you wouldn't be able to pay me."

"I will pay you. As soon as I can. That's all I can tell you."

"You must have some tanned hides you could give me—or something I could turn into a little cash. I would even take Nauvoo scrip."

"If I had something, I'd give it to you." He put his hands on his hips. "You don't sound much like a brother in the gospel to me, Will, staring me in the eye like that, telling me what I've *got* to do— and *when* I've got to do it."

"I thought a brother in the gospel kept his promises. Did I get that wrong?"

"I'm sorry, but I'm going to have to ask you to get off my property. You can't talk to me that way. You opened that land for me, and I appreciate it. But I won't be planting until next spring. When I see a harvest from it, I can pay you then."

"So you're telling me to wait a year before I see one penny from all the work I did for you. Is that it?"

Will realized that he had moved in a little too close to Brother Lancaster, and the man took a step back. "Will, that's enough. I'll pay you something this year if I can. But you have to be reasonable, and—"

"Reasonable? I need to live *now*. I've got a baby coming—"

"And I've got a whole houseful of children to feed—grown boys who can eat more than you and me put together. I've given you my answer, and if you don't like it, take me to bishop's court. But the bishop will tell you just what I did. We're all brothers in the gospel and we have to move ahead together as best we can."

Will stepped back. He took another breath. He knew he didn't want to go before his bishop and report that he had knocked a brother down—and he was feeling close to doing just that. He took another few seconds to collect himself, and then he said, "Brother Lancaster, a boat came in this morning. Some Church members named Johns arrived, and they had a little bedding and a few pots and pans—but mostly they had *nothing*. They took over that old cabin Liz and I lived in at first, and I told them they could have half of what they harvest from the garden I planted. I told Brother Johns I could give him a little work. When people are destitute, we have to stand with them and help them every way we can. But it's different to live the way you do, and to hire me to do your work and not give me a farthing for it—and then tell me I'm not a good brother in the gospel because I expect to get paid before a whole year has gone by."

"Will, there's nothing more to say. I can't pay you right now."

"All right, then. You're a religious man. Go back in your house and kneel down and tell the Lord that that's how you plan to operate. If you feel all right about yourself after you've done that, let me know."

"I can pray just fine. I'm an honest man, and I've been honest with you. I think you're the one who needs to do some praying— and repenting."

Will came close. His fist doubled and he brought his arm back. But he didn't swing. He slowly dropped his arm, and then he turned and walked away. But all the way back to his pregnant wife, he tried to convince himself that he was a good enough man to live in Zion—without knocking down some of his brothers. And he tried to think how he was ever going to build Liz a house if he couldn't get paid for his work.

CHAPTER 2

Abby Lewis shut her eyes and took a long breath. She was exhausted from her labor, which had lasted all day, but now fear was setting in. The pain had finally ended, and she had heard the baby cry—and that was a relief to her—but the delivery room had filled up with people in scrubs or white coats as the birth had neared. Abby had the feeling that all these nurses and doctors were ready to grab her baby and run, but she wanted to see him first. When she raised her head to see what was happening, she saw a nurse carrying him across the room. Abby was about to protest when she heard Dr. Hunt's voice. "Just a minute, Abby. We need to check a couple of things, and then we'll let you see him."

Abby looked at Jeff, who was still holding her hand. "Did he look all right?" she asked.

"I think so. I didn't get a really good look at him."

"New babies are kind of purple," Dr. Hunt said, and he laughed, "but your little boy looked fine. "He's not very big at this point, but you knew that."

For months now Dr. Hunt, the pediatric cardiologist, had been telling her that something was wrong with the baby's heart, but Abby and Jeff had been praying every day. She wanted to believe that everything was all right now.

A nurse was saying from across the room, "We'll bring him to you. Just give us another minute."

Abby looked toward the voice and saw a little huddle of people in plum-colored scrubs. The baby wasn't crying now, and that made her nervous. What if his heart suddenly stopped and she never got a chance to hold him while he was still alive?

Jeff was wiping the sweat from Abby's face with a damp cloth. He leaned down and kissed her gently. "Thank you," he said. "I'm sorry you had to go through all this."

She knew what he meant. He had been there the whole time, watching her struggle with the pain and effort, but she was struck with how little a man really understood. All that was behind her now. What she needed was her baby.

At last the nurse was coming. "What's his name?" she asked as she stepped to the bed.

"Moriancumr," Jeff said, and he laughed.

"What?"

"Not really. It's just our little joke. We haven't decided on a name yet."

Abby was reaching for the baby. He was already wrapped in a blanket, and she didn't want that. She wanted to see his body, see if he looked all right. She wanted to sit up and hold him, but she was still in the stirrups, and the doctor was down there stitching her, she supposed—with way too many people looking at her. Still, she held her little boy, and she looked at his wonderful little face. His nose was flat, his cheeks puffy, his eyes closed, but he was beautiful, with pretty little lips and an earnest look about him. He was like Jeff, she thought. So sweet. So little and sweet. She opened the blanket to look at his arms and hands, his skinny little legs—like a frog's—which he began to kick about. She knew that new babies had fingernails, but she was still sort of astounded to see all the detail of his body, how perfect it all was.

"He's all right, Jeff," she said. "I can tell he's all right. I don't think *anything* is wrong with him. You blessed him, and he's perfect now."

"He does *look* okay," Jeff said. "He's beautiful."

"Watch how he grabs my finger. He's strong."

Jeff laughed. "That's my boy."

But Dr. Hunt was standing next to Jeff by then. "We need to take him," he said. "We'll do the echocardiogram and then bring him back to you."

"How long?" Abby asked.

"The better part of an hour, I'd say. We need to do some tests, and we need to make sure we get a good image so we can tell you what the options are. But if surgery is necessary, it will be at least a couple of days before we do it. So you'll have plenty of time with him."

Abby wrapped up her baby again, and then she held him close to her chest and placed her cheek on his warm little head. She didn't want to let him go. When she did, she handed him to Jeff, not the doctor, and she said, "Hug him, Jeff. He needs to know who his daddy is before all these doctors start poking at him."

It was disheartening to think that the first things he would experience in this world were hard tables, machines, and needles. Her impulse was to grab him back and tell everyone to leave her son alone. She would take care of him, and his heart would be not only strong but pure.

• • •

Jeff was standing a few steps into the parking lot in back of the hospital—Blessing Hospital, in Quincy, Illinois. He had gone outside to get better reception on his cell phone. The sun was already down, and the air was bitterly cold. It was his mother who answered the phone at home in Las Vegas. "Has the baby come?" she asked without even saying hello.

"Yes. And he seemed all right. They took him away to check him out, so I'll know more in a little while."

"Is Abby doing okay?"

"She's kind of upset. She keeps telling me she's sure that he's all right. But I think she's scared."

"We're all scared, Jeff. If they have to operate, when will they do it?"

Jeff heard a change in the background sound and knew another phone had been picked up. "Is that you, Dad?" he asked.

"Yes. What's your doctor saying?"

"He's going to tell us what's going on in an hour or so."

"Should I come out?" his mother asked.

"No. Not yet. He'll be in the hospital quite a while if they operate, and besides, Abby's mom keeps saying she wants to come. Abby would rather have you, if you want to know the truth, but how is she supposed to tell her mother that?"

"Well, just know, I'm ready if you need me."

"I know that, Mom. Thanks." Jeff hadn't brought a coat outside with him, and it was a cold January day. He tightened his arms to his chest as best he could while still holding the phone to his ear.

"Have you picked out a name yet?" Dad asked. "I wanted to submit his name to the temple, and didn't know what to write down."

"I call him Mahonri Moriancumr—just to get Abby's goat—but

she keeps coming up with Kadin and Macon and all these 'with-it' names that I hate."

"What about William?" Dad asked.

A big pickup truck, black and rumbling, was passing Jeff. He stepped back to the sidewalk and waited for the noise to quiet. "Why William?"

"After your great-great-great Grandfather Lewis. You know, because of the Nauvoo connection."

"'William' sounds a little too formal to me, and I don't think I want to call him Bill."

"Grandfather Lewis was always known as 'Will.' My aunt Mary told me that."

"Does she know a lot about him? I haven't come up with much information about him out here."

"She has a life history that he wrote. It's in his own handwriting. I've never seen it, but—"

"Could I get a copy?"

"Probably. She told me a while back that she was typing out a transcript for the family, but she's never mentioned it again. I don't know if she finished it or not."

"Tell her I'd like to have a copy of whatever she has so far."

"Okay. I'll call her."

Will was still thinking about the name. "Actually, 'Will' sounds good to me. I'll see what Abby thinks."

"Honey, first things first," Mom said. "Don't bother Abby with that right now. Go take care of her. And then call us the minute you know anything."

"All right." Jeff was starting to shiver. "I'm standing outside, freezing—and I *do* need to get back to Abby. But I'll call as soon as I can."

"We're fasting," his father said. "Your mom called me right after you called and said you were heading for the hospital. I came home so I could start our fast immediately. Julie and Cassi started when they got home from school too—and we called Rachel, up in Provo. She's joining in. We're all praying—and waiting. And we do feel like things will work out okay."

"Thanks," Jeff said. Suddenly he was choking up. It hadn't occurred to him until that moment how exhausted he was, how tense. He had been awake since two that morning. What he wished was that his parents were not so far away.

Jeff took the elevator back upstairs and then waited outside Abby's room until a nurse and an orderly finally wheeled her in. It had been almost an hour since the team had taken the baby away. Jeff sat down next to Abby's bed and took her hand again. He told her about the phone calls he had made to her parents and to his, and they talked a little about that, but gradually they quieted as time continued to pass and their unexpressed nervousness mounted.

"Jeff, you felt what I did, didn't you? I think his heart is fine."

Jeff didn't know what to say.

"Didn't you feel it?" she asked again, and she turned her head on the pillow to look at him. Jeff saw the innocence in her face, her round brown eyes, childlike, and hints of her dimples showing, as though she wanted to smile and couldn't quite manage it.

"Honey, I'm not sure. He looked great. But we know *something* was wrong. I don't know if it would just go away, or—"

"You *blessed* him. God *took* it away."

Jeff nodded, but he looked past Abby. He couldn't bring himself to make any promises, and he felt ashamed that he couldn't give her what she needed at the moment. Still, he also knew how devastated she would be if he promised her that the baby was all right and then Dr. Hunt came in with a different story. "I do believe God knows what's happening. He cares about us and He cares about the baby. I just try to trust in that."

That was painfully neutral, and Jeff knew it. But for once in his life he decided it was better not to say anything more. It was not the right time to discuss the whole matter of faith and blessings again. They had done that too many times these last few weeks. So they waited, and Jeff heard every squeaky nurse's step on the hallway floor outside, every muted voice. The smell of the place was all around him: the scent of laundered sheets and something antiseptic, like hand sanitizer—clean but vaguely unpleasant. The truth was, the tests were apparently taking longer than expected, and that couldn't be good. Jeff felt more emptiness than faith.

When Dr. Hunt finally did come in, Jeff watched his face and saw that he wasn't about to say, "Everything is just fine." He stood with his legs spread wide apart and a clipboard clamped in his arms in front of him. He was still wearing his green scrubs, with his mask hanging around his neck. "This is a tricky one," he said.

Jeff glanced at Abby and saw her eyes fill with tears.

"I'm going to meet with some other cardiologists and we're going to try to figure this out. We're dealing with coarctation, or narrowing, of the aorta, along with atrial septal defect—what you'll hear people refer to as a 'hole in the heart.' But there are some other things going on. The left ventricle isn't well developed, and yet, it doesn't look like hypoplastic left heart syndrome. I think we—"

"Dr. Hunt, I don't know what you're saying. How bad is it?"

"I'm sorry, Abby," Dr. Hunt said. He took hold of her right hand. Jeff was still holding her left one. "It's all so hard to explain without—you know—using that kind of terminology."

"Is he going to live?"

"I think so. I really do. But I can't promise you that, Abby."

Jeff stood up. "You talked about one procedure that involved three operations. Is that what you're thinking you'll have to do?"

"Maybe. I don't know yet. It might be that we could repair the aorta and the increased blood supply would expand the left ventricle. But the hole is quite large. One of my colleagues thinks we should go in one time—open heart—and fix the aorta and the ASD, and do what's called biventricular repair. We're seeing—"

"When will you know?" Jeff asked. He was still watching Abby. He could see that she wasn't doing well. Her eyes were full of panic.

"We don't have to operate for a few days. I want to send our pictures to a couple of pediatric cardiologists I know—and get some more opinions. The one thing I can say for sure is that we *must* do surgery."

Abby was breaking down, finally crying. "I'm sorry. I'm sorry," she said. "I'm just so scared."

Dr. Hunt leaned over her. "I know, Abby. I didn't want to keep you waiting any longer, but I knew when I headed up here that I wasn't really ready. I need to confer with other surgeons and make sure we identify the best possible approach."

"When can you tell us what you're going to do?"

"I won't just *tell* you. I'll give you the options and offer a recommendation."

"When?"

"Today is Tuesday. I'll schedule the OR for Friday. Today and tomorrow I'll confer with my colleagues, and then on Thursday I'll show you the echocardiogram pictures and I'll bring in some charts that explain the way the heart works. We'll make a decision then—day after tomorrow."

"We'll get online and do some reading about all this stuff," Jeff said. "I want to understand everything I can, and I'm sure Abby does too."

"That sounds good." Dr. Hunt nodded, stood for a time, and then added, "I know you kids are religious. I just want you to know that I am too. I'll spend these next two days thinking and talking with smart people, but I'll also be praying—the same as you. We'll find the right answer, and I promise I'll do everything I can to save this little boy's life." He smiled. "You better come up with a name soon, so we'll know what to call him besides 'baby boy.'"

"I'm thinking we might want to name him 'William' and call him 'Will,' if it's okay with Abby." He looked at Abby, who was staring at him. "You know, after my Grandfather William Lewis. I found out just now that he was always called Will."

"When did you—"

"When I talked to my dad. He was the one who came up with the name, and it seemed right to me—since we live across the street from my grandpa's house."

Abby looked at Dr. Hunt. "Well, then, I guess his name is William." She smiled just a little. "It's okay with me. I don't mind the name."

"I like it," Dr. Hunt said. "I like the old names myself. I'm not too big on all these made-up names people are coming up with these days."

Jeff smiled at Abby, but he knew better than to list some of the names she had been thinking of. Abby didn't admit to anything. She told Dr. Hunt instead, "What matters to me is that he grows up."

"I know. I promise to do my best. And I have a good feeling, Abby. I do. I think we can fix that little heart of his."

"Thank you, Doctor. I needed you to say that."

"All right, then. I want you to stay in the hospital until Thursday. You'll want to be nearby anyway, and you need a full day of rest. But I promise, by then we'll be able to sit down and talk about the options."

"Okay."

"I'm sorry about all the medical jargon. I understand what you're going through right now." He patted her on the shoulder.

"It's okay. I have a lot of faith in you."

"Just put your faith in God. And pray for me."

"I will."

He patted her shoulder again, nodded to Jeff, and then he left.

As he walked out, Jeff asked Abby, "Are you sure you like 'William' for a name?"

"It's okay. You like it, and your dad does, and I'm sure my parents will like it a lot better than Kadin. My mom almost died when I told her that was the name I liked."

"But if you—"

"No. It's good to give him a family name. Maybe Grandpa Lewis will look out for him."

"Well, we need to think about it some more. We don't have to decide right now." But Abby seemed far away in her thoughts, not really concerned with the name. "I'm glad Dr. Hunt prays," Jeff said. "That made me feel a lot better."

"Me too. But just tell me—what are *you* feeling? Dr. Hunt said he had a good feeling about things. Don't you?"

"Abby, it's hard for me to know what to say. I do feel positive about Dr. Hunt, and I do feel like everything will come out okay. But I can't say that I've had any particular reassurance—you know, anything spiritual. You wanted to believe that nothing was wrong with his heart, but I couldn't say that. I just didn't know."

"And you were right. There *was* something wrong."

Jeff heard her frustration. She didn't say it, but he knew she wanted him to command the baby to be well, and he simply hadn't been able to get those words out. "I wasn't right, exactly. I didn't know what to expect."

"Jeff, I just don't want you to be so *logical* about everything. You're praying, too, aren't you?"

"I am, Ab. Constantly."

"Well, that's what I want to trust in. The Lord can heal him. We need to believe that."

"I do, Abby. Don't think that I don't." But he knew what she wanted from him. It was what he wanted to give her: more strength, more conviction. The problem was, he still felt no assurance that everything *would* turn out all right. And he wasn't going to lie to her about that.

• • •

On Thursday morning Abby was in the process of being released from the hospital. She got dressed and then sat down to wait for Dr. Hunt to come by with his pictures and diagrams. Jeff had sat by her bed with his laptop much of the day Wednesday, and he had explained a lot of biology and anatomy that Abby had thought she already knew—but he added a myriad of details about defects and surgical repairs. She asked him a few times not to tell her any more. What she read between the lines—and what she knew he was withholding—was that some defects were just too severe to be repaired.

When Dr. Hunt arrived, he asked Jeff and Abby to walk down the hallway to a little office. Jeff was armed with a dozen questions, and when they reached the office, he leaned over the desk and the diagrams with Dr. Hunt. The discussion turned technical and detailed. Abby understood what the two were talking about, but she didn't want to wade through all the possibilities. She wanted to know what Dr. Hunt was recommending. Abby was still embarrassed by her emotional responses on Tuesday, so she didn't interrupt the conversation.

What Abby was wondering was whether her attempts at faith

had really been misplaced hope. She was well aware that God's intentions couldn't be overruled by sheer stubbornness. Still, she wished Jeff would show more evidence that he trusted God. Most of what he had said for two days was science-based. He hardly seemed aware of what she was going through, even though he kept telling her that he was.

Since the first time Abby had agreed—tentatively—to the baby's name, he had become "Will" to Jeff. She actually liked "William" better, and she thought of him that way in her own mind, but it didn't really matter. He was finally "someone." She had been allowed to hold him a few times in the last two days, and she had never seen anything that indicated his little heart was so distorted. All she knew was that she loved him as though she had known him forever, and there was no science that could explain to her why she should now have to give him up.

That very first night, after the birth, she had nursed her William. No question, he had the impulse to suck, but he wasn't very good at it. He was catching on fast, though, and her milk was coming in. She was going to run home for a little while today, but she wanted to be at the hospital most of the time so that William could feel her warmth and know that she was there to feed him, to love him.

"Okay, let me see if I can summarize all this," Dr. Hunt was saying. He looked at Abby. He finally seemed to be aware that he hadn't included her the way he should have. "We think what we have is hypoplastic left heart *complex,* not 'syndrome.' It sounds about the same, but there's a big difference."

That set off another long series of questions from Jeff. What became clear gradually, however, was that Dr. Hunt was recommending that a team of doctors perform a long surgery and correct several defects. The hope was that once the aorta was repaired and the hole was patched, the additional blood pumping into the left ventricle would open it up, and William would be normal in time. Abby liked that idea better than a series of operations, but she finally asked the one question that mattered to her.

"Doctor Hunt, what if it doesn't work?"

"Well . . ."

"He'll die, won't he?"

He finally nodded. "Yes."

"Could you try something else that isn't so dangerous?"

"Yes, we could—and that's one of the options. But I really believe that William's best chance to have a normal life is for us to do open-heart surgery. We could try some other repairs, but I don't see a good long-term outcome."

"How many babies make it through this operation and grow up to be normal?"

He didn't answer for a time, and he didn't look at her. "I haven't seen any exact figures," he finally said, "but I have to tell you, it's probably only a fifty-fifty kind of thing."

"But you prayed about it?"

"Yes."

"Is it what you would do if he were your little boy?"

"Yes. It is."

Abby didn't want to talk anymore. She just wanted to move ahead. Looking at Jeff, she asked, "Will you give him another blessing?"

So the decision was made, and Jeff and Abby left, but that afternoon they came back to the hospital. Abby nursed little William again and held him for a long time. When Malcolm and Kayla showed up that evening, Malcolm rubbed a spot of consecrated oil on William's head, and, as Abby held him, the two men placed their fingers on his little head. Jeff blessed him with heartfelt words, shedding tears in the process, and Abby was touched. But she still wished he could find the faith to say, "Be healed."

On the following morning Abby let a nurse take William from her. She followed him to the door of the OR, but she wasn't allowed to go beyond. She walked back to the waiting room, and she and Jeff sat there all day. They got up from time to time, ate a small lunch, made phone calls, and they received a few reports that all was going well, but there was no telling from that what the final outcome would be. Eight hours went by, and then, down the hallway, Abby noticed some scurrying going on. She stopped a nurse and said, "What's happening? Is the surgery finished?"

"Uh . . . yes," the woman said, but she was already hurrying away. "I can't answer questions. You'll have to talk to your doctor."

Almost immediately the phone rang in the waiting room and Jeff picked it up. Abby saw his face lose color and she almost passed out herself. "Is there something you can do?" he gasped.

Jeff listened, and then he put down the phone. He came to Abby and took her in his arms. "The surgery went okay, they think, but Will's heart won't start up. They've shocked it, but it didn't work. They're trying something else—and then they'll call us back."

"Is he dead?"

"No. I mean . . . maybe. They're still working on him."

By then Jeff and Abby were dropping to their knees together. There were people at the other end of the room, but Abby didn't think about that. "Please, Father," she whispered. "Please. Help my son. Bring him back to life."

"Please, please," Jeff was whispering, and the two clung to each other and cried.

Then Abby heard Dr. Hunt's voice at the door. "It's okay. His heart started beating."

Abby jumped up, rushed to Dr. Hunt, and threw her arms

around him. What surprised her most was what she had heard in the doctor's voice. He was crying too.

Dr. Hunt patted her back, let her cry for a time, and then he said, "I think we did a good job. We felt good about all the repairs."

"Does that mean he'll be all right?"

"Everything depends now on that left ventricle expanding as blood is forced into it."

"How long will that take?"

"A while. It will take at least a couple of weeks before we can say for sure that it's happening. We'll keep a nurse with him every second for now—and leave his chest open, just in case we have to go back in—but once we close him up, it's just a matter of giving that little ventricle time to respond."

"Why wouldn't his heart start?" Jeff asked.

"Who knows? I can explain the biology of circulation, but I have no idea what spark makes a heart decide to beat."

"I think he'll be okay now," Jeff said. "God kept him with us. I don't think He'll take him away now."

Abby spun from the doctor and grasped Jeff. Those were the words she had wanted to hear from him.

CHAPTER 3

Will and Liz were relieved as the weather began to soften at the end of summer. They also felt blessed not to have fallen ill. Most conversations with neighbors began with news that another infant or child in the city had died, or, not uncommonly, that an adult had succumbed and left children in difficult circumstances. There had been dozens of deaths again this year.

Late in August Joseph Smith had emerged from hiding and had surprised and thrilled Church members by appearing at a Monday morning gathering at the grove west of the temple. Two days later he had spoken at the grove again, this time to the Female Relief Society. Liz had been invited to join the society, which now had around a thousand members, and she was delighted to attend and hear Brother Joseph. What moved Liz was the emotion in Joseph's voice as he expressed his gratitude to the sisters for their prayers and their letters to the governor on his behalf. He also proclaimed his confidence that members of the society were fulfilling their purposes by practicing holiness. As she walked home that day she wondered whether she hadn't fallen short of holiness during this summer of discomfort. She knew she hadn't been as kind to others—especially Will—as she might have been. She told herself she had to do better.

She also wanted to be more involved with the sisters, even though her time of confinement was not far off. Will sometimes returned from work in time for prayer meetings, held in homes around their neighborhood, but more often than not, he felt he couldn't quit his work that early, and Liz hesitated to attend alone. She knew of social gatherings, too, and visitors who lectured in the upper room of the brick store. Will promised that in time he wouldn't have to work quite so hard, and they could become more involved, but Liz wondered whether that would ever happen. For now, attending Female Relief Society meetings was a joy to her, and she wanted to offer all the help she could to people in need—and there were many.

One day early in September a storm rolled in across the Mississippi—purple clouds filling up the sky—and the heavens let loose with a torrent of rain so hard that it ripped leaves, even branches, from the trees around the Lewises' house. Lightning flashed and sizzled, and a thunderclap crashed so close overhead that Liz thought for a moment the house had been struck. The following morning was clear and bright, and the air was much cooler. Autumn was in the air.

Some of Liz's energy returned as the temperature subsided. Though she felt awkward with her great belly, she decided to keep her resolve to look beyond the confines of the little clearing in the woods where she lived. One morning she walked down from the bluffs to the house where she and Will had lived the first few months of their time in Nauvoo. Will had promised to help with the garden and share in the harvest, but he had rarely found time to keep his promise. Liz needed some of the root crop Will had planted, and she hoped for some of the pumpkins she had watched grow all summer.

But how could she ask for anything if she and Will didn't do any of the work? She thought she could hoe for a time this morning and it would do her good—and help the Johns family. Will had told her that the entire family was sick. Brother Johns had worked a couple of weeks for Will, but he had had to leave one day with a burning fever and hadn't come back.

When Liz reached the garden she didn't see anyone stirring yet, but it was early—even though Will had long since left for work on a road project he hoped to finish soon. She found a hoe leaning against the little garden shed and went to work without announcing her presence to Brother and Sister Johns. She had been hoeing for almost half an hour, taking her time, trying not to exert herself too much, when Brother Johns appeared from around the house, looking gaunt and pale. He stared at her, seeming confused, but he didn't speak.

"I'm Sister Lewis. I met you at the—"

"I know you, Sister Lewis. But what is it ye're doing?"

"Will promised to help you with the garden, but he hasn't come very often. I thought I could weed just a little this morning before the heat comes on."

"But you shouldn't . . . be doing that."

He didn't mention her condition, of course, but she knew what he meant. "It's good for me," she said. "I've been so indolent lately, I feel as though I'm losing my strength."

He continued to stare at her as though he were struggling to think what to say. "The garden's not been looked after," he said. "We're all down sick. Every one of us."

"I'm so sorry, Brother Johns. Have you food and water?"

"We've gotten by. One of us can most often make it to the well. And our neighbors have brought us food."

"Let me speak with your wife. I can help you. I have time these days."

He didn't answer, just stood as he had before, his mouth gaping. "Are you a lady?" he finally asked.

Liz laughed. "No. Not at all. I'm a common person—the same as everyone here."

"But you talk like a lady—so fine. I thought you was a angel when I first seed you out here. I had to rub my eyes."

"I'm far from being an angel, I fear, but may I speak with your wife?"

"Aye. Surely. But she's down this mornin'. Do you mind comin' inside?"

"No. Of course not."

So the two walked inside the dark little cabin. Sister Johns seemed as surprised as her husband had been to look up and see Liz standing over her. Liz knelt by the bed and took hold of Sister Johns's hand. "Is your fever bad this morning?" Liz asked.

"Not as bad as yesterday. I must get up today. I must look after my little ones."

"Let me make breakfast for you. And I'll see how the children are faring. You rest some more."

Brother Johns had built a small fire. Liz mixed up cornmeal with a little salt and water, kneaded it into dough, and then set the dough, in lumps, on a board in front of the fire. While the cakes cooked, she changed the baby's diaper, and she washed the little girl, Eliza, who was shockingly hot to the touch and seemed comforted by the cool water. Afterwards, Liz hoed again, and by the time she climbed up through the woods to her own house, she was exhausted but feeling much better than she had felt for quite some time.

All the next week Liz walked to the Johns's house each morning, and Brother Johns always called her "our angel." Liz told him not to talk so, but she liked that she could help them. She was needed, and that was important to her. She hadn't known until this summer that she could work, even work hard. She liked to think she could serve. She didn't want to be a weakling. She wanted to be part of this place.

• • •

On Sunday, September 11, Will and Liz walked to the grove, arrived early, and found themselves a place to sit on a split log in the shade of an old burr oak. It was a nice place, only thirty or forty yards from the wooden stand at the top of the hill, but as a large crowd gathered, Will gave up his seat to an older sister, Mother Greene, and sat a little aside on the grass. Liz wanted to do the same, but he told her she needed to have a seat and convinced her to stay where she was.

Will hoped that Joseph Smith would attend again, but not long after he had spoken to the Saints the last time, sheriffs had arrived in Nauvoo and searched for him. William Clayton had told Will the story: A visitor at Joseph's house had answered the door when the lawmen had knocked. The visitor had delayed the lawmen while Joseph slipped out a back door, ran through a cornfield, and made his way to safety upstairs in the brick store. Since then, Joseph had been in hiding again.

Hyrum Smith, Joseph's older brother and Patriarch of the Church, was presiding at the meeting this Sunday. He called the Saints to order. It was a meeting like the camp meetings Will had sometimes attended as a boy among the United Brethren. Thousands of members sat on the hillside or in their wagons or oxcarts.

Will never felt more a part of Zion than when he saw the assembled Saints and heard Apostles and other leaders preach the gospel. They would often proclaim a new understanding they had received on doctrine and eternal matters. It was never a matter of showing up to hear the same old sermons the way Will had been used to in his growing-up years.

What Will loved most about meetings in the grove was the sense he felt that "the gathering" really was taking place. Good people from many parts of the world had been caught in the gospel net, and they had given up all they had to come here and build the temple at the top of the hill. The walls were not very high yet, not even visible from farther down the hill, but the work was going on every day except Sundays, and people were sacrificing to pay tithes so the temple could be completed. It was true that Joseph sometimes reprimanded the Saints who failed to offer their tithes of income and labor, but Will knew how many had been ill lately and how difficult it was for most people merely to sustain themselves.

The Saints sang "Redeemer of Israel" in strong voices, and then Brother William Marks, Nauvoo's stake president, offered a mighty prayer. Brother Hyrum asked for a sustaining vote for several men who were to be advanced in the priesthood, and then he read a recently written letter from the Prophet Joseph explaining that his enemies, on the basis of lies "of the blackest dye," were pursuing him relentlessly. He had left Nauvoo for his own safety and for the safety of "this people." Hyrum's voice was like Joseph's, and so was his stature. Will felt a thrill, as though Joseph were speaking these strong words himself.

Joseph explained in his letter that he would return when the troubles had passed. Such trials were not a new thing to him. "But nevertheless," he wrote, "deep water is what I am wont to swim in. It all has become a second nature to me."

The letter also admonished the Saints to continue their work on the temple, and then Joseph demonstrated that he was continuing to lead the Church, even in exile. He taught the Saints that each baptism for the dead must be performed before a witness and carefully recorded.

Will was reassured to know the Prophet was still guiding the Saints, and he enjoyed the sermons that followed. But when the meeting ended, having lasted three hours, he could see that Liz was weary. She had begun to shift and squirm about halfway through. She had finally moved over to him, seeming to find more comfort on the softer surface. He helped her up after the closing prayer and she laughed at herself. "I feel like an old milch cow when I try to get up on my feet," she said.

"Maybe you should have stayed home—and had yourself a real day of rest."

"No. It's good to see everyone and remember how many of us live here."

"The truth of it is, I wish some of the people had left their boys home."

"Now, Will, you were a boy once yourself, you know." She wagged a finger at him and gave him a sly smile.

"I know. But my father didn't let me run about during the sermons. I had to sit and listen." He laughed. "Or at least, sit."

Just then Will heard a voice behind him. "Will and Liz, hello. It's good to see you."

Will turned around and saw Jesse Matthews. He was striding up the hill, and Ellen, with their children, was not far behind him. "It's good to see *you*," Will said, clapping his arms around Jesse. "It's been *weeks*. Are you faring well enough?"

Jesse's smile died away. "In truth . . . I can na' claim that we are. We're livin' with the family that took us in at the beginnin'—the Lovelesses. We're crowded up into one room. I have na' had much work—surely not enough to keep us thrivin'."

"I'm sorry to hear that, Jesse." Ellen was approaching now with

Jesse Junior and Mary. Liz hurried to them and embraced Ellen.
But Ellen looked tired. She was still very thin and her clothing
looked worn, the blue of her cotton dress now almost gray, her shawl
tattered.

But Liz was already inviting them home for Sunday dinner, and
Ellen seemed cheered by that. Will saw young Jesse's eyes come alive
as well, and he wondered whether the family had had enough to eat.

"Did you walk into town or—"

"How else can we go about?" Jesse asked. "We ha' no horse, no
cart. Nothin'."

Will heard something in Jesse's voice—a hint of resentment—
and that worried him. But he decided not to ask too many questions
for now. "I bought an old mare," Will said, "and I ride her out to my
work, but we walked here today. Let's go as far as our place, and then
you can rest and eat before you start your walk home."

So they all walked toward the crest of the hill. Many members had gathered at the stand to greet the Church leaders, but
Jesse showed no interest in doing that, so Will didn't stop either.
They walked on past the temple, and Will commented on the slow
progress lately with all the sickness in town. Jesse said, "Aye. 'Tis
true. I work on the temple oft. Work for pay, that is. But the wages
is na' much—and it's a mighty long walk comin' and goin'."

"I only put in my one day in ten. But I like to think what it
is we're building. You heard what Joseph said about it in his letter
today."

"Aye. It's a fine thing, I ha' no doubt—but na' the kind of work
I need."

They continued along Mulholland through the little business
area east of the temple. A number of stores and shops had opened
there on the bluffs, although some of the Saints said that it was taking business away from Main Street, which Joseph had intended as

the commercial part of the city. Shop owners, however—some of them settlers who had lived in Commerce before it had ever been called Nauvoo—liked this area near the temple, away from the wet ground near the river.

Will and Liz's place was about a mile from the temple. Will picked up little Mary after a time, and she leaned her head on his shoulder and soon fell asleep. Young Jesse tramped along as best he could. He was five now, but small for his age, and his boots were falling apart. As they walked south on Rich Street through a gulley between Mulholland and the hill where the Lewises' house was, Will expected Jesse to pick up the boy and carry him through a muddy area at the bottom, but Jesse hardly seemed to notice—which wasn't like him. So Will picked up Jesse Junior in his other arm and carried him halfway up the hill.

As they neared the house, Jesse did say, "It's a fine spot you chose here, Will. Did you build the house yourself?"

"No. I ne'er could have. I was still too weak. Some brothers helped me finish getting the logs ready, and then they raised the house. When you're ready to build, be certain to let me know. I learned a good deal about building a block house. I can help you—and other men will do the same."

Jesse nodded, but it was Ellen who said, "An' how should we do that, Will? Brother and Sister Loveless tell us we can have a parcel of their prairie land and they will na' ask us nothin' for it. But where do we get timber out there on the prairie, and how can we feed our family 'til we harvest a crop?"

"We need to talk that over," Will said. "I have some thoughts on it."

"It's too late for that, Will," Jesse said. "We're pullin' out. We walked to the grove this mornin' just hopin' someone would say somethin' that might change our thinkin'. But it was what we've heard afore. Back in England it was all tol' ta us like we was comin' to the Garden of Eden."

"Maybe that's more the way we wanted to think of it than anything anyone actually told us. And this is good land, Jesse."

"It is if you can afford it—and pay someone to plow it the first time. An' that I can na' do."

"Well . . . let's sit down and have a cool drink of water. Liz started a stew this morning, and we only have that and some cornmeal to make johnnycake. We have no wheat flour just yet, but there's plenty of stew, and that ought to make us all feel better. Then we'll talk."

So they all went inside. Will carried Mary to the back room and laid her on their bed; Jesse Junior soon joined her and fell asleep too. Ellen looked as though she would like to do the same. But she talked with Liz while Liz began to mix up the cornmeal dough. Will stoked the fire a little to make sure the stew would be hot. Then he walked out to the well, dropped a wooden bucket down, and cranked the winch to bring up the water.

Jesse and Ellen seemed to enjoy the cool drink, and the four talked quietly and let the children sleep for a time. Each had news from various friends and family back in Ledbury, and they shared what they knew. Will thought he saw their spirits rise a little, and when they finally gathered around the table to eat, Will was surprised just how much all of the Matthewses could gulp down. Even little Mary awakened to the smell of the johnnycake and stew and ate as though she hadn't had a good meal in a long while. Jesse Junior ate almost as much as Will did. After dinner, he seemed greatly revived, and he and his sister walked outside to look about.

It was Jesse who came back to the subject that Will had delayed. "I can na' say that any'un lied to us back in England, but they painted the picture too rosy," he said.

"But you can own land here, Jesse, and you never could have back in Ledbury."

"It's true. A man wants to give me a piece of land for nothin'. That sounds too good to be true. But I don't have a farthin' to my name. How can I build a house? For a true farm, I need a bigger section of land. And then I need animals to plow with—and everythin' else it would take to get started. Before we left England, I was tol' ever'one would work together and make such things possible. But we're all so poor, who can help som'un else get a start?"

Will knew what Jesse was saying. He didn't try to talk Jesse into anything. He took his time and just asked a few questions. Jesse described what had happened since he and Ellen had arrived. John Benbow had encouraged them to come to the prairie, by the "Big Mound," a bump in the prairie beyond Joseph Smith's farm at the east end of Parley Street. Out there they could be close to the Saints from the Malvern Hills. The Lovelesses had given Jesse and Ellen a place to live, but that had been intended as a temporary solution. Jesse had assumed he could work for someone and build up a nest egg to buy some farmland. But the little work he found did no more than keep his family fed, and sometimes not that.

Will sat across the little wooden table from Jesse. He listened and kept nodding and saying, "I know what you mean." Finally he asked, "What about the Big Field that you can plant for free? You live not far from it."

"But I have no equipment, no oxen or horses. And my children need to eat now—not next year. What am I to do all winter?"

"What are you thinking of doing? If you leave, where would you go?"

"I wish we could go home," Ellen said. "But I can na' face the ocean again. I can na' bear to lose another child."

"Aye. I understand. I'm sorry we didn't do more to help. We didn't know things were so bad."

"We've been able to get by. And many a one has brought us cornmeal and potatoes, e'en table and chairs. But a man likes to stan' on his own legs. All I want is work. Some people we knowed in Herefordshire is leaving here and heading to St. Louis, down the river. There's work there, they say, an' a good many Saints live there besides. We will na' ever leave the Church. We on'y want to go where we can find a way to live."

"But this is Zion. The temple is here."

"That's all well and good. But if it's such a fine place, why can na' the Lord bless His people? I hate to say such words, Will, but the Lord—or Joseph Smith—chose a sickly place. An' some of the people here is not so righteous as they pretend. They act about the way people do anywhere—and we was told they would be better."

Will knew all too well what Jesse was talking about. He still hadn't received a single dollar of the forty that Brother Lancaster owed him. He had seen men as drunk as sailors, and he knew for certain that one of his neighbors on the flats had struck his wife and blackened her eye. "But Jesse, people did bring you food," Will said. "And someone did take you in. That wouldn't happen everywhere. Most people do try hard to live the gospel. We have to look down the road a little and imagine what Nauvoo *will* be—and not be too disappointed by what it is so far. So many have come here, so fast, that the city can't keep up with all the demands."

"That's true enough. Too many has come. An' maybe some needs to leave."

"Maybe. But before you make up your mind, listen to what I'm thinking." Will wanted to say this right. He set his elbows on the table and looked into Jesse's eyes. "Here's our situation. I have six yoke of oxen. I've been plowing farmland for people and I've started grading roads. I'm also farming at the Big Field, out on the prairie by you. But I cannot get everything done. I hired a man, but he's down with the ague now, and he won't be much help to me during the harvest. I'm thinking, you and I could work together—join up as partners—and both be better off."

"I do na' see that. What could I bring to a partnership?"

"For one thing, I'm boarding my oxen with a farmer out east of town, but that only cuts into my profit. Maybe I could board those oxen with you, at this place Brother Loveless wants to give you. I'll return the favor by opening up some land for you at the Big Field. It's too late to plant this season, but right now I could use a man to work with me to get these county roads cut before winter sets in. Plowing—or grading, either one—with that many oxen, is too big a job for one man to handle. Three men would be best, and maybe that's what we'll have by next spring."

"Do you need me, Will, or are you only wantin' to—"

"I need you, all right, and I can pay you a dollar a day. That will help you lay in a few stores for winter. I've got timber here on this land, too, and we can fell some more trees—which will open up more grazing land for my animals. We'll use my oxen to haul the logs out to your place and you can hew them and get them ready. Before snow comes we could gather up some men to raise you a good little house. After a year or two, you could put some money down on a bigger farm of your own."

Jesse was staring at Will, his eyes wide. Ellen's eyes had filled with tears. "Is it true you really need a man to work for you?" Ellen asked.

"I do. I've been working sunup 'til sundown, but I cannot keep up with all the roads I've promised to grade before snow flies. I definitely need a man now, and I'll still need one once Brother Johns comes back to work. If you're willing to work with me—partners in everything—I cannot tell you how much I'd appreciate it."

Now Jesse's eyes had also filled with tears. His face looked older than it had back in England. He hadn't shaved for a time, and his skin looked hard and brown from the summer sun, but now his eyes were getting back some light.

"You need a cow and some hogs and chickens, and you'll need to plow up a garden there by the house we'll build for you. I can help you get some animals, and then next spring you can pay me back with your work."

"Will, you can na' do all that. You told me yerself, you want to build a brick house here on your lot. If you help me that much, you will set yerself back."

"Not at all. We're all going to prosper together. We just have to work hard enough to make it happen."

Will could tell that Jesse was still embarrassed to accept the offer, and yet he was so thankful he could only keep repeating how good it was of Will to help him this way. Will tried to shed all that, but when he saw the change in the man—and in Ellen—he felt reassured that it was the right thing to do.

As it turned out, Jesse and Ellen stayed all afternoon. Will and Jesse talked in considerable detail about the work they would do together and the things they could accomplish over the next few years. When Jesse finally walked away, he was carrying Mary on his shoulders, and Will saw some bounce in his stride.

Once they were out of sight, Liz turned to Will and wrapped her arms around him as best she could with her bulging front in the way. "Do you really need a man to work for you?" she asked.

"You know I do."

"Maybe one, but do you need two?"

"I've needed two men all along. I only thought I'd save up more money if I did everything myself."

"And what about this cow you're going to buy for Jesse? And pigs and chickens? Where's that money coming from?"

"He's going to need some animals, Liz. That's all there is to it."

"That's not what I asked you."

"I have wages coming for these roads I'm grading. If it's all right, I'll use some of the money I was going to put aside to buy bricks."

"I'm fine with that, Will. I've told you, this house is good enough for me. But are *you* all right with it?"

Will didn't want to answer. The truth was, he felt sick. He had already begun to realize that he couldn't build that new house next year, but now he wondered when it would ever happen. Still, how could he turn his back on Jesse and Ellen when they needed to get started too?

"This is Zion, Liz," Will said. "Jesse needed to understand what that means."

"Yes. And so do we."

"Aye. It's what I'm thinking, too." He put his arm around her shoulders. He was pleased that she was willing to help Jesse and Ellen. He only wished that he hadn't been so slow to be willing himself.

CHAPTER 4

Liz's pains had begun—hard ones—and she was frightened. It was still September, and she had calculated that the birth would not come until late October. What frightened her more was that Will was working on a road several miles south of town and probably wouldn't be home until after sundown. At first she had told herself that the pains would pass, but she was increasingly sure that that wasn't going to happen. There was nothing to do but seek out Nelly Baugh—her neighbor just down the hill to the west—and ask her to send her son to fetch Mother Sessions.

The trail through the woods to Nelly's house was not long, but a pain struck Liz along the way. She grabbed hold of a slender birch tree and hung on. Suddenly she felt a gush and knew that her water had broken. She hurried on then, and when she reached Nelly's open front door, she said, "Nelly, my baby's coming—and it's too soon."

"Don't tell me. Tell the baby," Sister Baugh said, laughing. But then she came to Liz and seemed to see how frightened she was. "Sometimes the sickness passes away. You can't be sure that the baby'll come today."

"My water broke, Nelly."

Nelly nodded. "Well, then, yes. It's a-comin', all right."

Just then another pain struck Liz. She thought for a moment that she would drop to her knees. She clutched her belly and moaned without meaning to, and she held her breath. This pain lasted longer than the ones before, her whole body seeming to clench. Nelly wrapped her arm around Liz and helped her sit down. "That's a real pain, all right," she said.

"Can you send Edward to get Mother Sessions?"

"Yes. An' I'll stay with you. But let's get you back home." She stepped to the door of her cabin and called, "Edward!"

The boy appeared quickly. The knees of his homespun trousers were wet and his hands were covered in mud. He pulled a dilapidated straw hat from his head when he saw Liz, and he nodded to her.

"Let your weedin' go for now," Nelly told him. "Run down to the flats to Sister Sessions's house. Tell her Sister Lewis needs her *right now*—and don't come back without her. If she's not at her place, track 'er down."

Edward was eleven, Liz knew, but he seemed older, and she saw that he took the command seriously. "Yes'm," he said, and turned quickly.

"Stop at the pump and wash yerself a little," Nelly yelled after him as he headed out the door. "But do it fast. An' run all the way."

Nelly gathered her younger children together—eight-year-old twin girls, a four-year-old son, and a baby daughter—and they all walked back to Liz's house, Nelly holding Liz with one arm and carrying her baby with the other. Along the way, Liz had another labor pain. "They's comin' a little too fast and too hard for my likin'," Nelly told her. "First babies come slow most times, but we best be ready in case Patty's off sum'eres with another birthin' and can't come the first minute she's called on."

Liz was frightened by all of this. She hadn't known how weak
she would suddenly feel, how confused, her mind seeming to lose all
concentration when the pains came. She wanted Patty Sessions, who
was always so calm and confident, and she wanted Will, just to be
there with her. But all that was nothing compared to the fear she felt
for her baby. If it was coming so early, would it be all right? Would
it be strong enough?

Sister Baugh took over. She chattered too much, worried out
loud more than Liz needed, but she was in control, and Liz had only
to follow instructions. She was thankful for that.

Nelly told the twins to keep the baby and little Arthur outside,
and not to come inside the house. Once inside, Nelly had Liz sit
down while she got the bed ready in the back room. She stripped off
the straw mattress and laid out flour sacks over the ropes of the bed.
Mother Sessions had told Liz to boil the sacks and keep them ready.
Nelly then helped Liz get her clothes off and lie down, and she covered her over with a quilted counterpane.

"Don't help the baby yet. Just let the pains come for now, and
we'll see how long before Patty gets here."

But it was hard not to push. Liz's body seemed to act on its own,
and each pain made her want the birth to happen whether Patty was
there or not. She clung to Nelly when her muscles clenched, tried
not to cry out too much but did at times in spite of herself. Time
passed—an hour or more, Liz thought—and finally Patty's voice was
at the bedroom door. "I wasn't planning to be here this soon, dear
Sister Elizabeth. How are you holding up?"

But a pain had struck again and Liz gasped, then grimaced as
she waited it out. It was Nelly who said, "I think it's coming awful
fast for a first one. I told her not to push."

Mother Sessions stepped close to the bed and took hold of Liz's
hand. She was an older woman, near fifty, with a stolid countenance

and a taut little body, but her voice was mild. "Liz, dear, just rest a minute now before the next pain comes. Don't worry about a thing. Let me pray for you, and then let's trust in the Lord after that."

Patty surprised Liz when she placed her hands on Liz's head. Liz had heard of women in Nauvoo laying hands on the sick, using the power of prayer to bless other sisters and children, but she had never received a blessing from a woman. The comfort was wonderful. Mother Sessions prayed softly for the Lord to watch over Liz and her baby and to help Liz withstand the pain. "May this dear spirit, about to take on a mortal body, be blessed to thrive and grow and live a righteous life," she prayed, "all according to Thy holy mind and will."

She ended her prayer in Christ's name, and then she stepped to the end of the bed and lifted the quilt that covered Liz. After only a few seconds of examination, she said, "Nelly's right. This baby is coming fast."

• • •

When Will walked toward his house that night—a little earlier than he had expected to return—he saw smoke coming from the chimney, and his first thought was that Liz had built the fire without him and was already cooking dinner. But when he opened the door, he saw Nelly Baugh at the fireplace, not Liz.

Nelly was stirring something in a kettle. She turned and said, "Oh, Brother Lewis. I'm glad you're here." She motioned with her hand toward the back room.

Will stepped to the bedroom door and looked to see Liz in bed. She raised her head in the dim light and smiled gently. Next to her, held in one of her arms, was a little bundle wrapped in a tan blanket—the blanket the sisters of the Female Relief Society of Nauvoo had brought to her. "What's happened?" were the words he heard himself say, even though the answer was obvious.

"Your baby's come already," Nelly said.

And in a softer voice, Liz said, "It's a little girl, Will. Come and look."

"Are you all right?" he asked as he walked to the bed. "I would have stayed today if I'd known."

"You couldn't know. I didn't know. But I'm fine. Nelly and Patty were here with me."

"Is the baby doing all right?"

"She's very, very small, Will. She looks like a doll—a tiny china doll."

Will knelt by the bed and took hold of Liz's hand. "You look so tired, Liz. Are you sure you're doing all right?"

"Yes, I think so. Mother Sessions said it was an easy birth, and I think it was—the baby being so small." She moved the bundle to the other side of her, near to Will. "Look at her, Will. She's so pretty."

Will took the infant in his arms and pulled the blanket open.

"Take her to the front door so you can see her better."

Will did as he was told, and when he saw the little one's face and arms and hands, he marveled as though he'd never seen a baby before. This was flesh of his wife's flesh—and his flesh, too. He remembered his little brothers and sisters, knew what new babies looked like, but this miracle seemed beyond all others. She was red and frowning, like his mother's babies, but still a little flower. She had a perfect face, with tiny rounded lips and ears folded against her head, perfect too, like the opening petals of a rosebud.

But her hand was tiny, and he sensed the danger. "Will she be all right?" he asked Nelly.

"Mother Sessions blessed your wife," Nelly told him. "And she told her after, sometimes the early ones do jist fine."

Will nodded. He understood what "sometimes" meant and

knew that Liz must be worried. He went back to her. "She's *beautiful*," he told her.

Liz took the baby back into her arms. "I want to name her Mary Ann. Is that all right, Will? I want her to grow up just as happy, just as comical and lively as my sister."

"That's fine. That's the name she'll have."

"Mother Sessions said the first week or two will be important— to see if she can gain weight." Liz had begun to cry. "Please give her a priesthood blessing, Will."

"I will."

"Do you have consecrated oil?" Nelly asked.

"No, I don't."

"I'll walk home now, and I'll send Warren back. He has oil, and he can anoint her."

"All right. I would appreciate that." Will thought of that little hand and wondered whether he was facing a force like the storm at sea. Was he being called to quell the winds and the waves again?

"There's beans cooking in the kettle," Nelly said, "and some bacon mixed in. And there's wheat bread I baked only yesterday, all ready to slice and eat."

Will finally noticed the smell of the beans, and especially the bacon, and he remembered how hungry he had been, riding home. "Thanks so much, Nelly. How did you know to come today?"

"It wasn't me. It was Liz. She walked down to my place when she first knew she was sick. She may sound like a highborn lady, but she hardly let out a whimper when it come to the pain of it. She's a strong woman, no matter how pretty she is."

Liz looked as frail as she had on the ship, and he knew how worried she was, but her face was perfect in that flickering light from the Betty lamp on the wall. "She's the most beautiful woman I've ever seen—no matter how many I ever look on," Will said.

"Look again," Liz said. "Look at the little face in that blanket. That's the prettiest face that ever was."

Will was thinking that *all* this was too wonderful to be true. He sometimes forgot how much he had wanted Liz, and how impossible it once had seemed that he could have her—and yet here she was, in love with him, and the mother of his own beautiful little girl. He had heard people say that things never turn out as well as we hope they will, but at this moment he couldn't imagine being happier.

Still, it was such a delicate joy. He needed both his wife and his daughter to get stronger now.

Nelly left. Will walked out and stirred the beans and used a wooden spoon to taste them, but they were still hard, not cooked long enough yet. So he took a chair to the bed and sat next to Liz. He asked her to rehearse the whole story, when and how she had known the baby was coming, and what had happened since then.

She was only partway through her story when Warren Baugh showed up. He had a little tin container of oil with him. Will asked Warren to anoint Liz's head, and then he sealed the blessing. He stated flatly that Liz would regain her strength quickly and live to bear many more children.

Will picked up the baby after that and held her so Warren could anoint her head in the same way. Will addressed his little girl as Mary Ann Lewis, and the words themselves made his voice shake. He pled with the Lord to bless her, to make her well, to allow her to live to adulthood and to have children of her own.

• • •

For the next few days Mary Ann seemed to do quite well, and Liz was hopeful. Nelly stayed to help her. She made a bed on the floor of the main room and kept the baby with her, only rousing Liz to nurse her. Liz needed to stay flat on her back for a week,

Nelly insisted, and Will needed his sleep so that he could go about his own work. Nelly's little daughter, almost a year old, slept on the floor with her. Liz knew what a sacrifice all this was for Nelly and her family, and what a blessing it was to have her there. She thanked Nelly over and over, but Nelly passed off Liz's words with a wave of her hand. "It's what us sisters do here," she would say. "Most times, we don't have family near to us, so we do what mothers and relatives would do."

Mary Ann didn't nurse very well, but she slept a great deal and seemed to be at peace. On the third day of her life, however, she began to cry. She started in the evening and continued all night. Will stayed awake with Nelly and Liz and they all three tried to comfort the baby. They kept her warm and dry, and Liz tried time and again to nurse her. Liz's milk had come in well enough, and Mary Ann would try to suck, but before long she would screech with pain and everything would come back up, already smelling sour. Then the crying would start again.

Liz had never experienced anything quite so frustrating or so heartbreaking. The poor little thing was not thriving, not comforted, and nothing Liz tried to do made any difference. She sent Will off to work each morning because she could see how much anguish he was experiencing and she couldn't stand to let him go through this with her. She knew, too, that he had contracted to finish grading two more roads before winter set in. He worried when he didn't move ahead on his work. Fortunately, too, Nelly not only stayed the night but part of the day, and some of the other sisters who lived on Parley Street, not far away, stopped in to offer help.

Mother Sessions also stopped by most days to look after Liz. She said that Liz was healing fine, but she also understood how worried she was. "Sister Lewis, you can only do what you're doing," she told her. "Some babies have colic. It's just the way they come to the world. Most often, we feed them as best we can and they finally keep down enough milk to grow on, and in time, they stop crying so much. But this pretty little thing is so small, she may not be able to keep herself alive. I don't like to say that to you, deary, but you need to know, if something happens, it isn't your fault."

"But there must be something more we can do for her."

"Not that I know of. I've tried a few things—herbs of different kinds—but nothing that ever seemed to make a difference. I'm afraid this world is full of heartache, my dear. I've birthed eight children myself and five are gone now. I lost a son who was sixteen years old and a little girl who was six. Only one was a new baby. The others I had time to know, and then it hurt all the more to lose them."

"I think I know my Mary Ann already," Liz said. But she didn't say the rest. She simply couldn't bear to lose her baby. She didn't know how Mother Sessions had given up five children; she only knew that if Mary Ann didn't live, she would want to follow her into the grave.

"I know, Sister Lewis," Patty said. "I understand what mothers feel." She smoothed Liz's hair with some gentle strokes, then rested her hand on her shoulder. "I see all these lovely babies born in Nauvoo, but I also see the ones that mothers lose, and I've never known a woman who didn't suffer as though she would die herself when it happens. We have the canker rash in in the city right now, and black canker, too. Sister Healey lost her daughter last week—the poor child's mouth and jaw all eaten away. And the chill fever is still taking lots of us. There's hardly a family that hasn't suffered with it."

"How do people get through it all?"

"We just go on. We do it for our husbands and for our other children—and for other babies still to come."

But Liz was not going to think that way. She pulled her baby closer and said, "I'm going to keep my Mary Ann alive, Mother

Sessions. I'll love her so much, she won't want to leave me. I'll hold her so close, she'll not let anything pull her away—not even heaven." But Liz broke down at that point, and Patty said no more, only stroked her hair again, and finally bent and touched her cheek to Liz's forehead.

· · ·

Day after day, things got worse. Liz exerted all her effort to let her baby know how loved she was, tried over and over to feed her, but gradually Mary Ann cried less, ate less, and seemed more peaceful—and weak. The quieter Mary Ann became, the more it was Liz who cried.

Will was Liz's greatest blessing now that Nelly wasn't staying through the night. He was patient with her and tender with Mary Ann. She saw in his eyes how worried he was for both of them. But she also heard at times, in his voice, that he wasn't expecting Mary Ann to live. She finally asked him to bless the baby again, and he did, but after, she saw no hope in his face. "The Lord heard my blessing," he told Liz. "Now we have to leave things in His hands."

But Liz didn't want to accept that. Why couldn't the Lord let her have this one thing she wanted?

Will was working every day and awake much of the night helping Liz, and she knew he was exhausted. One morning he said he wouldn't work that day, and she knew what he was saying: that Mary Ann was almost gone and he needed to be there when she took her last breath. But Liz was not ready to accept that. She almost forced him to leave. "She's doing a little better this morning. I'm sure of it. Her breathing is better."

"I'll help Jesse get started," Will told her. "Dan Johns should be there. They can manage without me. I'll be back before noon."

"All right then," Liz said. "But you don't need to worry quite so much. She's making a turn for the better."

But it wasn't true. They both knew it. All that day Liz watched her little sweetheart dwindle, her breath so shallow that her chest hardly moved. Liz would panic at times and try to wake her, try to make her nurse, but it was no use, and gradually Liz was beginning to admit to herself what was coming.

Late that morning she heard a little rap on the door. It was likely one of the sisters, coming to console her, but Liz didn't want that now. Still, she opened the door and found Emma Smith standing before her—the great lady herself. Liz had met her, chatted politely with her on several occasions, but she thought of Emma as too important to befriend, and a little too aloof to draw close to anyway. But there she was, tall and firm and pretty.

"Sister Smith, please come in. I heard that you were sick. I'm surprised to see you."

Emma stepped inside. "I have been sick, but I'm on the mend now." She smiled. "Or at least that's what I tell myself. The ague has a way of coming back for another visit or two even after we think it's gone."

"How do you manage everything with Joseph gone?"

"Eliza Snow lives with us now. She teaches the children and keeps them busy all day. She's been a great help to me, too."

Liz had never lit the Betty lamp in the main room, although the day was overcast. The firelight had been enough, early, and Liz hated the smell of coal oil when she burned the lamp. Now she was self-conscious about the dim light and the humble furniture she had to offer. But even in this light, Liz was seeing something. She hadn't known that Sister Smith was in a family way.

Emma smiled. "I see what you're noticing. It's a condition I know very well. That alone never slows me down very much."

"It must be difficult to be so sick at the same time."

"It hasn't been easy. But Joseph stayed with me. He was in danger every minute, but he wouldn't leave my side while I was down. He's had to hide away again now, so it's good I'm doing better."

Liz was filled with admiration. Sister Emma had the look of someone who had been deepened by her life's experience—like Joseph—and yet, her smile was gentle and her touch remarkably soft as she grasped Liz's forearm and then drew her close and embraced her. "Sister Sessions told me that your baby has had a hard time of it," she said. "I wanted to visit you sooner. I hope the little one is doing better by now."

Liz was crying too hard to answer. She had wanted her mother all these months—since the day she had set sail from England, but especially this week—and Emma was now embracing her the way her mum had once done. Liz's body seemed to know these arms, this voice in her ear. "I'm so sorry," Emma was saying. "Is she getting worse?"

Liz held on to Emma for quite some time—so long she was embarrassed, and then she knew she had to show more strength. She stepped back. "She's dying, Sister Smith," she said. It was the first time she had said the words, even to herself. She led Emma into the bedroom and to the bed where Mary Ann was sleeping.

Liz picked up her baby, in her blanket, and handed her to Emma. "Oh my, she's *so* beautiful," Emma said. "She has your lovely face."

"I know that I have to be stronger, Sister Smith. I—"

"Call me Emma, and, if you don't mind, I'll call you Elizabeth."

"Even better, call me Liz."

"I'll do that." Emma handed Mary Ann back to Liz.

The two walked back to the main room. Liz pulled a straight-backed chair away from the table and motioned for Emma to sit down, and then she sat in front of Emma and held her baby close to her, her cheek against her little head. "I know you've lost some of your babies, Sister Emma. I often think how strong you've had to be."

Emma nodded, her eyes cast down. "Joseph and I have lost four of our newborns, and we lost a little boy we had taken in as our own—Julia's twin brother. He was our son, too, so it's been five that have left us."

"It seems too much to bear."

"What choice do we have?" Liz saw that tears had come to Emma's eyes. "But that's not what I came to say to you, Liz. The day was fair, and I wanted to walk a little, and I thought of you, away from your family, and facing this trouble. I have a little advice for you, I suppose."

"It's what I need, Sister Emma. I'm missing my mother so much right now."

"I suppose the Lord sent me, then." Emma seemed to think for a time, and then she said, "Each time one of our little spirits left this world, women would say to me, 'My baby died too. I know how you feel.' And I would always wonder why they thought that it might help me to know how much grief there is in this world. When death visits us, we don't feel the world's pain; we only feel our own. We can grieve with others, and they can grieve with us, but we cannot take away one another's pain."

"But I've been feeling too much pity for myself."

"No, Liz. Don't tell yourself that. That's what I wanted to say to you. Words of that kind only add to the ache you already have to go through. It's not wrong to feel sorrow for your loss."

"Maybe once it *is* a loss, I can school my feelings. But all I can think is that I still have my baby and God doesn't have to take her away. He can restore her if He wants to."

Emma smiled softly. She was wearing a loose dress. It was a print in shades of tan and brown, and she was wearing a dark brown knitted shawl over her shoulders. Her black hair had begun to gray just a little, but the curls by her ears were dark against her skin. The light from the west window was emitting just enough light across her face that Liz could see the creases that were starting to form at the corners of her eyes. She was nearing forty, Liz knew, and she was still one of the best-looking women in Nauvoo, but she looked weary—and too thin for a woman expecting a baby.

"Think of me, Liz. I'm married to a prophet of God—and over and over the Lord has blessed me with babies, only to take them back. I told Joseph more than once that he should demand better treatment." She smiled. "But Joseph tells me that he and I have to know pain, too, no matter what his calling is."

"It all seems so clear to me," Liz said, "that pain is part of life and all will be made right. But I look at this sweet little thing and I don't want to let her go. Right now, I can't think of anything else." She watched Mary Ann, who hardly moved at all now, finally beyond pain.

"That's what you should feel. You're a mother."

"She could still get better, don't you think? Miracles do happen."

"They do," Emma said. "I've seen it happen. I'll ask the Lord to help her, and you keep asking too."

"Why do we have to beg the Lord for what only seems right?"

Emma nodded, as if to acknowledge the irony. "In Missouri," she said, "the mob took Joseph and put him in a stinking little dungeon of a jail in Liberty. I begged the Lord every day to let him live, and I promised I would never complain again if I could just have him back. And then he did return. But by the time he did, I knew one thing." She looked down at her hands, which she had gripped together, and then she looked back up, now with tears in her eyes again. "I knew that my dark days were not over, that more grief would come. So many of the prophets have had to suffer. It almost seems to be part of the covenant they make. It's what softens them and hardens them at the same time. They learn to listen to God in humility, and to listen to the cries of their own people."

"And now he's having to hide again—the same people still chasing him."

"Yes."

"The suffering never seems to stop."

"No, dear. That's not true. Joseph is with me at times, and we appreciate our blessings more than ever. So I feel comforted. But the testing never ends. And it's the same for all of us—both the pain and the joys. I don't doubt that the illness you suffered in crossing the ocean brought on this baby's weakness. But you came to Zion all the same, knowing what it might cost you. I hope you believe it was worth it."

"I do. At least most of the time, I do."

It was an honest answer. Liz had been thinking lately that she might have stayed in England and the baby might have been all right. She and Will could have lived in a better house, and they could have had an easier life. She had told herself all summer that the effort had been worth it—that Zion was worth it—but these last few days she had not been so sure.

"God is still with you, Sister Liz. It's what I wanted you to know. I didn't come to give you false hope. I merely want you to know that God will get you through."

"Thank you. I do believe that." She looked down at little Mary Ann again. She told herself she had to prepare—had to accept—and not let herself fall apart.

Before Emma left, she took Mary Ann in her arms again, and

she prayed for her. She asked that Liz might have the faith and strength to accept whatever came.

• • •

Will arrived home before noon, just as he had promised. But when he stepped through the door, he could tell that something had changed. His first thought was that Mary Ann had died, but Liz was holding her and crying softly. She wasn't upset the way she had sometimes been the past few days.

"Come and hold her for a little while and I'll fix us something to eat."

"Is she any better, or—"

"Will, she's almost gone."

"I could bless her again. I could—"

Liz shook her head.

But Will wasn't sure he was ready to give up. He had worried so much about Liz that he hadn't thought enough about what this loss was going to do to him. All he could think was that when Mary Ann was gone, there would be an emptiness in their lives, and he had no idea what would happen to Liz. He had brought her here, put her on that miserable ship that had almost killed her. Everything he had done since they had married seemed to have worked against her. He had wanted her more than anything—for himself—and she had given herself to him, but what was the result going to be?

The rest of that day they took turns holding Mary Ann. Her breathing was ever more shallow, and finally, late in the night—without Will or Liz ever knowing the moment when it actually happened—she was gone. Mary Ann didn't seem different when her spirit left her. Her face was still as delicate as a newly opened rose.

CHAPTER 5

Abby had stayed at the hospital every day—and most nights—since William's birth more than a week earlier. Because of Jeff's work, he couldn't stay all day, but he drove to Quincy each evening, and twice he had stayed overnight so that Abby could drive home, shower, and get a better night's sleep. In the Neonatal Intensive Care Unit, parents could sleep on a little pull-out bed when they chose to stay, but the trouble was, activity at night slowed but never really stopped. Sleep was difficult. Doug Vincent, Jeff's boss, had been understanding about Jeff's absences at the time of the surgery, but others at the company were not patient when their computers acted up. That meant on nights when he stayed at the hospital he had to leave early to make it back to Fort Madison, Iowa, across the river from Nauvoo, by the time people came to work. Abby knew Jeff was running on the last fumes left in his tank, but he didn't complain. He seemed to worry more about Abby and how tired *she* had to be.

Friends in Abby and Jeff's Nauvoo ward had rallied around them. Kayla had shown up at the hospital every other day or so. She had brought Abby things she needed and usually stayed a few hours to help Abby pass the time. On those days, Lois McClelland, an older woman in their ward, had taken Kayla's children for her. When Jeff got home at night, a meal was always in the oven. Sister Lawrence, the Relief Society president, had borrowed the extra garage-door opener, and she used it each day to get into the house with a hot meal.

What Abby learned was that Sister Caldwell, the senior missionary from Idaho who had become Abby's friend, had been making some of the meals and had also involved other senior missionaries. They were busy people, Abby knew, so she was touched to think of them finding time to help her.

As Jeff was getting ready to leave on a Monday afternoon, Dr. Hunt happened to come by. He told Jeff and Abby that William was doing all right and they both ought to go home for a good night of sleep. Abby was reluctant, but Jeff told her the baby was in good hands, that she had to give herself a break. And then he didn't take no for an answer. He got her coat and walked her out to the car. It would be good to have a little time alone, to talk—except that the conversation turned to the usual subject. Abby could never stop thinking about William's heart, and she was always trying to interpret even the subtlest of words the doctor or nurses used, even their body language. She knew she did too much of that, but it was what filled her head all day, and when she finally had a few minutes with Jeff, it was what she always felt a need to discuss.

When they got home, before Abby even had time to sit down, the phone rang. When Abby answered, it was Sister Caldwell who said, "Oh, Abby, it's you. I was expecting Jeff."

"We both came home tonight," Abby said. "It's the first time we've done that."

"That's wonderful. You two need that. The only thing I wanted to ask was how William is doing. Everyone wants to know."

"I think he's all right, Sister Caldwell," Abby said. "But I really don't know. The doctor just says he's 'holding his own,' whatever that means. They did close his chest, so I guess that means they aren't so worried about him as they were right at first."

"Can you hold him and nurse him and—"

"No. Not right now. He's got lots of tubes and wires running in and out of him. But I rub his little head and talk to him. They say he's not in pain, but I watch him and I wish I could just . . ." Abby stopped. She had had a long day.

"I'm so sorry," Sister Caldwell was saying. "You need to get to bed. I'll bet you're jist worn to a frazzle."

"I'm fine. I just wish we'd start to see . . ." She fought against her tears. "I'd like to see some progress. That's all."

"I can jist imagine. But honey, I pray every day for him—so do all the missionaries—and I jist know he's going to be all right."

Maybe. But so many people said such things. Abby was weary of looking for evidence of God's will. "Sister Caldwell," she said, "thanks so much for the food, and thanks for calling."

"Did your meal come today?"

"Yes."

"Okay, that's good. Sister Rosewater said she'd do it, but jist between you and I, she's gittin' a little forgetful. She forgits her schedule and don't show up where she's s'posed to be. And you oughtta hear her version of the scripts. I heard her start the Lucy Smith script in the bakery one day and I had to cough like I had the pneumonia to git her to stop and think."

Abby laughed. "Well, she remembered the meal. Jeff's getting it out right now, and it smells really good. Thank her for me—and all the sisters who've been helping."

"I'll tell you what I've learned about these sisters in our mission—because I sit and talk to 'em all day this time of year when not many come 'round for our tours. Ever' single one of 'em has had her heartaches. And when they hear about your little guy, they want to do something. That's the sisterhood of the Church, Abby."

"I'm learning that, Sister Caldwell."

"This life has a way of schoolin' people. And when school is about out—the way it is for us older folks—we remember what it was like to make it through the hard times. So we want to help. I know I talk too much, but ever' time I think about you, I jist want to say, 'It's all worth it, Abby dear. It's a good life, even if it's hard, and someday you'll look back and be thankful for ever' single thing—even all the hard things."

"Thanks, Sister Caldwell. I love you."

"I love you too, honey."

But Abby couldn't say all she wanted to say; she was too touched. Just once she wished her mother would call her and sound as kind and caring as Sister Caldwell.

Abby set the phone down and looked across the kitchen at Jeff, who had been dishing out the ham and cheesy potatoes he had taken from the oven. She knew that he was wondering about her tears, so she said, "She's such a dear soul. I don't know how I'd go through something like this if I didn't have the Church—and the sisters."

Jeff nodded. Abby was struck by how tired he looked, and it occurred to her how lonely he must be. She walked to the table, where he had set two plates. She held his hand while he said a blessing, and then, after they had eaten, she told him to forget the dishes for now, and she led him to the couch in the living room. They sat down together, and he tucked her tightly to him with his arm around her, and for a long time they didn't say a word. She liked that. It was what she needed.

• • •

The days since William's birth had been tough for Jeff. He called Abby at the hospital several times each day, and always, he hoped that she would have good news—just some indication that William's heart was beginning to function more efficiently. But every morning the nurses administered an echocardiogram and a blood saturation test, and nothing seemed to change. William's left ventricle had to expand, but so far that apparently hadn't happened. Dr. Hunt said that he wasn't too surprised, that it might take time, but Jeff just wanted to hear something positive after all this waiting.

Jeff wanted life to return to some sort of normality. He wanted the baby to come home, and he wanted Abby to be there, too. He had felt cut off from her for such a long time now. He knew he had disappointed her—hadn't given her the comfort she needed at crucial times. He had wanted to tell her that he *knew* everything would be all right, but he *hadn't* known—still didn't know—and he was sure that faking something like that could only do damage in the long run.

Now she had cuddled up under his arm and was holding him around the middle. He had some things he wanted to tell her, but he didn't want to break the mood. He just wanted to cling to her the way she was clinging to him and feel that the two of them were all right with one another—and that if something happened to little William, they could get each other through the experience.

After a time, Abby asked, "What happened at work today?"

He liked that she was remembering that his life was still going on, that he had things to do each day, but it wasn't what he wanted to talk about. "Nothing much," he said, and then he realized that he needed to let her into his life a little. "Everyone needs me at the same time—or no one does. One of the engineers had his hard drive crash today and he almost came unglued. I finally recovered a file he thought he'd lost, and I swear, I was afraid he was going to kiss me."

"It's great that you can help people."

Jeff had felt a little of that. But mostly it seemed that he was doing nothing at all. So much of his work seemed mechanical. And he could guess what that engineer's reaction would have been had he not been able to find the file. But he also knew it was the wrong time to complain about his job. He only said, "It did feel good to get the guy back up and running. I gave him my little talk about backing up his files, and he said he would do that. Maybe he learned his lesson."

Jeff heard the furnace fan kick on and realized it was running almost all the time now. He really needed to add insulation in the attic and ask Brother Robertson whether he wanted to put in double-pane windows. He had hardly thought about the house lately, and Abby hadn't done anything about redecorating. He really wondered whether they were earning their free rent.

"Are you okay, Abby?" Jeff finally asked.

"I don't know what I am, Jeff. My whole world seems wrapped up in little William right now. At first I was scared every minute. Now I just sit there and wait—and worry. I tell myself that lots of people have lost babies, or they've had older children die. I keep trying to believe I can handle it if I have to, but then I think about coming home without him and I go into a sort of panic."

"This whole thing is frustrating for me too," Jeff said. "I feel like I'm on edge every second."

"But you don't fly off the handle the way I do."

"I think you've been really steady, Ab. Sometimes I can tell you're right on the edge of falling apart, but you've never done it. You've been tough. I just wish I could respond better to what you need from me."

"No. Don't say that. I know I get mad at you for being logical—but one of us has to be."

Jeff had always wanted to believe that logic and faith could work together, even strengthen one another, but he was not so sure anymore. He felt as though two parts of himself were warring inside. He had learned, though, that he couldn't be so open about his struggle, especially right now. Abby needed strength, not confusion.

Jeff's mind went back to the life history he had received from his Aunt Mary that day. He had wanted to mention it on the drive from Quincy, but it had seemed trivial compared to all the weighty matters she was worrying about. Still, what he had read had felt significant—something he wanted to share with Abby. "I wanted to tell you, Ab, my aunt emailed me something interesting today. It's the first part of that life history of my Grandpa William Lewis—the one my dad told me about."

Abby actually didn't sound terribly interested when she asked, "What did you learn about him?"

"It was interesting how he came to join the Church. He grew up in this beautiful valley—Wellington Heath. He was in that group called the United Brethren who all joined the Church together—the ones that Wilford Woodruff converted. Do you know about that?"

"No."

"There were about six hundred people, all waiting for what they called 'light and truth,' and Woodruff pretty much converted all of them. But Grandpa only went to church because his dad made him go. He thought the people were crazy—ranting and raving and falling down on the floor. He believed in God, but he didn't think much of religion."

"What changed his mind?"

"Actually, I think it started with Grandma. She must have been a real knockout. He said she was the prettiest girl he ever saw." Jeff squeezed Abby a little tighter. "Of course, he never saw *you*."

"That's true. And just look how gorgeous I am right now."

Jeff knew how self-conscious she was about the weight she had gained during the pregnancy. Jeff didn't care about that, but he did hate to see her look so tired. "Well, she was apparently *very* pretty, and her dad was a solicitor—which is a kind of lower-level lawyer— and Grandpa was just a tenant farmer. He wanted to raise his station in life, so he went up to Manchester to look for work in the factories, but he ended up on a crew that was building a railroad line. He was working in a tunnel when it collapsed and his right hand was smashed. Then he got an infection from that and almost died. He was in really bad shape when he heard a voice telling him to go home. So that's what he did, even though—"

"What do you mean, a voice?" Abby turned a little more toward him, and he could tell that she was getting more interested.

"It was like his own voice in his mind. But it kept saying 'Go home,' so he walked all the way back to his farm, and that brought him in contact with Wilford Woodruff and the Book of Mormon. But he felt like he wouldn't have been ready for it if he hadn't gotten injured and was facing death. But the story gets even more amazing from that point. He and Grandma were on a ship coming here to Nauvoo and a big storm came up. It was so bad he thought the ship was going to sink. But Grandma told him to get out of bed and command the winds to cease. So he did. He raised up his arm and rebuked the storm—and when he did, the winds calmed down and the she ship was saved."

"Wow. Those pioneers had *so much* faith."

"I guess. But that's not how he told it. He said that when Grandma told him to stop the storm, he didn't think he could do it. He said it was her faith, not his, that made him say the words."

"Still, the winds stopped."

"I know. But it's interesting to hear him talk about it. My dad always says that he was this great stalwart, and in a way he was, but he struggled with doubt all the time, even after he joined the Church—especially when he was a young guy. What I kept feeling was that he was a lot like me. I know I disappoint you sometimes—because faith is so hard for me—but when I read about him today, I kept thinking that I'm not a hopeless case."

Jeff felt the awkwardness when Abby didn't say anything for a time. She was looking across the room, not at him, when she said, "Maybe things have always been the same. Women want their husbands to be the strong ones."

"I don't know. Grandma was the one who sounds strong. She went through some hard things herself and never lost her faith. She'd had a nice house in England, but when she got to Nauvoo she had to live in a little log cabin. It was a huge comedown for her."

Abby remained silent for a time again. Then she asked, "If your grandpa doubted so much, how could he command a storm to cease?"

"If you don't know the Lord's will, I guess you just ask for what's best. But if you *know*, you have a right to command. So I don't know—maybe he didn't know, but he trusted that Grandma knew. Does that make sense?"

"I guess. But would the Lord let the ship sink when his people were on their way to Zion?"

"That's the question I was thinking about today. But ships do sink. It's not like Mormons are protected from bad things that happen." Immediately Jeff realized that he had said the wrong thing, so he added, "Of all the ships that crossed the Atlantic with LDS immigrants on board, though, not one ever went down. It wasn't that uncommon for ships to sink, but none of the Mormon ships did."

"But some of the people died on the ships, didn't they? Especially babies."

"Sure. In fact, almost every ship lost some people—because of all the seasickness and diseases. My grandma was pregnant on the ship. She got really sick and almost died, and Grandpa contracted cholera on the riverboat coming up the Mississippi. Both of them came close to dying."

"But they made it."

"They did. My aunt said she'd send me some more of the story when she gets it transcribed. I don't know too much more about what happened to them, but I do know that they both lived fairly long lives."

"Can I read the part you have?"

"Sure. You can take it down to the hospital tomorrow." But Jeff worried what conclusion Abby might draw from all this. He felt he needed to tell her the other part of what he'd learned. "Abby, I looked something up today. I got wondering about that baby—the one Grandma was pregnant with on the ship. So I looked at Family Tree online."

"Did she miscarry?"

"No. But the baby only lived about two weeks."

Jeff saw the change in Abby. She slid away from him and turned to look at him more directly. "Why did you want to tell me that?"

"I don't know. It's just the rest of that story. Grandpa Lewis did learn to trust in God—but that doesn't mean he never had to face any more hardships."

"So what are you trying to say to me?"

Jeff realized the trap he had worked himself into. He had intended his story as a little lesson, but he didn't want to say what that lesson was. "It's not exactly a parallel, Abby. I don't mean to say that it is. Things are very different now."

"Babies still die."

"But not nearly so many. Look what the doctors have been

doing for William. In Grandpa's age, there would have been no way to—"

"Doctors can't change God's will."

"They've changed the death rate tremendously. Mothers rarely die in childbirth now. That used to happen a lot."

"So what are you saying? That's where we have to put our trust?"

"Partly, but . . ."

"Jeff, let's not do this again. We always come back to the same conclusion. We just have to wait and see what God wants to do." Abby got up. "I accept that. You don't have to tell me again. William may not live, and that's the reality you want me to learn to live with. I appreciate your reminding me." She walked toward the hallway, and there were tears in her voice when she said, "I'm going to bed. I'm really tired."

"Abby, don't misunderstand what I'm saying. I believe in blessings. And I believe in miracles."

Abby turned back and looked at Jeff for a few seconds. Tears were running down her cheeks. "Maybe it's wrong of me," she said, "but I want to be like your grandma. I just want to say, 'Jeff, command the winds to stop.' I know that makes you feel bad, and I'm sorry, but it's what I feel."

Jeff, still sitting on the couch, watched her go. He couldn't think what to say to her. He thought of praying, even thought of raising his hand in the air and commanding his baby to be healed. But his own story didn't really make sense to him. It was true that the waves had calmed, but after his ancestors had gone through all that, their baby had still died. Why?

Finally, Jeff got up, and, without retrieving his coat, he walked out through the kitchen door and closed it softly so Abby wouldn't know he was gone. He walked across the street. There was some packed-down snow on the nature trail in the state park, and the temperature was biting, but Jeff needed to do something, and this was the only thing that had come to mind.

He left the trail at the spot where he always had before. He pushed through the dead grass and ferns and made his way to the little clearing. He thought of kneeling down, but he wasn't sure he had come to pray. "Grandpa," he said out loud, "what am I supposed to do? I want to command little William to live, but I can't get myself to do it. I don't even know why."

There was nothing. No sound of wings. Not even any stars in the sky. It was a black night, no moon, and not a sound in the trees. The air was so cold it hurt.

He waited, but he soon knew that this wasn't his answer. Grandpa was dead, and maybe at times there was some solace in ruminating out loud, here on this spot. But Grandpa Lewis wasn't going to say anything to him, and if he did, what could he say?

Jeff suddenly felt not only cold but foolish. Abby loved him, but she didn't respect him, and he understood that completely. He had done nothing so far to earn her confidence.

• • •

Abby knew she had said the wrong thing—again—but why had he told her that story? She already knew that bad things happened to people, even to people who kept the faith. She didn't need to study Jeff's family history to understand that.

What Abby wanted was to trust the Lord and the gospel and live accordingly—the way she had promised to do in joining this Church—but maybe it wasn't in her. Maybe other people accepted the will of the Lord better than she did. During all these days in the hospital she had sat and prayed, but there was little William all the while, full of tubes. She could not think of one good thing that could come from her losing him. What kind of design was it, to create life and then take it back? Sometimes she wanted to scream at the Lord that He had no right to steal her baby away from her.

But Abby didn't like herself when she let those kinds of thoughts pass through her mind. She needed to tell the Lord she was sorry, and then she needed to apologize to Jeff. And she would, when she was ready, but she wasn't in control just yet.

Jeff was making no sound out there in the living room. Finally, she heard the kitchen door close, and she thought he was going out to the garage. But she heard him sit down on the recliner, which squeaked a little, and she knew he had actually just come back. She knew where he must have been. He liked to walk across the street to the spot where his grandparents had lived. He had even admitted to her that he sometimes talked out loud to Grandpa Lewis. She couldn't imagine what good it did to go out in the cold and confer with someone who had been dead for a hundred years.

She let more time pass, and gradually—very gradually—she began to think more about Jeff and what he was feeling. Talking to Grandpa was probably a joy after trying to talk to her. She knew she had to go back to him, but she also knew she had to say something that would bring them together, and she would have to change her mood to do that. So she slid off the bed onto her knees, and she told the Lord how sorry she was.

She wasn't prepared for what happened.

She felt no consolation at all—the way she usually did when she prayed. What she felt was only that life was ever so much harder than she had expected. There were nasty things to survive, and they seemed to come without any reason. Maybe God didn't send hardships. Maybe they just came. Maybe it was merely the law of averages. It was her turn, apparently, to go through a trial, and she had to prove she could do it.

Abby finally broke down; she cried harder than she had through this whole ordeal. She could deal with anything, but not with the feeling that God didn't care—that she was only a statistic. She had believed in prayer since she had first tried it. It was the thing that had brought her to the Church: the realization that she wasn't alone. So she prayed again and this time didn't say anything except, "Please, Lord, I need to know you're still with me."

She waited, but it was Jeff's voice she heard, not the Lord's. "Are you okay?" he asked.

She got up and went to him, still sobbing.

"I heard you crying," he said.

"I don't know if I can do this, Jeff. I don't know if I'm strong enough."

Jeff held her. He had never been so scared in his life. He had been feeling the same way about himself. It seemed as though the whole structure he had built his life on was falling away. And yet, he knew he had to be strong for Abby. "We'll be okay," he said. "We just can't turn on each other."

But that was only half an answer, and he didn't know what the other half was.

CHAPTER 6

Liz didn't cry when little Mary Ann died. She told herself not to let go, not to stumble into the darkness that hovered around her. She sat and held her baby for a time, and then she reminded herself of the things she had to do. "We need a coffin," she said to Will. "And we need to let Jesse and Ellen know."

"Do you want a funeral?"

Liz had already thought about that. "There are too many funerals in Nauvoo," she said. "We can just take her to the cemetery. Someone can say a few words at her grave."

"We could ask Brother Woodruff," Will said, as though he had also thought about it.

"He would be good, if he's well enough. But he's been so sick. Maybe Brother Benbow could do it. Or you could."

"No. I don't want to."

Liz understood. It would be too hard for Will. But she didn't want a lot of words anyway. What she had feared had come now, and she knew there was nothing to do but move forward.

Things happened. They just came, whether you wished them

away or not. Now she would do whatever came next. Life would be that way for now—maybe not forever, but for as far ahead as she could see.

• • •

Will felt the loss of the baby, but even more, he felt the loss of his wife. He had watched her shut herself off from him, from everyone. He sat up with Mary Ann most of the night. It had felt wrong to him to leave her little body alone. He was tired, but his mind was busy, and he knew he couldn't sleep anyway. Liz had gone to bed, and she slept as though she had never slept before.

Will kept trying to think about the future. He and Liz would have more children, and all their hopes could still come about. That was the thing to remember. He kept pushing away the memory of the young Liz he had known in Ledbury: her happy walks to the market, her playing the pianoforte or chatting happily with her sister. She had been so spirited, and she had laughed so much. He wondered what life was doing to her, and whether her choice to marry him was going to take away her joyful nature.

Will remembered all the advice he'd given Ellen when her baby had died on the ship. It was strange to think how wise his words had seemed at the time, disheartening to realize that he felt no more consolation than Ellen had felt then. Ellen was going forward now. She seemed all right. But he wondered how much she had been changed inside. There was a face that people presented to the world, and there was resoluteness in that public appearance, but he suspected that in the course of life people collected more and more grief, and much of it hung from their shoulders like the weight of a harness, pulling them down. In the end, no wonder that people were finally ready to return to their Maker.

Toward morning Will thought he would sleep a little, so he lay down next to Liz, but it was useless, so he got up to see to the burial. He walked off the hill to William Huntington's stonecutting shop on Main Street. He found no one in the shop, so he knocked on the door of the house, which was behind the shop. Brother Huntington showed up at the door looking as though he had still been in bed when Will had knocked. "I'm sorry to bother you so early," Will said. "Our baby died last night. We hope to bury her today."

"I'm sorry to hear that, Brother Will," Brother Huntington said. He let his hand settle on Will's shoulder, didn't seem to mind that he had been pulled out of bed. "Have you purchased a burial plot?"

"No. Where do I do that? I thought it might be here."

"You'll have to see Brother Hyrum at his office across from his house—the one where he gives blessings. We're digging graves every day these days. We have some men starting early each morning. Pick out a plot, and Hyrum will get word to the diggers. I'd give them until afternoon before you try to bury her, though."

"That sounds about right. I still haven't built a coffin."

Will and William looked at stones after that and settled on the simple inscription of name and dates, and then Will walked to Hyrum Smith's house. He didn't knock at the door; he waited outside the office, not wanting to rouse Hyrum too early as he had done with Brother Huntington. Will was wearing an old waistcoat that he used for work. The cool air penetrated it as he waited; he found himself shivering. Nauvoo was still asleep, but the rising sun was glowing from behind the bluffs, the mist along the river turning amber in the angled light. The river was more than a mile wide here where it bent around the city. Its surface was muted in the soft light, seeming docile, but Will always felt a sense of the river's inexorable power. It was like the force of life he had been thinking about all night, the inevitability of certain things he simply couldn't change. At least this morning he was reminded how beautiful the river could also be.

Will was still looking out toward the river when he heard a door shut. Hyrum Smith had stepped out of his house, and now he walked across the street. "I just now saw you waiting out here, Brother Lewis. Why didn't you knock on my door?"

"I thought you might still be in bed—where you rightly should be," Will said.

"No. I'm an early riser. But I almost hate to ask why you're here this early."

"It's our new little baby. She's gone already."

"I'm sorry," Hyrum said. He nodded, waited. When Will finally looked into his eyes, he saw that Hyrum's words were not empty. He *was* sorry.

Hyrum was not as forceful and jovial as Joseph, but he was reliable and *good*—and Will always felt that when he was around the man.

The two walked inside, and Will used a chart of the cemetery to choose a burial plot. He thanked Hyrum, promised to pay for the plot as soon as the county paid him for his roadwork, and then continued on to Wilson's sawmill, on Lumber Street at the river's edge. He had to wait a while for someone to show up there, too. He bought a few boards and carried them away on his shoulder.

The town was finally waking up. Thin plumes of gray smoke were rising from the chimneys and drifting eastward, hanging against the bluffs. People were beginning to emerge from their houses to winch water from their wells, to feed their animals, to work in their gardens. Will saw a boy cutting corn and a man digging his root crop from a garden. A woman was milking a cow that was tied to a "worm fence," the rails in a zigzag. She was leaning her head against the cow's side as though she wanted just a few more minutes of sleep—or maybe a bit of warmth. He could see the steam of her gentle breath.

This was a good place and these were good people. Will felt

that. But there was also something sad about all of it—so much work, so much willingness, and yet, so many trials.

The Woodruff cabin was on the way home, just under the bluff. Will stopped there and found Brother Wilford up, eating breakfast. He lived in a simple log house, nicely furnished and kept very clean. Will had often talked to him about his dream—the same as Will's—to build a fine brick home on this lot.

But Brother Woodruff looked emaciated now, after his weeks of illness, far from ready to take on such a project. He was genuinely sorrowful when he heard the news about Mary Ann. "Yes, yes. I'll come," he told Will. "I'm getting my strength back. I can mount my horse now, and I'll ride out."

"Don't feel that you have to say much. Liz said she wants things kept simple."

"Yes. And simple is what I have to offer right now." He chuckled to himself.

"Would two o'clock this afternoon be all right?"

Brother Woodruff thought about that for a moment. "Yes, I can do that. I want to put in a little time at the print shop this morning. Brother Taylor hasn't been well either, so we're each doing what we can to get the *Times and Seasons* out. But that will give me the morning to work a little. I'll meet you at the cemetery at two."

Will thanked him and shook his hand, and then he walked back up the hill, through the woods. He hammered together a little pine box before he entered the house and found Liz awake and making breakfast. He ate a little cornmeal mush, and then he set out to let Jesse and Ellen and the English Saints know what had happened. He made the ride out in less than an hour, stopping by John and Jane Benbow's place and Jesse and Ellen's, and then he returned at the same speed. He kept wondering what he would find when he got back. He half expected Liz to have broken down, but when he got back to the house, she was just as quiet as she had been earlier.

The Female Relief Society sisters had found out about the death by then. Nelly had stopped by that morning, and she had probably spread the word after that. Two sisters had walked up from the flats and helped Liz wash little Mary Ann, and now they were clothing her in a simple muslin dress. Liz had sewn it that summer, intending that it would be the baby's blessing dress. Somehow the thought of that brought tears to Will's eyes—but not to Liz's.

When the sisters were gone, Will said, "I thought we could put Mary Ann in the little coffin and carry her out to the cemetery in the oxcart. I think Socks can pull it all right, and you can ride. But if you think she needs something better, we could—"

"The oxcart is good."

Will had thought so, too. It seemed rather "processional" to carry her that way, but humble at the same time.

"Are you doing all right, Liz?"

"Yes." But she turned away.

"Should we invite people to come back here after the burial?"

"No, Will. The sisters wanted to bring food, but I told them not to do it. People can't stop their work every day just because of one more death."

"It's all right to feel sorrow, Liz. It's only natural. We miss her, and—"

"After we bury her," Liz said, "I think you should go back to work. It's a clear day, and we may not have many good days left. I can walk back from the cemetery by myself, and you can still get some work done. I'm going to advertise my school now. It's time I start taking pupils."

"That might be good, Liz. I think it will. But I'm coming back here today. I don't want you walking, and I don't want you to be alone."

She turned around, and her look seemed to say, "Yes, and what about tomorrow?" But she said nothing. He hardly recognized her face. There was no life in it. She was as pretty as ever, but pretty like a porcelain figurine.

Liz kept herself busy tidying up around the house and then heating water so she and Will could bathe. She took her bath in the bedroom in the tin tub they used. She stayed longer than usual, and when she came out she was dressed in her pretty green Sunday dress. Will cleaned up too, and he shaved, and then he put on his suit of clothes.

Liz seemed to forget about eating dinner, and Will didn't want to say anything, so they didn't eat. Shortly after one o'clock, Will set the little coffin in the back of the oxcart. He walked and Liz rode in the cart as they made the slow trip east on Parley Street. Near the cemetery they passed through a little valley that in summer had been as green as Wellington Heath. The woods were brilliant yellow now, with a smattering of red maples. Nature was always the same, it seemed, bright cardinals flitting about, finches enjoying the good day as it warmed, the blue jays making their usual irreverent noises.

Liz must have been thinking the same thing. "Life just goes on," she said—the only words she spoke during the entire trek.

• • •

Men were still digging graves when Will and Liz arrived at the cemetery, and one of the men showed them the little grave where they would bury their Mary Ann. It was on high ground among a scattering of white oaks and hickories. It was a nice spot, but Will found himself looking into the black earth and hating the thought of shoveling that heavy soil over the top of his little daughter.

The Benbows soon arrived with Jesse and Ellen, all having ridden in the Benbows' carriage. By then, Will spotted Brother Woodruff as he tied his horse to a sapling near the road and began his slow trudge to the crest of the hill. Will hurried down to take his arm and help him along. Will appreciated that these good friends would take time to come, and he was surprised that several other of the English families had showed up. Four women from the Female Relief Society also arrived, including Sarah Kimball, all having walked the two miles from the flats. They embraced Liz and told her how sorry they were, and Will saw a little emotion return to Liz's eyes.

Brother Woodruff preached only a few minutes. He talked about the Lord's great plan for His children, and he spoke of the Atonement. Tears came to his eyes when he said, "It was when I was with you in England that I received word that my little Sarah Emma had passed away. I knew everything then that I've said here today, but still, I missed her as though my heart would break, and Elizabeth and Will, I know that's how you feel today. I wish I could tell you that I no longer miss my little girl, but it isn't true. I'm sure you understand that. Still, what I've said about the Atonement is true, and it's the great comfort we have. You will see her again. She isn't lost to you forever."

These were good thoughts for Will, and again, he saw a small reaction in Liz. He knew she was trying not to think too much—not to feel—but surely she was glad for any measure of consolation.

• • •

Liz felt a little peace by the time she left the burial ground. She didn't want to watch her baby being lowered into the ground, so she turned her back and walked away, but she was warmed by so much love. She didn't say it to Will, but she was relieved that he didn't go back to work that day. He led the horse again, and he didn't say too much to her. And then, after he took care of the horse and cart at home, he came inside and held her in his arms. She was glad she had married such a man as Will, who looked out for her, loved her, and seemed to understand, or at least respect, a woman's feelings more than many men she had known in her life.

But ahead of Liz was a rutted road like the one she had been staring at all the way home. She would have to get up in the morning, and every morning all winter, without her lovely daughter. That was the reality she couldn't escape. She was not going to fall apart; she was not going to ask, "Why me?" She was not going to complain. But she would not see Mary Ann for an entire lifetime, and nothing could change that, even the faith that she would, in fact, see her in the next life.

Nelly came by that afternoon. She was carrying an evening meal for Liz and Will. Somehow, this kindness touched Liz more than almost anything. "Get back to normal, just as soon as you can," she told Liz. "That's the one thing that helps most, to do our chores and bake our bread—and all those things. I know you have no oven, but you make your cornbread and your ash bread, and it eats good when a man comes home. I'll come by every day, just to see if I can carry water and the like, or if you need to say somethin' that's on your mind, I'm good at hearin' those things."

Liz smiled a little, and said, "Do come by. I would like that."

And then Nelly went out, and Liz was alone. Will had gone outside, probably to look after his animals. Liz looked around her cabin and tried to think what chores she could do, since she had tidied up that morning and Nelly had brought pork and potatoes and a loaf of bread. Then she saw Mary Ann's little cotton blanket, resting on the cupboard near the fire, and all her resolve was suddenly gone. She picked it up and smelled it, and she started to cry. She told herself that she could only do that for a minute or two and then she had to put the blanket away. But she held it close, rubbed its softness on her cheek, and broke down. She sat at the table and sobbed as though she hadn't talked to herself all day about not doing that.

When the door opened, she looked up, tears still on her face. She was ashamed to have Will see her that way.

But Will stepped to her and touched her hair. "It's all right," he said. "It's what you need to do." Then he said, "Liz, there's someone here who wants to talk to you."

"No, Will. I don't want to see anyone else today." She got up, refolded the blanket, and walked to the cupboard.

"I think you'll want to see this man. It's Oscar Clarkston. He lived in Bishop's Hill, in Herefordshire. You remember him, don't you?"

"Yes. He married Rosemary Richens, from Twigworth."

"Well . . . yes. But he has something he wants to talk to you about. And it must be now. It could be something good for you."

Liz had no idea what to think of that, but Will was insisting, and Liz didn't have the strength to resist. "That's fine," she said. "Give me just a minute."

Will nodded and walked out. Liz tucked the blanket away in a cupboard drawer, and then she poured a little water in a basin and washed her face. She dried her hands and face, took a long breath, then turned and waited. Will granted her more time than she had expected, but when he finally opened the door, she could see that he was changed—almost eager, she thought. It was Brother Clarkston who looked thinner than she remembered him. He took his hat off and held it in one hand as he reached out to shake hands with Liz. "I'm sorrowed by what's happened to ye," he said. "Will says yor little girl was pritty as a picher."

Liz nodded and thanked him. "How is Rosemary?"

"Well . . . that's what I wanted to talk to you about." He stood straight, with his feet square under him, and he held the brim of his black hat with both hands. "Rosemary give birth to a child—a little boy—a week ago yesterday. But everythin' went wrong, an' . . . well . . . by the time it was o'er, she was too weak. I lost her, Liz. She took her last breath with me holdin' her in my arms." His lips were shaking, but he didn't cry.

"I'm so sorry, Brother Clarkston. I knew Rosemary all my life."

"She was sick all the way 'cross the sea, and she was wore out from that, I think, and then she was just so tiny. It was like she wasn't big enough to have a fine big boy for her first child."

"Is the baby all right?"

"Aye, he is. He come through fine. But he's not thrivin'. Some of the sisters what live 'roun' me try their level best ta help, but he do na' like cow's milk. He's losin' weight, and he cries aw the time. I know he's 'ungry."

"I understand." Liz was starting to realize why Oscar had come.

"Some'un said this mornin', you lost a baby, and them sisters said I should talk to ye—because you could do it. I mean, you could feed 'im that way."

All day Liz had been feeling pain from her milk. Certainly, she could nurse the baby, but what was he asking? "Did you want to leave him with me for a time, or . . . what did you have in mind?"

"Well . . . I don't know what you feel 'bout this, but I do na' see how I can raise 'im. I have to keep my farm a-goin', and I can na' be wif 'im all day. More'n 'at, the sisters is sayin' he'll die if he do na' have nourishment."

"But how long would you want me to have him?"

"I'm thinkin' you could take 'im as yor own. Raise 'im instead of the little girl you lost. And give 'im love the way a woman can. I hear some has done it, and it works out awright. The sisters said Emma Smith done it, and it was a blessin' to her."

Liz really didn't know. It wouldn't be her baby, wouldn't smell the same. Maybe she couldn't love it the same. But something was coming awake inside her.

"Do you want to see 'im? Sister Reynolds has 'im out in the wagon. I thought na' to walk right in with 'im, not 'til I said everythin' what I was thinkin'."

"Wait just a minute," Will said. He had stepped over next to Liz, and now he put his arm around her waist. "I have a question. And maybe Liz has some of her own."

"Good. Go right on an' ax me."

"You're likely to find another woman to marry. Supposing Liz has the baby for a few months or a few years, and you have a wife by then, and you get thinking you want your son back. What then?"

Brother Clarkston shook his head. He tucked his hat under one arm and said, "No. I thought on that. I never will marry now. I can na' feel the same about any other lass. My way of thinkin' is, I might leave here and go some'ere where I do na' think on Rosemary ever' minute of ever' day. If I give my son over, I do na' plan to come back for 'im. I might like to see 'im someday, and know what kind of man he is, but that would be aw."

"You might not feel that same way after a while."

"I can only tell ye what I feel now, Will. And I'll tell ye what else. I'd sooner let Liz have 'im forever than to watch him dwindle down and die, and I'm scared that's what he's a-doin' now."

"Well . . . I know," Will said, "but we need to have the right understanding before this all starts. I don't want Liz's heart to be broken all over again."

But Liz didn't need these men negotiating for her. "Will, how do you even know I want the baby?" she asked.

"I don't know."

"Let me see him. I could help him right now and worry about the rest later."

Will looked wary, seemed ready to say something else, but Brother Clarkston walked out and before long was back with Sister Reynolds, who whispered her condolences to Liz and then handed the baby to her, wrapped in an old brown blanket, not as soft as the one Mary Ann had had.

Liz was frightened, but she took him.

"He's fallen asleep along the way—from the rockin' of the wagon," Sister Reynolds said.

Just as Liz looked at him, however, his eyes opened. He was surprisingly bright eyed; if he was dwindling, he certainly was stronger than Mary Ann had been. "Oh, he's pretty," Liz said. "He has his mother's eyes."

"He's got more hair than most," Sister Reynolds said, "and look how dark it is, like yours. People will think he's your own son."

Liz wasn't sure about that, but he was a fine-looking boy, with a good head, and hands twice the size of Mary Ann's. He began to whimper, and his face wrinkled up. Liz laughed a little at how sad he looked, and she tucked him close to her. "Get Mary Ann's blanket," Liz said to Will. "I put it in the bottom drawer." She pointed to the cupboard.

"Liz, let's think this over just a little," he said cautiously.

"He needs to eat, Will. All of you walk outside. I'll feed him."

"Aw right," Brother Clarkston said. "Are you thinking that—"

"I don't know what I'm thinking, except that he needs to be fed." She looked at Will. "You go too. Just give me a few minutes with him."

Will got the blanket for Liz, but before he followed the others outside, he said, "This might be just the right thing for you, Liz. But only do it if you're sure it's right."

Liz wasn't looking at him. She was gazing down at the little boy. "I know," she said. "I understand what you're saying."

Liz dropped the coarse wool blanket on the floor and wrapped Mary Ann's soft blanket around the baby, and then she opened her dress and sat down on her bed. She held the little boy to her breast, and he knew immediately what to do. She had always wanted Mary Ann to nurse that way. She felt the tugs, more painful than she had expected, but liked the little grunting sounds he began to make. "You *were* hungry," she said, and she laughed. And then tears spilled onto her cheeks.

• • •

Will was worried. When Brother Clarkston had shown up and posed his question, Will's first thought had been that this was an answer to prayer, that this was what Liz needed. But almost immediately, he had begun to wonder. Could she love this baby the way she had loved Mary Ann? If he turned out to be belligerent or stupid, would she blame herself—or even Will—for taking him?

Outside, Sister Reynolds was saying, "He's a lovely baby. I'd take him myself, 'cept we have three little ones already. I can't give him what he needs right now."

"Will," Brother Clarkston said, "I can na' think what else I kin do. I don't know any other woman like this—who might want a little one and who has her milk."

This all sounded too much like a farmer sticking a calf under a strange cow. "There's more to it than that," Will said. "This is a decision that will last a lifetime."

"I know. And I do na' want to give up my li'l boy. But I fear for his life, an' I can na' hold on to 'im while he stops his breathin', same as Rosemary done." His voice had begun to shake.

For the first time Will saw that this really was difficult for Oscar.

He put his arm around the man's shoulders. "Let's just see what she says, here in a few minutes."

So the three waited as the sun began to set and fill the woods with burnished light. Will thought about having a son, teaching him, playing with him. But how could he ever feel that this was really his son when he knew that Oscar was his father? Oscar was a small man, not built very strong, and he was certainly not a scholar. What sort of son would this baby turn out to be?

After a time Liz opened the door and asked everyone to come back inside. And Will saw that she had her answer. The color had come back to her skin. She looked satisfied. "I want to raise him," she said. "He's a good little soul, and he needs a mum. What's his name?"

"We was goin' to call him Jacob, but that was the name Rosemary liked. I guess you could call him somethin' else."

"No. It's a good name, and Rosemary should have that much—the right to name him. I hope she knows, right now, that I'll raise him up to her, and always honor her name in our house, once he's old enough to understand."

"That's what I would hope," Brother Clarkston said. "An' I would like it if he can know he has a dad, if that would be aw right."

Will wondered. How confusing would that be? But Liz was assuring Oscar that that would be fine with her. Will had wanted to talk to Liz first before this all happened, but it was no use. There was no way he could disagree with her decision at this point. Her sadness seemed gone, and he hadn't expected that to happen for a long time.

Liz and Sister Reynolds talked then, and Sister Reynolds carried a few of Jacob's things into the house. The two discussed feedings and nappies, and whatever else. Liz had handed Jacob to Will, and the little fellow was sleeping now. He didn't look anything like Mary Ann, wasn't delicate, wasn't a rose, but he was a strapping boy, and he was saving Liz's life. That had to be the right thing.

CHAPTER 7

Will returned to his roadwork the next morning. It had not been an easy night with little Jacob waking often, but Liz had fed him well, and as Will had watched her in the dim light emitted by the fire—which Will got up and stirred a couple of times—he saw in her face a contentment he had not expected. She had always been lively and busy, but as she sat in her rocking chair by the fireplace and watched the little one nurse, he had the feeling she had found a peace she had never known in her life.

Will was behind schedule now, and there was a great deal to accomplish. He was cutting a road through prairie ground southeast of Nauvoo. There had been a few trees to fell and stumps to pull, but most of the work was plowing through heavy sod, and then, once it was turned and had dried, scraping a level path with an oxen-drawn grader.

Grading was slow work, done mostly one surveyor's 66-foot chain-length at a time. The problem was, Will's corn at the Big Field had been ready for some time, and a fair part of it had still not been harvested. Will had set Jesse and Dan to work cutting the corn, but that meant he had to work alone on the road. He used three or four teams at a time, used voice commands, and scoured his own blade. It was tedious to work that way, but it was what he had done before he had hired anyone. He was just thankful that the weather was fair and he could make good progress—as he was able to do throughout most of October.

On October 28 Will heard that Joseph Smith was home again, and two days later, on Sunday, Joseph preached to the Saints in the temple. The walls of the temple were only about four feet high, but a shipment of white pine had arrived from the pineries in Wisconsin, and workers had hurriedly put down a temporary floor on the joists that had been set earlier. Joseph spoke about the importance of the temple, of baptisms for the dead, of Zion in these last days. Sometimes Will worried about the weakness of some of the Saints, but on this wonderful day, with the colors of fall rich and golden along the river below, Will knew why he had come here, and he felt certain that in time the Saints really would prosper together just as Joseph so often promised.

After the meeting, Liz and Will walked back to their house. Will was carrying Jacob. "This boy is heavy," Will told Liz. "He's getting fat."

"Oh, Will, he's come so far," Liz said. Jacob was not yet six weeks old, but he had grown so much that he hardly seemed the same baby. Liz was smiling, her pretty green eyes full of light. "But do you think I feed him too much?"

"He's good and strong, Liz—and he never would have survived without you."

Liz took hold of Will's arm. "I think he's happy, too. I play with him, and he makes little sounds, almost like he's learning how to laugh."

Liz laughed herself, and Will watched her, happy to see her so pleased. "I don't doubt it for a minute. I'd be happy too if you'd play with *me* that way."

She tightened her grip. "Oh, don't be jealous. I still love you the most."

Actually, she had seemed much closer to him lately, the life coming back into her chatter and her affection for him returning. "I have nothing to complain about," he said. "Except that I have to spend such long days away from you and Jacob. I'm almost looking forward to the first snow, just to spend some days at home."

"That's my hope too, Will. Jacob and I get along fine, but the days do seem long when you're gone so many hours. It's good that I have my schoolchildren. They keep me busy."

"And wear you out."

"I have been tired lately. But who isn't? That's just the way life is."

Will had tried to convince Liz not to start a school now that they had Jacob, but she liked the idea of contributing something to their income. She was teaching only five students, but the children's parents paid her $2.00 each for a twelve-week term of reading, writing, and spelling. Three of the children stayed longer for grammar, geography, and history, and they paid another $2.50 each, so that was $17.50 for the term. People paid her mostly in chickens and produce and the like, but those were commodities she could either use or trade at the general stores in town. Besides, she liked the children, and Will noticed that she liked to tell people she was a teacher.

"Tell me this," Will said. "Did we do the right thing in coming here? Should we have stayed at the Crawfords' farm?"

"We put our hands to the plow, Will; there's no looking back now." She walked a little faster and playfully pretended to pull him along. "You just didn't know it would require quite so much plowing."

It was true. Will had liked being the farm manager, not the plowman. "But back in England," he said, "we never would have heard a sermon like the one we heard today. It's what we hoped for in coming here, and it all seems worth it when Joseph is with us."

"I do feel blessed," Liz said. "I wondered for a time if the Lord had forgotten us, but I know better now. I won't be so quick to question Him in the future."

"And yet, you still miss little Mary Ann, don't you?"

"I'll always miss her, Will. You know that. But Jacob keeps my mind off her, and I love him more than I ever thought I could."

"Aye. It's how I feel, too."

But Will knew that it was easy to trust the Lord after a test had ended and better times had returned. He still wondered what other tests might be coming in their lives.

• • •

Liz had thrilled to the Prophet's words, and she had drawn strength from such a large gathering of Saints, but as days passed afterwards, it was not easy to remain quite so satisfied with life. She enjoyed her time with her pupils most days, but every morning she had far too much to do. Will left so early that she didn't have a chance to get breakfast for him. He would pack corn pones or a loaf of ash bread from last night's fire and cut himself a large wedge of cheese to take with him, and then he would be off for the day. Most days Liz was still very sleepy from being up with Jacob during the night, and she had to feed and bathe him in the morning while she was also planning out what she would teach the children.

What was worse was when Will would slaughter a hog and leave her with the meat to cure, or she would have fruit to dry, and every day there was milk to churn and butter to make. She was learning all these arts, but she was still not very good at any of them, and she was inefficient. Nelly advised her or came over and helped her, but Nelly was a busy woman too, and Liz felt bad when she asked too much of her.

Will was good about felling trees, chopping firewood, hauling in water from the well, and all the rest—but the man rarely did anything but work, and she never liked to ask him to do more than he was already doing. That meant that every morning, while everything else had to be done, Liz had to carry Jacob out to the cowshed, lay him in a little box she kept for that purpose, and then milk the cow. More than once she had nursed the baby and done her best to milk "Sister Brown"—as Will called the cow—at the same time. She had spilled some buckets that way, too.

Was she happy? She didn't really ask herself that question very often. Sometimes she realized, however, that she felt more useful, more worthwhile, than she ever had in her life. And Jacob, demanding as he was in his way, provided a joy she had never known anything about. Those minutes she would steal to laugh with him and bounce him were the best of her day.

One morning, after Jacob had gone down for a nap, Liz was churning butter when someone knocked on the door. She expected to see Nelly Baugh, but when she opened the door, she was surprised. It was Eliza Snow—a woman she knew from the Female Relief Society meetings she had attended. She hadn't thought that Sister Snow had even known who she was.

"I'm Sister Snow. I—"

"Yes, I know. Come in. It's so nice of you to stop by."

"You might not think so after I explain what I have in mind," Eliza said. She smiled and glanced down at a brown-paper bundle she was carrying under one arm. She had always seemed rather formal to Liz—and serious. Liz wondered what she might want.

"What is it I can do for you?" Liz asked. She motioned to a

wooden chair near the fireplace. The weather had turned cold the last few days, and Liz was now keeping a fire all day. "Sit down, please."

"I won't stay long. No doubt, you're very busy." Sister Snow was wearing a heavy, dark cloak with a hood, which she now pushed back. Her face was flushed from the cold, and no doubt from walking up the hill, but she was a handsome woman, thin and fairly tall, with dark eyes and dark hair parted down the middle and pulled tight against her head. Liz guessed that she must be around forty, even though she looked younger. She sat down, but she held herself erect on the chair, looking quite prim. "Sister Lewis, I heard about the loss of your baby. And now I've been told that you've taken in a child not your own."

"Yes. The Clarkston baby. His mother died in childbirth."

"I want you to know, it was a noble thing to do. You saved a life. Emma Smith herself told me that, and I'm certain that it's true."

"I hope it is," Liz said, but she could only think what an honor it was to have Eliza Snow in her little home. Sister Snow was known for her intelligence. She wrote hymns and poems that appeared in the *Times and Seasons* and *The Wasp*. There was no woman in Nauvoo better known—except for Emma Smith herself—and no woman more highly respected.

"Emma thinks you are the prettiest woman in Nauvoo, and that's been my impression, too, but I'm glad I've seen you this morning with your hair falling out and a smudge across your face. You're just as pretty, I dare say, but it's good to know your feet are on the ground." Sister Snow began to smile, and Liz saw, to her surprise, something sly in her eyes. Maybe she wasn't always serious, after all.

Liz rubbed at her face, wondering whether the smudge was from adding wood to the fire or maybe a white smear of cream from separating milk that morning. "Everyone seems to think I was a fine lady in England," Liz said, "but it's not true. I was a solicitor's daughter, that's all. But it is true that I did very little work growing up, and now I'm trying to learn how to be a farmer's wife—and failing, for the most part."

"No, no. You're a mother in Zion, and you've chosen to do the things that will bring you exaltation in the celestial kingdom. That's the work of this life—serving in every way we can." But that sly look returned. "That's my introduction to a request. Did you sense that already?"

"I do think I saw something coming," Liz said, and she smiled too. "But I'm honored you would think of me."

"Do you know about the Necessity Committees?"

"I heard them mentioned at the meetings."

"We have had them in each of the four wards, but we're about to be divided into ten wards in town, and three more east of the city limits. We need a committee for each, and we would like you to serve on the one in your ward."

"What would I do?"

"Visit the sisters, assess the needs of those sick or otherwise afflicted, and communicate to our leaders what service can be rendered."

Liz nodded. She was honored, but worried how she would manage everything. Still, she said, "I would like to do that, Sister Eliza."

"Good. Now another question. Have you learned to sew?"

"Only a little. I do some mending."

"We need women to sew shirts for the men who work at the temple. It's one of the services we've been doing since we first organized last spring."

"Yes, I am aware of that, and I've often thought it's something I should do, but I don't have the first idea how to get started."

"That's fine. This is not refined work. It's something I can show you rather quickly. The question is, do you have time to sew some shirts if we supply you with material and thread?"

"And also serve on the committee?"

"Yes. If it's not too much for you."

Liz took a breath. "You may not know, I've started a small school here at home."

"Ah." Sister Snow stood, rather abruptly. "No, I didn't know. I'm a teacher myself, you know, and I understand how much time that takes. If I had known, I wouldn't have asked you."

"No. It's all right." Liz stood too, and faced Sister Snow. "Please. Show me how to do it, and then I'll try to sew as often as I can. I should have more time this winter. I do want to help."

"All right, then. But let's put off your service on the Necessity Committee for now, and only ask you to sew as much as you can find time."

"I'll try to visit sisters, too. It's something I like to do."

"You're a true sister, Elizabeth. I can tell it from your willingness to serve—but I also feel it in your spirit." She stepped closer and took Liz's hand in hers. "Now, let me give you our shirt pattern and show you a trick or two that will help."

Liz was moved by the kind words. She liked to think that she was doing her part, and liked to think that she could become some- one as accomplished and righteous as Sister Snow.

Eliza and Liz studied the pattern together for a time, and Eliza explained some of the tricks of fitting the sleeves to the yoke and of cutting and stitching around the buttonholes. She gave Liz some yards of heavy denim material—for winter wear—along with thread and needles and buttons. Before she left, she asked, "I know your baby is sleeping just now, but could I peek at him?"

"Certainly," Liz said. Little Jacob was sleeping in a makeshift cradle, more a box than a piece of furniture, on the opposite side of the fireplace from where Eliza had been sitting. Liz picked up Jacob, and he stirred a little and then settled in against her and continued to sleep. She pulled back the blanket and let Sister Eliza look. But then, when she saw Eliza's obvious joy at seeing him, she handed him over to Eliza, who tucked him close to her and gazed into his round little face.

She was a poet and scholar, but Liz saw in her face that she was also a mother in her way—that she loved Jacob as instantly and naturally as Liz had. Liz felt she knew Eliza now, and she also knew that she would never forget this moment.

• • •

In the middle of November, a hard rainstorm moved in and stayed for a couple of days. A cold, clear day followed, and then more rain. Will's crops were in, but his roadwork was not entirely finished. He didn't have snow to deal with yet, but mud was worse. He wondered whether he could plan on more good days before a hard frost came and his work would have to stop for the winter.

Will felt blessed when the November rains abated and the mud dried enough to let him finish his work before snow began to fall. But then winter set in hard, with fierce cold. The river froze over earlier in the fall of 1842 than anyone ever remembered. Will had work to do around his place in town, but he didn't relish working in such harsh cold—worse than anything he had ever experienced in England. Still, he told himself he needed to learn to enjoy this quiet time, with more days available when he could help Liz with her chores and help with Jacob. He needed to spend more time reading the scriptures this winter. Sometimes, working every daylight hour, his spiritual life seemed mostly put aside.

In spite of Will's resolutions, his first days cooped up inside turned out to be tedious. One morning he told Liz, "If you don't mind, I might walk down to the brick store to see if Brother Clayton is there. He told me he could let me look at the city plat maps." In September William Clayton had become the temple recorder and Joseph Smith's secretary. He split his time between the recording office, a little building near the temple, and another office at the brick store. "I'm thinking, when all the harvest money is in and I get paid for my roadwork, I just might have enough extra to put a few dollars down on a farm lot of our own, maybe out by Jesse's place."

"I thought you were going to wait on that."

"I was. But I thought I'd be putting my money into buying bricks. Since we don't have enough savings to start a house, maybe we could manage a first payment on some land. Brother Clayton tells me I ought to pick something out before too many people move here and there's nothing left."

"Well, fine. Go talk to Brother Clayton. You can't stand to be in the house for two hours. That's the truth of it."

Will was glad that she was smiling—at least a little. "Aye. It's true," he said. "But I didn't want to admit that to you." He grabbed his coat and cap from a peg on the wall and gave Liz a quick kiss. "I won't be long," he said. "And that's a promise."

That only made her laugh all the more.

The day was very cold, so Will walked as fast he could, partly to get out of the cold and partly to get his blood flowing. He took the path through the woods and straight west to the flats. Now that most of the leaves were off the trees, he could see the full breadth of the town. A great many new houses had gone up that summer. There were more brick houses under way now. Brigham Young's, down on Granger Street, was progressing nicely, and Jonathan Browning, from Quincy, had bought a brick house in town and had been converting it into a gun shop. With the corn cut, it was easier to see all the block houses, mostly painted white, and the few two-story houses, brick or frame, that were changing the look of the city. At times like this, Will felt as though he could see Joseph's vision, this muddy land actually turning into a civilized place: a beautiful city and a sizeable one. The great river was vast and white this time of year—a field of snow—but it was craggy, not smooth, after the days of freezing and breaking up before the hard freeze had set in.

Will walked to the store and entered through the back door, but when he found no one in the counting room, he hiked up the back steps and was surprised to see Joseph Smith himself sitting at his little desk with his back to the door. He twisted around and looked at Will and said, "Ah, Will Lewis. Did Brother William send word to you that I wanted to talk to you?"

"No. I stopped by to see him, but he's not in his office."

"Yes, he left not long ago, but I must say, it's more than a coincidence that you found me here," Joseph said. He sat back and smiled. "The Lord sent you here to see me. I have something I want to ask you."

Will felt a little quiver run through him—maybe excitement, or maybe fear. He was pleased to know that the Prophet had been thinking of him, but he wondered what he could have in mind.

Joseph stood and shook Will's hand, and he motioned for Will to take a seat. He waited and then sat in his own chair again. "How was your harvest?" he asked.

"Not bad, considering I had a late start. I was able to grind enough grain for the winter, and Brother Matthews, from our branch in Ledbury, worked with me. He's settled for the winter too, and we even made a small profit from the corn we sold."

"I heard that you also gave Brother Johns some work."

"Well, yes. I'm surprised you know about that."

"I hear about most things, Brother Will. But in this case, it was Brother Johns himself who told me how much he appreciated the work. And Jesse Matthews told me the same thing. He praised your name—said you hired him when you didn't need to, and kept him from leaving us."

"Oh, but I do need him. More than I thought at the time."

Joseph sat back and folded his big arms across his chest. He was watching Will carefully, as though he wanted to look inside his head. "Tell me this," he said. "Is Sister Lewis feeling well?"

"The death of our little daughter cost her dearly, Brother Joseph, but she's doing well enough. She's teaching a few students and working harder than I ever imagined she could."

"Has she taken well to the Clarkston boy you're raising?"

"She loves him as her own. He's a chore for her, but I don't know what she would have done without him."

"She's grabbed on, hasn't she? Our women carry too much of the load as we try to spread the gospel in this world, but the Lord sustains them. They'll receive a just reward, your wife and mine, and all the fine sisters; I can promise you that."

Will agreed, but his mind was on another matter. There had to be a reason why Joseph was asking about his well-being, his wife's strength. He realized what the Prophet was about to ask him to do. But he couldn't do it, not this year.

"Brother Will, I thought you might be able to serve a short mission this winter—leave soon and be back before planting time."

"I could go next winter, I'm sure, but I can't leave Liz now, not when she finally has my help for a while. She's not strong enough to brave the cold weather and haul in water from the well, chop wood—and all the rest of it. She did a good deal of that this summer, but she needs to catch up on her rest now."

"Is that your answer, then?"

"I'm sorry. It has to be."

"That's fine. But I want you to think for a moment about those brethren who sailed to England and brought the gospel to you. Most of them were sick when they left this place, and they left women behind—and families—who were down with the ague, shaking so bad they couldn't get out of bed. I thought the Lord had asked too much, and I tried to tell Him that we just couldn't send away the strength of our church—not quite so soon. But what if the Lord had rescinded His call? Where would we be now? Those brothers dropped everything and obeyed the Lord—and they brought *thousands* to the gospel. You and the other English Saints have breathed new life into this church. So the sacrifice was worth it. We know that now."

Will had no idea what to say. He only knew that he couldn't bear to walk back home and tell Liz, after all she had been through this year, that he was leaving her now.

"Don't answer me just yet," Joseph said. "Ask the Lord, and talk to Sister Lewis. I have in mind the Southern states, where the weather's not so bad in the winter. If you left soon, you would have about four months to travel and preach. That's not nearly so hard as heading out for a year or two, the way so many have done."

Will felt ashamed that he wasn't saying yes right then and there. But again he thought of Liz. "Let me talk to her," he said. "And let me think about it."

"I wouldn't think too much. I'd pray. But don't assume that the answer is yes. The Lord will speak peace to you if it's the right thing."

"All right."

Will was about to stand up when Joseph said, "There's something else I wanted to ask you."

Will waited.

"Are you hearing all the rumors in town—all the talk of 'spiritual wifery'?"

"Aye. Of course. But I don't listen to John Bennett's lies."

Joseph sat quietly for a time. His eyes had gone shut. Finally he looked back at Will again. "I need young men like you—men with leadership ability—to stay true to the Church."

"You don't have to worry about me on that account."

"But people talk. And some are turning against me."

Will wondered whether he had given the Prophet any reason for concern. "I'm not one of them, Brother Joseph. I promise you that."

Joseph's eyes went shut again for quite some time, and he began to speak before he opened them. "There are things I know—things I have permission to teach, but that not everyone is ready to know or to understand."

Will felt his breath catch in his chest. What was he saying?

"Do you think it's wrong to kill, Brother Will?"

"Of course."

"So why did Nephi kill Laban?"

"The Lord told him to do it."

"That makes a difference, doesn't it?"

"Yes."

"But why would the Father tell the boy to do such a thing? The Lord could have put the plates into his hands some other way."

"I don't know why. I've wondered about that."

"The thing is, we do what the Lord tells us to do, and we don't always know the reasons why. Wouldn't you agree with that?"

"I'm not very good at that, Brother Joseph. I like to know the reason."

A subtle smile came to Joseph's face. He had looked a little rough this morning, not having shaved for a few days and his eyes so full of weariness, but those blue eyes were clear now and seemed to bore into Will's own eyes. "We're much alike, Will. But I've learned, over time, I don't have all the answers. Why did the Lord sanction some of the early prophets to have more than one wife?"

Will saw the logic, but he didn't want to hear it, and he looked away. "I don't know. I suppose that was a different time. But the Book of Mormon says we should have only one wife."

"And that's usually God's law. But at times he has instituted a different standard. We may not know all the reasons, but we know he's done it. You know that from your Bible reading, don't you?"

"Yes."

"Brother Will, look at me."

Will looked back into Joseph's eyes as Joseph leaned toward him. "Do you believe I'm a man of moral character?"

"Yes, I do."

"Do you believe that I follow God's law?"

"Yes."

"Then let me say only this much. I promise you with all my heart that I would never do the immoral things John Bennett has accused me of doing. Bennett seduced women by claiming that God sanctioned illicit relations. I would never enter into immoral behavior of that kind. I never have and I never will."

"I believe that." And it was true. Will felt Joseph's simple honesty—heard it in his voice and saw it in his clear eyes.

"Just wait for a time, Will. Truths are being revealed every day. And many more will come. There will be a time when things that are incomprehensible today will be plain and simple once we understand them. So I ask you to trust me for now. I'm not the man I'd like to be, Will. I'm all too human. But I've been called of God. Do you believe that?"

"I *know* it."

"All right. Go home. Talk to your wife. Decide about this

mission I've asked you about. But no matter what else you do, never turn on me. Never turn on the Church."

"I won't, Brother Joseph. I promise you that."

• • •

Liz was not surprised when Will stayed outside for quite some time. She heard him chopping wood out there, and she suspected he was waiting for the schoolchildren to leave before he came in. He had been getting a great deal of wood chopped and ready for winter, but every time he decided he had enough, he would give a load away to someone who lived on prairie land, with no timber. Jesse had already come and hauled two loads off to his house. Will had told Liz that he would have to start charging seventy-five cents a load for wood, the same as others did, but when the time had come to ask for money, he had never been able to do it.

Liz loved that about Will. The man could be impatient with his brothers, but when he knew that people were in need, he was the first to give them what he owned, or to offer his time and muscle to do work that had to be done.

As it turned out, he actually did come in before her pupils left. He brought in an armload of firewood, set it down by the fireplace, and then laughed with the children. He even sat down and helped one of the boys read from his primer.

What she saw in Will, however, was that he had something on his mind. He seemed nervous, a little distracted. When the children were finally gone, he talked about the firewood supply and about the fence he needed to repair before winter, but his eyes seemed adrift, as though he couldn't concentrate on what he was saying. Finally, he said, "Liz, while I was down at the store, I had a chance to talk to President Smith."

"That's wonderful, Will. How is he?"

"He's fine, I think. We didn't talk much about that. He wanted to know how we were doing. I told him you were recovering well, but you still had a long way to go. Would you say that's true?"

"I suppose. But I feel quite well. Every new mother is tired, no doubt, and I only have one little one to look after."

"But you've never had to work so hard. You're just learning to do that. I think you need me here this winter, don't you?"

Liz understood instantly. She had picked up a stick of firewood and had been ready to place it on the coals left in the fireplace. But now she stopped. "What does he want you do to, Will?"

"He said I could decide—according to how you're feeling, and whether you need me."

"What is it? A mission?" She felt as though the blood were flowing away from her head. She had known this would come, but she hadn't expected it now. She wanted Will for herself for a few months.

"Yes. He thought I could go to the Southern states—and come back in time for spring planting. But I told him this was not the right time. You need me this year. I can go next winter."

But Liz didn't want to be the reason that Will turned down the Prophet. So many other women had unselfishly let their husbands go. She thought of Wilford Woodruff, who had left for such a long time when his family had hardly been established in Nauvoo. "Will, you cannot tell him no," she said. "We've been blessed, and now it's time for us to make a sacrifice."

"It's up to me to look out for you, Liz. I told your father I would make certain you had a good life."

"I don't want to hear about that again. I'll be fine. You said yourself, we have enough food and the house is tight and warm. You have no idea what to do with yourself all winter. Now you have your answer. And it's only a few months. How could a mission be easier?"

"But you'll be alone all winter with the baby and—"

"And with my pupils. I'll have plenty to keep me busy." But the truth was setting in now. Will would be gone all those dark months, and she would be here in the woods, waking up every morning without him. She would have to feed the animals, milk the cow, and haul wood—and all the while take care of little Jacob. It was overwhelming to think about, but she wasn't going to let Will know that. She fought her tears away and added some sticks to the fire.

"Liz, I can't do this. I just can't leave you here like this."

"The sisters will look after me, Will. And some of the men will help me with the firewood and the animals. I'm sure they will."

"I already told him, I don't see how I can possibly go."

"It's not Joseph who called you, Will. It's the Lord. How can we turn Him down? You know what He's done for us. We both came close to death, getting here, and each of us begged the Lord for mercy. Now He's given us a little test—hardly any sacrifice at all—and we simply cannot say no."

• • •

Will had come to the same conclusion out in the yard while chopping the wood. But he had only admitted it to his heart and not yet to his mind. Still, he had known exactly what Liz would say. And he knew she was right.

So the following morning he walked off the bluffs and down to the brick store again. Joseph was sitting in the same spot. "Brother Joseph," he said. "I've decided to accept your call."

"I know," Joseph said. He didn't even turn around.

"I suppose you do. You're a prophet."

Joseph stood then, and he turned to look at Will. A broad smile had spread across his face. "I suppose I did have a vision," he said. "In my mind I saw Sister Lewis, and I heard you trying to explain to her that she was too weak to let you go. That's when I saw her toss you head over heels out the door. Am I right? Is that how it happened?"

"More or less," Will said, and he laughed. "She told me we've been blessed and we can't turn down the Lord when He finally asks something of us."

"I try to be a fair man, Will. But when I asked you to go home and talk to your wife, I knew very well how this would turn out. I put you at a terrible disadvantage."

"I guess I knew how it would turn out too."

"When can you go?"

"Soon. Give me a day or two and then I'll set out."

"Thank you, Brother Will. The Lord knows your heart. You'll be a fine missionary."

Will wondered. Beneath all his concern about Liz was also fear for himself. He wasn't at all sure that he would have the courage to approach people, to teach, to face the skepticism that he knew he would meet.

CHAPTER 8

Abby was still spending almost all her time at the hospital in Quincy. Little William was almost three weeks old now, and he didn't seem in immediate danger, but he wasn't improving, either. Dr. Hunt said that his heart was only about the size of a walnut, and the tiny left ventricle might have expanded a bit, but it was hard to say for sure. Each day when the nurses took William's oxygen away and tested his blood saturation levels, there was no sign of improvement, so his heart wasn't functioning well enough for him to thrive and begin to grow. Dr. Hunt never said it, but Abby and Jeff remembered what he had told them in the beginning: if his heart didn't start to improve soon—after a couple of weeks or so—it probably never would, and he would not survive. Now it was well past two weeks.

Abby didn't really need to be at the hospital all the time, but the worst thought of all for her was that her baby would die and she wouldn't be with him. So she stayed all day, every day. She spent most of her time reading, but a kind of torpor had set in, her body exhausted and her mind almost numb. She told herself she needed to feel more connection to the Lord, more spirituality, needed her prayers to have more meaning, so she kept her scriptures close and read at least an hour in the Book of Mormon each day. Sometimes that helped, but as she reached the book of Alma, she didn't like all the wars and the evil of the Gadianton robbers. She skipped over to 3 Nephi and read about Christ teaching the people, blessing the children. She followed that by reading the Gospel of Matthew in the New Testament. She loved to read of Christ's tenderness with the people who came to Him—and the miracles He performed.

But the scriptures raised questions for her, too. She believed in all those miracles, but she would sit next to William and watch him, and he always seemed the same. She just wanted the Lord to touch him with His finger and make him well. How could she pray over and over, all day, and yet see no change? Still, she had stopped pressuring Jeff to step in and change things, and she was trying not to be critical of him, even in her own mind.

The fact was, she was tired of asking questions, tired of worrying, tired of waiting. Sometimes she read the magazines Kayla brought her, or she read bestsellers other friends had lent her. Now and then she even walked out to the waiting room and watched silly daytime television shows. It was a strange existence, all the days seeming long. Jeff would usually arrive late in the day, would always ask about changes, and she would have to tell him that nothing had happened—again.

One morning, after a fitful night of sleep on the pull-out bed, she got up and looked at William, then asked a nurse how the night had gone. "Just the same," the woman had said. "No change."

She was a nice woman—all the nurses had been very kind to her—but she sounded unconcerned. "Shouldn't there be a change by now?" Abby asked. "If he's going to . . . live, shouldn't we start seeing better numbers on his oxygen tests?"

The nurse, a gray-skinned woman named Louise, was older than most of the nurses in the unit. Surely she had had a tedious night, but she answered laconically, "I don't know, Abby. Ask the doc."

Somehow the words were just too unfeeling for Abby. She wanted to shout at the woman to *care*. But she said nothing; she only walked away. She tried to read her scriptures but soon gave up. She sat and stared, and something within her said, "It's over. I've sat here as long as I can stand it." She got up, grabbed her coat, and walked down the hall, and then she walked out to Broadway Street in front of the building. She didn't know where she was going, but she needed to move, to do something besides wait.

It was very cold outside, clouds scudding toward her, a storm building up. She headed west, walking fast, and soon put several blocks behind her. By then, she knew she wanted to hike all the way down to the Mississippi River where two big bridges linked Illinois to Missouri. She had been in the little park on the river between the bridges, seen the stone monument to the Mormons who had crossed the river into Quincy and then received help from the local people. She remembered what she had felt when she had stood in that spot, and she wanted those feelings back.

By the time she had descended the hill, crossed the railroad tracks, and made her way down to the river, she was warmed somewhat by the walk, but she felt the wind, even stronger, coming off the water. She thought of those early Saints fleeing from the "extermination order" in Missouri, making their way across the state in cold, wet conditions and then crossing the river any way they could. Emma Smith had crossed in February when the ice had still been solid, and she had walked with two children huddled next to her and two more in her arms. Jeff had told Abby about Emma sewing the manuscripts of Joseph's translation of the Bible into her skirts.

What Abby also knew was that Joseph had been in the Liberty

Jail at the time. Emma had surely prayed that he would be released, but it hadn't happened, and she had trudged across the ice with her children, not knowing what would come of her prayers. She had simply done what she had to do.

There was a painting of all this. Abby had seen it in a book that Jeff had shown her. In the picture, Emma was about to step onto the riverbank, and according to the inscription on the monument, that would have been about where Abby was now standing. She tried to picture it: this woman of faith accepting her lot in life, continuing on for the sake of her children, not knowing whether she would ever see her husband again. Abby didn't know whether she resented Emma for her tenacity or loved her. She had heard way too much about the noble pioneers being better than modern women. But what she was picturing in front of her, she realized, was what she had walked all the way down here to experience. She wanted to feel the cold, and think about the ice, and she wanted to feel, as she had the first time she had stood here, that a strong woman didn't have to mope about and pity herself. She didn't have to lie down and give up. She could accept the Lord's will and move forward.

"Lord, I accept," she said out loud. "Thy will be done."

She thought she had said it in anger, but the words had turned into a whisper. She felt a change in her mind and emotions. She was the one who was clinging to William. Everyone else seemed to understand that sometimes babies died, and there was only so much that human beings could do about that. She had to face reality. More than anything, she didn't want to watch the poor little thing lie there, hardly alive, while *technology* kept his heart beating. In any other era in history, he would have returned to his Father in Heaven by now. It was only the people of this age who had made up their minds to overrule nature's decisions, and maybe even defy God's will.

And then she told herself the truth: "I'm thinking of myself, not William." How could she know what the Lord had in store for this little spirit? How could she presume to know better than God?

"If it's the right thing, please take him," she whispered out loud. "But please, do it soon." She waited to see how that idea felt, and she knew she was all right with it. "I want to keep him, Father, but it's not for me to decide. You love him too. Please do what's best for *him*."

She spun around quickly and turned her back to the wind. She felt relieved, but now the cold seemed to penetrate her more deeply than before. She walked all the way back to the hospital, striding even faster than she had on her way down. And she fully expected that when she returned, Louise would say to her, "I'm sorry. He's gone."

But it wasn't so. The monitors were still reading out numbers, the IV still dripping, the feeding tube still in his mouth, and William was lying still, rarely moving. Nothing had changed.

• • •

Jeff had gone to work early that morning, so he managed to get away at three that afternoon. He stopped at home for only a few minutes and then continued on to Quincy.

There were times when he loved the Illinois countryside in winter. There was something dramatic in the bigness of the land, all the beige and gray in the lifeless stubble in the fields, and the black of the empty, gnarly tree limbs. The farmhouses stood amid those leafless trees as starkly as the landscape in the *American Gothic* painting. The fences and barns and oversized hay bales were the only intrusions in the seeming barrenness. All the green would return in the spring, he knew, but right now the land looked as stolid and resolute as the people he met at Duck's Market in Nauvoo. It was like the beauty of the desert, in a way, but it also spoke of regeneration, as though the land had to breathe awhile before it could produce such vibrant life all over again. There was no sign of any of that rebirth today, however. The landscape felt austere. Bulging clouds had progressed across the sky all day, west to east, and now light snow was blowing about. He suspected that the storm would intensify before he headed back that night, but he had learned that big snowstorms were rare in this river valley. Rain could dump inches in minutes, but snow rarely piled up very deep.

Jeff had had a bad feeling all day. Abby had called him before noon and said that nothing had changed. But something had changed in her. He heard the quiet sadness of her voice. He had asked her about that, but she had only said she had something she wanted to talk to him about when he reached the hospital. She had been so hopeful at first, so full of faith, that she had carried him along, but lately she had been discouraged, and today she sounded as though she were giving up. Of course, Jeff knew why. Too much time had passed with no sign of improvement. He suspected that his son's heart had come to earth just too deformed to keep his little body going.

When Jeff reached the hospital that afternoon, he washed up and entered the NICU that he knew so well. He found Abby sitting where she usually did, next to William. She was sitting straight, gazing toward him, but seemingly lost in thought.

Jeff knew better than to ask her whether anything had changed. "Are you okay?" he asked instead.

"Yeah. I am."

He stood next to her and touched his hand to the back on her neck. She reached up and took hold of his hand. "Have you eaten anything?" he asked her.

"A little. I got a bag of potato chips out of a machine."

"So what's happened to the health-food queen? Fall off the wagon?"

"I guess so," she said.

"Abby, let's not . . ." But he didn't know what to say.

"Jeff, there's something I've been thinking about today. We need to talk about it. Come with me." She took his hand and led him out to the waiting room. No one was in the room now, but they still went to a far corner, to one of the ugly orange couches.

Abby sat down and then pulled Jeff down next to her. She held his hand in both of hers. "I love you," she said. "I'm sorry I've been so hard to live with."

"You've been fine. This is stuff we never imagined ourselves going through."

"I know. But it's time to deal with it. You told me once that prayer is finding out the Lord's will—not changing it. I think we have to accept whatever it is the Lord has in mind for William."

"I know. But there's no reason—yet—to assume the Lord is going to take him."

She looked over at him. She didn't seem frantic or discouraged; her eyes looked calm. "They said two weeks, Jeff. In two weeks they should know how he was going to do."

"I think he said, 'at least two weeks,' or something like that. It wasn't *exactly* two weeks."

"Well, it's almost three now."

"I know."

"When I ask Dr. Hunt, he starts into all his left-ventricle-and-aortic-arch talk, and when I finally try to pin him down, he comes up with his usual, 'Let's give it some more time.'"

Jeff nodded. Dr. Hunt had said something similar to him. "But what would it take for him to finally say, 'This just isn't working'?"

"I don't know, Jeff. I asked him that, almost in those words, and he just hemmed and hawed and cleared his throat. I think he's losing hope and doesn't want to tell us."

Jeff thought so too, but he knew he had to be careful. He had seen Abby pass through a lot of moods in the last few weeks. He didn't know whether this calm acceptance was only a mask for her frailty. Maybe she was about to fall apart.

"I walked down to the river today," Abby said.

"That's a long walk."

"I know. And it was cold. But I needed to get out of here. And I wanted to see the river again—you know, where the Saints crossed."

"Why, Abby?"

She sat back on the couch and let go of his hand with one of hers. "When we were there last fall, you told me about Emma Smith crossing the river with her children. I just remembered how I felt about her and what she was able to do. She had watched four babies die by then. And she lost two more in Nauvoo. I can't hate God if I lose one. I have to be stronger than that."

"We both do."

"Do you think Emma wondered why she had to go through all that?"

"Of course she did. I'm sure Joseph did too."

"But they didn't whine about it. They accepted God's will."

"We don't know that, Abby. They might have complained plenty. They were human. I'm sure they grieved. Maybe they were just plain mad at times."

"Okay. Maybe. But they didn't give up their faith—so they must have accepted God's will."

"They did." Jeff had been coming to this point for several days now, but he had tried to fight the despair, tried to tell himself there was still hope.

"We don't know God's will, but it would help so much if we could find out."

Jeff stared at the floor. He didn't know what Abby expected him to do.

"I'm willing to accept whatever I have to. I decided that today. But I don't know what it is. Are you getting any answers at all?"

Jeff drew in some air. He kneeled down next to her. "Today, I've not felt very good about the whole situation, but I don't know. I'm never very sure that—"

"Maybe it's time we both *become* sure."

"We can't just . . . you know . . . demand an answer."

She was looking at him curiously. "But are you asking?"

"I keep praying that he'll live."

"But not asking to know whether he will or not?"

Jeff tried to think what he had done. He had asked for strength—for Abby, especially—and he'd pleaded with Lord to preserve William's life. "I don't know, Abby. When I blessed him, I tried to know what to say, but I've told you before, I just didn't get a clear feeling."

She didn't say a word, but he saw the look in her eyes.

He felt the same old disappointment in himself, and then he knew what he had to do. He stood up. "Isn't there a little chapel in the hospital somewhere?"

"I think you should go to the river," she said. "And I think you should walk."

He wondered, *why not drive?* But he wasn't going to say that to her. He simply nodded and walked from the room. He knew it was more than a mile to the river, maybe two. But it did seem right. He wanted the time, and he wanted to pay a price, even if it was only a small one.

So he stepped outside, zipped up his parka, turned the collar up around his ears, and began to jog. He ran for two blocks before he settled into a fast walk, but the run had warmed him, and the weather, with snow coming a little harder now, spoke to him. By the time he reached the river, he had the picture in his head: all those Saints, cold and beaten up by the trek across the state of Missouri, facing storms and wind, but crossing the Mississippi and then camping in Washington Park, there on the bluffs above the river.

His Grandfather Lewis hadn't been part of that. He and Grandma had come later, straight to Nauvoo, but they had made the hard voyage, and they had boarded a riverboat that had steamed its way right past Quincy. Grandpa had probably looked out upon this very land, sick as he was, and known that he and his wife had almost made it to their destination. But he must have wondered, exactly as Jeff was wondering, what was coming next in his life.

Jeff stood by the river and pictured that riverboat passing by, and he pictured Emma with her children, and Joseph finally crossing the same river to reunite with his family. The Mississippi rolled through Mormon history like a great divide, always testing the mettle of a people already downtrodden and driven from place to place. Jeff knew he needed to be as courageous as they had been.

Finally, he knelt down. There might have been people in the restaurant that overlooked the park, or there might have been people driving by, but no one was out in the park in the falling snow. He didn't care anyway. He needed to kneel.

"Father in Heaven," he said, "I need to know—and Abby needs to know—Thy will toward our little William. If it's time for us to give him up, we'll do it, but we would rather keep him here with us. Just tell me what to want."

He felt the answer like a break in a great storm, as though a wind suddenly stopped, and calm filled up the place where it had been. He had felt so much strain and confusion for such a long time, and all that lifted instantly. He heard no words, received nothing he could even turn into words. He simply felt his body fill up with warmth and calm, and he knew that all was well.

He thanked the Lord and got up. He stood for a moment and took another look out across the water—which looked different now, as though ice had formed and created a bridge. He turned and walked, steadily at first, and then faster. He lost his breath as he ascended the steep hill, but he kept up his pace. He had always laughed at the exaggerated image of those stern pioneers marching forward with hard-set jaws as they leaned against the handles of their handcarts, but he rather liked the idea now. He wanted to get back to Abby, but he wanted this feeling, too, that he was marching forward, unafraid.

When he reached the hospital, he stood in a hallway and warmed himself. He knew what he wanted to do, and he didn't want to do it with cold hands. He didn't want to come in huffing and puffing. Abby needed to sense the calm he was feeling. So he waited in the lobby for maybe ten minutes, and then he walked to the NICU. He left his parka in the waiting area outside, washed again, and walked back to where Abby was still sitting by William.

As he approached, she watched him closely, and he knew what she was wondering, but he didn't want to say anything yet. He wanted to turn his assurance into words, and he wanted to believe them the first time he said them—not force anything.

"I want to give Will a blessing," he said.

He watched her react, sort of startled, and he knew what she feared: that he had come back to release little William from this world. But he didn't explain. He merely held her hand for a moment and nodded to let her know that everything was all right. And then he stepped closer. He had no consecrated oil with him, but he placed as many fingers as he could on William's head—on all the dark hair. "William Jeffrey Lewis," he said, "in the name of Jesus Christ, and with the power of the holy Melchizedek Priesthood, I command you to be healed. I bless your heart to function and to carry your blood throughout your little body. I bless you to grow to manhood, to receive the priesthood, and to receive all the holy ordinances of the true and living gospel."

He closed in the Lord's name, and then he stepped away and took Abby in his arms. She was sobbing. "Oh, thank you, Jeff. Thank you."

But nothing happened. There was no change in little Will. For an instant, a doubt fluttered through Jeff's mind, but he told Abby, "He's going to be all right."

• • •

Abby decided she would go home that night. She and Jeff drove through the snowstorm. Snow was beginning to stick to the road. Jeff was concentrating on the road, but he also seemed to be in a pensive mood. Abby wanted to question him, ask him what had happened at the river, but she had learned that he didn't like to talk about such things, as though he feared that analysis might set in and disrupt the spirit he was feeling.

She did finally say, "You knew for sure, didn't you?"

"I did," Jeff said. And then he added, "I still do."

Abby was relieved. She had checked one last time before they had left the hospital, and William appeared exactly as he had all along. It was hard for her to trust that something actually had changed. What worried her a little was that maybe she had finally forced Jeff into saying what she wanted him to say. But Jeff sounded confident, and that was what she needed tonight. It was too terrible to imagine that nothing had really changed and she would still lose her baby.

• • •

Jeff went to bed that night still basking in the confidence he had felt there at the river. William would grow up. His heart would beat. He would be a normal child. That knowledge had come to him as an image more than a thought, and he had had no doubt. He held Abby in his arms now, loved the warmth of her and the comfort of knowing that he could be the husband Abby needed. He had too many faults to count, but this one trait—the capacity to believe—made all the difference, if he could only hang on to it.

But in the night Jeff awoke with a thought already in his head. What if nothing happened? What would Abby think of him then? Maybe the calm was only a reassurance that he and Abby could withstand the pain, should they lose their baby. He knew he had been granted a wonderful calm assurance, but maybe he had applied the wrong interpretation.

That possibility was so frightening that Jeff lay awake the rest of the night, until he finally got up early. "Abby," he whispered, "I'm heading over to work now—so I can leave early this afternoon. Do you have a ride back to Quincy?"

"Yes. I called Kayla last night, and she couldn't go, but she called Sister Lawrence, and she said she would do it herself."

"Okay. Call me after a while." He didn't admit that he was worried. He hoped she hadn't heard that in his voice.

"Let's have prayer together before you go."

"Okay." He knelt down by the bed as she slipped out from the covers, and they joined hands. "Will you say it?" he asked.

When she prayed, she thanked the Lord for the great blessing that had come to them, that their son's heart had been healed. Jeff loved the purity of her words and voice, and he hugged her afterwards. He felt a surge of confidence again that all would be well.

During Jeff's drive to his office, he held off any tendency he had to doubt, but he was nervous. He felt as though life was on hold, that he couldn't really relax until word came that his faith was warranted. He worked—took care of a few things—but couldn't concentrate well enough to accomplish a great deal. He kept guessing when Abby might arrive at the hospital. He figured that if something had changed, he would hear from her right away. But nine o'clock came, and then ten, and his phone didn't ring. He simply didn't dare call her. He finally lowered his head at his desk inside his cubicle and asked again to know.

The calm he had felt the day before filled him up again. He was sure again that it was real.

Jeff sat back in his chair, breathed in the spirit he was feeling, and wasn't surprised when the phone rang.

"Jeff, he's all right," Abby was saying. "Dr. Hunt just told me."

"How does he know? What's changed?"

"The nurses noticed something on all those screens they have—something about the volume of blood that was going through his heart. They took the ventilator off for a whole hour, and the oxygen is getting better. So Dr. Hunt ordered another echocardiogram. He said the left ventricle is finally enlarging. The blood is filling it up and that patch is holding, where the hole was."

"That's my boy," Jeff said. "I'll be wrestling with him before long."

"You *will not.*"

"Well, not for a day or two."

"Jeff, I told the Lord He could have him, if that's what was right. I quit being so selfish and just said that I would accept whatever came."

"I know. I did too." They both cried for a time before Jeff added, "Maybe we had to do that first—before the miracle could happen."

"Say a prayer, Jeff. We need to thank the Lord."

So Jeff prayed over the phone, thanked the Lord, and then told Abby how much he loved her. He went to his boss after that. "Doug, our son is doing better," he said. "My wife just called, and the doctor thinks he's going to be all right."

"That's wonderful."

"But I can't concentrate. Do you mind if I take the day off? I'll come in longer the rest of the week."

"Get out of here," Mr. Vincent said. "Go to your wife." And then he added, "Jeff, all of us around here—we've *all* been praying for this."

"Thanks," Jeff said. He was a little embarrassed to cry in front of the man, but he felt better when tears started running down Mr. Vincent's cheeks too.

CHAPTER 9

With Will away on his mission, Liz stayed busy each day, but evenings in December were extremely long. She was surely thankful that she had little Jacob, but after he fell asleep each night she tried to stay up for an hour or two. It was that or she would awaken long before the sun came up and then lie in bed feeling desolate and sometimes afraid. There seemed to be more sounds in the night when Will wasn't with her. Even in the day the cabin felt cut off from most people. Nelly stopped by often, and sometimes Liz bundled up Jacob and walked to the Amos Davis dry goods store on Mulholland, or to one of the stores on the flats. That was good for her—the time outside, the walk, and, above all, the chance to see people—but many days were so cold she simply didn't dare take Jacob outside. Trips to the outside privy on such days were an ordeal. She chose times when the baby was sleeping, or, when necessary, bundled him up and took him along—which was never simple. On snowy days, her schoolchildren didn't always tramp over to her house, and it was on those days, when she saw no one, that she felt especially lonely.

In America people didn't seem to make much of Christmas. It was sad to Liz not to have that merriment to enjoy, but worse was thinking of her family at home. She had thought she had overcome her homesickness, but letters arrived from both her mother and Mary Ann in December, and even though the letters had been written almost two months earlier, both Mum and Mary Ann mentioned how much they would miss Liz, away from them for the first time on Christmas.

Liz had heard from her family a few other times that year, and she had tried to be good about writing back, but it seemed more likely than ever that she would never see them again. When she had left home, there had been talk of at least Mary Ann following her, and even though her father had been dubious about the idea, Liz knew that her mother was open to it, and Mary Ann had clearly hoped to come. Mary Ann continued to mention the possibility in every letter, but Liz knew her well enough to suspect that when the time came for a decision, she would hesitate to leave the comfort of her good home.

Since Will had departed, on foot, only three letters had come from him. He seemed to be spending most of his time walking from town to town, covering many miles. As often as possible, he stayed with people who would let him into their homes, but he was often sent packing once they knew what he preached. Twice he had slept outside, once in a haystack and once in a barn. He had walked through southern Illinois and down across western Kentucky, and in his last letter had been in Nashville, Tennessee, but he was planning to travel deeper into the South, where the weather would be warmer.

Liz hated to think of all that: her husband being rejected and disrespected and going without food at times. But he had closed each letter with a testimony that he was doing the right thing, and he knew that if he brought one soul to the gospel, his time would be well spent. Liz knew she had to take that same attitude and not waver. The better part of a month had already passed, and that meant only about three more months until he returned. It really wasn't very long. Or at least that was what she told herself until evening came again, when she felt so very alone.

It was John and Jane Benbow who saved Liz from sadness on Christmas Day. John had stopped by a few days earlier and invited her to come to his and Jane's place for Christmas dinner, and then he came with a horse and sleigh and carried her and Jacob out past the cemetery to his house. Other friends among the English Saints also came to visit and feast together, and the day passed better than any since Will had been gone.

Liz's joy faded the next day, however, when she learned that Emma Smith had given birth to a stillborn child. The poor woman had lost six babies now—five of her own and one adopted. Liz wondered how Emma could sustain herself through all her worries and all her losses. To compound Emma's pain, Joseph had been arrested again the same day. On the following morning, Liz learned, he had departed with Hyrum and some other brothers to appear in court in Springfield.

Liz felt discouraged for a couple of days until she talked to Warren Baugh, who said that Joseph had actually gone willingly, hopeful that the matter of the extradition to Missouri could be settled. The new governor of Illinois, Thomas Ford, was not sounding like a friend to the Saints, but he seemed to be less convinced than Governor Carlin had been that the extradition was legal. As it turned out, a week or so later, good news came back from Springfield. Nathaniel Pope, a federal district court judge, had freed Joseph Smith and dropped all charges against him. He had ruled that if any crime had been committed, it had to have happened in Illinois, where Joseph was accused of colluding with Porter

Rockwell to assassinate Governor Boggs. Joseph had never traveled to Missouri during this time, so he couldn't be guilty of a crime in that state. After months of hiding out and sneaking in and out of town, Joseph was finally free to return to live openly with his family and his people. He arrived from Springfield on January 10, 1843, and celebrated with Emma and Church leaders. Then, on January 17, a day of "humility, praise, fasting, prayer and thanksgiving" was proclaimed, with prayer meetings held in homes in each of the wards in Nauvoo.

Having Joseph home, ready to lead the Church again, and under no condemnation from the government, changed everyone's mood. After a day of fasting, Joseph sponsored a day to celebrate his legal victory and his and Emma's sixteenth wedding anniversary. Emma fed people in their log home all day long. Liz felt a little envious of those who had been invited, but she held no illusions that she was important enough to deserve such an invitation. What she did do, for her own little celebration, was write immediately to let Will know.

Liz was also finding her strength, and she was beginning to feel some satisfaction in her capacity to deal with hardships. She taught her pupils each day, and after they left, she saw to her chores. During Jacob's naps, she hurried out, chopped firewood, and stacked it. She knew there were men about who would help—and did, from time to time—but she didn't seek help. She felt rather proud of herself that she could go out in the cold, wield an ax, and haul in armloads of wood. She also carried in heavy pails of water for the night, and in the evening she sat by her fire and worked on the shirts she had promised to make for temple workers. She was surprised at how quickly she was learning to cut the cloth and stitch the pieces together. Every time she finished a shirt she told herself that she had helped the cause of Zion—and more days of Will's mission had passed.

One afternoon she packed up the shirts she had sewn. With her parcel under one arm and Jacob in the other, she walked all the way to the flats and out to the river, where Sarah Granger Kimball lived. Sister Kimball, according to what Liz had heard, had been the first to suggest a women's organization in Nauvoo, along with Eliza Snow. Under Joseph Smith's direction, the organization had blossomed into something much larger than a benevolent society. Joseph had admonished the women to prepare the Saints for the day when the temple would be ready and members would be blessed to make covenants there. The women were to educate one another, but also to prod the brothers as well as the sisters in Nauvoo toward greater spiritual commitment.

Sarah Kimball was involved in almost all the charitable work that happened in Nauvoo. Liz had been introduced to her at the grove one Sunday and had been surprised, after learning about her prominence, to realize that she was not much older than Liz. Still, her husband was one of the richest men in town, and her two-story frame house, though not a large place, was ever so much nicer than Liz's log house.

Liz knocked on the front door and waited, a little nervous, although she wasn't exactly sure why. She knew her shirts weren't as expertly sewn as she would have liked, but she wasn't ashamed of that. She was, however, a little self-conscious about presenting herself to Sarah, a stately woman, tall and straight, self-assured and very intelligent. Liz wanted to be liked by such women, but she felt herself a newcomer to the gospel and not a truly educated woman.

When the door opened, however, Sarah didn't seem so austere as Liz had expected. She was wearing an everyday wool dress covered with a white apron, and even though she seemed tidy and correct, she smiled at Liz as though genuinely happy to see her. "Oh, Sister Lewis," she said, "have you shirts for me?"

"I do." Liz held out the parcel to her.

"Come in. Rest for a minute and warm yourself. Did you walk all the way off the bluffs to bring these? It's *very* cold, isn't it?"

"Not quite so cold as it's been. This seemed my best opportunity to get these to you."

"I'm so thankful. I haven't received many lately, and the men wear through their shirts faster than I ever could have imagined. There's not much work on the temple now, but men are still quarrying stone when the weather allows for it." She motioned for Liz to walk into the little parlor just left of the front door. "May I see your baby?"

Liz laughed. "He's a heavy weight to pack around. But he's not yet five months old, so I suppose he *is* a baby."

Little Jacob was squirming by then, eager to see where he was. Liz pulled his blanket away and let him sit up on her lap. His head swung about as though he wanted to take everything in.

"Oh, what a fine boy," Sister Kimball said. "He's big for his age. We have a son too, you know. He's a year old. I'm happy to say that he ran down, like an unwound clock, just a short time ago. He doesn't always nap these days, but I'm thankful when he does."

"I won't take your time. I know how valuable those minutes are when a little one finally goes down."

"But stay a bit. I've been wanting to know you. Sister Eliza tells me you're an intelligent woman—and I'm only too happy to hear it. We need more sisters who can think and lead. Too many have been raised to believe they should cook and clean and serve their husbands—and other than that, keep their mouths closed."

Liz was a little surprised by this assessment. "I don't know, Sister Kimball. Sister Snow may have given me too much credit for intelligence. What I wish is that I were better prepared to keep a home running."

"What makes you say that?"

"I didn't learn any of the household arts in my home. We had help to do those things. So I've had to learn to cook at a fireplace, milk a cow, and make butter—and everything else. When it came to sewing these shirts, I was all thumbs at first. I hope they've gotten a little better as I've gone along."

"Oh, Sister Lewis, don't worry about that. If you want to know the truth, I have a seamstress, Sister Cook. Margaret and I started this project to sew for the workers, but she's the one who does most of the sewing, and I usually do the organizing. I can sew well enough, but—and let me whisper this—I don't really like to do it."

This made Liz laugh. She had a whole new appreciation of Sister Kimball.

"Sister Lewis, I wasn't—"

"Please call me Elizabeth, or better yet, Liz."

"I will. And call me Sarah." She had a lovely smile, and she seemed very much at ease. Liz liked her. "As I was saying, I wasn't raised in a well-to-do family. I was fortunate that Mr. Kimball took a liking to me and provided me with the time and means to do some good in this world. But God didn't create women so they could work like plow horses with a husband behind, cracking a whip. I believe with all my heart—and I know Brother Joseph believes this too—that women are capable of much more than they're usually allowed to do. And I might add—as my own opinion—they often correct what men make a shambles of." She laughed, and suddenly she sounded mischievous.

"I've suspected the same thing all my life," Liz said, and she laughed too. "But I didn't ever dare to say it."

"Well, you just learned something about me. I say things. I

believe in the goodness and refinement of spirit I see in women—but I also know they can understand anything men understand. When I was fifteen, in Kirtland, Ohio, I attended one of the sessions of the School of the Prophets. I met women there who were able to test the wits of the priesthood holders who taught us."

Liz wanted to hear more of this. She had wondered since entering the Church—and had wondered as a member of the United Brethren—whether women always had to listen quietly to the things men had to say, whether they couldn't speak their opinions openly.

"When President Smith created the Female Relief Society of Nauvoo," Sarah said, "he told Emma—and all of us—that the Church had never been fully organized until the women had been established after the manner of the priesthood. When the temple is completed one day, women will receive a new endowment, the same as the men. I've heard Joseph promise that."

"Sister Kimball, I don't know what an endowment is."

"I know something about it. But most members don't so far. There was a ceremony in Kirtland—a series of promises made to God, and from God—but Joseph has received a full form of that ceremony now. We'll all hear about it soon. I'll tell you, just between the two of us, that some of the leaders have already received it. But once the temple is completed, we'll all have our opportunity."

Jacob was still squirming, and he was whimpering a little. Liz wondered how long it would be before he would be howling. The walk back to her home would take her at least half an hour, and he might not let her get away with that.

"If you need to nurse that baby," Sarah said, "I'll give you some privacy."

"I do need to, I think. But don't let me take more of your time. I can just sit here, and you go about your work."

"That's fine, but let me ask about you a little more before I do."

"Certainly," Liz agreed. Sarah seemed entirely at ease, but she sat very straight in her chair. She appeared almost regal. Liz found herself sitting up a little straighter herself.

"Are you managing all right by yourself?"

"It's not so bad. I keep busy. It's the night I hate. I don't like to be alone."

"I know. I've experienced that when Mr. Kimball travels with his business, which he does a great deal. He's not a member of our Church, you know—not yet, anyway." She smiled. "So he won't be called away on a mission, but I know what it is to be home with a baby. May I give you some advice?"

"Yes. Of course."

"Use that time in the evenings—when your baby is asleep—to learn more than you've ever known before. I have some things you can take home if you like: books and pamphlets by the Pratt brothers—brilliant men who open up this world and the next with their understanding of the eternities. And by the way, I have it on good authority that Brother Orson has resolved his difficulties with Joseph Smith and will soon be rebaptized."

"I'm glad to know that."

"But my point is, we women can't teach the gospel unless we know it, and if we lag behind and let the men do all the thinking in this life, we'll miss our chance to be all we're capable of being. Some may tell you that you're not wise or bright enough to understand the grand truths, but it isn't so. This Church—and this nation—will prosper as men and women think and work together. And it's we young women who will have to see that change through to the end. Our mothers were too content to sit by the fire and do needlework."

Liz thought of her own mother, who deferred to her husband on everything. Liz had sometimes worried that she was too quick to assert her own opinions, but she had the feeling that Sarah—and Eliza and Emma—were showing her what women could become.

• • •

Will was standing at the pulpit of a little country church. A congregation of about thirty people from Pleasant View, a small Alabama town, had gathered to hear what he had to say. But he had sensed from the beginning that the preacher who had arranged the meeting had also warned his people against the doctrines Will would teach. Will wasn't sure why the man wanted to bother people that way, if that was his attitude, but he didn't ever pass up a chance to preach.

Will was learning. He had rarely had a chance to explain the gospel to anyone, especially doubters, but in the last several weeks he had begun to find a way to organize his presentation and engage the interest of his audience. He had begun this meeting by raising questions about common Christian beliefs. Were babies really damned if they died unbaptized? Was the afterlife really a time for nothing but peace and rest? How long would that make a person happy?

Then he introduced the idea that prophets were needed on this earth. There were important questions to ask, important doctrines to understand, but the various sects were merely inventing their own interpretations of scripture. "We need someone in our own time who can talk with God and bring us truths, just as the prophets of olden times were able to do. Why would God speak to the children of Israel and not to us?"

But a man sitting near the front, in a center pew, suddenly stood up. "Enough of this," he shouted. "You're a blasphemer." He was a plain man, hardly noticeable until now, but his voice scratched like claws.

"And how so?" Will asked.

"It's for God to know how He'll speak to us, not for some char-latan to make claims that he's a prophet. In the last days there will be wolves in sheep's clothing who will try to lead the people away from the Lord. That's what your Joe Smith is. Don't speak of him in the same breath as Isaiah and Jeremiah. It's a wonder God doesn't strike you down."

Will had been praying for patience every day of his mission. He knew that this would be another moment to prove that he could be humble and kind in his response to such animosity. "Sir, what do you know about Joseph Smith, and where have you learned it?"

"I am the editor of our local newspaper, Mr. Lewis. I receive reliable information from all of the great newspapers of this land. I don't listen to rumor and innuendo; I listen to those who have looked into this matter and know the truth."

"So you believe what John C. Bennett has been saying. Is he your source of truth?"

"He *is* one source. The man lived in your city, and he led your church alongside this Joe Smith. He knows your people in and out, and he proclaims that Smith is a seducer and a liar. He enriches him-self at the expense of dupes like you, and he steals from women that which is most holy and sacred, as no prophet would do."

Will felt that old fire of his temper, but he gritted his teeth and waited, tried to calm himself. He thought of Joseph living in a log home in Nauvoo, serving his people, and it was infuriating to think of this man who knew nothing about him believing a scoundrel like John Bennett. "Mr. . . . may I know your name?"

"Erastus Mikkelson," the man said. "Everyone here knows me. They know I'm fair-minded and honest. But when I've heard enough, I've heard enough. What you've told us so far is all lies."

Mikkelson may have thought of himself as fair-minded, but his eyes were aglow with anger. He was a middlish man, of no special distinction, except that his long forehead seemed to draw attention to those fiery eyes. He was dressed better than anyone in the room, however, and clearly he thought it his right to speak for the rest.

"Mr. Mikkelson, you should read a recent statement by one Mr. James Arlington Bennet, not a relative of John C. Bennett's. James Bennet reports, in a nationally published editorial, that John C. Bennett has been untrue to his wife and is a notorious liar, a man set on feathering his own nest at any cost. He admonished this nation to give John C. Bennett no heed. Mr. James Bennet, in fact, tells of meeting with Joseph Smith and finding him to be a man of intelligence and humility—exactly opposite of the person you describe."

"A charlatan can often deceive the unwary."

"Then let me speak for myself and offer my own testimony. I know Joseph Smith well. I have watched him as he leads our people. He speaks with wisdom and inspiration. He lives simply and does nothing to improve his own lot in life above the rest of us. And sir, I have looked into his eyes and received, through the spirit of the Holy Ghost, a confirmation that he is, indeed, a prophet. I proclaim it on my honor, and I hope you see in me a man who has no desire to speak anything but the truth."

"Unless you come here on the same mission as your Joe Smith. I suspect you want to teach *our* daughters the damnable doctrine of 'spiritual wifery.'" Mikkelson took his time and looked around at the congregation. "This false teaching would sanction *licentiousness.* Is that what we want our daughters to be taught?"

This impassioned accusation brought some murmurs from the little gathering. Will had thought the people had been rather interested in the things he had said at first, but now he saw them stirring, whispering to one another. And Mr. Fields, the minister, looked pleased. He was a heavy man with whiskered jowls and a huge bulb of a nose. He had lost a couple of his dark front teeth, and the gaps were visible now even though he seemed to be making an effort not to smile.

"My friends," Will said, "I assure you that my purposes are honorable in every way. May I explain, as was my intent from the beginning, some of the tenets of my faith?"

"We get our tenets from the Holy Bible," Mr. Mikkelson announced. "Why should we ask to learn from someone who has cast the Bible aside for a crazy book written by Joe Smith?"

"I know you're speaking of the Book of Mormon," Will said. "But let me explain a little of what that book is, and how Joseph Smith came to receive it—and translate it."

"We don't need to hear anything about that," Reverend Fields said. "I asked you to tell us what you believe—but not if you want to preach from some trumped-up scripture, and not the Holy Bible."

"That's fine, sir. I'll use the Bible. I raised a question earlier about life eternal. Perhaps I could say something more about that. Some would have you believe that in the eternities we have nothing more to learn or accomplish. But the Lord's great plan of happiness assures us that we can continue to grow and become more like Jesus Christ."

"I see where you're going with that, and it's wrong," Reverend Fields said. "It's by faith that we're saved, not by works. And not one of us can ever be *like* God. We are so far beneath Him that we can only throw ourselves on His mercy and hope that He raises us up to heaven—not for anything we've done, but because He condescends to bless us through His grace."

"I don't disagree with that, sir. It's through Jesus Christ, and only Jesus Christ, that we are saved. But didn't He say to his disciples, 'Come follow me,' and what did He mean by that? Does He not invite us to follow His teachings, humble ourselves as He humbled Himself, and do good works that—"

"You were right, Reverend Fields," Mr. Mikkelson said. "It's a doctrine of works—the very thing you said it was. This man is only here to distort the truth. I've heard enough. I do believe everyone has."

Will thought he noticed a few who actually wanted to listen, but Reverend Fields was saying, "Yes, indeed, we've heard enough. I invite all who profess the true word of God to enter our doors and proclaim the gospel, but this is a waste of our time."

Will looked around for support. "Would anyone like to hear what I have prepared to say?"

"I would," one young man said, and his wife was nodding.

But this only angered Reverend Fields. "No, you wouldn't, Jake Winthrop. I told you already, we've heard all we want to hear. Pick up your false scripture and whatever else you brought with you, Mr. Lewis, and leave now. I'll take your place this evening, and teach truth—so these believers will not go away disappointed."

Will considered for a moment. He thought of pronouncing the word of the Lord, loudly and forcefully—no matter who tried to interrupt him—like Samuel the Lamanite calling sinners to repent. But he knew better. He would only satisfy himself and win no one over to his point of view. So he merely said, "That's fine. I thank you for letting me say a few words."

Will felt good about that. He hadn't taken offense. He had behaved as a true Christian should, humble and willing to accept this man's disdain. But still, he wanted to salvage something from the evening if he could. "May I simply add," he said, "that if any of you do want to hear my entire message, I would be happy to visit you in your homes or in any—"

"You'll not lead my people astray," Reverend Fields growled. "Calvin, throw him out."

A big man, built like a workhorse and dressed in a heavy,

worn-out coat, stood up and approached Will, clutching him by the arm. "Out with you," he said.

Will grabbed his Bible and his Book of Mormon and stuffed them into his valise. He began moving toward the door, but Calvin seemed to think that Will ought to walk faster. He pushed him from behind. Then a man opened the back door and Calvin gave Will a hard shove. Will stumbled forward. Just as he caught his balance, he felt two big hands slam against his back again, driving him, off balance, into the door frame. Will stayed on his feet, but he had dropped his scriptures, which he bent to retrieve. "I'm leaving, sir," he said. "You need not push me."

"I'll poosh yuh if ah choose to," Calvin said as Will stepped onto a front step. There was a muddy path ahead, and when the big man's hands landed on his shoulders, Will knew immediately that he was about to be shoved face-first into a puddle of water not far ahead.

Will responded by instinct. He suddenly ducked down, broke Calvin's grip, dropped his valise on the ground, and then twisted and came up facing the big man. "I'll make my own way from here," he said.

Calvin tried to lunge at Will, but Will dodged quickly to one side, and then, as the man lost his balance, gave him some help with a hard shove on his back. Calvin went sprawling into the puddle, on his chest, and floundered in the mud.

By then Reverend Fields had come to the door. "What kind of man are you, Lewis?" he was shouting. "How could you act this way at the very door to my church?"

"It was your man who tried to push me into the mud. I only moved more quickly than he did."

"And you pushed him from behind. I saw that."

It was true, and Will couldn't deny it. "I'm sorry, sir," he said. "I shouldn't have done that. But he was after me—and I simply reacted to his charge."

Calvin was up by then, his face and coat splashed with mud, but he appeared surprisingly unwilling to take Will on again.

"I really am sorry, Calvin. I shouldn't have done that. But you shouldn't have pushed me that way. I told you I was leaving."

"Clear out," Fields was barking, sounding almost wild with anger. "The devil take you, *Mormon. Blasphemer. Agent of hell!*"

So Will picked up his valise and walked around the puddle and then on down the road. But he did glance back to see the young man who had expressed some interest—Jake Winthrop. He was standing near the door watching, and Will told himself that somehow he would find this man and teach him and his wife.

But as Will walked on down the country lane, he also asked himself whether he would ever learn to take a blow and not return it.

CHAPTER 10

By the beginning of March, 1843, Liz had begun to hope that Will would soon return from his mission. Still, she had done well by herself—better than she had expected. She had liked what Sarah Kimball had told her, and after their conversation, she had read and studied the gospel and the scriptures almost every evening. She had also made excuses to visit Sarah more often than she actually needed to. The two were becoming friends, and Liz loved the strength she gained from the time they shared. Sarah told her one day, "It's right that we should miss our husbands when they're called away, but it's also good that they find out we can take care of ourselves."

Female Relief Society meetings hadn't been held during the winter, but they would be starting up again now, and Liz looked forward to meeting with all the sisters again—and hearing from Emma and the other leaders.

Liz enjoyed being called on by the Necessity Committee to help sisters in her ward. Liz's food was holding out well, so she gave a good deal of it to those who had not been able to put as much away. Even though she had her schoolchildren to teach and Jacob to look after, it was a rare week when at least once she didn't march through the cold and snow to visit someone. She prepared meals for families, carried in water, chopped wood. The winter had been extremely cold and hadn't let up yet, and she had worried about carrying Jacob out into the weather, but he was thriving, and he was a good-natured boy who seemed to accept a little discomfort as part of life. She knew she left him to himself a great deal when she was teaching school, but he was good about playing with whatever wooden spoon or rolled-up stocking she gave him.

It was on a bitter spring day when a dirty-faced boy in home-spun trousers and wool coat came to her door. "Ma'am, are you Sister Lewis?" he asked.

"I am."

"Sister Goodrich axt me to carry this here letter to yuh." He was holding a folded sheet of paper, which he extended toward Liz.

"Thank you very much. And did Sister Goodrich pay you something for your efforts?"

He grinned, showing teeth the color of smoke. "Yes, she did, and she tol' me you shouldn't pay me a penny more. So now I've said it." But he waited, as though to test her resolve.

"All right, then," Liz said. "Thank you."

The boy doffed his cap and then ran off, as though in a hurry to stop somewhere to spend whatever Martha Goodrich had given him. She was the leader of the Necessity Committee, and was surely writing to let Liz know of someone in need.

The letter explained that a woman on the bluffs, Hannah Murdock, had lost a child to whooping cough the week before, and now she had lost a second child. Sister Goodrich thought that Liz might be able to help her through some hard days.

Liz didn't know Sister Murdock, but there were directions to her house in the letter, and it wasn't far away. What Liz didn't like was carrying Jacob into a house where he might catch whooping cough. Still, she knew she had to help, so she took off her apron and tidied her hair, and then she wrapped a heavy shawl around herself and a blanket around Jacob, and she hurried down to Nelly's house. Nelly agreed to watch Jacob for a time—"not more than two hours," Liz promised. She handed him over to Nelly and then set out with her bonnet tied tight and her shawl close around her. She found the house close to Mulholland Street. It was a log cabin, but one that had never been properly chinked, and it had animal skins stretched over the windows, no glass.

Liz knocked at the door. No one answered for a time. Finally, a boy of seven or so opened the door and looked out. "My ma ain't well and cain't come to the door," he said.

"May I come in for a moment and speak to her?"

The boy shook his head and was about to shut the door, but Liz stepped forward, and he gave way. There was only one room in the cabin, with a bed in the corner, and Liz saw a face, gray as the bedding around it, looking out but not seeming to see anything.

"Sister Murdock, I'm Sister Lewis. I heard about your grief. Tell me what I can do for you."

The woman didn't answer, so Liz stepped closer to the bed. "Could I cook something for you and your family?"

It was only then that Liz realized that someone else was in the room—a man in a dark corner, sitting hunched over in a chair. "She don' wanna talk," he said. "She won't say a thing to me neither. When we lost our son las' Wednesday—our second oldest—she kept on a-goin' all the same. But then our li'l girl give out too, early this mornin', an' that was the end of it. Hannah went to bed, an' she ain't said a word all day."

Liz knelt by Hannah's bed, took hold of her hand, and held it to her face. "I lost a daughter last fall," she said, and she thought to say, "I know how you feel." But she remembered what Emma had told her, and she said instead, "It's the worst pain I've ever known, and it only goes away a little. I'll never be the same person I was; I know that."

Liz saw Hannah's eyes move, angle toward her without her head moving at all. But she didn't speak.

"I must say, though, Sister Murdock, I've learned from the pain. I hope I'm a better person. I'd trade the lessons I've learned to have my Mary Ann back, but there's something to gain from it all the same."

"But it's two," Brother Murdock said. "One was bad enough, but two was too much for 'er. We thought when we come here, God would carry us along on the wings of angels, but it's been nothin' but hardship since the day we set foot on this ground. I built this cabin quick, when winter was comin' on, but it's not held out the cold. That's what's brought on the sickness. We come too late to put in a garden an' we had no ready cash to buy animals. So food's been short all winter."

"Brother Murdock, I'm so sorry," Liz said. She looked about, now that her eyes were getting accustomed to the dark. There was bedding on the floor but only the one bed, and only one other chair—nothing else. There was not even a crane in the fireplace, or a kettle. She wondered how the poor woman had managed to cook anything.

"We ain't the only ones. I guess we can suffer for the truth. But I never thought it would be like this." There was a flatness in Brother Murdock's voice that seemed beyond grief—some version of wonder.

"I can bring you some smoked pork," Liz said. "And cornmeal. Should I go back and bring it now?"

"No. We have a little bacon left from what our neighbors give us, and we make ash bread. I know enough to do that. We'll get by for now."

"But I'll bring some other things. You need pots and kettles, and a crane for your fireplace."

"Yes. An' we'll get all them things in time. But for now, I jist hope you could do something for my Hannah."

Liz looked at her again. She had no idea what to say, so she reached under the old quilt and pulled Hannah into her arms. She pressed her cheek against Hannah's face and held her tight. "God hasn't forgotten you," she said. "He's sent your sisters to help. We'll be here as much as you need us, and we'll help you every way we can."

Liz felt no response. Hannah's thin body was stiff, and she didn't speak, didn't cry. Liz continued to hold her for a time, but she wondered whether she were only bothering the poor woman, so she slid her arms back from around her.

Someone *was* crying. Liz looked back at the boy, who had stayed by the door. "She's gonna die too," he said. "She tol' me this morning, she don't want ta live."

Liz stood up and stepped over to the boy. When she embraced him, he grabbed her around the waist and clung to her. "She doesn't want to die," Liz said. "Not really. She only feels that way today. But she loves you, and she'll get up tomorrow—or the next day—and she'll look after you. And for right now, I'll come with more food, and I'll do everything I can for her—for all of you."

The boy continued to grip her, continued to cry.

"Tell me your name," Liz said.

"Alfred," he mumbled.

A few more seconds passed, and then Liz heard Hannah stirring in her bed. "It's all right, Alferd," she said. "I'm gettin' up." She let her legs slide over the side of the bed, and she sat upright. "I need to wash Lucinda and get her ready," she said to Liz. "Could you help me with that?"

Liz hadn't known the dead baby was still there, but the father stood. "It's all right," he said. "I can get her ready. I just haven't wanted to—not just yet."

"Do you have a coffin?" Liz asked.

"No. But I have wood. I'll take care of that, too.'

"Please. You build the coffin," Liz said. "Let me help Hannah. We'll get Lucinda ready. I prepared my own little girl. It was the last thing I had a chance to do for her, and it still feels right that I did it."

A long pause followed. Finally Brother Murdock reached for an old blanket coat that was hanging by the fireplace. "I'll get some fresh water," he said, "and I'll bring in some firewood. We'll warm the water a little."

"Yes," Liz said. "Do you have something that she can wear for her burial?"

"Only the little dress she wore every day. Nothing else."

"Then let's wash her and wrap her up in a blanket for tonight. Tomorrow I'll bring something we can dress her in."

"The ground's froze. There's no burying her 'til warmer weather comes on."

"I know. But Brother Huntington keeps the bodies at his place. Lucinda can be buried properly when the ground thaws." She turned back to Hannah. "Let's do what we can for now."

Hannah stood. She looked more dead than alive, Liz thought, but she was on her feet.

• • •

Will wasn't having much success as a missionary. He had heard Wilford Woodruff's stories, knew that opposition was part of the work, but he also knew that Brother Woodruff had baptized thousands in England. Almost all missionaries came home with inspiring stories of miraculous conversions. Will was contending either with people who cared nothing about religion or with fanatics who had been admonished by their ministers to consider all Mormons the offspring of Satan. He had spent one night in jail—for no reason other than that a local minister had accused him of preaching devil worship and the sheriff had taken the man's word for it. In another little town Will had been chased by young ruffians who threatened to tar and feather him. He had run faster that night than he ever had in his life—as though God had given him wings—but it was not quite the inspiring story he wanted to tell when he returned to Nauvoo.

But Will hadn't forgotten the young couple back in Pleasant View, Alabama, the Winthrops. On the night that he had been cast from the church, he had made up his mind that he would teach them—since they had expressed an interest. He had stayed about the area in spite of Reverend Field's warnings, and he had used two bits from his limited cash to pay for a night's sleep in a local tavern. Then he had asked the proprietor on the following morning if he knew a young man by the name of Jake Winthrop.

"What are you?" the proprietor had asked.

Will wasn't sure what the man wanted to know, but he doubted it was wise, in this case, to admit his purpose. "I'm an Englishman," he said. "I've been in this country less than a year, but I consider myself an American now."

"And what is it you sell?"

"I'm not a salesman. I met Winthrop at a church meeting, and he encouraged me to stop by his place so we could talk religion."

"Oh, yes, he's religious, all right."

"Then you know him?"

"Yes, I do. He and his young wife have a farm west of town. It's a mile, maybe more, out on the road. It's a little white house with a red barn, newly painted."

So Will had walked back that way, and he had met Jake Winthrop, found him outside feeding his animals. Jake had invited Will in for a good breakfast, and he had apologized for the behavior of Reverend Fields. By the time Will had left, Winthrop and his wife, Faith, had listened and asked questions for three hours. They had also accepted Parley Pratt's pamphlet, *A Voice of Warning,* and promised to read it.

Will had had other experiences of that sort, and he had even baptized three families in a little town in Georgia. There had been a small branch of the Church established there, and some of the members had been spreading the word to their neighbors. What Will had learned was that when he stood before a group that was willing to listen, he could profess the doctrines with considerable clarity, and even more, with conviction. He sometimes longed to tell the story of how he had commanded the winds to cease, but it didn't seem right to do so. He didn't want to make himself out to be a tower of strength. But the experience at sea had brought him confidence in the power of the priesthood, and he drew on that when he preached. What he loved to do was to tell of Joseph Smith—describe the kind of man he was, in contrast to the lies about him—and he loved to tell people that he had looked into Joseph's eyes and the Holy Ghost had whispered to him that Joseph was, indeed, a man chosen by God.

Will knew that he had changed a few hearts, that he had countered some of the lies about Joseph. The problem was, the evil of those lies had spread far and wide. Will realized more every day that hatred for Mormons was unreasonably strong. Only Satan could have stirred up such feelings, he felt sure, and Satan would never stop his work.

By late March Will decided it was time to make his way back toward Nauvoo so that he would be there when the weather broke. He had felt the sting of a hard winter, even in the South, and Liz's letters reported extreme cold in Nauvoo. He didn't want to head too far north before warmer temperatures returned, but he also wanted to be home as soon as the planting could begin. More than anything, he wanted to be back with his wife and little Jacob, and he wanted to have a place to sleep each night and not be forced to ask strangers to take him in.

But before he headed north, he wanted to see the Winthrops once more. So he worked his way west from Georgia, continuing to preach when he could, but often walking all day. When he reached Pleasant View, he knew that he might have trouble if Reverend Fields or Mr. Mikkelson knew of his return, so he looped around the town and made his way to Jake and Faith's farm. He knew how these matters could go, however. If the Winthrops had become seriously interested, they may have shown Parley Pratt's pamphlet to Reverend Fields and asked his opinion. Once that happened, many a person who had taken an interest at first pulled back and then told him, on his return, to keep going.

Will knocked on the Winthrops' door late one afternoon, and he found them home. "Elder Lewis," Jake said, looking bright with happiness, "we feared you would never return. There's so much more we want to know. Come in. Come in."

Will shared a fine supper with the Winthrops. He got better acquainted with their three little children—two daughters and a son—laughed with them, taught the whole family some of the hymns of Zion, and then discussed the gospel all evening. The following morning Will accepted Faith's offer to fill a tub for him so that he could have a bath. Faith also washed his two shirts and brushed his vest and coat, and Jake cleaned and polished his boots. Will hadn't felt so refreshed in a long time.

After breakfast Will sat down with Jake and Faith in their little parlor. "We wish to be baptized," Jake told Will. "We've thought so since we read the pamphlet you left us, but after our talk last night, we are sure of it—both of us."

Jake was not yet thirty, Will was sure, and Faith was perhaps twenty-five or so. They were a handsome couple, well spoken, and seemed to be devoted to one another and their children. Will had learned a little about them, that they had come west from South Carolina, where they had been raised. Both had attended country schools and had been raised on farms, and they both had been taught to attend church every Sunday. But they had seen too much pettiness and hypocrisy in the churches they had attended. "That night when you preached," Jake told Will, "you seemed different from the people we've met in our church. You were respectful and patient, even when Mr. Mikkelson and Reverend Fields tried to make you look foolish."

"But I never should have tossed that big fellow in the mud."

Faith laughed. She was not so pretty as Liz, but she was a bright-eyed young woman, with deep dimples. "He had it coming," she said. "I thought maybe the good Lord gave you just a little help."

"I doubt he helps a man in such an unworthy purpose."

"Oh, I'm not so sure. The Lord must like to see a bully like Calvin receive a little of his own medicine."

"You sound like my wife," Will said. "She's a better Christian than I am, but she's not disappointed when I kick a man in the seat of his trousers—if he has it coming."

"So is that something you often do?" Faith asked, and she laughed again.

"I won't admit to that." Will grinned. "But it has happened before. I must admit, I was surprised when you said I was patient. It's what I try to be—but it's not my natural way."

"I'm a little like that myself," Jake said. "But, Brother Will—may I call you that?"

"Yes. By all means."

"We saw something in you that night. They gave you little chance to speak, but we heard the conviction in your voice—and you raised the very questions we had been posing about our own religion. When you said that a prophet of God was living today, my head told me not to believe it, but I felt my chest swelling all the same. I knew that you honestly believed it, and I wanted to believe it too."

"I hope you can meet Joseph someday. You'll know it then as surely as I do."

"But we don't want to wait for that," Faith said. "Can you baptize us today? There's a pond on our farm."

"Yes, of course."

"Are there others of your faith anywhere here about?" Jake asked. "Can we find meetings to attend?"

"Not close." Will thought for a time, and then he knew what he believed. "Come to Zion," he said. "Join with the Saints in Nauvoo."

"We've been wondering about that. We're not sure we can sell our farm for enough to get us started there, but it's what we're thinking we would like to do."

"Come, and don't worry yourself about getting started. I'll help you. I have oxen to open fields for you. I'll gather men to build you a house."

"But is it truly as good a place as Mr. Pratt claims it is?"

Will had to think for a time. Finally he said, "'Yes,' on the one hand, and 'not yet' on the other. You'll see a temple there, still being built, and you'll meet a people doing their best to look out for one another. But the Saints are not perfect. They're like me. I preach of Jesus and then toss a man in the mud. But I'll tell you what I know. We're trying to build a society like none other on earth—a people who follow Jesus Christ and love and respect one another."

Jake was thinking, and Will gave him time. "We have the Book of Mormon you left with us," he finally said, "and we can continue to read it. But I do want to bring my family to Nauvoo—not this year, but probably a year from now."

"That would be a good time to come. We have a plot of land that anyone can use for farmland when they first arrive. I'll plow twenty acres for you in the fall, then harrow it in the spring. It will be ready to plant when you arrive."

"That's more than I could have hoped for," Jake said. He looked at Faith. She was nodding, looking sure of herself. So that afternoon, Will baptized both of them in the little pond on their farm, and then he said good-bye and began his trek home, feeling more satisfied with his mission.

• • •

Spring stayed very cold. As Will traveled north, he learned that the Mississippi was still frozen, so he kept going on foot and was relieved when a thaw finally came. That meant hard slogging on muddy roads, but he arrived in Carthage on the last day of March. He thought he might stop there for the night but was surprised at the hostile responses he received. The uneasy feelings about the Saints in Hancock County seemed to be getting worse. He decided to continue on, and he trudged through much of the night on the Nauvoo-Carthage road. Late in the night he slept for a couple of hours alongside the road, but he awakened very cold. He thought of those nights long ago in England when he had tramped all the way home from Manchester with an infection raging through his body. Back then he had been almost hopeless, and today he knew he would see Liz, that she was his wife, that the miracle he had hoped for back then had actually come about.

Even though he was tired and cold, he set out walking again long before sunup, and he arrived at his house when he thought maybe Liz would be cooking breakfast. He was hungry, but it was not the breakfast that excited him. He wanted to hold Liz in his arms, and he wanted to see little Jacob. He tried to shake a little of the dried mud off his coat and trousers—with little success—and then stepped to the door. He didn't want to open the door and startle Liz, and he didn't want to knock on his own door, so he spoke from outside. "Liz," he said, "I'm home." He tried the door then and found that it was latched. "Liz?" he said again, and suddenly the door flew open.

She was still in her nightgown, her hair down, and she was as beautiful as he remembered—maybe more. "Oh, Will," she said, and she stepped toward him just as he grabbed her up in his arms. Her body, in his arms, fired the longing he had been feeling. He kissed her, and then he stepped back enough to look at her again.

"This is the moment I've waited for every day I was gone," he said.

"It was the same for me. It seemed such a very long time, but it wasn't, not really." And then she spun around. "Look at Jacob. Look how he's grown." Jacob was sitting on the floor, looking rather alarmed. Liz picked him up. "This is your father," she said. "Remember Daddy?"

Jacob brightened as Will leaned toward him and said, "Hello, little man. You've grown so big." And it was in that moment that Will realized, this was not his adopted child. This was Jacob, his son. Somehow God had made it so.

• • •

Will had arrived home on a Saturday morning, and he had hoped to hear Joseph preach in the grove on Sunday. He soon learned that Joseph was in Ramus, an outlying settlement east of Carthage, holding a conference with the members there. But on the following Thursday, April 6, 1843—the thirteenth anniversary of the founding of the Church—a special conference began in the temple. The walls of the temple were no higher than they had been in the fall, with work having stopped during the winter, but Will had been told that a great deal of stone had been prepared and hauled during the cold months, and the work was set to move forward quickly now.

The congregation on the main floor of the temple was packed tight, and Will felt fortunate that he and Liz and Jacob had arrived early enough to get inside. Will found a seat for Liz, with Jacob on her lap, and then he stood along the wall with many others who were collecting in every space they could find. To Will's disappointment, at eleven o'clock, when the meeting opened, Joseph Smith had not yet arrived. The word spread through the crowd that he was officiating at court and would arrive as soon as he could. Brigham Young, President of the Quorum of the Twelve, conducted the meeting. Will had been able to greet Hyrum Smith when he and Liz had arrived, along with several of the Apostles. He felt warmly welcomed by all of them as they asked him about his mission. Will especially enjoyed seeing his old friends Wilford Woodruff and Willard Richards.

It was almost an hour after the meeting had begun when Joseph Smith, Sidney Rigdon, and Orson Hyde arrived. Elder Orson Pratt was speaking at the time and seemed ready to say much more, but he ended his sermon rather quickly, and Joseph Smith stood and greeted the congregation. When he stepped to the little raised platform, he seemed changed to Will. He was more relaxed. Maybe it was because he no longer had to fear his arrest every day. He was wearing the same suit of clothes Will remembered from times past, but the fit seemed tighter, as though he had been eating well this winter.

"We all ought to be thankful for the privilege we enjoy this day," he said, "of meeting so many of the Saints, and for the warmth and brightness of the heavens over our heads. It truly makes the countenances of this great multitude to look cheerily, and gladden the hearts of all present."

Will's heart *was* gladdened. He was happy to be home, happy to be among people who loved the gospel and held the same beliefs he did. He knew his faith was stronger because of his mission, and he would always be thankful for some of the things he'd experienced, but he was also weary of being hated. The good, warm day was exhilarating, too, just as Joseph had said. Will had heard the claim that the ice on the Mississippi was still two feet thick, at least straight west and north of the city. Many had crossed on the ice from Zarahemla to attend the conference. Just south, however, the ice was finally breaking up and Will knew that new immigrants would finally be arriving.

After a hymn by the Nauvoo band and choir, Joseph Smith told the members that there were a number of matters of business to take care of. First, he wanted to ascertain the standing of the First Presidency. "Are you satisfied," he asked, "with the First Presidency in so far as I am concerned, as an individual, to preside over the whole church; or would you have another? If I have done anything that ought to injure my character, reputation, or standing; or have dishonored our religion by any means in the sight of men, or angels, or in the sight of men and women, I am sorry for it, and if you will forgive me, I will endeavor to do so no more. I do not know that

I have done anything of the kind; but if I have, come forward and tell me of it. If anyone has any objection to me, I want you to come boldly and frankly, and tell of it; and if not, ever after hold your peace."

After a motion to sustain Joseph Smith as President of the whole Church was introduced and seconded, Brigham Young called on the congregation to sustain the motion, and as far as Will could see, every hand was raised high. Will felt a surge of confidence as he glanced about and saw the earnest faces of such a big congregation, united in their support of the Prophet.

• • •

As things turned out, it was not until the third day of the conference that Joseph finally gave a full sermon. He spoke of the beasts in the book of Revelation. He gave a lengthy explanation of the symbolic meanings of those beasts, and that was interesting to Will, but when the sermon ended, the words that remained in Will's mind were Joseph's comments on the subject of knowledge. He said that useless knowledge sometimes made people "puffed up" and prideful, and led to contention. But true knowledge could do away with darkness. "In knowledge there is power," he said. "God has more power than all other beings, because he has greater knowledge."

Joseph saw danger in knowledge that led to pride; and yet, knowledge was not to be feared but to be sought. Will felt the rightness of that. He was glad for a religion that didn't fear learning. He had wished all his life that he had more education, and now he wondered whether he couldn't find time in his schedule to take some of the classes offered by the Nauvoo University. Joseph was studying German these days, and Will wasn't sure he wanted to do that, but he knew he wanted to understand Hebrew, and he wanted to understand the scriptures at a deeper level. Still, planting had to come next. His only hope was to take a class the following winter.

After three days of conference, Will returned to his daily work, but this time of jubilation had been just what he had needed. He had proclaimed the gospel and held firm in the face of great opposition. And now, as he associated with the Saints again, he felt a sense of being one with them. Above all, he felt sure that he and Liz had made the right choice in accepting the gospel and coming to Nauvoo. What pleased him, in addition, was that he had returned to a wife who was stronger and more sure of herself. She too had grown during the time he had been gone.

CHAPTER 11

J eff had picked up his mother-in-law at the St. Louis airport early in the evening, and now he was driving west on Interstate 70 and watching for the turnoff to head north toward Nauvoo. It was a long drive, upwards of three hours, and not one that Jeff was excited about sharing with Olivia Ramsey. For a couple of weeks now Olivia had been wanting to help, but Abby had told her over and over that there was nothing she could do so long as little William was still in the hospital. Now that he was home, Dr. Hunt had suggested that he not have visitors, that he be protected from any sort of virus or illness that might be going around. Abby had tried to suggest to her mom that even she should wait a while before she visited, and that had brought on an icy, angry sarcasm that had frightened Abby. She had quickly changed her tune and invited Olivia to come, but a day of pouting had followed before Abby had called again, apologized, and invited her mother in the most sincere voice she could bring herself to use. And now, here she was.

Jeff had always found Mr. Ramsey quite easy to talk to, and, at her best, Olivia could be charming and funny. She liked that Jeff was a Stanford graduate, and she made a point of introducing him with that credential: "This is Jeff, my son-in-law. Abby met him at Stanford." But tonight Olivia was tired after a two-legged flight with a rather long layover in Cincinnati, and apparently still put out that Jeff had talked her out of the morning flight she had originally planned to take. Their first conversation, after Jeff had greeted her, had been anything but pleasant.

"This was a *ghastly* flight," she said. "I got out of Newark late, as always, and I worried I'd miss my connection, but then we sat in Cincinnati for an extra hour without so much as an apology, let alone an explanation."

"That's too bad," Jeff said. "I'm sure you're tired. Maybe you can sleep a little in the car."

"I don't sleep in *cars* and I don't sleep in *airplanes*. Not in those horrible seats. That's why I wanted to fly in the morning. They have a direct flight then, and they don't seem to have delays that time of day."

"I'm really sorry about that," Jeff said, and then he slipped away to grab her suitcase off the carousel. It was one of those huge bags that people use for international trips. He wondered how long she was planning to stay. He tugged the big bag off and returned to her, and then decided he had better try to explain about the schedule. "My concern about your flying in the morning was that I didn't want you to have to wait here at the airport too long. I didn't feel like I could get off work until at least two, and that was pushing it."

"Won't those people you work for give you a little time off for something like this? What kind of boss do you have?"

"Actually, he's been great, Olivia. He really has. I'm new there, and yet he's let me leave early a lot with Will in the hospital all the time."

"Is that what you're calling him? Will?"

"That's what I call him sometimes. Abby calls him William."

"I would think so."

Jeff let that one go. He saw the mood his mother-in-law was in, and he made a quick decision not to converse any more than he had to. A light snow had started that afternoon as Jeff had driven down to the airport. He knew the traffic would be a bit of a trial coming out of St. Louis, and he could be seeing more serious snow as he headed north. He decided he would keep his mind on his driving and avoid all the dangerous areas of discussion that Olivia tended to bring up.

He pulled up the handle on the big bag and rolled it behind him as he walked ahead of her to the parking lot. The sun was down now, with only a hint of twilight in the western clouds. At least the snow was not falling any harder. Once he got out of the city traffic, he figured he could make good time going back.

At the car, Jeff called Abby and let her know they were on their way, and then he watched the signs as he worked his way out of the airport and onto the freeway.

"These people don't know how to drive in city traffic," Olivia complained.

Jeff tried to think what that meant. Didn't St. Louis qualify as a city? Or did she mean that they were all hicks who had wandered into town? Maybe New York was the only real city, and this was "out west," where people by definition weren't as savvy. But Jeff didn't want to argue with her, so he merely said, "Yeah, I guess so."

"You can go much faster than these cars are going, as long as everybody does. That's what we do on the Jersey turnpike."

"I've noticed that," Jeff said, just trying to think of something to say. "People really get out and go back there. It's the same in California, unless things get bogged down—which happens a lot."

"People out there don't know how to drive either. I've never seen so many crazy drivers as we ran into in California."

Jeff's actual opinion was that California drivers were aggressive but quite polite—at least compared to Las Vegas drivers. But he decided to say nothing more. It wasn't worth it.

"Didn't you find it that way?" she asked.

"Well, I don't know. It seems like there are crazy drivers everywhere. We all seem to think we drive better than everyone else on the road."

But this was the wrong thing to say, and he knew it immediately. She looked straight ahead and didn't respond. Olivia was an attractive woman—more well-dressed and put-together than pretty, but she made a nice impression. She had beautiful dark hair, though Jeff knew it was dyed now, and big, dark eyes. But she wore lots of makeup, which looked sort of baked on. When she looked stern, as she did now, her face seemed to take on a petrified appearance.

Jeff found his exit and headed north. The traffic gradually lightened. He made an occasional comment about the snow letting up, or he estimated the time it would take to get back to Nauvoo, but Olivia only offered polite responses, nothing more. She clearly was in no mood to chat.

It was almost two hours later, after crossing the Mississippi and passing by Quincy, Illinois, on their way toward Carthage, that Jeff made his mistake. "This is where William was born, here in Quincy," he said.

He expected her to glance toward the lights of the city, but she didn't. She only asked, "How big of a town is it?"

"I think it's maybe forty thousand—something like that."

"I'm surprised they even have a hospital."

Jeff should have let that one go, but he still felt defensive about some of her earlier statements. "They have a good one, actually. Their heart and vascular center is the best in this whole region."

She laughed in a little sound like a cough and said, "I don't doubt that."

Jeff tried to laugh too. "I know you look out there and see nothing but corn and soybean fields and you think there's not much going on around here. But Dr. Hunt is one of the nation's leading pediatric cardiologists. I don't think we could have done any better. He made good decisions. William's going to be a normal kid, from the way things look now, and—"

"Yes. From the way things look now. But Jeff, you took a gamble with your own *son*. You could have brought him to Princeton or Johns Hopkins—anyplace you wanted—and John and I would have paid for anything your insurance didn't cover. This country doctor of yours *may* have managed the job, but we won't really know for a long time, and it's something we shouldn't have to worry about." She took a loud breath and then added, "I haven't said anything, Jeff, because Abby gets so upset when I do, but I feel like I have to get it off my chest with you. You promised to look after our daughter and to provide for her. And now you've moved her out here a million miles from civilization and you've taken a job with no future. I have to say, you've given me lots of reasons to wonder what kind of life my daughter is going to have."

Jeff felt rage and defeat at the same time. There was a certain logic in what she said. He hadn't given Abby much so far. But there was a nastiness in her attitude that he wanted to defend himself against. For the moment, he kept driving, breathing, waiting to see what might come out of him. He told himself, *Don't say a thing, not a single word,* but he did finally say, "I'm sorry you feel that way. I hope, in a few years, you'll feel better about me."

The words were humble, but the tone was icy, and they didn't relieve the tension. Still, Olivia did seem to sense that she had gone too far. "I'm sorry to be so blunt with you, Jeff. I like you. I really do. But I want you to start making better decisions."

Jeff let that one go too, and he let everything run through his mind. He decided there was one thing she really did need to know. "Olivia, Abby likes it here. She's the one who would really like to stay. I haven't forced her into this situation."

"I know that, Jeff. I talk to her all the time. But that doesn't change anything. I want you to show some leadership. You can get a better job, if you really look, and you can move your son to a place where he'll get the kind of constant care he's going to need."

"Dr. Hunt says that his left ventricle is expanding and the aorta is normal now. He won't need special care. He's a normal—"

"I can't even stand to hear this, Jeff. Don't do that to me. This baby, hardly out of his mother's womb, has already had his chest sliced open. Don't tell me that's normal. This little boy is going to need careful attention all his life. I know a number of cardiologists. They tell me you should have taken my daughter to a top expert. They've never heard of this hospital you took her to."

It was no use. Jeff would not speak to this woman again. He played with a little fantasy of opening her door and pushing her out, but he couldn't get himself to find any humor in any of this. So he drove on for another three or four minutes before Olivia said, "I know I've said too much. And you'll hate me forever. But right now I don't care. I'm going to say one more thing and get it over with."

She waited another minute or so, and Jeff watched the head-lights on the other side of the divided highway. He could see flakes of snow streaking through the light of his own headlights, not thick, not piling up on the highway, but sort of mesmerizing to watch. Sensing that the next insult was going to have something to do with his religion, he readied himself and repeated in his mind, *Don't respond. Don't respond.*

"I know you Mormons like to fill up your houses with a dozen kids, but don't do that to my Abby. Your baby is going to need full attention for a long time. And Abby is a wreck right now. If she wants to have one more child, that might not be so bad, but don't force your Mormon ways on her and make her have another baby for at least *several* years."

Don't respond, Jeff was telling himself again. *Don't respond.*

Again some time passed. Jeff knew they were still the better part of an hour away from Nauvoo, and he wondered how he could hang on that long without exploding, but his silence was something of a defiance, and that would have to be his only satisfaction.

But it wasn't over. "Jeff, will you promise me that?"

"Promise you what?"

"That you'll have no more than one more child, and that one, if you have it, will be down the road a few years."

"No."

"No, what?"

"That's not your decision, Olivia. It's our decision—Abby's and mine."

"So you want a big family. Is that what you're saying?"

"No, I'm not saying that. I'm saying that however many children we have will be up to us—and I don't plan to consult you or anyone else. Except God."

"And this God of yours believes in a dozen babies—and maybe even a few extra wives. Is that it?"

Jeff took a very deep breath, and then in the most controlled voice he could manage, he said, "No, Olivia. That's not what God wants from me. But you know that. At this point, you just want to be offensive. So let me ask you to make a promise to me. Please, don't say another word until we get back to Nauvoo—or better yet, for several years down the road."

"Trust me, you have my promise," Olivia said. "But don't trust me when I tell Abby what I think she should do with you. If my husband had ever talked to my mother that way, I'd have kicked him out of my house."

Jeff thought of a dozen things he might have said at that point, but he voiced none of them. And it didn't take long for him to realize what a tense situation he had created by saying what he had. He only hoped that Abby *wouldn't* kick him out of the house.

• • •

Abby had been watching the clock all evening. She had calculated that Jeff and her mom would arrive no sooner than eight-thirty and, she hoped, no later than nine. The baby was still at a stage when he needed to be nursed quite often, and he was always awake at least a couple of times in the night. So she was sleepy. William was asleep now, and Abby worried that his grandmother would want to look at him when she came in—and wake him up. What she worried about much more was what kind of mood her mother would be in. She knew that her mom hadn't wanted to take this later flight, and she knew how cranky Olivia could be when she was tired. She also knew that her mother was likely to give Jeff plenty of "advice" about getting out of Nauvoo and finding a better job. It was what she had harped about a great deal lately, to Abby, and she wasn't likely to miss a chance to give Jeff a piece of her mind.

Abby had been overjoyed to bring William home, but she had found the adjustment quite frightening. A nurse had been assigned to visit her three times a week and help with his incisions and check his vital signs—and that would help a great deal—but not allowing any visitors would mean long days for Abby as she tried to figure everything out for herself. These first three days at home had been difficult. Jeff had gone to work extremely early and come home in the afternoons to help, but he was new at all this too.

Abby had called Kayla at least ten times in the last few days and had even broken down and cried on the phone a couple of times. "I don't think he's eating enough," she had told Kayla. "He nurses and falls asleep, and then, in just a few minutes, he wakes up and cries again. It seems like he's always hungry."

"They have to *learn* to nurse, Abby," Kayla had told her. "He's had a tube down his throat all his little life, and I'm sure he's still tired from all he's been through. He just falls asleep before he fills up. He'll get better."

It was the kind of information Abby needed, but she wished that Kayla could pop in from time to time so she wouldn't feel quite so much on her own. Still, William was doing well. He had gained a tiny bit of weight before he left the hospital, and now she just wanted to make sure he ate well and continued to get stronger.

As it turned out, Abby was asleep when the kitchen door opened and her mother stepped in from the garage. She had thought she would watch TV for a few minutes, but she had sat down in a recliner and fallen asleep almost instantly. As soon as she opened her eyes, however, she knew that something was wrong. She saw it in her mother's stiffness, her clamped jaw. Olivia was ready for a fight—or, more likely, had already been in one. "Hello, Abby," she said, but she stood by the door as though she were thinking of leaving without saying anything more.

Abby hurried to her mother and tried to hug her, but Olivia stood stiff and straight. Abby looked over her mother's shoulder and saw Jeff standing just outside, unable to get through the door with Olivia staying so close to the entrance. Jeff gave Abby a little shrug and a roll of the eyes that seemed to say, *I don't know what happened.*

It was all exactly as Abby had feared. "Come in, Mom," Abby was saying. "I'm sure you're tired. Do you want to go to bed early, or—"

"Am I staying here?"

"Of course you're staying here. I've got a bedroom ready for you. Come and see. Jeff will bring your things in."

"He doesn't need to. I can carry my own luggage."

Olivia turned as though to head back to the garage, but Jeff said, "I've got your suitcase. I'll take it to your bedroom."

The two women stepped aside, and Jeff carried the bag without pulling out the handle. Abby turned back to her mother. "Is everything all right?"

"I don't think I should stay here. Your husband has asked me not to speak to him. I certainly want to comply."

"Oh, Mom, I'm sorry if something went wrong, but please, we do want you to stay with us. That's why you came—so you can help me with the baby."

"I can come over after he goes to work each day—and leave before he comes back."

"Mom, it can't be that bad. I don't know what—"

"It *is* that bad. I've never been spoken to so rudely in my entire life."

Abby knew that Jeff could say the wrong thing sometimes, but he was not mean-spirited. If the two had had words, she knew very well that it was her mother who had instigated the argument. But she also knew how difficult this was going to be. Abby would have to watch her every word now. She would talk to Jeff when she could, and see whether some sort of apology might help, but her guess was, he was actually the one who had been abused.

By now Olivia was looking the place over. Jeff had removed the window unit from the kitchen window once the air conditioner had been installed, but the woodwork around the window had been warped and scarred, so Jeff had torn out the framing and had not yet replaced it. The little kitchen had worn linoleum on the floor, which would also be replaced in time, but hadn't been yet. Maybe worst was the carpet in the living room, which Olivia could surely see from where she was standing. It had been worn out before Jeff and Abby had moved in, but now, with all the tramping back and forth as Jeff had worked on the house, a dirty path ran past the couch. Abby had seen no reason to get the carpets cleaned when the plan was to replace them soon, but she had known before her mother arrived that she would have to apologize for the way things looked.

"Mom, Jeff has done a lot of work on the house, but most of it has been in the basement. He's put in central air conditioning and he's repaired the basement walls, which used to leak like crazy. You can't believe how hard he's worked, but there's still a lot to do. We're getting new carpets as soon as spring comes, and we're replacing almost all the woodwork in the house—even the kitchen cabinets. I know the bathroom looks awful, but that's another project Jeff will get to before long."

"If he says so, it must be true."

"Mom, I hope you—"

"Where's the baby?" Olivia asked.

"I have him in our bedroom for right now. He's asleep. He wakes up a lot, and I just can't stand to have him in another room for now. Do you want to see him?"

"Of course I want to see him, but I won't wake him. I'll get up with you in the night if you need me, but that means I better go to bed now. Where am I sleeping?"

Jeff had returned to the living room. He sort of gestured toward the hallway beyond, but he didn't say anything. "It's down here," Abby said. She walked ahead and took her mother into the extra bedroom. What Olivia couldn't have known was that there hadn't even been a bed in the room until the day before. Abby had been setting the room up as a nursery, but once Olivia had insisted on coming to help, Abby had wondered out loud to Kayla where they could get a bed. Kayla had sent Malcolm to their hometown, Augusta, Iowa, with his pickup truck, and he had brought back an old bed frame and mattress they had left stored with her parents. Malcolm had come in and set it up while Jeff had been at work.

But when Olivia looked at the bed, she asked, "How hard is that bed?"

"Uh . . . actually, I don't know. It might be softer than you like." Abby had been so happy to have something, she hadn't thought to worry about that.

"You know how my back is. Maybe I should look for another place right now. Is there any kind of hotel in this dumpy little town? We drove so long, I thought we had reached the edge of the world, and then we drove another fifty miles."

Abby was starting to feel that enough was enough. When her mother was like this, she expected everyone to bow down and try to please her, but it was never possible. Fortunately, she usually came back to her senses, at least to some degree, once she realized that she wasn't getting what she wanted.

"Mom, you'll have to make this bed do for tonight. If it's not hard enough, Jeff can try to fix it tomorrow. I'm sure he'll do anything he can to make you comfortable."

Abby didn't stand up to her mother very often, but she had spoken with some sternness this time, and she hoped her mother heard what she meant: *If you keep this up—or say anything against my husband—I just might throw you out.*

Olivia seemed to get the message. "Just let me settle in a little, Abby. I'm mad right now. You can tell that. But I have good reason.

All the same, I'll bite my tongue, and I'll help you in every way I can." She glanced around the room. "Is there no TV in this room?" she asked.

"No. I'm sorry."

"Why am I not surprised?" she asked with that icy sarcasm of hers, but she added quickly, "It's all right. I'll go to bed."

"The bathroom is right next door to you, but we only have one—and Mom, the grime on the shower tile just doesn't come off. I'm sorry, but—"

"How can you live this way, Abby? I don't understand."

"We've talked about all this, Mom. We'll have a nicer house someday. But—"

"Never mind. Just leave me alone. I need to calm down."

"Okay. These towels on the bed are for you, and if you need anything else, let me know."

"Fine." But as Abby walked out, she heard her mother say, "I need some things, all right."

Abby almost spun around to tell her what she thought, but she resisted. Instead, she walked back to the living room, where Jeff was sitting in his recliner looking as though he had been knocked over the head with a hammer.

"What happened?" Abby asked him, and a long, whispered conversation followed. Abby heard nothing that surprised her, and when she heard the remark about Mormons, she threatened to sock her mom in the jaw.

"It's okay," Jeff told her. "I'll apologize in the morning and tell her it was all my fault. I don't want to fight with her anymore."

"Don't do that," Abby said. "You can't tell her that she has a right to decide how many children we have, and if she says another word about our house, I'm going to tell her to fly straight back to New Jersey—on her broom."

Abby's night turned out not to be an easy one. William woke up every two hours or so. Jeff got up one of those times and gave the baby a bottle as a supplemental feeding, but Abby couldn't sleep, so she came out to make sure William was taking it.

Abby never heard a sound from her mother, so the bed must have been all right, and Jeff left at six to head for work, long before her mom got up. When Olivia finally got up, she seemed subdued. She had to know that Jeff would have repeated to Abby the things she had said, and she also had to know what Abby would think about that.

"Was the bed all right?" Abby asked.

"Just tell me you have coffee in your house."

Abby laughed. "I bought some yesterday. I knew you'd never make it through this without coffee."

Olivia actually smiled. "Abby, I'm not a nice person," she said. "You know that already. And I was in a bad mood when I got in last night."

Abby wasn't going to let her off the hook quite that easily. She only said, "I fixed some scrambled eggs. Do you want me to scramble some more, or—"

"No. Just coffee. And a slice of toast."

"It's just instant coffee. Is that all right?"

"Anything dark and ugly and full of caffeine."

Abby got the bread out. Olivia sat down at the little wooden table in the kitchen.

"I have some opinions, Abby. And I think I'm right. I'm not sorry I said something. But I overstepped last night. I know I did. And you may think I had a good night's sleep, but I didn't. I spent most of the night thinking about some of the things I said, and the way I said them. I thought about getting up, but I didn't want to face your husband. I know he hates me."

"Well . . . he probably doesn't like you much right now. I'll admit that. But he saw the worst of you last night, and he doesn't know the best of you as well as I do. But Jeff's a gentle man, and he's very forgiving. You may not know it, but I got very lucky when I found him."

"He got up with the baby last night, didn't he?"

"He did, and I'm sure he will every night, as long as he needs to. He was up at five thirty to go to work, too, so he can get home and help me this afternoon. And he spends half the time he's home working on this house—because he promised to do it."

"I don't think you should have another baby right away, Abby. That was all I meant to tell him."

"And he happens to think that's not your decision."

"Where in the world did he get that idea?"

Abby shook her head. But her mom was smiling, and so was she.

"Coffee! Where's the coffee?"

"The water's heating," Abby said.

Abby got up and checked the water, waited for a time, and then poured a cupful and stirred in the coffee. But Olivia had only finished half the cup when Liz heard William. "Do you want to see your grandson?" Abby asked.

"Oh, yes."

They walked into the bedroom and Abby picked him up and gave him to her mother. "He doesn't look like a single thing is wrong with him," Olivia said. "He's tiny, but he looks just perfect."

"Dr. Hunt says that even the scar will mostly go away. He's going to be a regular kid. He can do anything he wants to do."

"It's hard to imagine," Olivia said. William had calmed when his mother had picked him up, but he was starting to complain now that nothing had touched his lips.

"I need to feed him," Abby said, taking him back.

"It's hard to believe. My little girl with her own little baby."

Abby took William to the living room, sat down in her recliner, and unbuttoned her top. She felt a little funny doing that in front of her mother, and she used the blanket to be a little more private, but her mom seemed to relish the whole thing. "He's got his world figured out already," she said. "The squeaky wheel gets the grease."

Abby wondered whether her mom was being a little ironic about her own tendency to "squeak," but she didn't say so. She had just heard the storm door open, and now there was a knock on the front door. "Could you get that?" she said. "It's probably just one of the sisters, with food, but we can't let anyone come in. Dr. Hunt said that you're the only exception."

Olivia got up and walked to the door. When she opened it, Abby heard Sister Caldwell say, "Oh, hello. You're Abby's mom. I'd know that if you was standing a mile off. An', of course, Abby said you was comin'."

Mom was stuttering, obviously confused about who this was.

"I'm Sister Caldwell, one of the missionaries. I have a dinner for you. I thought I better bring it now before I head down to preparation meeting. I wasn't sure I'd ever make it back here the rest of the day. Just stick that casserole in the oven at 350 or so about an hour before you want to eat it."

"Thank you," Olivia said, taking the pan.

"I don't think you can carry that all at once, but I cain't come in, not without spreading germs."

"I'll come back and get the rest," Olivia said. She carried the covered dish to the kitchen.

"Hello, Sister Caldwell," Abby called. "I'm nursing William or I'd come and say hello."

"That's fine. I sure want to see that little guy one of these days. But I'll stay right here for now."

Olivia came back and took a bowl and a little basket with a cloth covering. "I don't understand," she finally said to Sister Caldwell. "Do you bring food every day?"

"No. *I* don't. But someone does. Either from Abby's ward or from the missionaries. We done it while she had to go to the hospital each day, and we thought we'd keep it up while the baby's still takin' all her time."

"I can take over now. I can cook for her and Jeff."

"I know. But let us do it a while yet. It makes us feel like we're helpin' a little, and we love your daughter like she's our own little girl."

"How did you get to know one another?"

"Down at 'Sunset by the Mississippi' one night. And then we live jist around the corner."

"That's so nice. I can't believe you'd be so kind."

"We jist try to look out for each other a little, that's all."

"I'm sorry. Who does?"

"Sisters in the Church. But I guess you know that."

"No. I don't think I did."

Sister Caldwell called out to Abby, wishing her well again, and then she said to Olivia, "It's so good to meet you. I'd give you a big hug, but that might carry some of my germs inside. Have a good day now, and enjoy that little angel. There ain't nothin' better in this world than bein' a grandma. I know that from *lots* of experience."

Abby saw Sister Caldwell through the front window as she waddled away like a plump mother duck. Then she looked up at her mother, who had shut the door and turned toward her. "They feed you every day?" she asked.

"Yes, and one of the women from our church drove me to Quincy lots of times so Jeff could take our car to work."

"How did you get to know all these people?"

"They're our brothers and sisters, Mom. We really believe that."

"But I've never met a woman like that in my whole life. Who is she?"

"She's Sister Caldwell, from Idaho. She and her husband pay their own expenses to live here for a year and a half. They conduct tours in the historic area, down off the hill."

"They *pay* to come out here?"

"They do. And they not only do the tours, they perform in a play in the evenings."

"I'm sorry, but I can't picture this. I just can't see her as a *performer.*"

"You'd be surprised, Mom. She does a great job. And I'll tell you what. I wouldn't trade her for a dozen of those women you play bridge with. She's all heart, and she's *good* right down to the bone."

Olivia was still looking rather wide-eyed, as though she couldn't imagine what she had just experienced. "I know people like that are probably very nice, in their way, but they don't seem the type you would want to make friends with. It just seems so strange."

"Mom, I've been trying to explain to you, I've found something wonderful. Jeff is as sophisticated as anyone I know. And so is his family. But when little William seemed to be dying, Jeff put his hands on his head and blessed him to live. And he did live. I believe in things now, Mom, and I didn't when I left our home. I've never been this happy in my life."

Olivia didn't say a word. But Abby saw a change in her mother's face. Jeff didn't need to be afraid to come home that afternoon.

CHAPTER 12

Will wanted to start farming the land he had purchased near Jesse and Ellen's place, east of Nauvoo. He would have to plow the land again and harrow it as early as he could, and then hope to bring in some sort of crop the first season—at least enough to make another payment on the property. If he put all his profit into the purchase, however, it would mean farming the Big Field for another year, and it would also mean procuring all the roadwork he could—but so far he had no promise of any further work for the county. He had ridden his horse to Carthage one day and talked with county officials, but they seemed more hesitant than they had been the year before. They spoke of opening up the work to bids this year, and Will wondered whether men from surrounding towns had complained about the work going to a Mormon.

There was nothing to do but wait for now. There had been some pleasant days that spring, but each time the soil was almost dry enough, a hard rain would delay his plowing again. Will was good at many things, but waiting wasn't one of them. He tried to help Liz all he could, and he worked on his fences and sheds, readied his equipment, even borrowed a rifle and hunted one day. He brought home a young white-tail buck and dressed it out. The fresh venison was a good change from the remnants of last year's cured pork, but he wanted to hear his plow cutting through dark loam. He wanted to get seed corn in the ground, and he wanted to plant the garden by his house.

One morning, after a downpour of rain during the night, Will walked down to the brick store. He wanted to ask William Clayton how much would be expected from him as payment on his land. He had made a small down payment in the fall, but he knew he would have to come up with more this year. He passed Joseph's log house and was continuing west to the store when he heard a big voice behind him. "Is that you, Will Lewis?"

Will turned around to see the Prophet. "President Smith, good morning," he said. Will waited as Joseph strode toward him, and they shook hands.

"I have to get away from my house these days if I hope to carry out my duties for the Church," Joseph said. "There are far too many folks living with us."

Will knew that Joseph had a houseful with Emma and their four children, along with Lucy Smith, his mother. Eliza Snow, who was still serving as the Smith children's schoolteacher, had moved out of the house not long ago, but on the same day, Lucy had moved in. In addition, there were Emily and Eliza Partridge, who lived in the house and helped Emma, and there were the four Walker children. Sister Walker had died the year before, and Joseph and Emma had taken in the oldest four of her ten children. Lucy and Catherine Walker worked in the house, and Lorin and William worked for Joseph and, among other things, delivered firewood to the poor. What Will had also learned was that during the winter, while he had been gone, the Walkers had played a big role in creating the Young Men's and the Young Ladies' relief societies.

"Your new house is coming along well, though," Will said. "Won't that give you more room?"

"Yes, it will. And I look forward to it, but we're adding rooms so that it can be used as an inn. Until we get the Nauvoo House built, we're going to need a place for travelers to stay." He clapped a hand on Will's shoulder. "It's good to see you," he said. "I heard a good report on your mission, but I've never had an opportunity to talk to you about it. How did you fare?"

"Let's just say that most people were less than welcoming. But a few embraced the gospel, and they made up for all the others."

"I know it was a hardship for you, but I think I see a little change in you—and for the good. Next time you're called, you may have to sacrifice a little more than you did this time, but I suspect you're ready for that."

The idea actually worried Will a little, but he only said, "I'll do what the Lord calls me to do. I promise you that." He grinned. "Liz won't let me do otherwise."

"Well, let's hope for a good harvest—both of grain and of souls. It should be a better year if we can just be left alone. What worries me is Thomas Sharp, down in Warsaw. He never misses a chance to complain about us in his newspaper—and far too many are taking up his attitude."

Will had been hearing about the trouble in the county, with more people saying that the Saints ought to be expelled from the state—the same as had been done in Missouri. When Governor Ford had been elected the previous fall, he had soon advocated that the Nauvoo charter be rescinded, and some in the legislature had grabbed at that idea. They had wrangled over the matter all winter while Will had been gone, and finally, this spring, those against the Saints had come within one vote of getting their way.

"We won't turn from this place unless they give us no choice," Joseph said. He glanced to the north, where everything was green and gleaming after the night's rain. The trees were in full leaf now, and the whitewashed homes were reflecting the morning sun. The mud was deep, and some of the sheds and outhouses looked weathered, but Will had learned to see the city with Joseph's eyes, and it was beautiful. "If trouble starts, the way it did in Missouri, we may have to locate a place where we can build our own city in our own way. I have men out looking at Oregon and the Rocky Mountains."

"But we can't be driven out this time, can we?"

Joseph now looked the opposite direction, out across the broad river. Will didn't know whether he was trying to decide how to answer or just being careful about what he said to Will. Finally, he looked Will squarely in the eyes and asked, "Have you joined the Legion, Will?"

"Not yet, I haven't. I don't know the first thing about the military."

"Every man between eighteen and forty-five, by Illinois law, is required to join a unit of the state militia—even new immigrants. But all the complaints I hear are that our army is too big. How can they have it both ways?" He didn't wait for an answer. "We may need to protect ourselves this time. It's clear that no government will stand with us. Every man in Nauvoo ought to be willing to lay down his life for his people—if it comes to that."

Will nodded. "I'm not a coward, Brother Joseph. I haven't thought of it that way. The Legion has seemed all parades and sham battles to me."

"And so it is—for now. But there could be real battles ahead.

The way I see it, though, if we make a show of force, many a man in Warsaw and Carthage might think better of marching their own puny militias against ours."

"You're right about that. Brother Joseph, I'll go ahead and join this year."

"Good. Die with me, if that's what it comes to. But better yet, let's live. Let's spread the gospel to the world—even if the devils of hell come against us."

"Aye. I gained a taste for preaching this winter. I want to do some more of it. But I do have to pay my bills. I came down to ask Brother Clayton for a little time to make the next payment on the farm I bought last fall."

"Go ahead and farm that land, Will," Joseph said. "It's yours. Pay the balance as your crops come in. But help others, as you've done for Brother Matthews and Brother Johns. Share in your prosperity; keep your eye on our higher purposes."

"It's what I want to do, Brother Joseph. Thank you."

So Will turned back and headed home. But he kept thinking about Joseph's words. He still wanted a better home for Liz, but he suspected the best thing he had done in Nauvoo, so far, had been to hire Jesse and Dan. The other words that also came back to him, however, left him uneasy: "Die with me, if that's what it comes to."

• • •

Liz didn't like the idea of Will joining the Nauvoo Legion. She didn't understand why Americans loved their militias so much. Young men in England joined the army, and they went away to train, but Americans seemed to revel in their titles and their uniforms and their weapons. Mormon men didn't gather at a pub and drink all evening, but they liked to go off and pretend they were shooting one another, like little boys.

Still, there was not much Liz could say, since Joseph Smith him-self had asked Will to join. And now that he had done so, Will was being called away to drills quite often. He came home talking of battle formations and drilling commands, and he soon began speak-ing of his need for a uniform. Liz did her best to sew one for him that was patterned after the fancy suits some of the others wore, but all the fabric and buttons and epaulettes didn't come cheap. What she managed to make for him remained rather simple—a blue coat with tails, a bit of gold trim, and a red sash. But he wore his every-day trousers and boots, and he had no hat to match the tall plumed ones that some of the men had purchased.

When Will came home from training one evening, he seemed hesitant about something. "Liz," he finally said, "I suppose I re-ceived something of an honor today—but one I could have avoided and perhaps been just as pleased."

Liz had long since finished cooking dinner. She dished out some of the venison he had brought home that spring, with some with-ered potatoes, almost the last of those that had lasted through the winter. "And what great honor is that?"

"Charles Rich spoke to me today. *Major General* Rich. He wants me to join a special brigade—the Escort Brigade of Light Infantry. We're supposed to be bodyguards for Joseph Smith."

Liz didn't like the sound of that. She set Will's plate on the table and watched his face to see whether he weren't more thrilled than he was letting on.

"It's not as dangerous as it sounds. Or at least I don't expect it to be. It's mostly parading near the front of the troops, close to Joseph."

"Why did Brother Rich ask you?"

"I can't say exactly. Men in the Escort Brigade need to have horses, and he knew I have a horse. Maybe that's all there was to it."

"Or maybe he's heard the stories about you fighting that man on the riverboat."

Liz saw Will smile just a little. "It could be that. I do have a reputation as a man who can hold his own in a fight. But that's not my worry. Brother Rich says I must have a full uniform, and I will have to drill more often."

Liz didn't like any of this. It was more money for a hat, more sewing to make matching trousers, probably a new pair of boots. But that wasn't what concerned her most. She was quite sure that Will actually liked the whole thing, no matter what he was saying.

"Brother Rich . . . *General* Rich . . . said he would have me fitted up with the uniform I need—and the weapons. I can pay the money back later on."

"What *weapons?*"

"I'll wear a brace of pistols and a sword. It's to look *important,* I think. It all makes me laugh, if you want to know the truth."

"It makes you want to burst your buttons, Will. You know it does."

He grinned. "I don't have any buttons, Liz. But when I get some, will you sew them on?"

"Oh, Will, we joined a religion, not an army. Where will all this lead?"

Will had found himself wondering the same thing, but he remembered what Joseph Smith had said: If they looked formidable enough, no one would come against them.

• • •

On Saturday, May 6, 1843, Will paraded with the Nauvoo Legion. Joseph led the way on his black horse, Old Charley. He looked resplendent in his blue coat, white trousers, high boots, and a tall military hat with a plume. A sword was strapped to his side, the scabbard hanging next to his leg. With him at the head of the parade were Emma Smith and half a dozen "leading ladies" of Nauvoo, and after that, Will's group, the Escort Brigade of Light Infantry. Then came the Legion brass band playing spirited marches.

General Smith led a force of more than two thousand men, the first cohort made up of mounted troops and the second, foot soldiers—and all in some sort of uniform, whether matching or not. Will knew that the soldiers must have been an impressive spectacle as the men marched out Parley Street to the parade ground beyond Joseph's farm. But in the past, hundreds of spectators had attended such parades, including dignitaries from Illinois and surrounding states. That had changed now, partly because it was a cold, windy day, but even more because the Legion, which had been greatly admired in years past, was coming to represent the very suspicion people felt toward the Mormons. What did General Smith—President Smith, Mayor Smith—want to do with this army? Men like Thomas Sharp said his plan was to build his own kingdom, to conquer his neighbors, and to rule over them.

At the parade ground, the cohorts stood in formation as Joseph Smith and his staff of officers—along with visiting dignitaries—rode past to review the troops. The women, in black velvet dresses, and with white feathers on their hats, made a grand sight, but no one more than the stately Emma Smith, who rode a horse beautifully. And yet, Will thought she looked troubled this morning. He wondered what other worries might be on her mind.

When Joseph spoke to the troops, he shouted against the wind and told them, "When we have petitioned those in power for assistance they have always told us they had no power to help us. Damn such power! When they give me power to protect the innocent I will never say I can do nothing. I will exercise that power for their good. So help me God!" Everyone knew he was referring to his experience with President Martin Van Buren, who had refused to redress the wrongs that the Saints had experienced in Missouri.

The mock battle turned out to be spirited, and Will enjoyed the day, but afterwards, as he rode his horse back along Parley Street to his home, he was glad Liz hadn't been there. He wondered if the men had enjoyed the display of power a little too much. He thought Liz might be right to worry about that.

• • •

On Sunday, June 25, not three weeks since the Legion parade, Will and Liz were enjoying the good weather and listening to a sermon on the floor of the temple when a rider galloped toward the building. "Nauvoo Legion soldiers," he shouted in a loud, urgent voice, "meet at the Lodge Room, immediately!"

The Lodge Room was the upstairs room in the brick store, where various events were held, including Masonic meetings. The cornerstone for a Masonic Hall had been set the day before, but construction was only just getting started.

Will turned to Liz. "I better hurry down there." He looked around and saw that men were already filing out before anyone got up to close the meeting.

"What could it be?" Liz asked.

Will saw her concern. "You take Jacob home," he told her. "I'll go to the meeting and find out what's happening. I won't go anywhere without stopping home first."

"Do you think it's—"

"I don't know what to think. But don't worry about me." Will fell in line with many others, and he walked with the crowds of men down to Main Street and then south to the store. By the time he got there, however, a man was standing in the front doorway, shouting,

"It's too crowded up there. Assemble on the green and form a hollow square. We'll meet outside."

As the men fell into formation, Will heard them speculating about what could be wrong. Everyone knew that Joseph was out of town with Emma and their children, but no one seemed to know where they had gone. By the time Hyrum Smith stepped into the square of men, a huge crowd had gathered outside the formation.

"Brothers, thank you for coming," Hyrum shouted, and the rumble of men's voices silenced immediately. "I need to explain quickly what's happened, and then we need some volunteers to ride north to protect Joseph."

There was a stir in the crowd, and Hyrum raised his hand to quiet everyone. "Joseph and Emma left last week for a visit with Emma's sister, near a town called Dixon, up north in the state. It's about two hundred miles from here, maybe more. We found out, after they left, that Governor Ford has given in to pressure from Missouri's governor and has issued a new writ for Joseph's arrest and extradition."

This brought on some shouts of anger, and one man called out, "That was all settled months ago."

"I know," Hyrum said. "They're coming at it in a different way this time. It's not about shooting Boggs. They've gone back to the old charge of treason—from the battles in Far West."

This incited more shouts and groans, and Hyrum held his hand up again. "I know all that, brothers. I know what you're saying. But please let me tell you what's going on now. We need to act quickly." He paused for a moment and then said, "We don't have many details yet, but we've learned that a Missouri lawman, Joe Reynolds, has partnered with Harmon Wilson, constable from over here in Carthage, and they've found Joseph and placed him under arrest. Joseph was able to hire a lawyer, and he's filed suit against the two lawmen for false arrest and abuse. From what we've learned, they roughed him up pretty bad when they took him in."

Will felt a low rumble of anger spread through the crowd. He felt the outrage himself.

"We're hearing that Reynolds has a gang of scoundrels ready to grab Joseph, and if they get him to Missouri, you know as well as I do that he'll never come back."

Someone yelled, "Let's get going, then. I can leave right now."

"Wait just a minute. Don't just ride off unorganized. We're asking the Escort Brigade to ride toward Monmouth—all who can—along with others who wish to join with us. We think that's the direction they're going to take."

Hyrum looked around at the men. "All right now. How many are ready to ride out tonight?"

Many hands went up—hundreds. And of course, Will raised his own.

"All right. But remember, we're not going out to fight anyone. We only plan to serve as protectors, to make sure that Joseph is not hauled across the river. Go home and get what you'll need and report back here in two hours."

So Will walked home and gathered up cheese, bread, and dried meat, and he rolled up a blanket. All the while, he kept promising Liz that he was not going off to battle. But when he strapped on his pistols, she asked him, "If it's not a battle, what are those for?"

"Just to show authority. Trust me, I'll have no cause to use them."

Will reached down and picked up Jacob, who was eight months old now. He loved to have Will toss him in the air, so Will did that three or four times, and Jacob laughed. Then Will kissed him and handed him to Liz. He was about to leave when Liz said, "Please, let's pray before you go."

"Of course," Will said. "But you have nothing to worry about."

"I am worried, Will. What's going to happen to us? You know how things got out of hand in Missouri. How can we interfere with constables and not get everyone around here up in arms?"

"What would you prefer, that we let our Prophet be murdered?" But he had sounded a bit too angry. He stepped to Liz and took her in his arms. "We're doing what's right, Liz. I promise you that."

But the truth was, Will was worried too—worried about what might happen not only today but in days and weeks to come. Until now, the growing resentment in the area had only taken the form of accusations and threats. This could be the end of all that.

Will held Liz and prayed, called on the Lord to look after her and Jacob, and to look after Joseph Smith and the men who were going to support him.

· · ·

The Mormon posse rode until late into the night, the men gradually becoming strung out along the trail. Socks was a sturdy old mare, but Will doubted she could beat him in a footrace. So he kept her on a steady walk and made up for her pace by continuing longer into the night.

The men slept where they could, wrapped in blankets or strips of canvas, and then they rode as long as their horses could keep going again on Monday. It was Tuesday afternoon when reports circulated back to Will that Joseph had been located—just up the road, a little short of Monmouth.

By the time Will reached the assemblage, he could hardly see Joseph for all the men on horseback who had gathered around him. A man named Turner peeled back from the crowd and brought his horse alongside Will's. "When we rode up to the wagon, and Joseph recognized us, he said, 'Gentlemen, I think I will not go to Missouri this time! These are my boys!'"

"Who are the other men with Joseph?" Will asked.

"That's what's making us all laugh. Besides sheriffs, it's mostly lawyers. The two lawmen arrested Joseph, but a sheriff from up in Dixon arrested the men who arrested Joseph. Now they're all heading to court together. I heard Joseph say that we're heading to Nauvoo—to appear at our own courts."

That night Will slept in a blanket alongside the road again, and the following morning the entourage headed on to the south. Will kept plodding along until he could take a turn at riding next to Joseph's wagon. He finally had a chance to say, "Hello, President Smith. I'm glad to see you're doing all right."

Joseph laughed. "Nice day for a ride in the country, don't you think?"

"Aye. It turns out that way. But I heard they roughed you up some."

"That they did. But I'm well enough. I pulled sticks at the camp last night. I pulled up everyone who gave me a try—and I only used one hand. I even took on two men at a time, and they still couldn't pull me up."

"Too bad I was na' there," Will said. "I would ha' showed what a Herefordshire lad can do for hi'self. I might ha' tossed ye over'n my shoulder, a li'l feller like you."

Joseph roared with laughter. "Get a stick," he bellowed. "Will Lewis wants to pull with me."

"Ah, no," Will said. "It's not right to stop the progress of this fine party. I'll do it another day."

"Yes, and don't forget. But I must say, I believe I'll use both hands when I take you on. I suspect I'll have to."

"Both arms and both legs, I'd say."

Joseph roared again.

"I heard those two sheriffs are not behaving quite so proudly as they did when they put you under arrest."

"True enough, but that's all right. We'll treat them as friends and see whether they change their attitudes a little."

And that was what happened when the posse reached Nauvoo. Word had gone ahead, and the Saints were waiting as the party approached the town. Emma and many of the city leaders had waited at Hyrum's farm about a mile east of the temple. They greeted Joseph and then proceeded west on Mulholland with Pitt's Brass Band and the Nauvoo Legion Band leading several carriages full of Church and civic leaders. Emma had brought Old Charley for Joseph to ride, and Joseph seemed to like that. He rode at the front with Emma and waved to all who greeted him, calling out their names and wishing them well, reporting that he was doing fine.

The men who had ridden out to meet Joseph had decorated their horses' bridles with wildflowers in celebration, and they were pleased with themselves, it seemed, however little they had actually done. Will understood. He felt proud that the people along the street were able to see him as one of the reliable men who had gone to protect the Prophet. The entire entourage rode past the temple as the crowds grew ever larger, then down the hill and south to Joseph's house, where a large group sat down to dinner—and at the head of the table were Reynolds and Wilson. Will was not invited to that gathering, but he heard afterwards that the two lawmen seemed nervous the whole time. Still, they ate up and accepted Joseph's hospitality.

After dinner, the Nauvoo municipal court judge, on a writ of habeas corpus, reviewed Joseph's case and set him free. Reynolds and Wilson were also released, and they got out of Nauvoo as quickly as they could.

That evening Joseph spoke to a large gathering in the grove. He laughed and even bragged a little, recounting his victories in pulling sticks, but he also became serious and made a legal argument that the power of the Nauvoo court came from the state, and the state's power came from the federal government. He spoke disparagingly of attorneys who didn't understand that. And then he said: "If our enemies are determined to oppress us and deprive us of our rights and privileges as they have done and if the authorities that be on the earth will not assist us in our rights, not give us that protection which the laws and Constitution of the United States and of this state guarantee unto us: then we will claim them from higher power from heaven and from God Almighty."

Joseph then told the Saints not to harm Reynolds or Wilson, and he argued that the law had now been shown to be on the side of justice. The Saints could feel confidence in that. But the words that stuck in Will's mind when the long speech was over were: "Before I will bear this unhallowed persecution any longer I will spill my blood. There is a time when bearing it longer is a sin. I will not bear it longer. I will spill the last drop of blood I have."

The audience gave a loud cry of approval, and Will joined in, but he also worried about the mood that was developing in Nauvoo. One of the complaints about the Saints was that they used the power of habeas corpus in their own municipal court to overrule judgments of courts that should take precedence. It was this "abuse of power," as some called it, that had caused many legislators to vote for repeal of Nauvoo's charter. Will feared that the power of the courts and the Constitution that Joseph had praised could at some point be turned against him.

Will had loved hearing Joseph take such a firm stand, but in the coming days, he was haunted by Joseph's description of the blood that might be shed. If it came to shedding blood, it might be the

Saints who would shed the most. The men of the posse had been very proud of themselves for saving Joseph and Hyrum, but Will wondered what accusations and threats were being spoken—even shouted—in all the other towns in Hancock County.

CHAPTER 13

On the Fourth of July, 1843, Will rode with the Escort Brigade in another Nauvoo Legion parade. The cost of his uniform had set his savings back, but his finances were looking better now. The county had offered him a new road to grade for the same rate of pay he had received the year before. All the talk of getting bids this year had come to nothing. No one seemed to have taken an interest—or perhaps no one owned enough teams of oxen to carry out the work.

The parade started at the old drilling field just west of Main Street. The troops marched north along Main Street and then up the hill toward the temple and the armory. All along the way the people gathered to wave handkerchiefs and cheer on the troops. Little boys marched alongside the soldiers with sticks over their shoulders, and mothers of little girls had washed their daughters' white aprons and bonnets and curled their hair as if this were Sunday, not Tuesday.

A massive crowd gathered in the grove west of the temple after the parade. Three riverboats with guests from St. Louis, Missouri; Quincy, Illinois; and Burlington—in the Iowa Territory—increased the crowd at least an extra thousand. The boats arrived at the lower landing, and Pitt's Brass Band played lively march tunes as it escorted the passengers to the grove. People brought picnic lunches, listened to speeches, and awaited the major address by Joseph Smith. The day was fair, but the heat, by afternoon, was anything but pleasant, and Liz hadn't been feeling very well lately. She hoped Joseph wouldn't speak too long.

Liz soon realized that Joseph was well aware that many people of other faiths were part of the congregation. He had to shout to be heard by so many people, but his tone was pleasant. He explained that he had not committed treason in Missouri, as he was accused of. He had never ordered his people to resist Missouri law. He also denied that he had had anything to do with the assassination attempt on former Governor Boggs. He was certainly aware of what people were saying about his leading a great army in Nauvoo and serving as a religious leader at the same time. He told the crowd that the Illinois law required men to enroll in a militia. Many men in Nauvoo carried licenses to preach, but the state had not been willing to excuse them from military duty, so that meant thousands of men were required to serve.

When the meeting ended, Will and Liz walked up the hill. Will told Liz, "I'd like to tell Joseph what a fine speech that was," but as they neared the stand, it was obvious that far too many others wanted to shake the Prophet's hand and congratulate him. Will and Liz were about to walk on by when Emma Smith, who had been sitting near the stand, greeted them. Lucy Smith, Joseph's mother, was with Emma. Will and Liz shook hands with both. Liz had met Mother Smith before, but she doubted that Lucy would remember that. "I'm Elizabeth Lewis," she said.

"I know that," Mother Smith said. "When I looked into your beautiful eyes the first time, I knew I'd never forget you."

"Oh, thank you," Liz said, but she truly was surprised. Mother

Smith was close to seventy, Liz knew, but her lively eyes—and her voice—made her seem younger. She was a little woman, and her hands were twisted with arthritis, but each time Liz had been around her, she had realized where Joseph's powerful personality had come from. Mother Smith spoke her mind freely, and she carried an authority that contradicted her age. Today she was wearing a black dress and an old-fashioned white cap with strings around her chin— all of which seemed far too hot in this weather—but she showed no signs of wilting in the heat.

"I was hoping to see you today," Emma said to Liz. "I want to invite you and Brother Lewis to go with us on board the *Maid of Iowa*—our new riverboat—and enjoy a short excursion. Afterwards, a traveling group, reported to be very accomplished, will perform a play in the upper room of the brick store."

"Oh . . . that would be very nice," Liz said, but she could hardly believe she had heard correctly. Why would she and Will be included?

"It will take place on the evening of July 15, a week from Saturday. We won't make a long trip of it, but there will be a band on the boat, and there will be some dancing—and certainly, a little something to eat."

"More than a *little* something," Lucy said. "I have no doubt of that."

Liz glanced at Will. He was nodding. "Aye. I'm certain we can attend," he was saying, and Liz could see how pleased he was.

"Good, then. We'll plan on you." And then she added, as though by explanation. "There are so many of us in Nauvoo. It's not easy to include everyone. But Joseph thinks very highly of both of you—and I've had such a good impression myself. We want to become better acquainted."

Liz was nodding. "Thank you. That means a great deal to us. I'm certain it will be a happy occasion."

"And how is your little adopted son doing?" Emma asked. "Tell me his name again."

"Jacob."

Jacob was perched on his father's arm. He turned his head shyly when Emma patted him on the knee. But Emma raised her voice a little and called, "Children, come and say hello to the Lewises—and to little Jacob."

Emma's children were playing nearby. Little Alexander, who seemed to be about five, was chasing after his sister, Julia, and his two brothers, Joseph and Frederick. The children dodged and ran about as he tried to tag them.

The children didn't stop their game immediately, and Emma became more demanding. "That's enough, children. You're perspiring like little heathens. Come here now."

Julia was the first to approach. Liz thought she must be eleven or twelve. Emma introduced all the children, then said to Julia, "This is Jacob. He's the little boy I told you about—the one who lost his mother."

Liz thought she understood. Emma wanted Julia to see how much Jacob was loved—just as she had been when Emma had taken her in after her own mother had died in childbirth. Julia immediately reached for Jacob, who surprisingly went to her, and he laughed when she spoke to him in an animated voice. "Well, aren't you a fine big boy," Julia told him. "May I be your auntie?"

Liz found the scene touching—these two motherless children so happy with one another.

Liz could see that the boys were less than entertained by this pause in their game. She thought it better if she didn't keep them long. "Thank you so much, Sister Emma," she said. "We'll look forward to the excursion on the fifteenth."

Will took Jacob back, and he and Liz wished the Smith family a good day and walked on toward the temple. As soon as they were distant enough, Liz asked Will, "Did she really ask us to go on the riverboat with them—and to *dance* and see a *play?*"

"She did, and I'm still trying to imagine that such a thing could happen. It must be because she likes you so much."

"Joseph keeps saying how highly he thinks of *you.*"

Will laughed and shook his head as if to say, *That couldn't be the reason.*

But Liz was still trying to accept what had happened. A picture came into her mind: her only Sunday dress so old and worn now. She decided she would have to do something with it to make it look a little fancier, but she wouldn't say anything to Will about it.

Will must have been thinking the same thing. "If I buy some material for you, could you sew your own dress—now that you're becoming such a seamstress?"

"I don't need a new dress, Will. I can wear—"

"You shall have a new dress. And that's the end of that conversation."

But Liz knew she could never manage to sew a fancy dress. She tried to think how she could explain that to Will. "Maybe Sister Cook can help me with it," she finally offered.

"I'll buy satin for you—to match your eyes."

"Oh, Will, we can't buy satin."

"Pale green satin, with a shine on the cloth, just like your eyes. You'll be the most beautiful woman there."

Liz liked hearing that, but she also knew there was something else she needed to tell him. It was a realization that had been coming on these past few days. "Will, there's something you might want to consider." She stopped and turned toward him. He stopped too. "That would be a great deal of money to spend on a dress that might not fit me very long."

She waited for his eyes to register the obvious question. "Liz, are you . . ."

"Yes, I believe so. In fact, I'm quite sure."

Will shifted Jacob to his left arm and wrapped his right one around Liz. "That's good," he said. "That's wonderful! And all the more reason to have a nice dress while you can still wear it."

"It may never fit me again."

"It will be worth it just to let everyone on that boat see the most beautiful woman in the world. How often do people have that chance?"

"Will, you shouldn't say things that are not true. The Lord might smite you for such an exaggeration." But in fact, she liked him saying such things, and she liked when he denied her accusation and claimed to be speaking pure truth. What she couldn't imagine was that there really was a man in the world quite so fine-looking as Will. And what was best, he had understood how much she wanted a new dress even when she had told him that she didn't need one.

· · ·

Will and Jesse had both planted their own fields, and they had also planted their acres at the Big Field, the profit from which they planned to split. They even planned to include Daniel's new land and make the split three ways, even though the newly plowed field wouldn't produce as much. Now the three were working on a road from Green Plains to Lima. A rough wagon trail had existed there for many years, but Will and Jesse had been hired to widen and level it. This road was farther from Nauvoo than Will had worked before, and he worried about finding safe places to keep his oxen at night.

Their own farms were simply too far away. But Will had found a farmer, Oliver Hyatt, who was willing, for a reasonable price, to let the oxen graze with his own animals.

Some nights the men slept on the ground near the road they were cutting rather than make the long ride back to their homes, but they only did that when they had alerted their wives that that was their plan. Liz worried that Will was working too close to Warsaw—where the greatest animosity toward the Saints had been building. Thomas Sharp, apparently in financial difficulties, had given up the *Warsaw Signal,* and a man named Thomas Gregg had taken over. He had renamed the newspaper the *Warsaw Message,* and although he was no friend of the Mormons, he didn't express such harsh opinions as Sharp had done. But Sharp had not left town, and rumor was, he was working to organize anti-Mormon citizens to take action in driving the Saints out of the county. Levi Williams, a Baptist minister in Green Plains and leader of a local militia, had also spoken at anti-Mormon meetings and warned that the Saints were trying to take over the county and would do it if they were not driven out.

Will understood why Liz worried. He had certainly felt the hostility of some of the people he met in the area, but he tried to be friendly. He hoped that something as simple as doing good work on the road would prove his good intentions—and represent the Saints as good people.

One morning in July Will slipped out of bed long before the sun was up. He told Liz to rest a little longer, grabbed some cheese and a loaf of bread, saddled Socks, and headed out for Green Plains. He followed the road along the river, passed through Montebello, and reached the Hyatt farm just as the sun was rising. He had told Jesse to check on Daniel Johns, at the Big Field, and then to meet him at the Hyatt farm—or on the road south of there. Daniel had one of the teams, and he was cultivating the corn. After a wet spring, the summer had turned hot and dry. If rain came, the ground needed to be ready, and the weeds had to be cleared out. Will was worried that the cornstalks might be drying up before the grain reached full maturity.

Will yoked three of his ox teams, walked them to the road, and then hitched them to his grader. He had already plowed the ground and broken up the sod along the sides of the old trail. Now it was a matter of leveling the ground.

Will had been working an hour or so when a lone horseman approached from the south. As the man came near, Will greeted him, but the man said something Will couldn't hear, so he called "whoa" to his oxen. "I'm sorry, sir," he said. "I didn't hear you."

The man laughed as he reined his horse to a stop. "Well, now, don't you have fancy ways," he said. "Where'd you come here from?"

"England. Maybe you've heard of Gloucester. I grew up not too far from there." Will knew very well that the man had never heard of any English city other than London, but he wanted to sound friendly. He even hoped they could converse a little, so he could show that he was no threat to anyone.

"Gave up yer queen, did yuh? And come here to kiss the hand of ol' Joe Smith?"

He was a grimy-looking fellow with a dirty shirt and no coat, and he wore a long, dark beard that fanned out over his chest. He sounded like some of the backwoods people Will had met in the South. Will decided that he needed to be careful—and not respond to the man's hostility. He took off his hat and wiped his face with the bandanna he kept around his neck. "I am a Mormon, if that's what you're asking."

"Is someone payin' you to make this road?"

"Yes, sir. Hancock County is."

"An' who decided you was the one to get the work?"

"I was asked to bid on it, sir, but as it turned out, no one else made an offer."

"No one tol' me. I'd like to have this work—and I kin do it, too. Why do they think they have to give it to the Mormons?"

"They didn't give it to the Mormons. They gave it to me. I have oxen. I've done similar work in England, grading beds for railroad tracks, and I offered a bid."

"It's the way thin's is now. You people come in here and take everythin' for yoursel's. An' we know what you got planned. You want to build up a place for Mormons and drive ever'one else away."

Will looked at the ground, the dark earth. There was so much of it, so many open fields, not yet plowed. Any Englishman would have longed for so much land and would have thought there was space for a multitude. "Tell me your name, sir."

"Why do you need to know that?"

"I don't *need* to know it. My name is Will Lewis, and I crossed the ocean to come here last year. As far as I'm concerned, I'm your neighbor, and I would like to be a good one. Shake my hand, and let's be neighbors and friends." He stepped toward the man, held out his hand, and asked again, "What's your name, sir?"

"Samples," the man said. "George Samples." And he did shake Will's hand, but with clear reluctance, as though caught off guard and not sure what to do.

"Glad to meet you, Mr. Samples. If I were you, I'd put in a bid the next time the county announces one of these jobs. If you're in Carthage, drop by the county office and ask them whether other roads are being opened for bid. I suspect there might be plenty of work for both of us these next few years. The governor has set aside money to improve the roads all through the state."

Samples didn't respond. The truth was, Will suspected that he didn't know the first thing about grading a road and probably had no more than a single team of oxen.

"That's all fine and fancy, the way you say it," Samples finally said, "but it won't be like 'at for much longer. Ever' Mormon votes the same, and more'n more of you is comin' all the time. It won't be long, you kin vote in yer people to run the county, and then who's goin' to get the jobs?"

"Some of our people are being elected—no question. But we can all work together, don't you think? That's what we want."

"That's what you say, but Joe tells yuh who to vote for, and you do what he says. That way, you put in yer own people or them what gives yuh what you want."

Will wiped the sweat from his forehead again. The morning had been tolerable, but the heat was building and the air was full of moisture. He knew he had to get his work done before the temperature was too high for his oxen and before the prairie flies came on thick in the afternoon. Still, he wanted to convince this man he wasn't his enemy. "George, it is true that we've had some concerns that most of us in our church share, so we have given our vote to certain candidates, but I promise you, President Smith has never *instructed* us to vote for a certain man."

"You say all that and you look jist as pious as a preacher, but all us 'roun' here, we know what's what. Yer takin' over. An' if we don't like it, you got yersel's an army big enough to run right over the whole state. What I say is, we better run you all off before it's too late. An' I'll tell yuh what. Most folks is sayin' jist what I'm sayin'."

Will wasn't sure this man could read, but whether he read the newspaper himself or not, he was taking up the attitude Thomas Sharp—and now Thomas Gregg—had been spreading. Will felt a terrible sadness about that. There was not one thing that would change this man's mind.

"I'll tell yuh somethin' else. Before all you people come, we never had no thievin' going on 'roun' here. But now, horses go missin'—cows, too, and even tools from sheds. You claim religion, but what you is, is a pack of wolves. You thieve for Joe, vote for him, dance to ever' tune he plays. Yer jist not Americans. In this country, a man works hard and looks out for hisself, but he don't band up with a bunch of others an' do the biddin' of some lyin' crazy man."

"George, I've tried to—"

"Don't call me George. Don't call me 'neighbor.' You cain't pull the wool over my eyes."

Will took a long breath. "Mr. Samples, I believe in Jesus Christ, and I try to follow Him. I don't want anything that's yours. I want to farm this good land, the same as you, and I want to worship as I please and allow you to do the same. Not everyone in our Church is as good as we ought to be, but I don't know a single man who wants to run you out of this county. I promise you that."

"Look, Mister, I've heerd all I'm goin' to listen to. But mark my word. I'm not finished with you. When I strike back, you'll know it's me. Me an' some more who think the way I do. I'd be watchin' out from now on."

"I'm sorry you feel that way," Will said, and he gave up on saying anything more. He called to his oxen to push ahead, and he gripped the handles as the animals trudged forward. George rode his horse on past and up the road.

Jesse showed up not long after that, and the two put in a good day of work, but the day became oppressively hot, and about three in the afternoon Will had to pasture his oxen. He watched them head straight to the only tree in the field, near a tall sod fence, and settle down in the shade. A cloud of prairie flies was already gathering around them.

Will and Jesse rode their horses back to their homes. Will got home early enough to put in some time in the garden by his house, and he ate a big dinner and waited out the heat a little, but he went to bed before the sun was even down. He was back up again early in the morning, and he and Socks made the ten-mile trip back to the Hyatt farm. When he got there, he spotted Oliver Hyatt out in the field. He was kneeling down, looking at something. As Will came closer, he realized that it was one of his oxen. Oliver stood up, waited until Will got down from his horse, and then said, "I heard two shots ring out last night, and I thought someone was hunting varmints. But I came out here just now, and it's one of your oxen, shot dead. I don't know who would do such a thing."

Will knew. He got off his horse and walked to Oliver. The ox was Billy, one of his strongest. But the damage was much greater than the loss of one ox. Shooting an ox was the same as shooting a team. It took time to train two oxen to work together. And the trouble was, Will needed six teams, not five.

Will tried to keep control. A fury was building in him. But he told himself that for once in his life he needed to be the Christian man he was supposed to be.

"Do you know George Samples?" he asked.

"I do. He lives south of here a couple of miles, him and his brother. Neither one has a wife."

"Well, he did this. He warned me yesterday that he didn't want me here. He said he would do something to run me off."

"I know George, and I wouldn't put it past the man to do such a thing—but how can you prove it?"

"I don't know."

"You might want to report this to the constable," Oliver said. "He could maybe stop by George's farm and tell him that he's suspected—and then he could warn him that if he tries something again—"

"Are you talking about Harmon Wilson? Is that the constable you mean?"

"Yes."

Will shook his head. "Wilson might *help* Samples," he said. "He doesn't think much of us Mormons."

"I doubt that. I don't think he would agree with a man who shoots another man's animals."

"I don't know what I can trust in anymore, Oliver. What do you think of our people? Do you think we're thieves and liars?"

"I live and let live, Will. The Mormons I've met seem about the same as any other people. I've heard folks say that they steal and all that, but I don't know that anyone's got any proof of it."

"We have some bad people among us, I'm sure," Will said. "And there's been some scoundrels who've moved in and made their home among us. They think they can use the place to do wrong and get away with it. But it's not what our church would ever approve, and we try to stop such things the same as any other town would do."

"I believe that," Oliver said. "There's wrongdoers in every place I've ever been. If there's thieving going on, it can't all be coming from your people."

"We can live together, can't we?"

"I don't know why not. I only worry that if too many of you come, that might upset people like George Samples more and more. It does seem strange for people to gather up like that. It may not be wrong, but it does cause suspicion."

Will nodded. He thought of Joseph speaking of going west, where Zion wouldn't impinge on anyone. But he also thought of the word *Zion*—what it had meant to him when he had heard of it in England. It was supposed to be a place of goodness and mutual support. He had never imagined that it could create such hard feelings.

"I need to think about all this," Will said. "I might have to give up this job. I can maybe afford to buy another team of oxen, but it will set me back and delay everything I've been working for. And if he comes after the rest of my teams, what would I do then?"

"I don't know, Will. You have to decide. But it's not right to let him win."

"I could ride down to his place and tell him that I know he did it, and I won't let it happen again."

Oliver shrugged. "I don't know. He might shoot you on the spot."

"Well . . . for now, I better slaughter this animal. If you and your wife want to brine this meat and cure it, I'll share with you half and half."

"That's fine. But you better work fast. It was a warm night, and the meat is going spoil fast in the sun."

Will knew that, but he hardly had the heart to get started. Billy was a friend. Will had spent a lot of days with the animal, working hard. Still, he couldn't just sit down and cry. And he couldn't let the meat go to waste.

CHAPTER 14

Shortly after Will began to butcher his ox, Jesse arrived. He had managed to buy a plodding old workhorse that he rode bareback. It was a slow means of travel, but at least he didn't have to make the long trek on foot. Will saw him lead his horse through the gate at the end of the field and then lift the reins from its head and let it go free in the pasture. As Jesse walked closer, Will saw the concerned look on his face. "What's happened?" Jesse asked. "Is that Billy?"

Will told him what he knew, and Jesse stared at Will in disbelief. "You mean he just shot your ox for no reason?" he asked.

"No, he had a reason. No doubt it was his way of telling me that I might be next."

Will was looking down the road as he spoke. He had spotted two horsemen riding up from the south. "It's George Samples," Oliver said. "Him and his brother."

The brother was bigger and oilier, with the same sort of dirty beard. George was unable to hide a grim smile as he came near. "Mornin'," he called. He had stopped his horse on the road beyond the pasture's sod fence, but he was not more than twenty yards away. "What you doin' with blood all over yuh like that?"

Will stood up straight and looked at Samples. He knew what he wanted to do. He also knew he couldn't do it. But he wasn't going to take any more of the man's gloating.

"George, you killed my ox. Are you—"

"Wait jist a minute thar, Lewis. Don't start makin' accusations. I don't know nothin' about killing no ox." He glanced at his brother, who grinned, showing only two teeth in front.

"What's next?" Will demanded. "Do you have in mind to kill more? Just tell me what you want from me."

"I told yuh yesterday what I want. I want yuh to clear out."

"You, and all the rest of yuh," the brother said.

It was Oliver who spoke up. "There ain't no call for all this. You Samples boys don't have a right to tell people who can live here and who can't. It's not right to kill a man's animals like that."

"How's yer ol' milk cow doin,' Oliver—and that ol' team of plow horses? They in good health?"

"Don't threaten me, George. I'll have the law on you."

"An' here's what I say. Jack Mormons should be run outa here jist the same as Mormons."

"Never mind," Will told Oliver. And then he walked to the fence. "George, what's your brother's name?"

"It don't matter to you," the brother said.

But George answered. "It's Blake. Blake Samples. Don't forget it. He's a man who keeps his word. He could tote you under one arm, walk all the way to the river—an' drown you thar."

"Is it the roadwork you want?"

"What?"

"Do you have enough teams? Could you do the job if the county hired you to do it?"

"I could do it good as you. That's fer shor."

"What if I tell them, over in Carthage, that I can't finish the job, but I know someone who can? Would that be the end of this?"

"They won't hire George," Oliver said. "Nor his brother. They've never done anything right in their lives. And never finished a job they started. Everyone around here knows that."

"I think I noticed that cow of yers is lookin' sick. She could die one of these very first nights, the way she looks."

"She could get *lead poisoning*," Blake said. They both grinned, but Will could see that George's anger was serious and that Oliver could end up paying for it.

"George, Blake," Will said. "I don't want trouble, and Oliver doesn't either. He told me himself he likes to live and let live. So let's end all this. I'll give up the road job, and you can see if it's something you could hire on to do. Then, as far as I can see, you have nothing to complain about. We can just go our separate ways."

"You kin go yer sep'ert way, all right. You can go straight to hell, you and ever' Mormon in this county."

"Maybe we *will* leave someday. But for now, let's just—"

"You better clear out now or I'll be making beef out of *you* and not your ox. An' then I'll have mysel' some fun with yer wife, and—"

Suddenly Will was over the sod fence. He grasped for George, caught hold of his suspenders, and jerked him down to the ground. He had him by the neck by then, one hand gripping his throat and the other fist high in the air. But he didn't strike the blow. He only stared into George's terrified eyes. At the same moment Will heard movement and knew that Blake was dismounting, but he glanced to see Oliver and Jesse both bounding over the fence, and in another few seconds Blake was prone on the ground too, Oliver on top of him. Both horses shuffled about, sending up puffs of dust. And then everything stopped.

"I'd like to slaughter you like I did that ox," Will growled. His fist was still hoisted in the air, and he had to fight his impulse toward driving it into George's face. "I won't do that. Not now. But if you ever come near my wife, I swear, I'll kill you. Do you understand?"

George didn't say a word—not with Will's hand around his throat.

Will threw his leg off George and then grabbed him by his elbow and jerked him to his feet. George must have felt Will's strength because he didn't make a move to take advantage of his freedom. "Let Blake up too," Will said, and Jesse and Oliver hoisted him upright, one on each side.

"Let's end this right now," Will said. "I told you yesterday I'd be your friend and neighbor if you'd let me. But since you don't want that, let's just forget all this ever happened. I won't speak to the constable this time, and you admit to yourself that a Mormon can be a fair man. I'm handing the road job over to you if you want to go after it."

"This *ain't* the end of *nothin'*," George said, but he walked backward carefully, reached his horse, and grabbed the reins. He pulled himself up by the saddle horn and then rolled his bulk into the saddle. "Let's go, Blake," he said. Blake's horse shied a little as he stepped toward it, but he chased it down and mounted it. The two turned their horses and headed back down the road, but they kept glancing back as though they were still wary.

Will and Jesse and Oliver watched for a time before Jesse said, "Will, I don't understand. Why give up our work? They have no right to take it from us."

"I've thought all night about it," Will said. "It's too far down here. We're taking too great a chance working this close to Warsaw. And more than that, it's working us—and our animals—too hard. Let's just farm our plots and take on some extra plowing when it comes. We'll get by." He looked at Oliver. "I know the Samples brothers won't listen to reason, but if you tell people we did what was fair, that might change a few minds about us."

"If you stayed on this road, those boys wouldn't let up," Oliver said. "They'd shoot more of your oxen, and maybe take potshots at you. But it ain't right to back down to them. It's what keeps men like that going."

"Christ taught us to turn the other cheek. I can't change those men, but I can do my part to end the trouble."

"Then you shouldn't have thrown him on his back," Jesse said. "He won't forget that."

Oliver was nodding. "He'll be waiting for you sometime. You can count on that."

Will folded his arms and looked out across the prairie. "I know," he said, "but that was too much, what he said about Liz."

"And that's why he said it," Jesse said. "He was pushing you until he got you to show your hand. He'll be drinkin' with some of his kind tonight, an' he won't say a word about bein' thrown down. He'll be tellin' about killin' your ox, and he'll be vowin' what he's going to do next. That puts Liz in more danger than ever."

"I know." Will had been settled with his decision the night before. He had told himself that if there was any trouble at all, he would give up the road job, but that sort of concession didn't work with a man like Samples. Will should have let the man have his little verbal victory. But the threat of that man harming Liz hadn't been anything he had expected. The truth was, he didn't regret what he'd done to George. He hoped maybe he had put some fear in the man.

• • •

Liz was surprised when she glanced out the window and saw Will riding toward the house. It was early afternoon, much earlier than she had expected him. What concerned her, though, was that she saw how worried he looked. He got off his horse, but he didn't walk it to their corral or pull the saddle off.

When Will came inside, Liz knew enough to wait. He had something on his mind, and he would tell her what he wanted her to know. She had learned that he didn't spill things out the way she did.

"You're home early," she did say, hoping that might at least start the explanation.

"I'm giving up the road I've been grading," he said. "It's too far south. It's not worth all the traveling Jesse and I have to do. If we ever get any rain this summer, we could still have a decent harvest. I'll pick up some plowing if I can, but I don't plan to cut any more roads this year."

"That's good, Will. It gets lonely when you're gone so long, and I always worry about you—with all the hateful talk we're hearing."

Will only nodded. Jacob had toddled over to him and was looking up. Will picked him up and tickled him. "Hey, how's my boy?" he said. He looked over at Liz. "He's walking better every day now, isn't he?"

"He is. He still tips over. But it never bothers him. He's back up fast and off and going again. He thinks he's big now, walking about."

"That's right. He's a little man, that's what he is." Will tickled him again, and Jacob twisted and laughed.

Liz loved watching that, but she knew there was more to Will's decision than he was letting on. "So did you just up and decide today that you weren't going to finish the road?"

"Aye. Jesse and I talked it over, and it seemed for the best. I sent him over to Carthage to tell the boys over there that they can give the work to someone else who wants it, and settle with us for the part we did."

"Won't they have trouble finding someone else to do it?"

"Maybe not. Someone might jump at the chance, especially with the harvest looking slim. I told Jesse to say that we wouldn't break our promise. If they could find no one else, we'd finish out."

"That's good. But if I know you, you'll still work too much."

"That could be true. My only worry is having enough work for Dan. But immigrants are still coming, and they need their fields opened. That should keep all three of us busy."

"Just hope that some of them can pay you."

"Aye."

And now she saw the worry again.

Will set Jacob down. "Liz, you might as well know, one reason we decided this way was that we lost one of our oxen. Billy . . . died . . . last night."

"Died?"

"Yes. Mrs. Hyatt is curing the beef, so I told Oliver we'd split it with him, but we'll get some meat from it—tough meat at that—but I'm afraid that's all. I can either buy a new team or purchase one ox and hope I can find time to train it to work with ol' Barney."

Liz laughed. "Those are my oxen, you know. So maybe I ought to decide."

"No doubt about it. What do you want to do?"

"I say, get another ox and say your prayers. The Lord will look out for us. Six teams have been good for us. No one else has so many, and it's brought business to us right along."

"That's true. It's what I was thinking too." But he was still hesitating, and she knew there was more on his mind. "Do you want supper now, or—"

"No. I want to ride down and talk to William Clayton about some business matters. I won't be long. I'll build a fire when I get back. Don't heat up the house any more than it is."

She was relieved to hear that. The block house had stayed fairly cool most of the morning, but the heat outside was sweltering, and she was feeling it now. She had been sick every day for the last couple of weeks. It wasn't as bad as the last time she had been pregnant, but then, she wasn't dealing with a tossing ship this time. Still, the heat didn't help her at all.

"All right, then. I'll be on my way, and we can maybe sit outside a little once the sun is down. We can let Jacob watch the fireflies. We haven't done that for quite some time."

"That's not so. He and I do that almost every evening. And Nelly and Warren walk over sometimes. You just haven't been here with us."

"I know. That will change now." He set his hat back on his head and walked to the door.

"Will?" Liz said.

"Aye."

"If the ox was sick, is it all right to eat the meat?"

"He wasn't sick."

She waited, but he offered her nothing more. Finally she said, "Will, something has happened. I knew it the minute I looked at you. Tell me why you really gave up your roadwork. I'd rather know."

Will nodded. He looked across the room, not at Liz. "There's a man who lives south of Oliver Hyatt's farm. George Samples. He saw me cutting the road and told me that he didn't like Mormons getting that work. He warned me something might happen. In the night, someone shot Billy. There's no question that he was the one who did it. Then he came back with his brother today, and I told him I didn't want any more trouble. He could have the work himself if he wanted it."

"Why did you give in to him?"

"For all the reasons I told you. That job is too far south, and the truth of it is, it's too close to Warsaw. You've been telling me that yourself. Let him have the work and then have no reason to resent me. He keeps saying he wants to run us out of the county, and I just figured I'd show him I wasn't spoiling for a fight."

"That's good, Will. I'm glad you didn't fight him."

But she sensed that he still didn't want to look at her, and she wondered what it was he hadn't said.

"One other thing," Will said. "I decided today, I'm going to buy you a pistol that you can keep here in the house. If a man ever came after you—and wanted to hurt you and Jacob—could you bring yourself to pull the trigger?"

Liz had never thought of such a thing. "Who would bother me, Will?"

"Some of these folks in the county are making claims—saying they want to drive us away, the way the mobs did in Missouri."

"But they couldn't do that again, could they—not with the Legion to defend us?"

"No. It's all just talk. But some might try to snipe at us, make us so unhappy we'd prefer to leave."

Liz was understanding now. "This man—this Samples. He made threats, didn't he?"

"He's all talk. He and his brother are both the same. But I would still feel better if you had a way to protect yourself if I wasn't here."

Liz had certainly worried about many things since coming to

Nauvoo—but never about this. She felt the fear in her stomach adding to the unsettled state it was already in.

Will walked back to her. "Don't worry, all right? I won't let anything happen to you."

"You just said, you won't always be here."

"I know. But Samples knows not to take me on. If he bothered you, he knows what he'd get."

"You fought him today, didn't you?"

"No, I didn't. But I threw him down—just to warn him, to let him know not to try anything with us."

Liz walked to the table and sat down. She felt faint. Jacob came to her as though he sensed something was wrong. She picked him up and hugged him.

"I didn't want to tell you all this, Liz. I knew how you would take it."

"How do *you* take it? You're telling me you want to buy a gun for me."

"I know. Just to relieve my mind a little. But the Lord will look out for us."

"I'm sure that's what the Saints in Missouri said too."

Will clearly had nothing to say to that. He told her he would not be gone long, and he said he was sorry to have frightened her. But when he left, Liz felt as though the world had changed. She had never imagined that anyone would ever want to hurt her. And she wanted nothing to do with guns.

• • •

Will had known as he rode his horse home that he needed to tell Liz certain things—about Billy, about giving up the roadwork—but he had wanted to do it without frightening her. And he had wanted to leave out all the worst details. The trouble was, he had also made up his mind to buy a pistol, and he hadn't known how to tell her that. Now he had told her pretty much everything, and he had seen how frightened she was.

Will knew that he never should have touched Samples, and yet, he hoped that he had shown the man that he was no one to take lightly. But now he had to worry about his wife every day, and he had had to scare Liz enough to prepare her to shoot a man, if it came to that. All his study of the Book of Mormon and the New Testament had opened his mind to a better way of thinking, but the Samples brothers had left him with no clear answers. He thought maybe he could turn his own cheek, but he would defend his wife and child no matter what it took.

When Will entered the counting room in the brick store, he was feeling the weight of all these concerns. But when Brother Clayton saw him, he said immediately, "Brother Lewis, it's good you came by. Joseph's in his office upstairs. He wants to see you."

That was the last thing Will wanted to hear. He couldn't go off on another mission, certainly not after the things that had happened today. He walked up the stairs, but this time he knew that he had to say no to the Prophet. "President Smith, did you want to see me?" he asked.

Joseph turned to look over his shoulder and then, when he saw Will, stood and extended his hand. "Yes, I do. Did Brother Clayton get word to you already?"

As Will shook hands, he said, "Just now he did, but I actually came down to speak with him. I had some things I wanted to mention to you, too, if you have the time."

"What's that, Will? Sit down."

Will sat in a chair by the door, and Joseph turned his own chair around to face him. Will told Joseph about his encounter with George Samples, about the ox, and about giving up the road job.

Joseph sat with his hands on his knees, his big chest expanded. He had taken off his frock coat and cravat, and his collar was open. He listened carefully, asked a few questions, and then said, "Don't worry, Brother Will. The Lord is in this, whether you see it or not."

Will waited and wondered. Joseph always had a way of seeing things from a broad perspective, discerning the purpose behind events. Will trusted him, but he wondered whether Joseph had understood the danger that might be ahead.

"I need you and your oxen," Joseph said. "That's why I sent for you."

"My oxen?"

"Yes. We need to increase our effort on the temple before the season ends this fall. We haven't pushed the work far enough ahead this year."

"The problem is, I'm still farming and still plowing for people. I could maybe help out a little, but I—"

"Don't tell me. Tell the Lord. He needs you, Will. And He needs those oxen to haul stones from the quarry up to the temple site. I'll find some money somewhere to buy you another ox—and that will repay you a little. But it's mostly a matter of putting first things first. It's not easy for any of us, but it's what we have to do."

Will hardly knew what to say. He couldn't do this. He had crops in the ground, crops he would have to harvest, and he was getting no savings ahead. By next year he still wanted to start the house he had promised to build for Liz. If he spent too much time hauling stone, he would be fortunate even to get enough food put away for winter.

But Will didn't say that. And he didn't ask for time to talk to Liz. He knew what she would say. This was simply something he had to do. Nothing was more important than finishing the temple.

Joseph laughed. "Come on, Will, don't look so down in the

mouth. What a blessing it is to work on the temple. And you will be paid. We can't pay you what you were making grading roads, but then, maybe that's why the Lord took that away from you. He knew that I needed you in town to build His temple."

Will was relieved to know he would be paid. But it wouldn't be cash. He would be paid in kind, he supposed—or with a draw from the storehouse. He also wondered how he and Jesse and Daniel could get their crops harvested if he was using the oxen at the temple.

Joseph seemed to know what Will was thinking. "Will, do as much as you can for us. Let Brother Matthews and Brother Johns take care of your farm. They're strong men and good workers. When you have to put your oxen to your own work, then do it. But I ask you to give every hour you can to the temple." He stopped, sat up straighter, and took a long look at Will. "Brother Lewis, we have to finish this temple. It's our offering to God—and blessings will flow from it for many generations. It's this generation that will build it, with blood and sweat, and your children and their children will thank you forever."

Will nodded. "All right, then," he said. "I drove the oxen away from the Hyatt place today. In the morning, I'll ride to the Big Field and bring them on in. For the next few weeks I can put in most of my days at the quarry, and then I'll just figure out a way to harvest crops when the time comes. If we don't get some rain soon, we may not have any crops anyway."

"Yes. We're worried about that. But thanks for your help, Brother Will." A smile came into Joseph's eyes and spread across his face. "Tell me this," he said. "What kept you from breaking that man's head open, right there on the spot?"

Will smiled a little too. "I didn't tell you quite the whole story. When he threatened Liz, I pulled him off his horse and threw him on the ground. I had a good grip on his throat, but I never struck the man. I let him go. I only let him know that I wouldn't hear that kind of talk about my wife."

"God will never punish you for protecting your family, Will. Don't regret that."

"But I want to be more like Jesus Christ, and I can't seem to find His ways anywhere inside me."

"You're more like Christ than you know. You merely have some rough edges on you." He nodded rather solemnly. "And I know all about rough edges."

Will liked that—liked to think that he and Joseph were alike in some ways. The man was a prophet, but he felt like a big brother, too. Will had the feeling that if they had grown up in the hills of England together, they would have been mates, would have trapped a hare or two together.

Will thanked Joseph, told him he'd give his whole heart to the temple, and the two shook hands again. It was all very unsettling to Will, this change in his plans, but he was learning to do what the Lord asked, and he told himself not to worry too much.

Will stopped in and talked to William Clayton for a few minutes—made sure he understood that Will might not be able to make a payment on his land this fall. Brother Clayton was wearing his full suit of clothes, in spite of the heat. He made no adjustment to his British ways, as Will tended to do. But Brother Clayton patted Will on the shoulder and said, "Pay when you can. Joseph understands that when he calls you to work for the Lord, you may not be able to meet some of your other obligations."

"But I will pay it, Brother Clayton. If we salvage some sort of harvest, I'll be able to pay some of what I owe."

"That will be fine."

Will walked out the back door of the store and mounted his

horse. He was riding away when he saw John and Jane Benbow in a little one-horse carriage. They were pulling up at the front of the store.

Will reined up his horse and swung himself down as Brother Benbow was stepping out of his carriage. "I'm so glad to see you," he told Will. "I see Brother Jesse quite often. He tells me how busy you two are. Thank heaven you helped him, Will. He and Ellen were getting ready to pull up and leave—and that wouldn't have been good for them. He says he's never known a man to work as hard as you, but he likes that. He seems happy."

Will didn't want to tell his story again, especially didn't want the story about the ox told around Nauvoo. He had thought about that and decided it was better not to build anger inside or outside the city. So he only said, "We're backing off some of our roadwork before harvest. Jesse might make it home earlier at night—so he can see his family a little more."

"Well, that's good too." Brother Benbow walked around the carriage and gave Jane a hand as she stepped down. Will followed and shook hands with Sister Benbow, who told him to greet Liz for her.

"I just spoke with President Smith," Will said. "He asked me to bring my oxen into town to help out with hauling stone to the temple. Maybe I can be a little closer to my own family now."

"That's good, Will. Very good," Sister Benbow said. She was a gentle little woman with a quiet voice, but Will knew how firm she was in all her convictions.

"Can you make time to do that, Will?" John asked.

"I'll find a way. But I'm still a little out of breath right now, just trying to think how I can get everything done."

"I know how you feel," Brother Benbow said. "The temple takes our money and our time, and I've heard men complain about it. But Joseph knows why it matters. We have to trust him."

"Aye," Will said. "I do trust him. I told him that. But I want to build Liz a better house before much longer. I promised Brother Duncan, back in Ledbury, that I wouldn't make her live in a log house too long."

"Back home in England, that's how you saw things, Will. You were taking a young woman away from a nice home, settling her in a wilderness. I don't blame Brother Duncan for making you promise, and I don't blame you for wanting to keep that promise. But there are more important things in life than big houses and fancy furnishings."

"You gave up all that for the gospel, Brother Benbow." Will knew that Brother Benbow had provided much of the money to print the British edition of the Book of Mormon, and he had used his own money to pay the passage for many of his brothers and sisters to emigrate.

"Don't make it sound so great a sacrifice, Brother Will. Jesus told the rich young man to give up everything and follow Him. If we call ourselves followers of Christ, we have to learn to put first things first."

"Aye, but you've given up more than most of us."

"That's not been difficult for me, Will. We're all the same here. And that's how it ought to be."

Jane laughed quietly, and Brother Benbow looked over at her. "All right, then. Jane's laughing at me," he said. "It's not been entirely easy for me to lose my 'place' in the world, as we thought of it back then. But if I can learn a little humility, that's something I can take with me into the next world. And a house, I never can."

Will nodded. He could wait a while longer to build that brick house, he supposed.

"I know how much it meant to you to own land, Will. And I understand that. You grew up on another man's farm, the same as I did. But it's not the land in Zion we came for. It's Zion itself. And I don't know about you, but I think I'm only just beginning to understand what that means."

Will agreed. As he mounted his horse again, he looked up at the temple, which had been rising slowly and steadily all summer. It occurred to him that the building meant more to him now than it had when he had gotten up that morning. It had been a strange day, and a frightening one, but maybe one that he would value even more as days passed. What he needed to do now was go home and have another talk with Liz, and this time, calm her fears and testify to his own faith.

But there was something else he had to do first. He had been telling Liz to buy herself some fabric to make a new dress for the little excursion on the *Maid of Iowa*. Liz had admitted that she had found some lovely green satinette at Pratt and Snow's new store, just north of the temple. "It's not really satin," she had told Will. "It's mostly cotton. But it's still far too expensive. I've thought some more about how I can alter my Sunday dress and make it look almost new."

But Will wasn't having that, and he was finally home early enough to stop at the store. He rode his horse along Main Street to the north and then up the hill on Young Street. The fabric Will found at Parley Pratt and Erastus Snow's store was green, all right, but a pale green, and luminescent—exactly what he had told Liz to find. What he also found was that it *was* expensive material, even if it was not real satin. But he didn't care. In the back of his mind were the ugly words he had heard from George Samples that morning, and the fear he had seen in Liz's eyes. He simply had to find a way to bless her life more than he had so far. She had accepted their plight better than he had, and she had turned herself into the hardworking woman she had never expected to be. He wanted to give her this one little pleasure. So he bought the fabric and carried it home to Liz. He knew she would tell him he had done the wrong thing, and he also knew she would be very pleased.

CHAPTER 15

Liz was becoming a better seamstress. A ball gown was quite a different chore from a man's work shirt, but with Sister Cook's help Liz had fashioned a beautiful dress. She had finished it the night before the riverboat excursion and had finally tried it on in front of Will. He had actually gasped when she walked from the bedroom. "Oh, don't pretend," she had told him. "My hair is not even curled. I'll be much more presentable tomorrow night."

"Any prettier and I'll pass right out," he had said, and then he had taken her in his arms and kissed her.

"I know I should have made it with an empire waist, to leave room as the baby grows, but it's just not the style now. Am I terrible?"

Will had no idea what an empire waist was. He only knew that this dress made her waist look very small, and the top was scooped a little to show her lovely neck. The fabric shimmered in the firelight as she spun around. "You'll wear it again next year. Look how slender you are now, after having a baby last year."

"That's what happens when I chase Jacob around all day."

"And work so hard around this place."

"It's good for me to work, Will. I can chop wood almost as well as Nelly now, and I carry water like a washerwoman. Feel how strong my arms are."

But Will felt bad about that. He didn't feel her arms. He pulled her close again and held all of her. She laughed and pushed him away. "Be careful with my gown, sir," she said, teasing him with her smile.

"I will, Mrs. Lewis," he said, and he almost admitted his secret, but he managed to keep quiet. What he knew, and she found out the next evening, was that he had borrowed a little one-horse carriage. He couldn't make Liz walk down the dusty streets in her new dress—or ride in an oxcart.

He worked at the quarry that next day, but he came home early with the gig they would ride in that night. He saw the delight in her eyes when she saw it. She had brushed and ironed his only suit of clothes, which had gotten a little tired during his time in Nauvoo, and she had shined his Sunday boots even though he had told her that he would come home in time to take care of them himself.

Nelly came to sit with Jacob, and after Liz had given her lots of instructions, Will took Liz's arm and walked her to the carriage. He helped her with her skirt as she got in, and then he proudly drove the carriage over to Parley Street and down the hill. He liked greeting the people he saw along the way—all of whom surely guessed that the Lewises had been invited to attend the special event with Joseph and Emma. Will believed with all his heart that one person should not hold himself above any others in Zion, but he also remembered seeing guests arrive at Joseph and Emma's house in the past, and he had always hoped to be included someday. He told himself this was his and Liz's turn—that was all. But he sat up straight in the carriage, feeling proud, and he watched the people look at Liz, even call out to her how lovely she looked.

At the wharf, livery boys took care of the horse and carriage, and Will walked Liz down the ramp to the boat, which sat below the bluff near the edge of the river. The Lewises were actually a little early, but it wasn't long before the boat filled up and even became crowded. Will thought there must be at least a hundred passengers. The Nauvoo Quadrille Band, made up mostly of stringed instruments, played as guests came on board. Most of the Apostles were on missions in the East this summer, but others of the Church leaders had been invited, and there were many, like Will and Liz, who were ordinary citizens of Nauvoo. Most of the women were wearing the same dresses they wore on Sundays, but even among those who wore fancier ball dresses, not one looked as lustrous as Liz—at least in Will's mind. He loved to see how many people glanced at her and then took a second look—or even spoke to others, who then looked her way.

Joseph and Emma greeted everyone informally as they stepped onto the boat, and then formally, as a group. A grand spread was set out on a long table, and Brother John Taylor was invited to offer an opening prayer and blessing on the food. Joseph invited everyone to eat whenever and as often as they chose, and then the band began to play again. Quadrilles were formed as soon as the boat was under way. Will had never been much of a dancer, but Liz had worked with him lately and taught him some basic dance patterns. Still, the two stood by the rail of the boat at first and only watched. The evening was warm, but the moving air coming off the river felt wonderful.

Americans had a way of performing quadrilles as though they were tromping grain on a barn floor, but they danced with more vigor than Will remembered in England, and they laughed more.

Mormons seemed to enjoy themselves more than any people he had ever known. After the second dance, Will was getting up the nerve to lead Liz to the dance floor when he saw Sarah and Hiram Kimball walking toward them. They had been dancing, and Will could see the perspiration beading up on both their foreheads. "We need a rest," Sarah said.

Will was about to reach out to shake Hiram's hand, but he heard Liz, in a voice more polished than usual, say, "Brother and Sister Kimball, how nice to see you. You have met my husband, Mr. Lewis, I believe."

"Yes, yes," Mr. Kimball said. "Nice to see you again." He shook Will's hand.

"I hope we can all come to know one another much better," Liz said. "Sarah was such a great help to me when Will was gone on his mission last winter."

Sarah was taking a long look at Liz. "Will," she said, "it's not right to let Liz have a new dress and to bring her here where she shines like the moon, and the rest of us are made to seem, by comparison, only tiny stars in the firmament."

"It's a sky full of beauty," Will said. "I've never seen so many pretty women in one room. Perhaps the Spirit does more than teach truth. It must change countenances."

Will feared that he had tried just a little too hard to sound as refined as his wife, but Sarah smiled as though she liked the compliment. Then she looked at her husband and laughed. "I know what that means, Hiram," she said. "Once you're baptized, you'll change in the twinkling of an eye. You'll be as handsome as Will here."

Hiram laughed too. He was much older than Sarah and rather thick around the middle. He was certainly not a handsome man. But he was congenial and good-natured, and he treated Sarah as though she were his crowning glory. "If I can look that good, it will be worth it," he said. "But I won't count on it."

"Are you going to be baptized?" Liz asked.

"Yes. It's taken me a long while to take that step, but I've promised Sarah, and I'll do it soon."

"Don't leave them with the wrong impression," Sarah said. "You always said you wouldn't join the Church just for me."

"That is true," Hiram said. "And I have come to that point. I *am* a believer." Liz could see that he was serious now.

The boat took a little bounce, throwing everyone off balance for a moment. But the dancers were quickly back in their formations. Will laughed with the others, but then he returned to the subject. "What brought you to the faith?" he asked.

"I've known Joseph Smith for four years now, and we've had our disagreements along the way. But working with him in the city, being around him, listening to his wisdom, and knowing what kind of man he is—those things have changed my mind about him. I honestly believe that he receives his guidance from God."

Will was gratified to hear those words from someone who had lived in Nauvoo since before the Saints had arrived, someone who had dealt with Joseph not only as a religious leader but as a man of business.

"But you two were about to join the dancers," Sarah said. "We'll sit for a dance or two, and you have your turn."

So Will walked Liz to the dance floor as the next quadrille was formed. He danced rather badly, he was sure, but no one was watching him with Liz twirling through the formations.

The excursion was not long, but the breeze on the river was refreshing, and more than anything Will enjoyed watching what an evening of entertainment did for Liz. He had taken her from a world of social pleasures and kept her in a little log cabin hidden away in a grove of trees. She did seem happy most of the time, but he had forgotten how wonderful it was to see her smile and chat and be the Liz he had first watched from a distance in Ledbury. He knew that somehow he had to offer her more pleasures of this same kind.

Will noticed also that even as Liz was shining, Emma Smith seemed to pull herself back. She simply wasn't as vivacious and friendly as he had always known her. Even Joseph seemed more subdued than usual.

• • •

On the following day, Joseph preached twice in the grove, and he said some things that Will didn't know how to interpret. On the one hand, he said that a man and woman needed to enter into an everlasting covenant if the man wanted to claim his wife in the next world. Then, in a solemn tone he added that he would reveal more on the subject if it were not for the unbelief of the members. Will found the idea that he could be sealed to Liz for eternity remarkable and inspiring, and yet, Joseph explained little about it, and instead dwelt much on the idea that a man's foes were often part of his own household. "The same spirit that crucified Jesus," he said, "is in the breast of some who profess to be Saints in Nauvoo." Most shocking of all was his statement that he would no longer prophesy, that Hyrum held the office of prophet to the Church as Patriarch, and he should be the one to prophesy to the people. Will thought he was saying that his own revelations were being rejected, so the Church could listen to his brother, if that was what they preferred.

Will was left confused and downhearted. He wondered which people close to the Prophet were making him feel so disconsolate. For so long Will had been hoping that better days were still ahead for Zion. Now he couldn't help but wonder what Joseph knew that was causing him such disappointment.

• • •

Liz didn't walk to the lower part of the city very often, but when she did, she usually stopped at Sidney Rigdon's house to see whether she had received any mail. One day in early August she entered the Rigdon kitchen through the side door and looked at the cabinet in the corner. In one of the cubbyholes, under the letter *L,* she found, to her surprise, two letters for her, one from her mother and one from her sister, Mary Ann. She waited to get home to read them, but letting Jacob walk created too much of a delay. She hoisted him into her arms and carried him up the hill, and then she opened her mother's letter as soon as she was back in the house. But what she read was anything but what she expected:

Dearest Lizzy,

I am sorry to tell you that your father was taken from this earth two days ago on June 8, 1843. He died at his desk, his heart simply stopping. I can only say, by way of consolation, that he looked peaceful and he seemed not to have suffered. He was not very old, but he has worked hard all his life, always concerned about providing for us to the best of his ability.

I was taken by surprise, of course, but we all must prepare ourselves to meet our Maker, and I have taken solace in knowing that your father served the Lord, was baptized by one having authority, and was counted among the membership of God's true Church. My one heartbreak is that he couldn't see you one more time before he left us. He expressed his wish, at times, that we might gather with the Saints in Nauvoo. Perhaps we never would have done it, and I certainly was part of the reason for that, my fear holding me back, but I did like to think of seeing you, and now I know, I never shall. What sustains me is my belief that life continues beyond mortality and I will see my dear husband again. I rest also in the comfort of knowing that if you and I never embrace on this earth again, I may trust that in the life after this one I shall yet hold you, my dear Elizabeth, in my arms once again.

Do not worry about me, dear one. Your father was careful with money, and he saved for this day. I have adequate income for my needs, and I have enough faith for the needs that go beyond money. I'm happy to know that you have joined the Saints in Zion, however much it pained me to see you leave. Give kisses to little Jacob and tell him that his grandpapa loved him very much, though he never saw him. I also send my love to Will, and I promise that never a day passes without my praying for his and your well-being.

Your loving mother,
Jane Duncan

Liz dropped the letter to her lap. She was already weeping, but now she gave way to sobs. She had known that she was not likely to see her father again, but this brought a finality she had not been prepared for. He was gone. She had prayed for him and Mother and Mary Ann every morning and night, and all the while he had been buried in the old cemetery in Ledbury.

Liz had set Jacob down, and he had picked up a little toy horse that Will had carved for him. He was pretending to make it run across the floor. But he had turned when he heard his mother's sobs, and now he had come to her knees and was touching her, looking up into her eyes. Liz picked him up and held him close. "Grandpapa will never see you, Jacob. And never your little brother or sister, either." Liz knew how much her father had wanted to have grandchildren. She had written to her parents about Jacob and told them never to think of him as adopted. He was their grandchild, just as he was her baby, as much a part of her as any naturally born child could be.

Liz had often felt the pain of homesickness, but never so much as now. She wondered all over again whether she had done the wrong thing in leaving her family. What was her mother to do? How could she manage without Father? Money she had, and faith she had, but Liz hated to think of her alone in the house once Mary Ann married. Mother was not yet fifty, and she may have many years to be alone.

"It's all right," Liz told Jacob. "Mummy's fine. Here's kisses from Grandmama, and from Grandpapa too." Jacob wrapped his arms tight around his mother's neck and held on to her for a moment, and then he hopped down off her lap.

Liz picked up the other letter. It was postmarked a week later than Mother's but had probably been shipped across the ocean at the same time. When Liz opened it, she saw that it was a long letter, but written on a single sheet. To save paper, Mary Ann had written in one direction and then turned the paper and written over the lines at right angles. It was confusing to read at times, but she made out the words:

Dear Liz,

By now you've heard the bad news. Mother, I'm sure, told you that we are fine, but that's the way she is. She has faith, it's true, and she wants no pity, but I hear her crying at night, and I know she's swallowed up in grief. Father didn't suffer, she keeps saying, and that's all well and good, but one instant he was alive and in the next, he was slumped on his desk for Mother to discover. It was hard to accept, and for a few days I thought we might lose her, too, she was so overwrought.

I don't want you to feel bad, but I need to tell someone

how awful things are for me. There's a man in Ledbury who thinks he loves me. The truth is, he wants to marry a member of our church, and I'm the right age. I don't think he knows anything about love—or any other emotion. He's stiff as a statue and about as interesting to talk to. He comes here to court me, and then he can't think of anything to say. I tried to run him off the way I did old Henry Parker, but he doesn't have enough sense to know that I'm laughing at him. I won't marry him, Liz; I simply cannot do it. But he's like a honeybee. He thinks I'm a flower and he won't stop buzzing around me, no matter how many times I swat him.

So I made up my mind. I told myself I was going to join you in Nauvoo as soon as I could. I decided I wanted one of those earthy American boys with their long vowels and big muscles. I had my mind all made up, and I had Father halfway talked into it, and then, suddenly, he was gone. I miss him with all my heart, Liz, I really do, but what's left for me now? Can I run off and leave Mother crying herself to sleep every night? I'm tied to her apron strings, tight as if they were a hangman's noose, and there's not one thing to do about it. She'll live forever, you know she will. I'll be looking after her when I'm sixty and still wondering what it's like to kiss a man. I would kiss the honeybee just to test my lips one time, but I doubt he'd taste like honey.

Tell Will that his sister Sarah wants to come to America. She and John Davidson both, whenever they can afford to get married. They can't get on here, and they don't have money for passage yet, but they are saving. If Will has become rich by now, you might tell him to ship a few guineas back to his sister. She and John might grow old before they raise the money themselves. Will's father hobbles about and does his share of work for a man of his age, and Daniel has taken the farm in hand and does well enough. They do have enough to eat, but little more, and Daniel sees no hope for him to marry anytime soon. Daniel speaks of emigrating too, but more than just a wife, he would like to bring the whole family. Of course, he knows of no way to manage such a thing, but tell Will to think what he might do to help someday.

As for me, I may yet decide to come to Nauvoo. Mother needs me, I know, but I also wear on her. I'm not as sweet and kind as you are, and sometimes she tells me to be more of a lady, or not to chatter on so. It might be best that she not have to hear me, if that's how she feels.

Oh, Liz, I'm a terrible person. I fear I always will be. It would be good to have you for an example. And if I came there, you could find me someone like Will. He's the only man I ever met who pleased me so much. But I am serious, even though it doesn't seem so; I do want to come to Nauvoo if I can, but not for another year, even though I'm aging very fast. I may never find anyone who wants to marry an old maid such as I'm becoming. I love you more than anyone, and love Will, too, and love Jacob. Tell Jacob he has an aunt who has stored up lots of kisses for him and wants to deliver them herself one day.

Your spinster sister,
Mary Ann

Liz was crying and laughing when she finished the letter. She loved Mary Ann so much, longed to have her around to keep her laughing, longed to have her nearby all her life. But she knew that Mother, however noble she had sounded, would cling to her daughter, and that hold would be hard to break. Mary Ann was not yet twenty-one, and hardly a spinster, but Liz understood her worry about that, with so few prospects in Ledbury. Liz was not entirely sure Mary Ann would find a young man to her liking in Nauvoo, but clearly, if she wanted to marry in the Church, she had a better chance in America than she ever would have in England.

Liz liked to think that her sister would finally come, and she liked to think that Sarah and John—maybe all the Lewises—would immigrate too, but she wondered what another year might bring. Mary Ann had no way of knowing what was happening here, that Will had bought her a pistol and taught her to shoot it, and that people had vowed to see the Mormons run off. What if the Saints did move on to the West, as Joseph had suggested they might? What would Mary Ann face then? Here on the river there was some evidence of civilization, but what was out west but wilderness?

· · ·

Will was now hauling stone to the temple every day, and he had come to like the work, but lately, progress on the building had not moved forward as much as Joseph Smith had hoped. William Player, a master stonemason, had become the principal setter the year before, but he had been sick all last winter. When spring had finally come, Brother Player had directed men in building runways for additional cranes. That had been important for the future, but it had kept the actual stonework from moving ahead in the short term.

Will understood why he was needed at the temple—he and his teams. He also thought every day of what Brother Benbow had told him. The Saints had to put first things first. Joseph Smith was speaking more about temple work now. He spoke of an endowment worthy members would be able to receive. These ordinances and work for the dead, he kept saying, were essential for the full restoration of the gospel. But Will heard enough complaints among the workers to know that not everyone had caught that vision.

Although Will had a better attitude than most, he had to admit that the work was hard in the August heat. Joseph Smith had provided Will with the new ox he had promised, and, as though trained by an angel, the new animal, Bobby, was already pulling with Barney without difficulty. It took six teams of oxen to wheel the heavier stones up the steady slope from the quarry, and then up the steep hill to the temple. Will knew enough not to push the teams beyond their capacity, so he rotated them when he had smaller loads, letting some of the teams graze and rest in the shade near the quarry as often as possible. But there was no rotating for Will himself. Once the stones had been dragged from the quarry with block and tackle and then hoisted by cranes and manpower onto a wagon, the tedious march to the temple started. The heat was almost more than a man could bear. Sweat would drench him as he helped load the wagon, and then, during the mile-long trek up to the temple, all his pores seemed to open and gush. He drank all the water he could and still felt drained at the end of a long day.

Rain came some afternoons, but the heat didn't back off much, and the air was steamy after a storm—and full of mosquitoes. Even worse was the mud—the greatest enemy to the poor oxen. A hard pull sometimes became an impossible one as rain turned the clay on the slopes into a slick muck. It was then that Will would sometimes gather other men and all of them would help push the wagons. That aided the oxen and carried some stones to the temple that might have had to wait another day or two, but the muck filled Will's boots, penetrated the legs and knees of his trousers, and splashed onto his chest and into his face. He came home some nights so filled up with mud that Liz wouldn't let him into the house. He would pull everything off outside and then trudge inside to wait while Liz boiled his clothes. He would wash himself—never quite getting all the stain off—and then he would lie down on the bed and try to retrieve his strength, but the heat in the house lingered not only all evening but all night.

Will was young—not quite twenty-seven—and powerful, and he told himself there never was a job that could get the better of him. No matter how tired he was at night, he was able to arise each morning, well recovered, and he could go after the work again the next day. "The Lord is blessing me, Liz," he told her one morning. "I know I'm a strong man, but God has lifted me up a notch or two. The men at the quarry talk about me as though I'm Samson, the way I can lift and pull and carry mighty stones."

Liz smiled at him. "I'm glad you're giving thanks to the Lord. Otherwise, I might think you're boasting a little."

"I'm sorry, Liz," Will said. "I didn't mean to sound that way. I do know it's the Lord who's given me such strength. I thought at one time that I would be a cripple all my life, but my bad hand works well enough for the work I do. I have the Lord to thank for that, too."

"Just don't push yourself too hard, Will. I fear you'll break your back and make a cripple of yourself yet."

Will grinned. "Don't worry about me. I never lift a stone that's bigger than I am."

But at the end of that very day Will felt more worn down than usual. He fell asleep before supper, and by the time the meal was ready, he could feel a fever coming on. By morning he was shaking with chills and then burning with fever. "I boasted too much of my strength yesterday," Will told Liz. "It's all gone now. I *am* like Samson. I was the strongest man alive yesterday, and now I can barely lift a finger."

"Maybe that's what illness is for—to remind us that we're not so powerful as we think we are."

"If it's so, the Lord wants to chasten His people. Half the men working at the quarry are sick again."

• • •

Liz didn't know why so many died in Nauvoo, why so much illness came each year at this time. She wished that this illness hadn't
come to Will now. She was not very well herself, feeling sick with
the baby, and she was aching with the loss of her father even more
than she had expected. She thought of her mother and sister every
day, wondered what they were thinking and feeling now. A letter
was only an expression of a single day—or just an hour—and she
knew that moods and attitudes could change quickly. Mother had
sounded accepting and stoic, but Mary Ann had told the other side
of it. Each night when Liz went to bed, she thought of her mother
alone and crying. She was likely to be alone a long time, and maybe
it wasn't right for Mary Ann to think of leaving. But if that was so,
maybe Liz shouldn't have left either.

God expected so much, it seemed. Liz had found the faith to
accept Zion, but she simply hadn't known that Zion would be so
hard as it was. She hadn't known about the heat—or the terrible
cold, either—and she hadn't known it was a place where people got
sick, and where so many of their babies died. She hadn't known that
people from neighboring towns would hate them, that she would
have to learn to shoot a gun to protect herself. She hadn't known
that members of her church would spread rumors, criticize the
Prophet, fall short of keeping their commitments and even the com-
mandments of God. She hadn't known that she herself would doubt
and fear and sometimes complain.

Liz didn't blame God. She didn't feel any resentment about the
choices she and Will had made. But she was homesick, and she was
worried for her mother and her sister, and she was pregnant, hot,
and tired—and now Will was sick again.

Strong men died of the ague. And Will was very sick. Liz told
herself she needed God again—and she reminded herself that it was
a good thing to need God. So as Will slept, Liz slipped down on her

knees and prayed, "Please, Lord, make him whole again. And give me strength."

When she opened her eyes, she saw that Jacob was watching her, and suddenly everything came back to her: almost a year ago now, she had thought she had lost everything, and the Lord had given her this gift, this lovely child. She couldn't indulge herself in self-pity. She had to keep her eye on what Zion was, in spirit, and not pay so much attention to the earth it was built upon.

• • •

After four days in bed, Will got up. "It was only a fever," he told Liz. "I don't think it was the ague. I've got to get back to the quarry."

"It will come back. It always does," Liz said.

"The ague does. But not a summer fever. I'm certain that's what it was."

But Will knew that Liz might be right. He had watched all the suffering in Nauvoo because of the "fever chills." Even in winter the attacks would return, and strong men and women would be brought down again. People would shake as though they were freezing, their teeth chattering and their limbs jerking. The victims could pull on any number of quilts and still continue to quiver, and then they would throw everything off as the fever came back. He knew also that once a person became sick with ague, they were never entirely free of it.

But this had been only a summer fever, he told himself, and he went to work. He put in a good day, not feeling all the power he had boasted of, but doing well, moving a good deal of stone. In his absence, others had driven his oxen, but the men at the quarry all told him that no one could move as much stone in a day as he could. The Lord needed him, Will told himself, and would sustain him. But that night the chills and fever came back. Will made it to work most days after that, but once or twice a week, he simply couldn't. On those days, other men worked with his animals, and they reassured him, the illness could put any man down.

Jesse and Daniel brought the harvest in—what there was of it. Before long they came and worked with Will and helped with the oxen. They needed the wages now, at least enough to put away food for winter. They did have their earnings from the roadwork they had done, but there was no more of that to expect. Will hoped some new immigrants would want their land plowed this fall and he could gather a little more savings that way. He thanked the Lord that he had partners who could keep some of his work going when he couldn't be there to help.

Each night Will also knelt with Liz and thanked the Lord that they were well off enough to make it through the winter. They had seen nothing of the Samples brothers, so he thanked the Lord that he and his family were safe and well. He thanked the Lord that the baby was growing and that Liz was feeling a little better now. He thanked the Lord that Jacob was a year old, strong and happy, and hadn't been sick this season. He thanked the Lord for the temple, and prayed that progress on it might be doubled next year, and the day would soon come when the people could enter and receive the endowments and sealings Joseph had promised. He thanked the Lord for Zion, for the prophets and apostles, for the truths they had received, for life itself. After all, he was getting a little stronger all the time.

Work on the temple continued through the fall. When the first hard frost came, the work had to slow, but stones could still be cut and hauled to the temple, ready for placement in the spring, so Will, along with Jesse and Daniel, still had work to do all winter—and that was a blessing.

As the colder weather came on, Will had fewer bad days, and he was able to procure some quinine powder from Brother McNeal, a druggist in town, although at a very dear price. Still, he could tell that the medicine was helping him. What he wanted now was for Liz to be a little happier. She had never been quite herself since she had learned of her father's death.

CHAPTER 16

Jeff had never been so tired in his life. William was six weeks old now and was making steady progress. He had gained a little weight and he was healing well. Other than being small, he seemed to be thriving in every way, and Jeff and Abby never failed in any of their prayers to thank the Lord for preserving his life. But that didn't mean that baby William—or "Will," as Jeff usually called him—slept very well at night. He was nursing better, and sometimes slept three or four hours without waking up, but he woke up two or three times during the night, and Jeff always tried to take one of those feedings. The trouble was, he had to be up early to drive to Fort Madison, and he was also feeling the pressure to start accomplishing more on the house. It wasn't right for him to continue to get free rent if he wasn't doing much work for the Robertsons.

After his mother-in-law had left, Jeff had decided to take on the kitchen, and he and Malcolm had spent some evenings planning all they wanted to do. Malcolm had enough to do in his own house, but their idea was, they would rework Jeff and Abby's kitchen and then do the kitchen at Malcolm and Kayla's house. They could save some money on materials that way, and the two of them working together could get more done than if they each worked alone on their own projects. The only catch to that was that they tended to inspire one another with their lofty ideas and to end up attempting things that were rather grandiose. The cabinets in both homes clearly needed to be replaced, and the Robertsons' house had no dishwasher. The additional plumbing was enough of a challenge, but as the two used graph paper to draw their plans, they began to realize that they needed to move a wall to get the cabinet space they wanted.

Jeff and Malcolm had taken their wives and kids with them to Quincy one night to look at kitchen designs at a home improvement store. That had turned out to be fun for both couples—especially with a stop for something to eat at the Steak 'n Shake that both men liked so much—but the women added more ideas, and the plans became all the more elaborate.

Actually, the hours working with Malcolm were some of Jeff's favorite times these days, but neither of them knew when to stop, and their nights got late sometimes. Jeff knew he wasn't getting enough rest, but he had been a night owl during his college days, and he always thought he could get by on four or five hours of sleep. He was finding now, though, that he sometimes had trouble keeping his eyes open when he sat down at the computer in his office.

Abby kept telling Jeff that he needed to take some evenings off and go to bed early once in a while, but the kitchen was all torn up and the house was a mess. Jeff really wanted to get the project finished.

One night, when William had gone to bed and Abby had fallen asleep early, Jeff and Malcolm were still working. Malcolm took a look at his watch and said, "Jeff, it's almost ten. I promised Kayla—*and* Abby—that we wouldn't work late tonight."

"I know. I told her the same thing. But Abby's asleep. You go ahead. Now that we've got these corner cabinets hung, I just want to secure them with a few more screws."

"Won't your drill wake the baby—and Abby?"

He laughed. "I know it won't wake Abby. Will might be another matter."

"If you wake the baby, you wake Abby."

"You're right. Maybe I better stop."

Malcolm turned toward Jeff and waited until Jeff looked back at him. When he did, Malcolm asked, "What's going on with you lately?"

Jeff was taken by surprise. "What do you mean?"

Malcolm unbuckled his tool belt and leaned back against the cabinet. "I don't know. You don't talk as much as you used to."

"Hey, that's got to be a good thing." Jeff laughed. "I'm fine. I'm probably just worn out from burning the candle at both ends these last few weeks. But then, you've been doing the same thing."

Malcolm nodded. He dropped his tool belt to the floor, as though he still had something he wanted to say. "On Sunday I watched you during the lesson in elders quorum. You started to raise your hand three or four times, and then you'd put it down again. Gary finally noticed and called on you, but all you said was, 'Never mind.' What was that about?"

"I don't know. I was thinking about something I learned in one of my college philosophy classes. But I decided it probably wouldn't add anything to the discussion. You know how those guys roll their eyes when I bring up stuff like that."

"You shouldn't worry about it. You know more than anyone in there. You talk about things I've never thought of. I like that."

"Yeah, maybe. Sometimes. But I'm better off if I stick with the scriptures." Jeff walked over and sat down at one of the kitchen chairs that had been pushed back against a wall. "I get people upset when I start spouting off."

"I love the stuff you tell about Nauvoo history. You know more about it than people who've lived here for a long time."

"But that's my problem, Malc. History is always a lot more complicated than people want it to be. We tell these stories, and they get passed along, whether they're true or not. Last Sunday I was reading a book about Nauvoo. There was a whole chapter about plural marriage and how Joseph first started preaching it—and practicing it—and it's really different from the way we all like to think about it now. It was a secret thing at first. The Lord had taught Joseph, but Joseph knew he couldn't tell the world—even most of the members—at that point. He understood the spirit of plural marriage, but guys like John C. Bennett were describing it as something really lurid. Emma actually agreed to the doctrine at one point, and then she changed her mind. She and Joseph really struggled over that."

"After Joseph was killed, didn't she claim it never happened?"

"Yeah, she did. Here's the thing, though. I want to know about those kinds of things, but a lot of people get really nervous when I talk about them—so it's just better if I keep my mouth shut."

"Maybe we *should* know all that stuff."

"I used to think so. But I don't anymore. People don't have to know everything, or understand everything. And they don't need to speculate as much as I do. They need to hear the whisperings of the Holy Ghost and recognize that's what they're hearing. That's what counts."

"Do you really mean that?"

Jeff sat for a time. He tried to think about that. "Malcolm," he finally said, "I spent a lot of time wringing my hands and wondering whether I had enough faith to heal our baby. But I finally received an answer from the Lord, and once I did, I knew what to do. If that didn't change me, it should have. All my philosophizing doesn't mean a thing compared to that."

"Yeah. I get what you're saying." Malcolm reached down and picked up his tool belt, and he walked over to the door that led to the garage, but he stopped and turned around. "There's another side to it, though."

"What's that?"

"When I was a kid, me and my dad used to fish a lot. And you know how fish are. Out of water, they flip around for a while, but then they start opening and shutting their mouths, like they're trying to figure out how to breathe when they're not underwater. I thought of that on Sunday. It's like you're trying to make the switch. You're trying to survive, but you're a fish out of water. You used to raise questions that made me pretty uncomfortable sometimes, but I watch the way you live, and you *do* live by faith. I think you can be smart and have faith, too."

Jeff nodded. "I know. But some things are worth thinking about, and other things are just word games. I'm trying to figure out which is which, and it's starting to become obvious to me how many games I've been playing."

"Okay. But don't worry about it quite so much. Just go ahead and say what you think. I don't think it hurts anything."

"Well, maybe that's right."

Jeff was surprised when Malcolm didn't leave. Instead, he pulled out another one of the kitchen chairs and sat down across from Jeff. "I've been thinking I need to go to college," Malcolm said.

"Are you serious?"

"Yeah, I am. Part of it is, I feel like I'm stupid. I didn't take school seriously because I always figured I'd do about what I'm do-ing now. But I don't know anything except tires and—"

"Malc, you're one of the smartest guys I've ever known."

Malcolm laughed. "No way. You're just—"

"I'm totally serious. It's not just that you can fix things. You remember everything you've learned. I'll read the instructions before I start to install something, and then I have to go back and read every step again as I go along. You take a look, you get it, and you know how to do it."

"Yeah, if I'm using my hands, I can—"

"No. It's your brain. Things stick there. If you can do that with an instruction booklet, you can do it with anything. You'll be a good student if you go back to school."

"I can't write an English paper to save my life."

"Sure you can. And that's something I could help you with."

Malcolm laughed again. "We're going to be building these two kitchens the rest of our lives. When will I have time to go to college?"

"Hey, we've got to get these houses finished. These projects of ours are going to do us both in."

Malcolm nodded, smiling just a little, but his voice softened when he said, "Jeff, I found out this week, I might be out of a job before long."

"Out of a job? Why?"

"I talked to the owner of our store this week. He says if our business doesn't pick up, he might have to close the shop. Our numbers are down for the third year in a row. It seems like everybody sells tires now, and places like Walmart are cutting prices down to a level we can't compete with."

"How long is he willing to stick with it?"

"I don't know. We talked about some new advertising gimmicks—four for the price of three and things like that—but if he doesn't see any sign of things improving, I don't think the store will last past the end of the year."

"What would you do?"

"I don't know. I can't go back with my dad. Two families could never live off of what he makes, and he's already wondering whether he'll ever be able to retire. He just hasn't been able to put enough away."

"So is that why you want to go back to school?"

"Yeah, sure. If I go looking for work, what do I say? I've been running a business, but I've never taken a business class in my life? How's that going to sound? The only thing I'm qualified for is some sort of construction or factory work, and who's hiring that kind of worker these days?"

"The economy is going to pick up one of these days, Malcolm. I really do believe that."

"Maybe so. But I'm always going to have the same problem if I don't get some sort of education. And I probably need to get started pretty soon."

"Here's another way to think about it. Maybe we could start a home remodeling business."

"I guess that's a possibility." Suddenly Malcolm grinned. "Or I could get into computers and we could invent some sort of software that makes us filthy rich."

"I think about that sometimes," Jeff said. "But I'm better at talking than I am at inventing. That's why I probably ought to be a professor. And you should be an engineer."

"We're two fish in the bottom of a boat," Malcolm said. "Both of us looking for enough water to go swimming in."

They were both smiling, but Jeff could see in Malcolm's eyes that he really was worried. "Well, we're both pretty lucky, too," Jeff said. "We've got wives who believe in us, and families that will back us up."

"Yeah. That's true."

"We'll figure things out."

For a moment, Malcolm looked directly into Jeff's eyes. "Thanks," he said. "You came to Nauvoo at a good time. I've needed a buddy like you."

"Yeah. Me too."

But now they were both embarrassed. Malcolm nodded and headed out the door.

• • •

A couple of nights later, on a Friday night in March, Jeff and Malcolm were busy in the Robertsons' kitchen again, and Abby had driven over to spend some time with Kayla. The idea was that Kayla would fix dinner, with Abby's help, and the men would knock off early so the two families could eat together. But it was almost nine o'clock now, and dinner had been drying out in Kayla's oven for well over an hour. The little girls had eaten earlier and were now in bed. Abby had called Jeff twice and asked him when he was coming, and both times he had said, "We're just finishing up; we'll be right over."

Finally Abby said, "Let's just eat. Who knows when those guys will get here?"

"I'll tell you," Kayla said, "those two *seem* like opposites, but in some ways they're two peas in a pod." She had cooked a big dish of lasagna, and she was using hot pads to pull it from the oven now. "This stuff looks cremated," she said.

"It smells great. The guys will put it away, no matter what."

"I'll tell you what I told Malcolm," Kayla said. "I think him and Jeff are both happier when they're working on the houses than they are any other time."

"I *know* that's true for Jeff," Abby said. "He still doesn't like his job."

"He doesn't? He always tells me he's okay with it."

"He thinks he has to say that—as much as anything, for my sake."

Abby stepped over to the kitchen cabinet where Kayla had dished out lasagna on two plates. Abby had made a green salad, and she used tongs to place some on each plate, next to the lasagna.

Kayla had also baked a big batch of dinner rolls that had been cooling on the counter. She placed one on each plate and then added a second. "I'm hungry, too," she said. "I keep telling myself I need to lose weight, but every day I decide I'll start tomorrow."

"It's so hard to lose weight after a baby, isn't it?"

"Oh, come on, Abby. Don't even say that. You're already back into your clothes.

"And stretching them out in the process."

The two carried their plates to the kitchen table and sat down. Kayla said a blessing and with a little humor in her voice prayed that their husbands would soon return home, safe and sound.

After, as they began to eat, Kayla said, "So what does Jeff tell you? Does he ever admit that he's not happy with his job?"

"No. Never. I've tried to talk to him about it, and all he'll say is that the Lord guided him to the job and he's blessed to have it. And then he starts counting all our blessings—William doing so well and everything—and he knows I'll agree with him. But I see it in his eyes when he leaves in the morning, and I hear it in his voice when he calls home during the day. He's going through the motions, making the best of life for now, but his career is not turning out the way he always pictured it. He won't admit that because he's trying to *provide* for me—and for William—but he's settling for what life has thrown at him, and he's just telling himself it's okay."

"So what are you going to do about that?"

"When Jeff lost his job, I felt like I was falling off a cliff. But I've decided it's time for me to grow up. Jeff's doing what he has to do for now, and he does *everything* to give me what I need. He's got to figure out for sure what *he* needs—and then I'm going to support him."

"For Malcolm, it's almost the other way around. I think he always figured that if he had a good job, and me and him was together—with kids and everything—that's what life was all about. But now he's scared. If he loses his job, he doesn't know what he'll do. He's afraid he won't be *able* to provide for us."

Abby finished chewing a bite of lasagna and then took a sip of milk. "Jeff told me about that. He said the tire store might close."

"Malcolm's really worried about it, and he's like Jeff: He doesn't say much because he doesn't want to worry me. But we might have to figure out a way for him to go to college. Maybe they'll both end up back in school."

"Well, one thing Jeff's losing his job has taught me is that we can get by on a lot less than I thought, and if things go wrong, we can figure something out and keep moving forward."

"That's what I keep telling Malcolm. I think he felt a little better after he talked to Jeff the other night."

"Well . . . it's good they've found each other. Jeff's never had such a good friend in his life."

"That's what Malcolm said the other day—that Jeff's his all-time best friend." Kayla wiped her mouth with a paper napkin. "But Malcolm's like me. We always worry that we're using bad grammar or saying something stupid when we're around you two."

"Oh, come on. I don't—"

"You notice. I know you do. Sometimes I know I'm saying things wrong, but I don't catch myself until it's too late. Besides, you're so pretty, and I'm frumpy as an old lady already. I guess I can live with that, but I wish there was one thing I could do that would set me apart a little."

"Are you *serious?*"

"Sure I am."

"Kayla, I call you every day to ask you what to do with William."

"I know, but that's just because I've had three kids now and—"

"No, it isn't. I watch you with your kids and I marvel at your instincts. You're good at everything I *want* to be good at. You're such a good cook, and you can make money stretch like no one I've ever met. Your house always looks perfect, and—"

"And you graduated from *Stanford.* You're a decorator, and you—"

"No, no, no. I don't want to hear any of that. You're good at so many things that *matter*, and I only recently started to understand what those things are. I didn't get ready to do what it turns out I'm doing. Kayla, I don't know what I would do without you. You've kept me going through this whole horrible winter." Abby's voice cracked, and she felt tears begin to trickle down her cheeks. "And now you're teaching me things I should have known all along."

"Oh, brother, I think you're exaggerating just a little."

"I love you, Kayla. I've never had a friend like you. God sent you to me, just when I needed you. We may leave Nauvoo sooner or later. But I know one reason we came—so you could take care of me."

"Well, I hope you always stay here. I hope we both do."

Abby nodded, and she wiped away her tears. She did want to stay in Nauvoo, but it probably wasn't what Jeff needed, and she didn't know how she could make both things work.

"Do you want another roll?" Kayla asked, and she laughed.

"No. I really shouldn't."

"I know. Me either."

Both sat for a moment, but Abby saw the hint of a smile coming into Kayla's eyes. "Should we split one?" she asked.

"Well . . . no. Let's each have another one, then eat a lot less tomorrow."

"Good idea. That's just what I was thinking."

• • •

Jeff and Abby tried to go to the temple as often as they could. When Sister Caldwell didn't have rehearsals or performances in the evening, she loved to take William, and Abby also had a good visiting teacher who would call up and say, "Let me have that little boy of mine tomorrow night, and you and Jeff go do something."

With all Jeff's busyness, that often didn't work out, but when they did go out, they liked to go to a session at the temple and then get something quick to eat before they went home. Jeff had never lived just five minutes away from a temple, and he had never found a place where he felt quite so comfortable and secure. The Nauvoo Temple was a wonder, inside and out. Jeff loved the woodwork, the details in the carpet and windows, and the murals in the endowment rooms. It had a different feel from most buildings constructed in his own era. It felt like a nineteenth-century work of art and craftsmanship, even if it was a reconstruction.

In this place that his Grandfather Lewis had probably helped to build, Jeff felt a connection to his family and to all the Saints who had lived in Nauvoo in the 1840s. Even in his busy life, he spent every spare minute reading about those days. He knew how hard the Saints worked to build a temple when they might have put their time and money and effort into building better homes for themselves.

The temple ceremony seemed, in some ways, to fit with that time, too. And Jeff liked to think about the meaning of all he heard. He was changing his mind about lots of the things he had thought mattered to him, but he was still struggling to know where he fit and what he wanted out of life. It was in the temple that he was able to push worldly thoughts aside and feel as though he were connected to the Prophet Joseph and all the early leaders, and at the same time, connected to the doctrines he loved so much. Jeff could question everything, but he knew he believed in the words of the Sermon on the Mount. He knew it was more important to be humble than to be important. He knew that kindness was a better trait than brilliance, and that serving others was more important than serving oneself.

Jeff had blessed his baby, and his baby had been healed. That had changed his way of thinking forever. He felt a security in his faith that he had never expected to experience.

At the same time, his mind was always full of questions.

Sometimes he still crossed the road and stood on his grandfather's property. He liked to talk out loud and test his thinking. He couldn't do that in the temple, but the temple was a place to be alone in the midst of others, and a place to divorce himself from the world for a little while. Grandfather's property, on the other hand, provided a place to think about himself. He was relieved not to doubt as much as he always had, but he seemed more aware than ever that he wasn't yet the man he wanted to be. He often felt lonely, too. He knew he didn't want to bother others with all his questions, but sometimes it was almost more than he could do to hold them all inside.

CHAPTER 17

The winter did not set in as severely as it had the previous year. Will was feeling much healthier as Christmas approached, and Liz was no longer sick every day. She had calculated that her baby would come in early March, 1844. She tried to trust the Lord and not worry about the baby's health, but she was apprehensive all the same. She remembered little Mary Ann, who had been so frail, and hoped for a stronger baby this time. She knew this one was bigger, and it kicked with more force than Mary Ann ever had, so she told herself all would be well.

Christmas was better too. With Will at home and his time a little more free, he and Liz sometimes visited the English Saints near the Great Mound east of Nauvoo. Their friends from the Malvern Hills decorated their houses with greenery and held little dinner gatherings in their homes, and on Christmas Eve there was caroling throughout the neighborhood.

Liz tried all day not to think about her father, who had loved Christmas so much. But in bed that night, her mind turned back to him. Father had always read the Christmas story from Luke on

Christmas Eve, just as Will had done that night. She knew that in some ways Will was a better man than her father. He wasn't quite so attracted to things of the world, especially now that he had worked so hard on the temple. She had watched Will change a good deal lately as his greatest desire had become his wish to see the temple finished and to receive the promised endowment. But still, her father had brought Liz's family to the gospel, had taken a chance as a solicitor to join a church that many in Ledbury had held in contempt. He had wanted the very best for Liz, and sometimes he'd been a little forceful in his attempt to guide her to someone other than Will. All the same, he had respected her wishes when he had seen how set upon them she was. And after all, now that she had a son, and a baby soon to come, she understood a little better that it must be hard to let children make their own choices. It was true that what he had feared from Will had actually come about. She was living in humble circumstances, just as he had predicted. But she suspected he wouldn't be disappointed now, not if he could know Will's intentions and understand his heart.

• • •

Will was still working at the quarry, and the winter had been quite open so far, with little snow. That had meant a steady pace of work had continued, with men cutting stone most days. It was not always possible to move the stone up to the temple, but Will worked on the days when he could. This meant he received some income in months when he hadn't had that before, and it gave him something to do. Still, the days were much shorter, so he was home evenings, and some days he was at the house all day. He worked outside a good deal, and he helped Liz with Jacob while she taught school, but the plan was to discontinue her school before the baby was born. Liz thought she could start up again in the fall, but Will hoped that would not be necessary. He didn't have the roadwork ahead of him, but he and Jesse were farming enough acreage now that he thought they could manage all right, especially if the harvest was better next season. He would also continue to plow for other men as often as he could

One turn of events had helped with finances. Brother Lancaster, in spite of the bad harvest, had actually come to Will with half the money he owed him: twenty dollars. He had apologized for taking so long and hinted that he thought he had paid Will enough now, so Will had told him they were "square" as far as he was concerned. He felt good about that. He still felt that Brother Lancaster had broken promises, but he wanted to be generous and forgiving, not judgmental. He had been reading his scriptures a good deal this winter, and when he did that, he saw a vision of the man he wanted to be: bold as Paul but humble as Jesus. He was not much like either one of them at this point, and he knew that, but he felt he had acted the way a brother should.

What worried Will was that he was hearing too much about disagreements among the members in Nauvoo and too much criticism of Joseph Smith and other leaders. In January, William Law was removed from the First Presidency, and he was vocal in his protests about the manner in which he had been released. Will had a feeling that Brother Law could end up leaving the Church. There had been trouble between Joseph Smith and Sidney Rigdon, too. During the Church conference the previous October, Joseph had actually spoken to the membership and asked that Brother Rigdon be released from the First Presidency. That hadn't happened, and since then, relations seemed to have improved, but the fact was, Sidney was hardly visible as a leader in the Church. Will had a hard time understanding how such harsh feelings could develop among Church leaders. He knew that people were weak, that they made mistakes, and that good people lost their faith—but it was one thing to see a member become a backslider, and it was another to see those at the highest level of the Church taking issue with the Prophet and other leaders.

Brother Clayton had told Will more than once, "They're men, Will. They're men like you and me."

Will thought he understood that, but one day Brother Clayton finally asked, "What about you, Will? Joseph always speaks well of you. What if you're called one day to serve as an Apostle—or in some other high calling? Will you leave all your weaknesses behind, or will you carry some of them with you, no matter where you serve?" Will had never thought of himself as someone who could serve in such a high calling, but he was struck by the rightness of the question. Sidney Rigdon, William Law—all the brethren, even Joseph Smith himself—they were strong, but they were human. He supposed it was his job to pray for them, not question them, and a lot more people in town should do the same.

• • •

It was February 26, early on a Monday morning, when Liz knew the pains she had been feeling were the real thing and that her baby would be born that day. She was glad that Will was with her and that Nelly was nearby. Patty Sessions came again, and all was much as before, except her labor was more difficult. This was a bigger baby, she knew from the beginning, and she wondered, before the ordeal was over, whether she could stand the pain. But her joy was greater, too, when she saw a big, healthy boy. He cried louder, nursed demandingly almost from the first, was more wide-eyed and aware, and, fortunately, also slept better than Mary Ann had done.

Jacob seemed a little unsure about what was happening. He liked to touch the baby's face and say, "Baby. Baby." But he also wanted to be held more often himself, especially when Liz nursed the little one. And he seemed to get into more things—as though he knew that being naughty would get his mother's attention. Liz hadn't realized how much more challenging her life would be now. But Will was at home more this time of year, and he was much more willing to help her than most men she knew. He gave Jacob more time than usual, and Jacob loved that.

As busy as she felt—and tired—she loved to think that they really were a family now. They chose the name Daniel for the baby, naming him after Will's brother but also after Daniel of old—a visionary man. It was Will's choice, but one that Liz liked very much. And she liked having her "three boys," as she called Will and the babies. As she recovered from the birth, she felt stronger than ever, and she was happy to think that she really was becoming a woman of strength.

• • •

In March, Jake and Faith Winthrop arrived in Nauvoo with their son and two little daughters. Will had plowed some ground for Jake in the Big Field the previous fall, just as he had promised, but the Winthrops had been able to sell their farm, so they came with enough cash to buy a lot in town and a small farm, already established, near Hyrum Smith's farm on the eastern edge of Nauvoo. For three weeks they stayed with Will and Liz and slept on the floors. But Jake and Will felled more trees and then, with the help of other men in the neighborhood, hewed the logs, hauled them to the town lot, and raised a cabin. Will and Jake talked a good deal about working together to build brick homes the following year. Jake had given up something much better for what he now had, but he was happy and optimistic, and the first time he and Faith heard Joseph Smith speak—and shook his hand afterwards—they were certain that they had done the right thing.

Will was pleased that the city was looking better all the time, and Jake and Faith seemed impressed. A rope manufactory had opened near the lumber mill on Water Street, and Lucius Scovil had opened a new bakery on Main Street. In fact, all sorts of businesses had been starting up: a comb factory and a brewery on the bluffs, along with new brickyards, and another drugstore and two more general stores on the flats. More brick houses were going up all the time, and Nauvoo University was offering more classes each year. Even though the university had not yet constructed its own building, the new Seventies Hall, with its museum and library, and the almost completed Masonic Lodge, with its cultural hall, offered places for classes to be held. Orson Pratt, Orson Spencer, and Sidney Rigdon taught classes in mathematics, philosophy, and English literature—and many other subjects—and Will had read the announcements for classes in Hebrew and other languages. Will often felt his lack of education, and he longed to find time to change that. He and Jake Winthrop talked about helping each other free up time to attend some of the classes. All that seemed to excite Jake. He had come to Zion for religious reasons, but he was surprised that it was also becoming a business center and a place of culture and learning.

Late in March, just as Will began to hope for a good spring, wet weather settled in again. Still, better days had to be ahead, and planting couldn't be too far off. He hoped there would be plenty of new immigrants who would want to open their newly purchased fields as soon as the weather broke. He decided this might be the year to advertise in the *Nauvoo Neighbor,* as the *Wasp* had been renamed, that he had oxen and could plow through deep prairie grass. So he rode Socks down to the flats and stopped at the print shop on the corner of Water and Bain Streets, across from the brick store.

When he walked inside, a young man was operating a press toward the back of the shop. "Good day," he said. "A moment, please, an' oi'll see to yor needs."

He was English, Will knew immediately, although he sounded northern, not from the midlands. The young man had been daubing ink on the printing type, and now he was using a handle to tighten a blank sheet of paper against the type. When he released it again, he picked up the sheet at the corners and carried it to a line where he could hang it up to dry. As he pinned it up, he said, "Now, then, what is it I can do to serve ye, sir?"

"I hope to print a notice in the *Nauvoo Neighbor.*"

"If you will kindly write out what—"

But from a desk in the back corner of the room, Will heard, "Is that the mother tongue I hear spoken in my office?" The man stood from his desk, and Will realized it was John Taylor himself. He was an Apostle—had served in England at the same time Wilford Woodruff had been there—and Will had heard him preach many times here in Nauvoo. Will had greeted him and shaken his hand from time to time, but the two had never become well acquainted. Apostle Taylor was tall and handsome, with carefully trimmed whiskers that ran down the side of his face and under his chin. To Will, he seemed the best-dressed man in Nauvoo, with tailed frock coats that were better cut, better brushed than the ones most men wore, and a shirt collar so white it gleamed.

"The purest languitch be spoken on'y in Herefordshire, England," Will said, "so aye, you heerd right."

Brother Taylor laughed and then walked forward. He always moved with a natural uprightness that seemed foreign here on the frontier. "I would claim Westmoreland for that honor, perhaps," he said, "but my own speech was no doubt corrupted by my years in Canada."

"Not a bit," Will said. "I love to hear your voice. You have the sound of a scholar."

"Not so. Not so," Brother Taylor said. "In spite of the editorial position I now hold, I was trained as a cooper and a carpenter, not as a man of letters." Then he added, "I know you're Brother Lewis. Is it William Lewis?"

"Aye. Or plain Will. But thank you, Brother Taylor. I didn't know whether you would remember me."

"There are good stories told about you. President Smith likes to tell about the time you fought and defeated a giant of a man on board a riverboat—a man who attacked you with a knife."

"I'm afraid the story has grown a little. The big fellow gave up the knife—handed it over to another fellow—before I took him on. And he almost killed me before I finally knocked him down."

"In any case, Joseph likes to joke that you're one man he doesn't plan to wrestle. But he also tells about your quelling the storm on the ship, and says you're destined to be a leader in the Church."

Will was taken aback. He had no idea that Joseph had said such things. He actually had to catch his breath for a moment. "I don't know about that, Brother Taylor, but as for now, like most of us, I'm a plowman. I want to advertise that my oxen and my two good arms—and one bad hand—are for rent."

Will no longer thought much about his damaged hand, but he was self-conscious now when he saw both Elder Taylor and the pressman looking at it. He found himself pressing it against his hip, flattening it a little, as he often did when he realized someone was noticing.

Elder Taylor motioned for Will to follow him. "Come back to my desk and write out what you want to post in the newspaper."

So Will walked with him, proved that he could use a pencil, in spite of his bad hand, and wrote out a little statement about his oxen and the plowing he could do for $2.00 an acre. He was waiting for Brother Taylor to review what he had written when he glanced up to see the sheets that the young man had been printing. "General Smith's VIEWS" was printed across the top. Will was trying to read the smaller print when Brother Taylor said, "That seems fine, Brother Will. We can print that in our next issue. The price is 25 cents."

Will nodded and reached in his pocket for a two-bit piece, but at the same time he asked, "What's this you're printing, if you don't mind my asking?"

"It's President Smith's views on government. It's a pamphlet he plans to distribute across the country. You know he's running for president of the United States, don't you?"

"I heard a man at the quarry say it, but frankly, I thought it was another rumor. It is true, then?"

"Why wouldn't it be?"

"I don't know. It's just that so many people seem to hate us. I'm not sure who would vote for him."

Brother Taylor leaned across the desk, looking serious, as though he were about to begin a sermon. Will had seen that expression before when he was ready to proclaim what he believed. But instead, he asked, "Brother Lewis, did you read my editorial in the *Times and Seasons* last fall—the one entitled *Who Shall Be Our Next President?*"

Will had caught up on the *Times and Seasons* during the winter, but he was having trouble remembering that particular piece. "I believe I did," he said, rather hesitantly.

That brought a smile back to Brother Taylor's face. "I probably editorialize more than I should," he said, "but that one was important. I raised the question as to whether any man lives in this country who would give us redress for the way we were treated in Missouri. I said that we should elect a man, if such an one could be found, who would assist us in receiving the rights we have under the Constitution."

"Aye. I do remember now."

"Joseph Smith sat down with President Van Buren and pleaded our case for redress, and he saw nothing from the man but fear and trembling that he might lose votes in Missouri. Since last fall Joseph has written to the leading men in this country—those who style themselves as likely candidates for the presidency. He's asked them who will stand up for us, and all we have heard from them—if anything—is timid arguments about states' rights and the will of the people. We were driven off lands we owned and farmed, driven away from a temple lot we had dedicated. That should never happen in these United States, and every right-thinking man knows it. But no one stands up for us. The federal government is far too weak, and governors have no courage."

Will was nodding, convinced not only by Brother Taylor's words but by the power of his voice.

"So we are taking action," Brother Taylor continued. "We have nominated Joseph Smith, the finest man this country has produced since the days of the Founding Fathers themselves. If no one cares about the rights of the downtrodden and the abused, *he* does. And that is exactly what he will stand for."

Will liked that idea very much. He remembered the abuse he had taken in England—with no one to stand behind him.

"So what do you think, Brother Will. Can he win?"

Will felt his face grow warm. "It does seem unlikely to me, Brother Taylor. I must admit that. But if it's the will of the Lord, I suppose—"

"The Lord certainly will approve. He's depending on the truth. I'm going to give you one of these pamphlets we're printing, and I want you to read it. Ask yourself whether men across this land won't read it and pronounce it the best document ever written on the subject. And then get ready. Missionaries will be called before long, and young men like you will be sent to all corners of the land to preach the truth about government and about the gospel. I'm certain you will want to be one of them."

Will's first thought was that he couldn't leave in the spring. He would have nothing to live on if he did. But he had thought he couldn't serve before, and the Lord had opened a way. Who knew what might happen now?

"Brother Lewis, we all have to expand our vision and think the way our Prophet does. These are the last days, and a government must be set up that will be ready for the Second Coming of the Lord. Joseph speaks of a theo-democracy, with a man at the head of the country who is also a man of God—a man who can lead us to be something much grander than we've been. Prophets of old led their people not only by wisdom but by revelation. Joseph Smith is the man who can prepare us for the times ahead, when Christ Himself will reign as King and Lord."

Will nodded. "I understand what you're saying, Brother Taylor. I've been trying to take a larger view since I joined this Church. But I still think about my crops and my family and the things of the world. I don't know how to do otherwise."

"Nor should you. You look after that good wife of yours, and you provide for your family. Those are your God-given responsibilities. But whether you accumulate wealth on earth will not matter when you receive your true reward on high."

Will was nodding again. And he accepted the pamphlet from Brother Taylor. He even read it as he rode his horse back along Water Street and on up to the bluffs. He was amazed at the things Joseph Smith had said. When he stepped through the door at home, he said to Liz, "Did you know that the Prophet is running for president of the United States?"

She was busy at the table, pressing butter into a mold. She looked up. "Speak softly," she whispered. "Daniel and Jacob are both asleep at the same time—for once." But then she asked, "President? Are you sure?"

"I was as surprised as you are, but Brother Taylor is confident that once people hear what he's saying, they'll rally behind him."

"What *is* he saying?"

"I have the pamphlet—all his views. Here, read it."

"I can't right now, Will." She held up her hands to show that they were covered with butter. "Come over and tell me what the pamphlet says, but do keep your voice down. If you wake up Jacob, I'll expect you to look after him."

Will felt a little deflated after all the excitement he had brought with him into the house. He didn't want to whisper these ideas; they needed to be *proclaimed*. All the same, he went to her and spoke in a soft voice. "Should I read this whole thing to you? It might be good to hear it in the Prophet's own words."

"No, just *tell* me a little about it now, and later on, I'll read it."

"All right." Will looked at the first pages of the pamphlet, wondering where to start. "Now, remember, these are the things he believes are right, but it actually doesn't say he's running for president. The title is 'General Smith's Views of the Powers and Policy of the Government of the United States.' Missionaries are going to go out and declare these ideas and teach that the nation needs a man of God as well as a man of government."

"Why call himself 'General,' then? That doesn't sound like a man of God."

"A man of God *and* government, Liz. He's *Lieutenant General* of the Nauvoo Legion—the only Lieutenant General in the United

States. People are more likely to listen to him when they hear a title like that."

Liz didn't respond, but she looked skeptical. Will decided not to argue the point. Instead, he said, "One of the main things he makes clear is that the national government should have protected us against the mobs in Missouri—and it should stand up the same way for all people who are mistreated."

"I agree with that," Liz said.

"Listen to this one. He says we ought to reduce the number in Congress by half.'"

"Why?" Liz asked without looking up from her butter.

"Because Congress would accomplish more if there weren't so many men to fight with each other. And here's the best part. He says we should only pay congressmen $2.00 a day. It's more than a farmer earns, so it ought to be good enough for congressmen. I think *everyone* would agree with that."

"Probably so. But isn't he swimming upstream? Men in Congress won't reduce their own pay, will they?"

"I'm sure they won't. But it's the right thing, and that's what he stands for. Listen to this one: 'Petition your state legislatures to pardon every convict in their several penitentiaries, blessing them as they go, and saying to them, in the name of the Lord, *go thy way and sin no more.*'"

"Is he serious?"

"Of course he is. It's the way Jesus Christ would rule. He doesn't want to put people in prison for stealing. He'd rather give them jobs to do on roads and public works, and that would teach them wisdom and virtue. He thinks only murderers ought to be imprisoned."

"I don't know, Will. Joseph thinks everyone is just waiting to repent. Maybe some people ought to be kept where they can do no harm."

"But he's asking people to be as good as they ought to be. He has the same attitude about slavery. He comes right out and says it's wrong. He wants slaves to be purchased from owners—so slaveholders don't feel cheated of their property—but then he says slaves should be set free to work for fair pay."

"He's right about that, but no Southerner will vote for him."

"Maybe they will. They must know it's not right to own a human being, and so long as they get paid for their slaves, maybe they could hire the same people and then treat them better."

"It seems a little too hopeful to me. It's not that easy to change the way people think."

"Still, we have to try. And some things just make good sense. He says we ought to use more economy in state governments and ask for fewer taxes, and we ought to create a national bank, so money will be the same all across the nation. And here's the one that matters the most. He says, 'Give every man his constitutional freedom, and the president full power to send an army to suppress mobs.' He even says that sometimes the governor himself may be a mobber, and the national government ought to be able to stop him. If we'd had that policy sooner, the Saints never would have been driven out of Missouri. The president of the United States shouldn't fear to do what's right just because he's afraid of the power of one state."

"It is what's needed," Liz said. But now she was holding her finger to her lips, reminding Will again to lower his voice.

"At the end he says that we ought to extend the nation from ocean to ocean—but we ought to get the permission of the Indians first. See how he always thinks about the people who haven't been cared for. Slaves and Indians and people who are mobbed."

"Well, that's good. I hope people will listen."

But her voice said that she didn't think they would, and Will was feeling some loss of his initial enthusiasm. He had come in wanting to say that he would serve another mission and carry these ideas to as many people as he could—but now he wondered. He still didn't know how he could leave before the spring planting.

"Liz, you have to remember, the people in Hancock County could drive us out of here, and when they do, our government, once again, wouldn't do a thing. Maybe this is the only way we can protect ourselves—work hard to get Joseph elected."

Liz was nodding, but she didn't say anything for a very long time, and Will wondered what she was thinking. Finally, she said in a soft voice, "Maybe it's already too late for that."

"Why? What do you mean?"

"I need to tell you. Something happened that has me worried."

"What?"

"I think I saw George Samples not long before you got home. He and his brother."

"What makes you think so?"

"They were two big men on horses—both with black beards spread out across their chests, exactly the way you described them."

"What were they doing?"

"They just rode by, along Rich Street, but I could see them through the trees, and they were staring back here, like they were looking for our house."

"What did you do?"

"I got the pistol out. And I watched and waited. They didn't turn in, and they haven't come back."

All the air was suddenly gone from Will. How could he ever serve another mission? How could he leave Liz here alone? Joseph could talk all he wanted about setting prisoners free, telling them to repent, but there were evil people in this world who would laugh in Joseph's face if he tried to preach to them.

CHAPTER 18

Will wasn't sure what to do about George and Blake Samples. He couldn't think of any reason why they would need to ride past his house. If they had been coming from Warsaw, they were likely to ride along the river, and if they had ridden in on the Carthage Road, they should have angled straight to Mulholland, not come in by way of Rich Street. What was worse, though, was that they had been staring toward the house, which seemed to mean that somehow they had found out where he and Liz lived. "I'm going to ride over to Mulholland," Will told Liz. "I want to see whether those boys are still in town."

"No, Will. You know what could happen. Just stay here with me."

"I'll be back soon—long before dark. But if I'm going to meet up with them, I want to do it on my terms, not theirs."

"Will, I've been praying, and trying not to be too scared. But I prayed mostly that you would come home. Please don't leave me again."

Will almost changed his mind at that point, but he didn't want to lie awake all night wondering what might happen. A Mormon farmer near Warsaw had had his house burned to the ground and been lucky to get himself and his family out in time to save their lives. "Let me just take a look around and see if I can't end this before it starts."

"Take the pistol."

"No. That's the last thing I want with me. I'm not going after them. But if they come after us, we may have to defend ourselves. Don't hesitate if you have to use it."

Will was sorry to leave Liz looking so upset, but he thought he knew what he had to do—if he could find them. So he rode Socks north on Rich Street and then west on Mulholland. He saw no sign of the men at any of the shops or businesses along the street, so in front of the temple he turned north again and headed for Pratt and Snow's general store. That was when he saw the big chestnut-colored horse with the worn-out saddle. It was George Samples's horse, and tied next to it was another horse about the same color. That would be Blake's.

Will tied his horse next to theirs and walked inside. There were not many people in the store, but the Samples brothers were standing at the counter. They had made a purchase, it seemed, and George was counting out coins as a clerk watched. Will waited. He was nervous, but he thought this might be a good place to make it seem an accident that he had met up with them. And they weren't likely to pull out weapons in the store.

The clerk, a frail young man of twenty or so, had wrapped up something in a brown-paper parcel. When George had paid, he grunted something that might have been a thank-you, and then he turned. Will was pretending to look at some bridles that were hanging near the door. He waited until George and Blake walked toward him, and then he glanced up and acted surprised. "Oh, George," he said. "Blake. How are you? I didn't know you ever came up this way."

Will had spoken in a friendly voice, and he noticed the brothers' confusion. Neither spoke, but George nodded a little in response, as though he didn't quite know what to do.

"This is a well-equipped store, isn't it? Is that what brings you this far up the river?"

Both brothers stared at Will, but neither spoke. A drop of tobacco spit dribbled from the corner of George's open mouth. Will could smell the two of them—a stench like rendered lard gone sour.

"Listen, George," Will said, "I guess you know I gave up that road I was cutting. Did you take the contract to do that work?"

George took his time, but he finally said, "No."

"Is that right? So you decided against it?"

George nodded.

"It's a big investment, isn't it? A man needs at least four or five yoke of oxen or strong horses, and six teams is even better. Do you know who took the job?"

"No."

"Well, I'm sorry it didn't work out for you. After we talked, I felt it was the fair thing to give you your chance. I hope we can consider ourselves all square now. There's just no reason we can't all live together in this county."

George finally gathered himself. "Get out of my way," he said. "Nothin's changed 'tween me and you."

"I'm sorry you feel that way, George. But let's declare a truce. We may not be best friends, but we certainly aren't enemies." Will held out his hand.

George stepped closer to Will and looked hard into his face. He spoke in a low grumble. "What you need to do is *git out*. You and this whole bunch up here. If you clear out, we'll jist let you go. But you stay and we'll *burn* you out."

"But why do we have to—"

"I know where you live, Lewis. I know where your wife is. And yer boys. I know all about that. So don't think you kin put a little honey on yer tongue and sweet-talk me into forgittin' what ya' done to me."

"George, listen, I'm sorry I pulled you off your horse like that, but you know what you said about my wife—and that would make any man angry. All the same, it's not too late to let it go. I think we all believe in Jesus Christ, and He would have us—"

Blake had been hanging back, but he suddenly bolted forward, shoving Will aside as he walked on by. "I've heerd enough of this," he said.

George grabbed Will by the coat and pulled him close. The smell of tobacco and decay was powerful on his breath. Spittle sprayed as George said, "You don't have any more time. There's a lot of boys in this county who feel jist like me and my brother. We're gittin' together to do somethin' 'bout it. Joe Smith ain't got long to live, and you don't either, unless ya' go some'eres else."

Will didn't respond. He had tried to take a higher road, but there was no dealing with a man like this. At least he had no impulse to knock him down again. He only felt sad that things had come to this. He watched the brothers walk out the door, and then he glanced to see whether the clerk had been listening. Parley Pratt was now standing next to the young man. "What was that all about?" Parley asked.

Will walked back to the counter. He shook hands with Brother Parley, a man Will had come to like very much. Since Parley had opened his store, Will had stopped by now and again while temple stones were being unloaded from his wagon. The two had always found things to talk about. Parley spent most of his time writing pamphlets and letters for the Church. He wasn't really cut out to be a man of business, Will thought, but he was a man of great intellect as well as faith, and Will never got tired of hearing him explain the deeper doctrines of the Church.

"Those are the Samples brothers," Will said, "from down by Warsaw." He explained to Parley the conflict that had developed while he had been grading the road in that area.

Parley nodded as he listened. He was a strongly built man with a broad face and a receding hairline, but it was his intense eyes that always engaged Will. When Brother Pratt listened to Will, his entire face showed his concentration. "It's happening again," he said solemnly, "just the way it did in Missouri."

"I don't understand it, Brother Parley."

"It's the gathering. People fear us because we come in such numbers. But that's going to change."

"What do you mean?"

"We have to think differently now. Joseph has been telling us lately that all of America, North and South, is Zion. Nauvoo is the center place, and the temple is here, but we need to start establishing stakes in all directions. We're looking to the west, but we're also considering Texas and the area where we cut pine in Wisconsin. We just can't keep bringing more and more people to Nauvoo."

Will had heard others speculate about going west, but he had never liked the idea. On the other hand, when he considered what George Samples had said about burning people out, he knew his family might be better off if they did leave. "How soon would any of that happen?"

"Soon. For over a year now, we've been exploring some of the places we might want to consider for settlements. We're still seeking redress from the government for what happened to us in Missouri, and we're going to help Joseph with his campaign for president, but a group of men—a council—is being called to consider our future and to move forward."

"I guess we have to look at all the possible choices."

"It's more than that, Will. Christ will reign upon this earth before much longer, and a government must be ready to welcome that reign. In the true order of things, the gospel and the government will not be two things, but one."

It was what John Taylor had said. "So is this a council that's separate from the First Presidency and the Twelve?"

"Yes, and it includes people of other faiths who live with us here. But not much of that will be voiced around. Suffice it to say, the Lord is preparing us. Joseph is receiving deeper truths every day. All will be manifest in time, and the Saints must be ready to accept doctrines that will introduce new realms of glory, new covenants."

"The temple is part of that, isn't it?"

"More than you know, Brother Will. We must finish the temple even as we look for other places to establish stakes. Think back on what Joseph has preached to us the last two times he's spoken at the grove. He's talked of Elias and Elijah and the power to seal. There's work to do for the dead in the temple, but we'll also be sealed up unto heaven with our families. It's all in the Bible, just as Joseph tells us, but it's a mystery to those who lack the prophetic power to see it. And I think you know, Will, some are being prepared, both men and women, to perform those ordinances when the temple is ready."

"Do you really think the end is coming soon, Brother Parley?"

"Soon, yes. But you heard what Joseph said. It's certainly not coming in the next forty years. There's too much work to be finished. And a great deal of the work lies on the shoulders of the Twelve. I can't be a merchant much longer. Last year, when I returned to Nauvoo, Joseph told me to take a year off from missionary work and to build a house for my family. I've done that now—right across the street—but it's time to be about my Father's business. I'm never so happy as when I'm serving the Lord with all my heart."

Will felt the words like an accusation, even though he knew Parley didn't mean them that way. "To tell the truth, Brother Pratt, I've concerned myself with settling in—building a house and establishing a farm—more than I have about serving missions. Maybe it's time for me to change the way I think."

"No question. We need houses, though, and we must provide for our families. It's the first thing to think about, especially for a young man. But you won't be able to hide away much longer. Trust me, Will, the Lord, in His own time, will come looking for you. Be ready."

Will liked hearing that in some ways, but the idea also frightened him. He had come to America to be with the Saints, but he had also wanted good land and a chance to rise in the world. He wasn't ready to give all that up—not the way Parley had done.

"Are those Samples brothers a threat to you, Will?" Parley asked.

"Yes. Not immediately, I don't think. But they will be."

"Then go home. Watch over your family."

Will had been thinking the same thing. He didn't think George and Blake were heading to his house now—they were too cowardly to try something in daylight or to attack someone in the midst of so many Mormons. It would be more like them to come at night, and if they burned farms, they would probably choose those in outlying areas. Still, they had left angry, and there was some reason they had decided to come to Nauvoo. Will decided to head for home.

"What did they purchase here?" Will asked.

"That's what I wanted to tell you," the clerk said. "They bought black powder. They said they use it to take out stumps on their farms."

"Can't they buy black powder in Warsaw?"

"I'm sure they can."

Will left immediately.

• • •

Liz kept checking out the window to the east—watching the trees and the road beyond, and listening for any sound outside. Jacob was restless, seeming to want her attention more than usual, and she found herself impatient with him. He had cried over some little thing and had awakened Daniel, who was ravenous, as usual. So she had nursed him, and now she was standing at the window, holding him wrapped in a blanket, but she had never stopped watching and listening.

When Liz saw Will through the trees, riding his horse along Rich Street, and then saw him turn toward the house, she was greatly relieved. While he had been gone, she had let her mind run to all the possibilities. What if Will were to take those men on and they pulled out guns or knives? He had taken no weapon, and she doubted very much that reasoning was going to work with such people. But here he was, seeming all right, and if the Samples brothers came now, at least Will would be with her.

When Will came inside, he pulled off his coat and hat and hung them by the door. "It *was* the Samples boys," he said. "I talked to them."

"Did you settle anything, or are they still out for revenge?"

"They want us out—no question about that. They think all the Saints should leave. But I don't think they'll do anything to us for now."

Liz heard something she didn't like—as though Will were trying to show confidence but straining to do it. "What do you mean, 'for now'?"

"They're big talkers. They say that we better leave the county soon or they'll . . . well, they don't say what it is they'll do, but they talked about burning houses."

"Burning? Would they do that?"

"They might. But they won't start with us. They don't have the courage to come into Nauvoo and start here. They know how many men we have in the Legion, ready and trained, and they don't want to face that kind of force."

"What will they do, then?"

"Mostly talk. That's what I'm expecting. Men like them might throw their weight around a little down by Warsaw or around Carthage, but I don't think they'll ever come against us."

Will did sound a little more confident now, and Liz took some comfort in that. And in the days that followed, she breathed more easily as she saw nothing more of George and Blake Samples. Her world was filled with her boys and her chores, and with sewing shirts whenever she had time to do it. But one day Sarah Kimball came by to see her, and she brought new worries.

Sarah had actually come by to talk about families in need and women who were sick or had sickness in their families. One of the new spring immigrants, a Brother Hastings, had lost his wife to a fever during the ocean crossing. Female Relief Society sisters were helping the husband care for three small children he wanted to keep. "I think he wants to find himself another wife, fast as he can," Sarah said. "I suppose I don't blame him, but if I died, I'd hope that Hiram might wait a few days before he looked around for a replacement." She laughed.

Then Sarah had admitted that she was worried about her husband. He had joined the Church the previous summer, but now he had entered into a dispute with Joseph Smith over taxes. He owned his wharf and the land around it, and he had been there before the

Mormons had come to Nauvoo. He saw no reason why he should be required to pay city taxes. He had hired lawyers and taken the issue to county officials in Carthage, and Joseph had taken an equally strong position, denouncing Hiram and his lawyers at a city council meeting. "I don't know where it's all going to end, Liz," Sarah said. "Hiram's a stubborn man, and he thinks he's right. I tell him just to pay the tax—to support the city—but he won't back down." And then she added something that took Liz by surprise. "There's so much of that sort of thing going on these days."

"What do you mean?" Liz asked.

"Some of the leaders—William and Wilson Law, Frances Higbee, the Foster brothers—they're speaking out against the Prophet."

"I knew William Law was dropped from the First Presidency, but I've never known why."

"It started, from what Hiram tells me, from bad feelings over the Law brothers selling land to immigrants—working for themselves and competing against the Church. The Church needs to sell lots to make its annual payments. But the issue has gone far beyond that now. William Law has told people that he believes Joseph is a fallen prophet—that he's teaching false doctrines."

"What doctrines?"

Sarah hesitated, then said, "I don't know all the details, Liz." She was sitting at Liz's kitchen table, and she was holding little Daniel, looking down at him. "He's such a sweet boy," she said. "He's growing fast, isn't he?"

"Yes, he is." But Liz was frightened. It was one thing to be hated by others, outside the Church, but she didn't want to know that leaders of the Church had turned against Joseph. "What doctrines bother them, Sarah? When I listen to Joseph, I think he makes so much sense, always."

"I know. But he's spoken about 'celestial marriage' lately. He says that it's possible for marriage to last into the next life. That's part of the sealing in the temple that he's spoken of."

"But what's wrong with that? It sounds wonderful to me."

"I know. But some people—the men I mentioned—don't believe it."

"There's more to it than that, isn't there, Sarah?"

"I only know what people say. It's better that I not spread rumors."

After Sarah was gone, Liz thought of asking Will whether he had heard any talk of plural marriage, which so often came up in accusations against Joseph Smith. She even thought of telling him that she would never accept such a teaching. But she didn't want to believe Joseph would actually ask the Saints to enter into such a practice, so she didn't bring it up.

What made Liz feel much better was listening to Joseph at the conference meetings the first week of April. On Saturday morning, April 6—the fourteenth birthday of the Church—Joseph addressed a huge congregation in the east grove, where the wooden stand had now been moved. Joseph stood near the corner of Robinson and Young Streets, and people filled the entire block in front and all around him. Joseph had to shout every word he said. He started by saying that people probably expected him to talk about some of the "petty difficulties" that had come up lately, but he wouldn't do that. Liz knew that he was talking about the dissenters who had been speaking out against him. "These things," he said, "are of too trivial a nature to occupy the attention of so large a body. I intend to give you some instruction on the principles of eternal truth, but I will defer it until others have spoken, in consequence of the weakness of my lungs."

Joseph often preached very long sermons, and his voice had

worn out at times. Liz understood why he wished to wait, but she was also relieved that he seemed to see the "difficulties" as minor. And she was especially moved when he said, "I feel closer in communion and in better standing with God than ever before in this life."

As she heard his voice carry through the air, she felt a rush of confirmation: the Spirit, which she had felt from Joseph so many times before. He was a prophet—she knew that—and she waited throughout the conference for him to speak again.

Fortunately, the weather, which had been quite wet, had cleared nicely this weekend, and the days were beautiful. These meetings were not easy with an infant and a little boy who liked to wander, but Will didn't stand with the men, as many did. He wore his Sunday suit of clothes and the tall beaver-skin hat he had finally purchased. Liz had teased him that he was paying more attention to styles these days, but he had merely muttered, "A man needs a hat, doesn't he? And what else is for sale?" But in spite of his serious man-about-town look—and his great interest in the sermons, both morning and afternoon—he still chased after Jacob when he had to.

It was fortunate that Jacob fell asleep by three in the afternoon on Sunday when Joseph rose to speak from the wooden stand where all the Church dignitaries were sitting. Will stood to see, and Liz, seated on a grassy incline, could only get a glimpse of Joseph if she raised her head high, but she could hear him quite well. The wind had come up in the afternoon and was blowing fairly hard, but Joseph's voice seemed unusually powerful as it penetrated the wind.

As everyone in Nauvoo knew, King Follett, a well-loved elder in Nauvoo, had died in a well-digging accident recently. Joseph announced that in light of that death, and the concern many had about the loss of friends and relatives, he planned to speak on the subject of death. But he said he needed to start from the beginning so that all could understand. The world didn't understand the true nature of God, and yet, "life eternal" was to know God and understand His nature. Liz followed his thinking as he explained what that meant, and she heard nothing she disagreed with, but then Joseph said something that struck her with force: "We suppose that God was God from eternity. I will refute the idea, or I will do away or take away the veil so you may see. It is the first principle to know that we may converse with Him and that He once was a man like us, and the Father was once on earth like us."

He then explained that each person could follow a similar path of growth. "And you have got to learn how to make yourselves God, king and priest."

Liz glanced at Will, who was looking down at her. She could see in his eyes that he was shocked and at the same time inspired, just as she was. Had God *become* God, and could mortals become gods themselves?

Still, she believed the doctrine instantly, not because the idea seemed logical or even necessarily all that appealing to her, but because she felt a forceful reassurance that Joseph was speaking pure truth.

The Prophet continued to open her mind. Man was eternal, he said, had existed with God forever and would continue forever. God did not create the world from nothing but from material that had always existed. When people died, their spirits separated from their bodies for a time, but those who had passed on were conversant with one another. All mind was susceptible to improvement and could go on and on, ever increasing in capacity.

And then Joseph ended with something that changed Liz's life: "Will mothers have their children in eternity? Yes, yes, you will have your children. But as it falls, so it will rise. It will never grow. It will be in precise form as it fell in its mother's arms."

Little Mary Ann. Liz would have her again. She would see her baby, just as she had been, and then, if Liz understood correctly, she would still have the chance to raise her. Liz gripped little Daniel tightly and knew within herself that she would someday hold little Mary Ann again the same way.

• • •

On the evening after Joseph's sermon, Will and Liz talked late into the night. Some of the things Joseph had said had opened up new ways of thinking for them. Will felt these days as though he spent too much time working with his hands, not increasing his understanding, but suddenly all eternity was opened to him—with the capacity to learn and comprehend *everything*. Each act of life seemed to mean more when he thought that it was part of an eternal scheme and necessary labor to get himself through mortality.

Like Liz, Will had felt the power in Joseph's voice, and he had felt the concepts enter him with a powerful confirmation of the Spirit. He had been troubled lately by the worry he felt for the Saints, the disappointment he experienced with some of them, but this way of thinking was bigger than any of that. If Joseph was bringing doctrines to the Saints that seemed a stretch to believe, maybe that was only because the members were not ready, not that Joseph was teaching falsehood.

Tuesday was the last day of the conference. In the final session, men were called upon to go out across the nation to preach the gospel and hold conferences. At the same time, they would be campaigning for Joseph Smith for president of the United States. Church leaders were convinced this was the only way the Saints would ever gain a measure of justice from the wrongs that had been done to them in Missouri. And what was encouraging was that Joseph's views on government had been distributed through all the major newspapers across the land, and many editors had written favorably about the content of the pamphlet. Will had never imagined that Joseph could win the presidency, but optimism was growing among the leaders that he had a chance.

Will had a hard choice to make. He didn't know exactly when the missionaries would depart, but he knew he had to get his crops planted first. As hundreds raised their hands to accept the call, Liz whispered to Will, "Raise your hand. You should go." Will almost did. But he held back, knowing there would still be time to express his willingness. He could plant soon if the weather cleared, and he could leave soon after, and Jesse and Daniel could look after the farms. But what about Liz? Could he leave her home with the two little ones? It was hard to put aside the thought of the Samples brothers and their bundle of black powder.

In the next two weeks Will talked to many of the Saints who had been greatly moved by Joseph's sermon, and who were excited about his campaign for president. He also learned, however, there were those who had not accepted the image of God that Joseph had preached, and who also thought it was folly to send missionaries out on campaigning missions.

Before the month was out, a dissident group headed by the Laws and Fosters and Higbees had formed. Having challenged Joseph publicly, they had been excommunicated. They had taken a position against the concept of gathering, arguing that it was this practice that led to so much hatred by others. And this new sermon on the nature of God was blasphemous, they said, evidence that Joseph was no longer a prophet. Above all, however, was the accusation that Joseph was teaching plural marriage, and that not only had he entered into plural marriages, but others of the leaders had as well.

The majority of the Church members continued to trust that Joseph Smith had been called by God, but the mood in Nauvoo had changed. Will had believed for such a long time that a Zion spirit would continue to develop to its fulness, that life in Nauvoo would become superior to any form of society anywhere. But this spirit of dissension filled the newspapers in every town in the area, and entered into every conversation. Will felt as though everything he had worked for was about to break apart, and he didn't want to believe that that could happen.

CHAPTER 19

Will had hoped that the weather would break and he could plant soon, but storms were coming often, hard thunderstorms that soaked deep into the soil. Twice Will had started to plow, only to see rains come again. And when he and Jesse had finally managed to plow some higher ground and start planting, a deluge of rain had washed out most of the seed corn. Will knew of other men who had agreed to leave on missions but were being delayed the same way. Others were departing in spite of not having planted. Most of the Twelve had set out before the end of May. Some farmers were promising to plant for others as soon as the ground was ready, and that would free up their brothers to serve.

Will continued to feel that the time had not yet come for him to leave. There was simply too much work to leave everything to Jesse and Daniel. Liz was encouraging him to go, but not with the same confidence she had shown when he had left on his previous mission. He knew she was afraid to be alone, and that worried him more than anything.

There was constant talk in Nauvoo about the dissenters and the attention they were receiving in all the newspapers in the region. The Law brothers and their friends were starting a new church that would reject some of the things Joseph had been teaching in recent months. Some of the dissenters had been excommunicated, and they were now preaching among the members and were gathering dozens of converts.

And then, on June 7, 1844, the dissenters began to publish a newspaper. It was called the *Nauvoo Expositor,* and it promised to set the record straight, to reveal Joseph Smith's sins and his false teachings. Seven long letters, plus a preamble to introduce the purpose of the newspaper, filled the pages, denouncing Joseph Smith in the most vehement language Will could imagine. Frances Higbee called the Prophet "Joe Smith," a name always used by enemies but never by the Saints. It was hard to believe that William and Wilson Law, with whom Will had served in the Nauvoo Legion, could become so bitter. Will had heard both bear powerful testimonies of the gospel of Jesus Christ and of Joseph Smith's role as Prophet of the Restoration. And now they were attacking Joseph as forcefully as they had once praised him.

That spring Thomas Sharp had bought back the Warsaw newspaper, and Will knew that any accusation printed in the *Expositor* would be printed in the *Warsaw Signal* and then would go out to newspapers all across the country. Just at the time when missionaries were campaigning for Joseph, this diatribe against him would reverse everything they were trying to do.

Still, the greater danger was at home in Hancock County. Some of the language of the *Expositor* amounted to a call to arms. One anonymous writer argued that if people arose and enforced the law, such a response should not be looked at as mob action. Will had seen the hatred that had been growing in the county, and he knew it would only take a spark like that to set off a conflagration. He knew now for certain that he couldn't leave Liz alone.

The *Expositor* had come out on a Friday, and word was, the city council had been called together to discuss the matter on Saturday. Will hoped the Prophet would speak on Sunday in the grove. He didn't do that, however, and everyone Will talked to that day was of the same opinion: Serious trouble was about to break loose. The Legion would have to be ready.

Will got up on Monday, unsure what he should do. But no muster had been called, and he had work to do on his farm, the weather finally having turned warm. He knew of nothing better to do than to pray for the Lord to intercede, and then to finish his planting. He and Jesse and Daniel put in a long day, and at the end felt good about their work. "I don't know what's a-comin'," Jesse told Will, "but it's best to go forward and trust in God, the way I see't."

"I feel the same," Will said. "But if I'm not here in the morning, you'll know the Legion has been called to guard the city. You might be called into Nauvoo too. I suspect anyone out here away from the city could be in danger."

"Aw right, then. We'll follow what the leaders tell us to do."

"If you're told to move into town, you and your family can sleep at our place, nice and cozy."

"Or my new house," Brother Johns said. "If you squeeze in with us, that would be cozy fer shor."

They all smiled, but Will felt the nervousness among them. All day Will had watched the road to see whether a militia—or a mob—might be marching that way. He had seen Jesse and Dan looking off in the same direction. They actually had plenty of daylight left to work later, but Will felt a need to get back to his family. He was sure the other men felt the same.

The ride took Will more than an hour. It was after seven o'clock by the time he got home, but he didn't put his horse away. He tied up Socks to a fence and walked inside. He heard a little tension in Liz's voice when she said, "I didn't think you would stay so long today."

"Good weather's been hard to come by," Will said. It irritated him a little that Liz didn't seem to realize how much work he had to do. Still, he hated to see her so worried. "Have you heard anything?" he asked.

"Nelly came over a little while ago. Warren heard that John Greene was raising a posse, but no one knew exactly what it was for."

John Greene was the city marshal, so that sounded like something official. Will wondered whether some action was being taken against the dissenters. "But no one came by to muster the Legion, I take it."

"No. But Warren says that will be next. He thinks you shouldn't leave town tomorrow."

Will wanted to know something official. "I'm going to ride down to General Rich's house. He can tell me what to expect."

"Do you have to, Will? I've had your supper ready for over an hour, and . . ." She didn't have to say the rest.

"I'll be back before the sun goes down. It's better to know something than to sit here and wonder."

She gave a little nod, but he could see that it was acquiescence, not acceptance. He almost stayed, but he needed to know what was happening, and he thought she would be less worried herself if he could report something accurate.

So Will rode down Parley Street. As he reached the flats he saw men on horseback, all heading south, probably toward the Mansion House. Will decided to follow and see what they were doing. Maybe the call-up had begun.

As Will reached Partridge Street and turned south himself, he rode alongside a man he knew from the Escort Brigade. "What's happened?" he asked.

John Benton was the man's name. He was a private, like Will, but a much better horseman and a crack shot. Will had often wished he had the man's skills. "Ain't yuh heard? We just tore up that printing place on Mulholland—the one them dissenters was usin'. They won't be publishin' any more of their lies."

"What do you mean, 'tore up'?"

"We carried the press out and smashed it up. And we scattered the type in all directions. They'll never print with that machine again."

"Were you authorized or just—"

"From the top. The city council had meetin's all day Saturday and agin taday. They said that newspaper was a danger to us all and had to be stopped. You know that's true if ya' saw what they wrote in it."

Will did believe the purpose of the paper was to invite mobs from the county to attack the Saints, but he wondered what would come of destroying the press. He could only imagine what Thomas Sharp would have to say about that.

There were dozens of men who had already dismounted their horses. They were gathering around the front of the Mansion House. More men were coming all the time. It seemed a huge number of people to carry out the order. Will thought maybe the men would be worried about what might be coming next, but they were rejoicing, slapping one another on the back, joking about "ol' William Law" being "shut up for good."

After a time, Joseph Smith stepped from the house, and a cheer went up. He stood on the front steps and waited for the men to quiet. He didn't seem nearly so joyous as the men were. He thanked them, however, and he told them that the only purpose of the *Nauvoo Expositor* was to spread libel and slander and incite indignation among the other citizens of the county. The paper, he said, was a nuisance that couldn't be tolerated. "I care not how many newspapers there are in this city," he told them, "if they would print the truth but would submit to no libel or slander."

There was a shout of agreement, and then Joseph wished them well. He waved to everyone and stepped back into the house. The men continued to talk among themselves. There was something exciting about all this, and Will began to feel it himself. Maybe this time the Saints were strong enough that they could stand up and defend themselves. He had been telling himself for a long time that he needed to calm his spirit and avoid his tendency to fight back when pressured, but Joseph had sanctioned this action, and it sounded right. Others would make of it what they wanted, but he felt certain that "nuisance" was the right name for the rag of a paper that had been published. If Warsaw wanted to get up a mob, maybe they would find out what the Nauvoo Legion boys would do about that.

He glanced across Water Street and saw that a group of young boys had gathered. He saw one of the boys pretend to shoot a rifle and then say something to his friends, who all laughed. This all must have seemed a great game to them: playing at war. Will suddenly saw the other side of all this. He thought of Liz and his two little boys, and he wondered, could a war, fought here in Nauvoo, be good for anyone? Was that what God wanted the Saints to engage in?

Will spotted Brother Rich walking across Main Street to his horse. He followed and caught up with him. "General Rich," he said, "I worked at my farm all day and haven't heard anything. Will the Legion be called up?"

Brother Rich looked solemn. "I would think so," he said. "We'll know in the next few days. I wouldn't go out to work on any outlying farms right now. Mobs will attack there first and then move on into the city. These boys of ours think they're in for some good sport, but they won't be so haughty once it all starts."

Any excitement Will had felt before was entirely gone now.

"At very least, we'll soon be setting up guard stations. So be ready. The Escort Brigade will guard the Prophet."

Will nodded, said he would be ready, but all the way home he tried to think what words he should choose to inform Liz what was happening.

• • •

Liz was glad that Will didn't go back to the farm on Tuesday morning. She could tell that he was troubled. He had been very careful the night before as he had told her about the things he had heard and seen. He didn't question the Prophet's decision, but she knew he was wondering whether the destruction of the press hadn't gone too far—and would bring on the wrath of everyone who hated the Saints.

But nothing happened. Twice that day, and twice again on Wednesday, Will sought out William Clayton at his office to learn what new developments might be at hand. He came home with little to report. Late on Wednesday Brother Clayton had received a copy of that day's *Warsaw Signal* and had let Will read it. When Will came back home, he told Liz, "Tom Sharp has gone mad, I think. He said that every man would have to make his own comment about what we did to the *Expositor*, but he said they ought to do it 'with powder and ball.'"

"What's he saying, that they should *kill* Joseph?"

"Not just him. He said that what *we* call the Missouri persecutions should be called 'Missouri justice.' So you don't have to guess what he thinks they ought to do."

Liz felt weak. Will seemed to see that. He came to her and took her in his arms. "Things are different this time," he said. "The Saints had no army in Missouri. The old citizens are calling for meetings in Warsaw and in Carthage, but they don't want to take on the Legion. Joseph already wrote to Governor Ford and explained why the press had to be destroyed. Ford may not agree with Joseph, but Brother Clayton thinks he might send state troops to intervene—to stop a war before it gets started."

"But we can't keep living this way—surrounded by people who hate us."

"No, we can't. But if some of our people migrate to other parts of the land and we stop adding to our numbers here in Nauvoo, things could calm down in time."

Liz could always tell when Will was trying to ease her mind. The truth was, he wasn't confident about anything he was saying.

• • •

On Sunday morning, rain was falling. Will said he wanted to walk over to the grove and see whether Joseph would have something to say, but he didn't think it would be a good idea to take Jacob and Daniel out into the storm. Liz agreed, so Will walked to the east grove by himself.

After a hymn and prayer, Joseph stood in the steady rain and thanked the people for coming. Will expected him to instruct the members on how to respond to the threats they were facing. But he didn't do that. He kept his tall hat on as protection from the rain, and he shouted his words loudly enough to be heard above the noise of the spatter in the surrounding trees. He said that he would take for his text Revelation 1, verse 6, which referred to "God and his Father." The "apostates," as he called the dissenters, had accused him of teaching "the plurality of Gods," but anyone who read the Bible carefully must know that it was full of references to multiple Gods. He pointed out that he had been teaching for a long time that God and Jesus Christ were separate beings, not one God. As he continued to describe Bible references to God and Christ being separate and Paul's mention of multiple Gods, Will had to smile. Joseph wasn't there to talk about the battles that might be ahead. He was preaching the gospel as it had been taught to him by the Spirit. That mattered most to him.

If Christ was a God, and he had a Father, he asked, why couldn't God the Father have a father? The fact was, for mortals on this earth, there was only one "God the Father" to worship, so it didn't matter if there were other Gods in other places. He wasn't blaspheming against God; he was opening up a greater truth. He refused to apologize for teaching something that was different from what most Christians taught. "I never heard of a man being damned for believing too much," he said, "but they are damned for unbelief."

The rain was gradually coming harder. Joseph said he could talk for three or four hours on this subject, but because of the downpour, he would have to close the meeting. By afternoon, however, the rains had abated, and at a four o'clock session Joseph stood up again. This time, as he often did in afternoon sessions, he dealt with some practical matters. Most important, he ordered Major General Charles Rich to hold the Nauvoo Legion "in readiness to suppress all illegal violence in the city."

At the close of the meeting, Will felt that the Sabbath had been a fitting escape from the rancor he had heard in recent days, but he wondered what lay ahead. He had told Liz that the ragtag troops from Carthage and Warsaw could never drive the Saints away, but what he hadn't told her was that the dissidents had filed suit against Joseph for the destruction of their press, and Governor Ford was demanding that Joseph appear in court—in Carthage, not

Nauvoo—to answer the charges. He had written Joseph that if necessary he would call out thousands of troops from all around the state. He could not, he argued, allow Joseph to take the law into his own hands and destroy private property without facing his accusers. Joseph and the city council, he said, may have had a legal argument for what they had done, but it was unlawful for Joseph to be exonerated by the Nauvoo Municipal Court.

The governor's position had plenty of merit, and Joseph Smith might ordinarily have been willing to comply, but what Joseph believed, and Will assumed was true, was that if he gave himself up and went to Carthage, he would never return.

• • •

Will decided not to work at his farm on Monday morning. He was worried that his crops had been washed out again by the storm on Sunday, but there was nothing to be done until the soil dried again. Even more, he found himself unable to give much thought to his work. Will talked to William Clayton on Monday afternoon and learned that Joseph had sent out representatives to all the communities in the area. These agents would try to explain the city council's actions against the *Expositor* and reassure leaders that peace could still be worked out. The reports coming back, however, were frightening. In Yelrome—the Morley settlement—there had already been burnt farmhouses. Joseph had told the Mormons there not to leave for now, but it seemed unlikely they could withstand the persecutions of Levi Williams, the lay minister from Green Plains, with his band of vigilantes.

Brother Clayton told Will that Joseph had declared martial law and thought that the Legion would be called up in the morning. That turned out to be right. The Legion assembled, in uniform, at the parade ground near Main Street on the flats. Will was at the forefront with the Escort Brigade. At about eleven o'clock Joseph Smith arrived on Old Charley, and then he led the Legion as it marched to the Mansion House.

Porter Rockwell had been building a barbershop and inn just across the street, south of the Mansion House. Only the foundation and first floor of Porter's building were in place, but it made an ideal platform where Joseph could address the Legion. Will's brigade stayed toward the back of the crowd with their horses. Will was still mounted on Socks when he saw Joseph, along with other high-ranking officers, climb a ladder to the platform. Joseph was wearing his full uniform, even his plumed hat. He appeared resolute and more solemn than usual. The soldiers lined up in the intersection of Water and Main and up and down both of those streets. They stood in formation in their battalions and companies, and Will thought they appeared a powerful force.

Before Joseph spoke, William Phelps read the declaration that Thomas Sharp had made in the *Warsaw Signal,* calling for citizens to arm themselves and drive Joe and Hyrum Smith and all their "infernal devils" from the county. Many had already read these words or spread them around verbally, but Will could see the resentment, even anger, in the faces of the men when they heard the entire editorial. Still, they remained silent in their military discipline.

Joseph projected his voice over the large assemblage, but he sounded reasonable, not angry. He explained that the purpose of some men in the county was to exterminate the Mormons because of their religion. He called upon the men to defend the Constitution of the United States and to defend their wives and children, fathers and mothers, brothers and sisters. He told the soldiers to arm themselves with whatever weapons they could find and be ready to protect their city. Gradually his voice had grown more forceful, faster in cadence. Finally, he shouted, "Will you all stand by me to the death, and sustain at the peril of your lives, the laws of our country?"

"Aye!" the mass of men shouted back.

He repeated the question twice more and received the same loud response each time.

He pleaded with the soldiers to defend their families, but never to spill innocent blood. Then he concluded by raising his sword in the air and shouting, "I call God and angels to witness that I have unsheathed my sword with a firm and unalterable determination that this people shall have their legal rights and be protected from mob violence, or my blood shall be spilt upon the ground like water."

He hesitated after that, and when he spoke again, his voice had softened. "You are good people; therefore I love you with all my heart." He ended by saying, "You have stood by me in the hour of trouble, and I am willing to sacrifice my life for your preservation."

Will was heartsick. Joseph was ready to die—all the men were—for the sake of the truth, for the sake of Zion. But how had everything come to this? How could these good people have possibly generated so much hatred in the hearts of their neighbors?

The troops were dispersed around the city after that, placed at entering points to the city or assigned to guard strategic buildings. Will and the Escort Brigade stayed at the Mansion House, and they stood guard in shifts, around the clock. Will saw the comings and goings of Joseph and those leaders who were still in town, but most of the Apostles were still out campaigning for Joseph's nomination for the presidency.

Will continued to speak with his friend William Clayton when he could. He learned that Joseph had been exchanging letters with Governor Ford. The governor had promised Joseph protection if he gave himself up in Carthage, but Joseph doubted the governor could make that guarantee. On Friday, Governor Ford came to Nauvoo, and John Taylor met to negotiate with him. The outcome was that the Legion was disbanded and a promise was made that armies being organized in Warsaw and Carthage would also be controlled by state forces. Will learned the next day, however, that Joseph, unable to believe that Governor Ford could keep him safe, had left with Hyrum and crossed the river to Montrose in the Iowa Territory. It was Warren Baugh who had heard the news, and he was not happy. "Here we are on the verge of war," he told Will, "and Joseph runs away to save himself. I don't understand it."

"Or is he trying to save us?" Will responded, rather forcefully.

"That's what some is sayin', but he told us he'd spill his blood to fight for us, and then he hides out. It don't seem right to me."

Will heard the same accusation from others that Sunday morning, but by afternoon reports circulated that Joseph was already back in the city. And later that day Will was called to the Mansion House again. Joseph had agreed to give himself up after all. Eighteen men had been indicted for the destruction of the press. Joseph and Hyrum, along with the others so accused, would be riding to Carthage Monday morning, June 24, and a small escort of Mormons would ride with him. The governor had changed his mind and was now offering no state posse for his protection, but Joseph had become convinced he had to go, had to answer the charges, and he would take along his own protection.

Will spent Sunday night back at home, but he returned to the Mansion House early in the morning to make the trip with Joseph.

• • •

Liz watched Will ride away that morning, and then she went back into her house, knelt, and prayed. She wanted the faith to trust that all would be well, but she had seen something in Will's eyes she

didn't like. He had promised her that he was in no danger, that she
need not worry, but he was not really sure of that, and she knew it.
She didn't know whether he was scared for himself, for her and their
little boys, or for Joseph. She doubted that he knew. What she did
learn was that he had asked two men from the Escort Brigade—
since only a few had been chosen to ride to Carthage—to stay near
her home and look out for her. She didn't think that a battle was im-
minent, with Joseph agreeing to give himself up, but that made her
wonder whether he had felt a need to have someone there for her,
should he not return himself.

She wondered even more when at midmorning Nelly showed
up just to see how Liz was doing. "How did you know that Will was
gone?" Liz asked.

"He told me. When he came back from the Mansion House
last night, he stopped here first. He asked me to watch out for you
a little."

"Why, Nelly? Does he expect to get himself killed?" The idea
that he would speak to Nelly irritated her. Why would Will never
admit to her how much danger he was actually facing?

"Oh, no. He said nothing of the kind. He only said you might
worry, and it might be nice if I kept you company a little."

Liz was holding little Daniel, who was almost four months old.
She had fed him, and now he was asleep. But she liked having him
close to her. Jacob came to her and leaned against her legs. Liz knew
she shouldn't have asked Nelly about Will dying. Jacob didn't really
understand death, but he must have heard the concern in her voice.

"There's nothing you can do for me, Nelly," Liz said. "Now I
just have to wait. And I do that best when I keep busy."

"I know. But a little talk don't hurt. An' maybe I kin help you
with whatever it is that you need to do taday."

Liz wanted to tell her no, to tell her that she was only going to make her nervous, but Nelly meant well. So Liz said, "All right. That would be nice," and Nelly stayed much of the day.

• • •

It was a sizeable party that rode north on Main Street and then climbed the bluff toward the temple. The entire city council had been indicted, along with Joseph and Hyrum. Willard Richards, Dan Jones, and Henry Sherwood were not accused, but they had joined the group to support Joseph. James Woods, an attorney from Burlington, Iowa Territory, was also with them, as were others, like Will, who were there to escort and defend the group. As they crested the bluff, Will saw Joseph turn his horse and look back at the city below. Hyrum was next to him on Sam, his white horse, and the two gazed out over the river valley and spoke for a time. They finally rode on, and John Benton came up alongside Will. "What were they saying back there?" Will asked.

"Joseph said, 'This is the loveliest place and the best people under the heavens.' I heard him say it, clear as anything, and exactly in them words. But he also said that the people didn't know what trials were ahead for them."

"Does he think the mobs will still come, then?"

"I don't know. He didn't explain."

The party rode east on Mulholland about a mile, where they connected to the Carthage road and angled southeast toward the cemetery and then out across the prairie. It was a solemn procession, but they met no enemy, and by ten o'clock they were only about four miles from Carthage when they met a company of men from McDonough County. Will heard Captain Dunn, their leader, explain to Joseph that he had been sent by the governor to collect the arms that had been issued by the state to the Nauvoo Legion. Will understood that the governor wanted to interrupt the preparations for war, but he also worried that the Saints would be giving up their chance to protect themselves.

But Joseph didn't argue. He agreed to give up the arms, countersigned the order from the governor, and sent Henry Sherwood to hurry back to Nauvoo and gather the weapons into the new Masonic Lodge. Joseph turned then and told his men that he would ride back to Nauvoo with Captain Dunn to make certain all would be peaceful.

Will wanted to ride with Joseph. It was his job to protect him. But Joseph didn't want to make all the men travel back and forth and wear out their horses, so he asked most to stay. He and Hyrum and about twelve others made the trip back.

For Will that meant a long day of waiting, with nothing to do but wonder about Joseph, wonder what might be happening in Nauvoo, and wonder how Liz was doing. Some of the men napped under some gnarly old cottonwood trees by a creek, but Will had never been good at sleeping when his mind was riled this way. He walked for a time, sat for a time, and talked to the few men who stayed awake. It was a humid day, and after a time, the shade of the trees was no protection against the heat.

It was one of the longest days of the year, so the sun was up until late, but as it was setting, Joseph and the others had still not returned. Will was pacing and ready to start riding back toward Nauvoo when Joseph, along with Captain Dunn's company, finally rode toward them. Joseph greeted the men, again more solemnly than Will was used to from Joseph, and they all continued on together.

John Benton, who had gone back with Joseph, rode alongside Will, and Will asked him how everything had gone in Nauvoo. "It took some time to explain to the Legion officers what was goin' on—and then to start haulin' in all the weapons—but more than anythin', Joseph wanted to see Emma. He went back to the house twice. He kept holdin' onto Emma and the childern like he didn't 'spect to come home agin. And then, when we got to his farm, there by the cemetery, he jist kept starin' out across his land. When we asked him why he was doin' that, he told us that if any of us had a farm like that, and knowed we'd never see it again, we'd want to take a last look too."

"Is he so sure he's going to die?"

It was Henry Sherwood, riding on the other side of Will, who responded. "I think he's ready for whatever comes. I heard him say, 'I'm going like a lamb to the slaughter, but I'm calm as a summer's morning.' And he is calm—like he's accepted what's coming."

"I heard him say some things like that, back in Nauvoo," John said. "But he tol' Emma that all would be jist fine, and Hyrum keeps sayin' that too. So I think they still hold out some hope. But Abram Hodge caught up with us not long after we passed the farm. Joseph had sent him on to Carthage to see what was goin' on over there. He told Joseph not to go on, that he'll never get out of Carthage alive. He'd talked to a minister who said the Carthage Greys was waiting to kill him."

"But Joseph decided to go on anyway?"

"I think he feels he has to," Brother Sherwood said. "It's as though he sees God in this, and he's carrying out what the Lord wants him to do."

But what did that mean? Will felt the soberness in Sherwood—in all the men. Will's instincts told him they should never let Joseph give himself up, that they should convince him to go back across the river again, get far away from this place. But Joseph had made his decision, and Will was going to stay with him, no matter what that meant.

It was almost midnight when the party arrived in Carthage.

Will had learned that Joseph was staying at the Hamilton Hotel for the night and would turn himself in the next morning—along with all the indicted men. The hotel was only one street east of the courthouse. As the band of men rode past the public square, Will saw that the local militia, the Carthage Greys, were camped near the courthouse. Along with them was the rest of the militia from McDonough County. All the men seemed eager to have a look at Joseph. Many of them came out of their tents and howled their insults. They vowed to have his life, called him every disgusting name imaginable.

Joseph didn't respond, but Will was infuriated. These men knew nothing of Joseph Smith. What possible reason could they have to hate a man—any man—that much, particularly one as good as Joseph was? Will understood why some of the local people resented the Saints, but this kind of hatred was beyond reason. The men seemed crazed, their voices—their eyes—full of rage.

Many of the men followed on down the street, trying to get as close to Joseph as they could, seeming to hope they could yell some insult directly into his face. Captain Dunn's troops surrounded him, however, and kept them back. As the mass of people reached the hotel, and Joseph, along with everyone else in his party, began to dismount, the roar of the mob reached a fanatic volume. About then a window on the second floor of the hotel came open, and someone yelled at the men. When they turned to see who was speaking, Governor Ford identified himself. "That's enough, boys," he shouted. "I'll bring Mr. Smith by for your review in the morning. You get some sleep now—and let me do the same."

Someone shouted, "Hurrah for Tom Ford," and three loud cheers went up. Will thought the crowd was about to disperse, but just as Will was trying to get close to the Prophet, to offer protection as they walked inside, a man broke out of the crowd and rushed forward. He shouted, "We're going to kill you, Joe Smith, an' ever' Mormon in these parts. We won't put up with you no more."

It was George Samples. Will jumped between him and the Prophet, but Samples slammed into Will, chest to chest. He was wearing a makeshift uniform and had a brace of pistols strapped around his waist. "Git out of my way, Lewis," he growled, and then he threw out his arm and tried to fight his way through. But Will grabbed him by the arm and spun him around. He was about to drive him to the ground when he felt a strong hand grasp his shoulder.

"No."

Will knew the voice, knew the firm hand. Will let go of Samples, who stumbled away and turned back around, hesitated, and seemed to reach a decision not to make another charge. He mumbled an insult and moved back into the crowd.

Will looked at Joseph, who nodded as if to thank him. But Will had heard the resolute tone of his voice, and he knew he was looking at a better man than himself. "It's no use to fight them," Joseph said. "It's what we have to learn—you and I both."

"I won't let any of them get to you," Will shouted over the continued roar of the mob.

Joseph leaned close to Will's ear. "I know. And I appreciate that. But we can't go to war with these people. The Lord doesn't want that."

"We can't just let them massacre our women and children."

"No, we can't. But if they have me, they won't attack Nauvoo. I'm the one they want."

"You'll never get a fair trial."

"That's all in the Lord's hands now. I tried to escape. Hyrum and I crossed the river. But my friends told me I was wrong to leave, and the Spirit told me to come back. I've accepted my fate, whatever it is."

Will looked into the Prophet's face, tried to read his eyes in the dark, but all he needed to know was in his voice. He was calm—and sad. Back in Nauvoo, he had raised his sword and vowed to fight, but something had changed in him now. He had accepted the Lord's will. It was that acceptance—that sadness in his voice—that stayed with Will as he waited out the long night.

CHAPTER 20

Liz had trouble sleeping with Will gone. She kept wondering what would happen if a militia from Warsaw or Carthage attacked the little escort force that was traveling with Joseph. She knew that Will was too much of a fighter. He would put his life in danger to protect the Prophet.

She finally gave up on sleeping and got up early. She knew that Will would probably still be gone again that night. She already expected the day to be endless, and she knew the heat, which had been bad in recent days, would be ever more oppressive as the day stretched on. She needed to do something besides wait and worry. So she dressed Jacob, nursed Daniel and got him ready, and then set out along Rich Street carrying Daniel and holding Jacob's hand. The going was slow—with Jacob stopping to pick up rocks and sticks—but Liz liked being out of the house. The birds were up early too, singing raucously in the woods. Surely, it seemed, Will couldn't be lying dead somewhere on the road to Carthage, not on such a beautiful morning as this.

Liz made her way to Hannah Murdock's house. She found her

outside hoeing in her garden. "Oh, Sister Liz," she said. "It's so good to see you."

"I haven't been a good friend lately, Hannah," Liz said. "Since Daniel was born, I haven't left the house much."

"I shoulda came to you. You set with me so many times when I lost my little ones. It oughta be my turn now." Daniel squirmed in Liz's arms. Sister Murdock smiled at him. "Look how big your baby is already."

"Do I see something you're hiding under your apron yourself?"

"Oh, yes, it's true. I'm glad to have a new baby on the way, but I worry about it. What would I ever do if something happened again?"

Sister Murdock stretched backward with a hand against the small of her back, and Liz wondered whether she should be hoeing in her state. But she looked much better than she had the year before. She had filled out, looked strong and healthy. "Let me take that hoe," Liz said.

"No, no. I'm stoppin' now. I've been out here a hour, and that's all I promised myself I'd do. Alferd's prob'ly awake by now an' I need to fix breakfast for 'im."

"Where's Brother Murdock?"

"Oh, gone since daybreak. He's workin' his fields, replantin'. How many times have we been washed out this year?"

"Too many." But Liz didn't say where Will was. She wasn't sure she could talk about that without breaking down.

"Has anyone heard anythin' this mornin'?" Hannah asked.

Liz knew what she meant—anyone in Nauvoo would understand the question. "I don't know. I haven't. They left early yesterday, but Joseph and Hyrum came back to turn over all the state weapons. Then they—"

"I know all that. But I'm wonderin' what's goin' to happen over there in Carthage."

"Will said, if the judge grants all the brethren bail, they might be free to leave."

"Will the mob let 'em go?"

"I don't know. That's what everyone is wondering."

Liz watched Sister Murdock, saw the worry in her face. It was the same look she had seen in Nelly's face, and Warren's, and in the faces of everyone she had talked to lately. People were going about their business as best they could, but time seemed suspended. It was as though a fuse had been lit, and everyone was waiting for the explosion.

"Walk inside with me a minute," Sister Murdock said. "It's so good to see you."

So they walked to the house and Hannah leaned her hoe by the door. What Liz saw pleased her. These were still cramped quarters, with hardly enough room for two beds and a table, but everything looked tidy. The Murdocks' garden was flourishing more than most in spite of all the rain that had come in recent weeks, and there were new pieces of furniture inside the cabin, and a new quilt on the bed. "You're doing well, aren't you, Hannah? You seem to be prospering."

"I guess we are. We're poor as church mice, but we've worked hard and our neighbors have looked out fer us. You brought us what we needed for cookin', but we didn't have a dry sink, so Brother Dawson, our neighbor jist east of us, helped my husband build one. He coulda jist looked after hisself and his family, but he thought of us. We plan ta pay 'im back a little with some vegetables as soon as we're pickin' from our garden."

Liz didn't know Brother Dawson, but she liked knowing that neighbors were helping one another.

Sister Murdock peeked at the bed in the corner and then

whispered, "Alferd was up too late las' night, with the sun up so long. I'll let him sleep a little more." She motioned to the table by the fireplace. "Sit down. Will ya' have a cup of tea?"

Liz was not sure how long she should stay. Jacob had been hanging on to her so far, but he would soon want something more to occupy his incessant curiosity. Daniel was also looking about, as though surprised by his new surroundings. "Oh, yes, tea would be nice, but I can't stay long. I just thought I'd walk out a little before the heat comes on. I'm alone today and . . ." But suddenly she was crying, and she had told herself not to do that.

"What is it, deary?"

Liz couldn't speak for a time. She held a hand over her mouth and let herself sob. "Will went with them," she finally managed to say. "With Joseph and the others."

"Oh, my. An' you thought of me this mornin'? I shoulda been down to yer house."

"I wish it were so, Hannah. Mostly, I needed someone to talk to. I've been missing my mother and my sister so much lately."

"I can imagine." Sister Murdock came to Liz, put her arm around her shoulders. "If we ever trusted God, we have to do it now."

Liz had thought so much about that during the night. "But what about Missouri, Hannah? Why did those things happen over there? Do you think the people here will try to drive us out again?"

"I don't know, Liz. I on'y know what ya' taught me las' year. When things happen, even things so awful we think we cain't go on, we do anyhow, no matter what."

All night Liz had told herself that God wouldn't take Will from her. But some of the Saints had died in Missouri. She couldn't trust that nothing bad would happen here.

"They've tried to kill Joseph before," Sister Murdock said. "An' the Lord pertected him. I jist think it will be that way agin."

Liz told herself that was right. But the fear wouldn't leave her. After she walked back home, she tried to work, but mostly she watched and waited—all day—and when night fell, Will was still gone. She told herself that if there had been bad news, she would have heard, but that thought didn't take away the sick feeling in her stomach.

• • •

In Carthage no one knew for sure what was happening in Nauvoo, but Will kept hearing rumors, mostly in the form of threats. He had been told a dozen times that an attack would soon begin, and according to some of the militia men shouting at him, armed soldiers were already in Nauvoo driving the Mormons into the Mississippi. It was terrible to sit around and wait when something like that might be happening, but he couldn't walk away and leave Joseph without protection.

Will had waited outside the Hamilton Hotel that first night in Carthage as a "guard against the guards": the Carthage Greys and the McDonough County boys. They were called militias, but they were a drunken, noisy band of ruffians, more mob than military force. They were there to protect the Mormons, according to the governor, but the majority of them hoped to see Joseph dead and the Saints run out of Illinois—and they didn't mind saying so.

On Tuesday morning Governor Ford marched Joseph and Hyrum before the two militias, as he had promised to do, but the militiamen became enraged when the governor addressed the Smith brothers by their military titles, as generals. Some of the men cursed in response and threatened violence that very moment. The governor put an end to that, but he hurried Joseph and Hyrum back to the hotel.

All those accused of "riot" for destroying the *Expositor* press were scheduled for a hearing at four o'clock that afternoon, and that meant another long day of waiting for Will. He stood guard outside the Hamilton Hotel and listened to the insults of both soldiers and citizens. One well-dressed man approached him and, without any hint of animosity, said politely, "You look like an upright young man. What's brought you to this? How have you allowed yourself to become so deluded?"

Will replied, with equal politeness, "Sir, I'm not deluded. If you could meet Joseph Smith and talk to him—or talk with any of us— about the things we believe, I feel certain you would change your mind."

The man stood silent for a time and stared into Will's eyes. Finally he said, "They're going to kill Joe Smith, you know. I don't approve of that myself, but you must see it coming. You can't be foolish enough to assemble yourselves in such great numbers here on the frontier and expect to be welcomed as though you were ordinary people."

"But we are ordinary people," Will said.

The man smiled. "I suppose you do see it that way. No lunatic *knows* that he's a lunatic." He shook his head sorrowfully. "Go home and protect your family, not these Smiths. Or better yet, leave the county before these other lunatics drop their ruse as militiamen and show their true colors. I'm a physician, and if you stay here, I fear that you'll need my services before another day passes."

But Will continued to wait—and worry—and then, just before four o'clock, a number of officials, escorted by armed soldiers with fixed bayonets, marched down the street to the hotel. Will learned that one of the men in the party was the man who would try the

314 · DEAN HUGHES

case, Justice Robert Smith. He had come to the hotel to protect
Joseph and Hyrum from having to walk to the courthouse, according to the wishes of the governor, who insisted that he wanted to
avoid armed confrontation.

As it turned out, the hearing didn't last long. Within an hour the
judge exited the hotel and walked back toward the courthouse. Will
wasn't sure what that meant, so he stepped inside and found John
Taylor in the lobby. "Brother Taylor, what's happened?" he asked.

"The prosecution wanted a continuance, so Justice Smith delayed the hearing. He set our bail at $500 each. I don't think he
expected us to produce the money, but our friends pledged their
property, and we've all been freed for now."

"Are we all going back to Nauvoo, then?"

"Most are. But a few of us are staying with Joseph and Hyrum.
The justice informed us just now that they are about to be charged
with a second crime. The dissenters are claiming they committed
treason when they called up the Nauvoo Legion against the citizens
of Illinois."

"To *protect* ourselves from those fine citizens of Illinois. It's what
the governor told us to do."

"I know. But the judge can hold a man without bail on a treason
charge. I heard Governor Ford tell Joseph that it was a groundless
accusation, but he felt he couldn't interfere with the legal system.
For now, he thinks Joseph and Hyrum are safer in prison anyway, so
after supper they'll be escorted to the jail."

"What can we do?"

"Nothing, for now. You should ride back with the men from
the city council. They may need protection themselves. Willard
Richards and I, and two or three others, plan to stay in the jail with
Joseph and Hyrum. Joseph told me to send everyone else home.
You're in more danger out here than we shall be in the jail."

"I'll wait to see you safely installed in the jail, then."

"Will, there's nothing you can do. How can you take on a whole mob, if it should come to that?"

Will nodded and walked out the door, but he couldn't stand to think of riding off, only to learn that a mob had attacked as soon as Joseph and Hyrum were led outside. So he waited, and he watched as the Smith brothers, John Taylor, and Willard Richards, along with Dan Jones, Steven Markham, and John Fullmer, were marched to the jail. But the prisoners had no more than entered when one of the Carthage Greys turned to Will and said, "What is it you're looking for—a chance to die with Joe Smith?"

Will didn't answer, but several more men looked his way, and one of them said, "See this finger." He held his finger in the air. "It's itchin' to pull a trigger. I want me some Mormon blood. You might jist satisfy that itch if you don't get yerself out of town. And I mean *now*." He slowly raised his musket, pointing the muzzle toward Will.

Will said nothing. He turned and walked away. He went after his horse, and he did ride out of town. What he knew was that most of the men who had escorted Joseph to Carthage had left well ahead of him. He worried about riding the road alone at night with so many angry men about, so he found himself a quiet spot in a little copse of willow trees and slept on the ground. Very early the next morning, he set out again for Nauvoo.

• • •

Will had barely slept the last two nights. He was only half awake as Socks trudged along. When they crossed a little stream with a rocky bottom, he paid more attention, and then he looked up as the horse began to climb out of the little valley full of willow trees. When he heard a loud clap and saw a flash off to his right, he didn't know what had happened for a moment. But Socks suddenly hunched, took a staggering step, then dropped to her knees.

Will fell off to the left and rolled to stay out from under the horse. At the same moment he heard another loud report, this time from the other side, and something—by then he knew it was a musket ball—slapped into the dirt just a few inches from his leg. He rolled again and then clambered on his hands and knees toward the brush on the side of the trail. But as he did, he saw a man step out of the trees. Will stopped, looked up, and saw that it was Blake Samples. "Stop right thar," he said.

And then there was another voice, behind him. "We coulda killt ya if we wanted to, but we di'n't. But if you try to run, we won't miss nex' time."

It was George, of course. Will couldn't think what to do. He stayed on the ground, turning back only enough to see George, who was reloading his musket, driving a cartridge into the barrel with a ramrod. George raised the weapon then, pointing it toward Will.

Socks was snorting wildly and flailing her legs.

"Don' move atall, Lewis," George said. "I need to put yer horse out of her misery. I don't like to see a animal in pain like 'at." He laughed.

But he waited, and Will looked to see that Blake was pouring black powder into the pan of his flintlock. He took his time, inserted a paper cartridge into the barrel, and then withdrew his ramrod and drove the cartridge into the breech. Clearly, George wasn't about to fire again until he knew that Blake was ready to stop Will if he tried anything.

Will straightened up but stayed on his knees, and he turned enough to be able to glance toward either man. He tried to think of some way to escape, but the only direction he could run would be back across the stream, with his back to Blake, an easy target.

"I know what yer thinkin', but don't try it," George said. He stepped closer to the horse, aimed, and fired a ball into her head. There was a splash of blood from just over the animal's eye, and then all movement, all sound stopped.

George turned and glared at Will. "We thought about jist shootin' ya and lettin' that be the end of it, but it jist did'n' feel like it was quite anough, after the way you done me twice now. The first thing I'd like ya to do is to tell me how wrong you was to show me up the way ya done." He was pulling another cartridge from the box that hung on a strap around his shoulder. He tore it with his teeth and then poured the powder.

Will's mind was working. He hated the idea of asking forgiveness of these two, but he had to buy some time, and he had to get back to Liz and his boys somehow. He knew already that he would say whatever he had to say.

"So what is it ya want to tell me?" George's musket was ready now and aimed toward him. There was no way to make a charge on one of the men without being fired on from both directions.

"Listen, George, I still say we can talk about this. You insulted my wife once, and I know I lost my temper about that—and I wish I hadn't—but I think any man can understand that—"

"Thass not a good way to go on, Lewis. When a man has a gun pointin' at yer head, it's not good to argue with 'im. Get on with tellin' me how much ya regret what ya done."

"I do regret it, George. That's the honest truth. I lost my temper, and I know I embarrassed you, throwing you down that way. I should have turned the other cheek and let it go. It's something I'm trying to learn."

"He ain't beggin' ya, George," Blake said. "He's goin' on the way he allus do. I think he ought to break down and cry, tell ya' how sorrowful he is, maybe even kiss yer boots or somethin' like 'at."

"Thass right. Thass more what I was thinkin' too. Beg me a little, Lewis. Thass what I want to hear."

Will's anger was mounting, but he knew he had to keep control. He gripped his knees, looked down. He heard the birds in the willow trees, the water in the stream. He felt the steam in the air—felt it all without exactly knowing it—and sensed that life was going on outside himself, and he couldn't make the wrong move and lose his part in all that. "George, I beg you to let me live. As you know, I have two sons. They need me."

"What about gittin' out of Hancock County, the way I telled ya to do. Ya ready to do what I said?"

"Aye. I can do that."

"That ain't no promise. Yer allus tellin' me what a Christian man ya are. Promise in the name of yer Book of Mormon, that yull leave this place."

"All right. I'm willing to do that."

"Swear it."

"I swear I'll leave."

"Swear on yer book."

"We don't swear on the Book of Mormon, George. I'd rather leave Illinois with my family than go through any more of this. That's all I can tell you. If you'll let me go, I'll leave as soon as I get back to Nauvoo, and you won't ever see me again."

"What 'bout that, Blake? Do ya believe 'im now?"

Will glanced at Blake, saw him grin. Will wanted more than anything to get his chance with these men, to fight them both without those muskets. But he had to save himself, for Liz's sake. He had to hold his temper for once in his life.

"I don' b'lieve 'im one bit, George. I say it's time he kisst them boot of yers. One nice big kiss on each boot."

George laughed, making a sound like gravel rolling out of his throat. "It do seem right to me. Crawl on over here, Lewis. Tell me how much ya want to live one more time, and then pucker up and kiss my boots."

Will stared at him for a time, watched George grin, his shaggy teeth showing through his beard. "All you want to do is humiliate me, and then you'll kill me anyway. If that's what you have in mind, just go ahead and pull the trigger right now."

"No, Lewis. I telled ya afore, I don' like ta kill a man. Not unless I hafta. You kiss my boots and promise that yer leavin' the state, and that'll be the end of it."

"Unless we change our minds here in a minute," Blake said, and he and his brother joined in a huge laugh.

But Will knew by then what he would do. He bent forward and crawled on all fours past Socks and over to George. He stopped a few feet away and raised his head. "I'm sorry all these things happened between us," he said. "I'm willing to humble myself before you to save my life. I ask you to spare me, and I promise to move away from here. And I don't mind kissing your boots to prove that I appreciate your kindness in letting me live. But you have to promise me that you won't let me kiss your boots and then shoot me anyway."

Blake and George were both roaring. "The way I see it, you ain't in no position to be askin' for any promises. But I like the way ya made it sound—like ya mean it and everythin'. You kiss them boots, and then jist see how it all turns out."

"What about *my* boots, Lewis?" Blake bellowed. "I think ya oughta slobber a little over me, too."

Will was quite sure he knew where this was going. They would never let him go. They would do everything to rub his nose in the ground, and then they would kill him. "I'll kiss your boots, too, Blake. Anything. Anything you ask of me. Just let me live."

But by then, George seemed to see the obvious danger. "Naw. No boot kissin', Lewis. I ain't lettin' ya get that close to me. I think we need to do ya the way we done your mare. We need to put ya out of yer misery."

Will raised up a little more. "Did you know someone is traveling with me?" he asked.

"I know the opposite. We watched ya leave and we followed ya. We saw ya go into them woods and we moved on ahead and waited 'til we could get the drop on ya when mornin' come."

"Think again. I hear horses coming. Look up the trail."

George only glanced, but in that instant, Will dove at his feet, grabbed both boots, and yanked with all his strength. George landed hard on his back with a great grunt, and Will rolled quickly to one side just as a ball stung him in the backside. But Will was up quickly and had hold of George's musket, which had dropped to the ground. George was struggling to get up, but Will was too quick for him. He swung the musket by the barrel and bashed the man in the side of the head with the stock. George dropped back to the ground like a dead man.

Will was turning by then. Blake had taken off running for the trees, not having tried to load his musket again. Will plunged through underbrush and caught up with him quickly. He swung the musket again, brought it down on the top of Blake's head, the thud sickening and hollow sounding, and the shock of the blow shooting through Will's arms. But he had seen all this in his mind, and he knew what he had to do. He wasn't going to stop and kill these men—if they weren't dead already. He was only going to get away, as fast as he could. He ran back to the trail and caught a glance of George rolled onto his side, his bloody hands grasping the side of his head.

Will knew that he had to get across the open prairie as fast as he could. If George and Blake roused themselves, they surely had horses tied up somewhere, and they would come after him.

He ran hard for a time, found another shallow valley with a stream, and then ran in the water northward, hoping to leave no trail, hoping to find another way across the prairie. He had many miles to go. What he didn't know was how bad his wound was and whether he was losing a lot of blood. He only knew that his backside was aflame with pain.

He ran in the stream for maybe half a mile, and then he slipped into the bracken under some cottonwood trees and let himself rest for a few minutes. He finally twisted around as best he could and saw blood on his trousers, but not as much as he had expected. So he didn't worry about treating the wound. He knew he had to make time while he could, before the wound began to cause him more trouble. He set off across an open field of grass, heading west. The grass was deep enough that he could drop down if he saw anyone, and someone looking for him out there would have a hard time picking out the spot. But the going wasn't easy, and he wondered how long he would last in the heat.

What Will was also thinking was that George and Blake were surely in bad shape. He had hit them with a viciousness that he had hardly known he was capable of. He heard the sounds again, felt those thudding blows. He knew he had wanted, for a moment, to kill them, but he hoped now that he hadn't done that. He was in great danger from them, not only today but in the days ahead, but he knew what Joseph had told him. He didn't want to be the one to start the killing. Where would it end?

Will walked all day. He rested each time he found water and cover but kept pushing himself as much as he could. The pain in his backside kept getting worse, but he told himself he had to get home as soon as he could. If George and Blake were able to ride, they may head straight to his house. But it was well into the afternoon when he made it to Jesse's place, and he knew he had to stop long enough to get some help.

Jesse and Ellen dressed his wound. The ball had cut a swath through the muscle, but it hadn't penetrated very deep. The blood had stopped flowing after a time. Ellen cleaned the wound with soap and water and then wrapped it in muslin cloth. By then Will was thinking ahead to his arrival at home. He had to be ready if the Samples brothers showed up—or even the county constable—but he also had to avoid alarming Liz and Jacob any more than necessary. He asked whether Jesse had a pair of trousers he could borrow— ones that weren't torn and bloody. Jesse didn't have any, but he ran to Benbows' house, and Brother Benbow returned with a pair Will could wear. He then borrowed Jesse's horse even though the pain of riding was much worse than that of walking.

When Will finally made it home, late in the day, Liz rushed to him, embraced him. "Oh, Will," she said, "I've been scared I'd never see you again."

Will understood that. He held Liz for a long time, and then he picked up Jacob, who had wrapped his arms around Will's legs. The pain in his wound was throbbing, but he wasn't going to bring that up yet. "It was bad over there," he said, "but it was worse to wonder what might be happening here."

"Is Joseph home now? Is he—"

"No, Liz. He and Hyrum are in the Carthage Jail. The governor is promising that they'll be protected, but I'm not sure he can make good on that."

"Sit down. I'll get you something to eat. But tell me everything."

Will didn't sit down, but he related the story briefly, told about arriving in Carthage late at night and about the Carthage Greys shouting insults at Joseph. He decided not to describe all the hatred and anger. And he said nothing of George and Blake.

He kept watching her, though, and he could see that she was starting to comprehend the reality of the situation. "Can't the Legion break Joseph and Hyrum out of the jail?" she asked.

"The Legion doesn't have many guns now, Liz. And Joseph keeps telling everyone to trust in the law. I don't see how anyone can trust Governor Ford, but Joseph says we have to. We can't start a war."

But Will couldn't stop thinking about the things that had been going through his head all day. If one or both of the Samples brothers were well enough, they would be coming after him before long. Maybe he had to keep the promise, even if he had made it under duress, to leave the county soon. The last thing he wanted was to give up the Zion he had worked so hard to become part of, but he also had to protect Liz and the boys. He had to think clearly, and yet, he was feeling weak enough to collapse.

CHAPTER 21

Will knew that he shouldn't say any more to Liz. She was frightened enough. But the truth was, things were ever so much worse than she could imagine. Fresh in Will's mind was what Brother Benbow had told him. Brother Benbow hadn't said much as Will described what had happened to him and what he had done to the Samples brothers, or even when he described what was going on in Carthage. But Will watched him, and the man looked broken.

"I thought we might find peace here," Brother Benbow had said, "but the Lord's not finished with us. We have more we have to learn."

"What is it yer expecting?" Jesse asked.

"I'm thinking, no matter what the Saints have been through before, we haven't seen the worst yet. I hope it's not true, but it's what I feel today."

Will had come away from Carthage feeling the same way. He had seen the hatred in the faces of those men in Carthage, seen it up close in George and Blake Samples. There was no way that all this could end well. He had saved his life and gotten away from

324

his attackers, but he had to think about taking his wife and at least crossing the river, maybe moving on to St. Louis or even farther away. Even if the Saints remained in Zion, he doubted that he could.

What Will hadn't expected was to hear Brother Benbow say, "We've brought much of this on ourselves. We didn't enter into friendships here. We came in and took over—or at least that's the way the old citizens see it. And we weren't humble about it. Even Joseph himself railed at Tom Sharp and made him an enemy. Maybe there was no avoiding that, but we all could have tried more than we did. We strutted our army about and we puffed out our chests. We showed our strength when we might have shown our goodness. I'm not sure we've learned yet to be followers of Jesus Christ."

These had been the hardest words for Will to hear. He had just described the crushing blows he had delivered to his assailants, per-haps with a little satisfaction—or at least relief that he had saved himself. But he wondered now. There had never been much hope of changing George Samples's mind, but if he had held back, hadn't fought the man the first time, maybe things never would have gotten so out of hand.

But Will was standing before Liz now, still trying to think what he could say to her.

"What's happened to you, Will?" she asked. "You have no color in your face. And you won't look at me—not straight on."

Will nodded, tried to think of the right words. "I was wounded over there—just slightly." He tried to laugh. "That's why I can't sit down."

"Oh, Will, what do you mean? What did they do to you?"

"Someone took a shot at me, but he nearly missed. It only took a slice from my backside. It's nothing serious."

"What aren't you telling me, Will? What happened? Was anyone killed?"

He took her in his arms again. "I do need to tell you some things, Liz. I'm not certain what we should do just now. We may need to leave Nauvoo."

She pulled back. "Leave Nauvoo? Why?"

So Will told her, as simply as he could, what had happened to him on the road back from Carthage.

When he finished his story, Liz asked, "How badly were they hurt?"

"I'm not sure. I know George was alive when I ran past him. But his head was bleeding, and he wasn't trying to get up."

"But by now, they must be on their way here."

"Maybe. Maybe they bled to death. Maybe they're in no condition to go anywhere. I just don't know."

Liz was the one who looked pale now. She was staring at him, her mouth open a little, her eyes full of fear.

"Liz, I had no choice. I begged them; I promised to leave; I tried to reason with them. But I don't think they were going to let me go. I think they followed me so they could kill me. They just wanted to humiliate me before they did it."

"I understand that, Will. You didn't do anything wrong. But if they're not dead, they'll never stop until they get revenge. And if they are dead, and someone figures out who did it, you'll be accused of murder."

What Will knew, and didn't say, was that it would not be hard to trace the incident back to him. Socks was lying dead at the scene, and he had left his saddle, too. "I know all that, Liz. Brother Benbow told me to come here and stay here. He's going to talk to General Rich. He thinks some of the Escort Brigade will be willing to guard the house."

"For how long? The rest of our lives?"

"That's why we might have to leave. I'm sorry."

"No, don't say that." Liz tucked herself back against him. "You're alive. You did what you had to do, and you came back to me. If we have to go, we'll go. I prayed for two days that you would come back to me, and I won't ask for more than that."

· · ·

The evening was very long. Liz redressed the wound, which looked worse to her than Will had made it sound. She also knew he was in much more pain than he was admitting, but he wouldn't lie down and rest. He kept watching out the windows, listening, holding a pistol in his hand.

Poor little Jacob kept clinging to him, obviously frightened and nervous. Will finally picked his son up and put his gun down. He talked to the boy, tried to make him laugh. He didn't have much success at that, but when Jacob finally fell asleep in his arms, Liz could see that Will was exhausted. She took Jacob from him and put him in bed.

It was still not dark outside, but Liz said, "You need to rest, Will. Lie down and go to sleep if you can. I'll keep watch."

Will didn't answer for a time. He kept switching from the east window to the one on the south. But finally he told her, "I think both brothers must have been hurt badly enough that they couldn't come after me. They may not dare to ride into Nauvoo right now anyway."

"I think that's right. Please rest before you faint."

"I'm not going to faint," Will said, but he did go to the bed and lie facedown. As he did, he allowed himself a little groan, and Liz knew that every move was hurting him. She quickly checked on her boys, and then she went back to the windows and watched as Will had done, making only a crack in the curtains so she wouldn't be seen from outside.

After a time, Will was breathing steadily, and she hoped he was asleep. But it didn't help Liz to have time to think. She had tried to sound brave for Will, but her mind was full of disjointed thoughts. What would happen now? Where would they go? How would they start over somewhere? What would happen to her babies? How could the Lord call them to Zion and then allow everything be taken away from them?

The light was finally fading, and Liz was still watching, beginning to believe that no one was coming, when suddenly she saw a movement outside. "Will," she whispered, "there's someone coming on a horse. He—"

Will was suddenly on his feet.

But by then Liz could see that it wasn't one of the Samples brothers. It was a man she didn't know. He had ridden directly to the house on a big, dark horse, and now he was dismounting. Will was next to her by then. "It's Jacob Backenstos," he said. He went to the door and opened it. "Hello, Mr. Backenstos," he said. "Come in."

• • •

Will had met Jacob Backenstos, had talked to him on a couple of occasions. He was the clerk of the county court in Carthage and widely known as a friend to Joseph Smith—and to the Saints. Some of the old citizens called him a Jack Mormon. He was running now for the state legislature, but Will didn't think this was a campaign visit. He saw how serious the man looked.

"Hello, Mr. Lewis," he said. "Could I talk to you for just a few minutes?"

"Of course. Come inside."

Mr. Backenstos was dressed only in his shirtsleeves, no hat, and even at that, his face and his shirt were wet with perspiration. "Hot night," he said. "Hello, Mrs. Lewis."

"Sit down," Will said.

"No, that's all right. I'll only be a few minutes."

Will nodded and waited. Mr. Backenstos was not a sheriff. He wouldn't be the one to arrest Will, if that was what was coming.

"Do you know Blake and George Samples from down near Warsaw?"

"Yes, I do." Will made a quick decision to say no more than he had to. He wanted to know what Mr. Backenstos knew.

"How is it you know them?"

"I cut a road down close to their place. They stopped and talked to me a couple of times."

"Was there any trouble between you?"

"What kind of trouble?"

"Listen, Will, I know what kind of men they are. I'm not here because I think they're innocent victims. But someone found them out on the Carthage Road this morning, both of them hurt very badly. They were taken back into Carthage. The bigger one, Blake, has a broken skull, and the doc said he may not live. The other one is down for a while, but he should recover in time. He's the one who's saying it was you who hit him over the head with a gun. He says you ambushed him and his brother and knocked 'em both out. He says you wanted to steal their horses."

Will was shaking his head. "So why are you here? Do you believe them?"

"No, I don't. But George says he's going to file a charge against you, and if that happens, they'll be sending Constable Wilson over to arrest you. I had to come to Nauvoo on other matters, but I wanted to let you know what might be coming."

"Mr. Backenstos, those men followed me and shot my horse out from under me. They threatened to—"

"I don't want to know anything else. But what you're saying makes a lot more sense than the story George Samples is telling. I'm going to talk to the man, when he can think a little better, and warn him that he wouldn't be wise to file a false complaint. But you know the mood over there in Carthage right now. I'm the only man who's likely to believe you and not him."

"What should I do?"

"I'll talk him out of filing the charge if I can."

"They wounded me, Mr. Backenstos—tore a hunk of flesh out of me." He glanced at Liz, who was looking worried, her arms folded tight, her lips pressed together. "Do they want to claim that I shot my own horse, and shot myself in the backside? It was George's musket I used to—"

"Don't say anything else. I'll remind George about the dead horse, and I'll tell him it looks like maybe he was the one who started the trouble. I'll warn him that he could be charged himself for trying to kill a man."

"All right."

"But if the word gets out, what he's saying, it might be other folks, not the law, coming after you. I would stay close to home for now."

"I'm wondering if we should cross the river and get away from here."

"I don't know. I don't know what's going to happen with Joseph and Hyrum in the jail. That's got everyone's attention for now. These firebrands down in Warsaw talk about war, but I don't see them marching into Nauvoo to face the Legion. I saw some men out on the road with guns. They said they're guarding your place tonight. If I was you, I'd get some rest and stay here in Nauvoo for now. I'll see if I can get this thing to blow over."

"But George and Blake Samples will never let it pass."

"That might be right. But you don't need to fear them for now. They're not in any condition for a fight. They may not want to take you on, ever." Mr. Backenstos laughed. "Someday I want to hear how you took on both of them and did that much damage—but don't tell me now. I don't want a judge to ask me what I know."

So Mr. Backenstos left, and Will breathed a little easier. But he knew he was facing an evil that would never go away. Maybe Brother Benbow was right. The Saints had made their mistakes. But how could Will have placated a man like George Samples? And there were many more like him, most of them gathered in Carthage right now. Will saw little hope for better days ahead.

Will was hurting, but he had had very little sleep in the last three days, and he now knew there were guards outside. So he went ahead and allowed himself to fall asleep. When he awoke in the morning, the pain in his wound had eased a little, but his trip to the privy was awkward and painful, and by the time he returned, the pain was as bad as ever. The trouble was, he couldn't sit down and he didn't want to lie on his face all day. He tried to take care of some chores outside but found he couldn't bend, couldn't manage to do much of anything. All the while, he was almost frantic to know what was happening in Carthage. Finally he told Liz that he needed to see what he could find out. He walked down through the woods to the Mansion House.

Will felt the strange change in Nauvoo. Here and there, standing in the shade, were little pockets of people, talking, but this place had always been busy, full of building and doing. Now, everyone seemed only to be waiting.

Robert Massengale, a man Will knew from the Legion, hailed

Will and asked what he had experienced in Carthage, but Will didn't
have the heart to say very much. Brother Massengale was standing
in the shade of a shabby shed, near the edge of his property, and
near the street. "I have things to do," he said, "but there seems no
reason to do them. All I can think is that a mob is coming and our
weapons are gone. Why hoe our gardens if we'll never have a chance
to harvest them?"

"We'll just have to trust in the Lord," Will said. "We can't pray
for the best and expect the worst."

Brother Massengale nodded. "I know that's right. But I can't
seem to change how I feel. If they kill Joseph, I don't know what will
become of us."

"So let's keep praying," Will said, and he walked on down the
street, but he didn't claim that Joseph wouldn't be killed.

Will found Brother Clayton at the Mansion House. "I won't
bother you long," he said, "but I'm wondering what you've heard
from Carthage."

"What's happened to you, Will?"

Will had tried not to limp as he walked into the room. He stood
with his hat in his hand. "Nothing. I'm fine."

Clayton sat back in his chair and looked up at Will. He looked
deathly tired. "A rider brought a letter from Joseph. He still trusts
Governor Ford. He thinks we should go on about our business and
not expect any trouble."

"Do you think the Lord is guiding Joseph in this?" Will asked.

"I don't know, Will. He sounded a little as though he wanted to
say good-bye. He said he wasn't worried because he felt justified in
his actions. It's as though he's answering to a higher power, not to
the men who will try him."

"I know that. It's the same way he talked to me."

The two men took a long look at one another, and Will felt the same gloom in Brother Clayton that he had been seeing in everyone else.

Outside the Mansion House, Will spotted General Rich and some of the other men from the Escort Brigade. Will greeted Brother Rich and then asked him what word *he* had heard from Carthage.

"The brethren are all right so far, last we heard," he said. "But the governor sent word he's heading over here."

"Why?"

"At first he said he was going to search every house in town to find out if we've got any counterfeiting equipment, the way all the newspapers have been claiming."

"So he believes Tom Sharp, I guess."

"Well, maybe. Mostly, he plays both sides, to convince everyone he's hearing their complaints. But now he's changed his mind about the search. He's decided he only wants our people to gather up so he can 'address' us, as he put it."

"Address us?" Will said. "Why?"

"I'm sure it's to warn us not to raise an army to go after Joseph. I just hope he didn't abandon Carthage so he can claim, once it's all over with, that he wasn't there when the mob attacked."

Will had no interest in hearing Ford's speech, and he didn't feel well enough to stand around very long—or to walk home and back—so he went home to Liz and stayed away from the flats that afternoon. Later, he learned from Nelly what had happened. Ford had stood where Joseph had, on the floor of Porter Rockwell's half-built building across the street from the Mansion House, and he had scolded Church members "like naughty schoolchildren," as Nelly had put it. "He told us to put up our guns and swords, and not to think about damagin' the property of those fine Law brothers and all the rest of them that caused all this trouble. To hear him tell it, armies is comin' in from ev'ry road to stop us if we even think of startin' a fight. He even made us hold up our hands to promise we won't start no trouble. We all raised our hands, but I wanted to yell some questions about what the other folks in this county is promisin'."

Will knew very well what those people were promising. He had heard their evil vows. But he didn't say that to Nelly.

•　•　•

That evening, Thursday, June 27, after the little boys were in bed, Will and Liz walked outside. They stood in the clearing and looked out toward the setting sun that was filtering through the trees and turning some feathery clouds yellow and pink.

Liz realized that something was wrong, but it took her some time to name what it was. "Will," she said, "the birds have stopped singing. And the locusts are quiet."

"It's the heat," he said.

Liz wondered. Birds were not as noisy this time of year, especially late in the day, but she had never heard the woods so silent. The locusts never stopped on summer nights. Somewhere in the distance, a dog began to wail, as though in grief. Will heard it too, and he looked at her. She saw the concern in his face.

"Something's wrong," Liz said.

"Maybe not. It's just . . . quiet. And hot."

But that wasn't what Liz was feeling. Something had happened, and she thought Will knew it too. Another dog had taken up the howl, and then another, and the plaintive sound continued all through the night.

Liz couldn't sleep that night. Maybe it was the eerie sound of those dogs—and the weighty feel of the air—but she wondered whether *anyone* was asleep. The Prophet was in the grasp of an enemy that seemed unwilling to accept anything but the extermination of the Saints. Joseph was putting trust in the law, but what would happen if he and Hyrum went before a jury of Hancock County men, and what if that jury *dared* to proclaim them innocent? Would the mobs let Joseph and Hyrum walk from the courthouse and return to Nauvoo? Would they let the Saints go on with their lives? There seemed no possibility of that. So what would happen? Would the Saints go west somewhere, as Joseph had talked about lately? How could they survive in a wilderness? If they gathered in Oregon or the Rocky Mountains, how long before populations built up again and all the old hatreds repeated themselves?

Liz thought of Ledbury, thought of her house, her family, her simple life. She had given it all up for Zion, but not for wandering in the desert.

Toward morning, Liz finally slept a little. But she sat up straight in bed when she heard a wild shout at her door: "They've killed Joseph and Hyrum!"

Will jumped up and ran from the bedroom and out to the door. But he turned back, shaking his head. "He's gone, whoever it was," he said.

Liz had followed Will to the bedroom door and was not far from him, but she couldn't make out his features in the dim light, couldn't see his eyes. He limped toward her and took her in his arms. Liz clung to him. She tried to tell herself that it wasn't so, that it was rumor—the kind of thing that might spread around at such a time. But she didn't believe it. She had heard the assurance in the man's voice. And the truth was, she had known something terrible had happened the night before, had known it all night. She pressed her head to Will's chest and began to sob.

"Listen to me, Liz," Will said. "We'll be all right somehow. We will."

But Liz didn't want to hear that. She knew that nothing would ever be the same. Everything the Saints had tried to build in Nauvoo felt meaningless, lost. She tried to stop herself, tried to accept this new pain the way she had accepted the others, but all she saw ahead was darkness, and her response was to cry all the harder.

Daniel had been crying since the first shout at the door, but Liz had not let the sound register until now. She knew she had to go to him—was even relieved to have something she had to do. She slipped away, picked him up, and held him close to her. She needed to nurse her baby, protect him, keep him safe. And she needed to comfort little Jacob, who was grasping her leg now, obviously frightened. These were the things that made sense to her now, but she wondered what the day would bring, what attacks might follow, whether anything would ever feel normal again—and how many more might die before the mob was finished.

Will got dressed, but he couldn't think what to do. What was going through his mind was that the war had only just begun, and now he would have to defend his family. The pain in his wound was throbbing now, after his quick run to the door, but that was not important. His wife and two little boys could be in danger, and he would have to keep them safe.

Warren Baugh came by before long. He had learned a few of the details. The murders had happened the day before—around five o'clock in the afternoon—at the Carthage Jail. John Taylor was badly wounded. Willard Richards had also been in the jail when it had been attacked, but he was all right.

Will knew that two good men had died—men he loved—but so much more than two lives had been taken away. Will and Liz had come to Nauvoo because of a prophet, because of Zion, because of the restored gospel, and now it wasn't clear whether any of that would go forward. It was possible the Church itself would die. There seemed no doubt that mobs would come next, and the Saints may well be scattered. Joseph Smith had always been the strength of the Church. His vision, his authority, were the forces that kept the Church together, made the connection from heaven to earth. There were fine men in the Church, great men, but they weren't the Prophet. No one galvanized the membership as he did; no one inspired them as he did.

· · ·

Friday was the strangest day of Will's life. He kept going back to Liz, holding her, and each time she would cry while Will fought against his own tears. He wanted to stay with Liz, but he felt crazy to know how this had happened and what to expect now.

"I want to talk to Brother Clayton," Will finally told Liz. "Will you be all right if—"

"Yes, go. But find out what we're to do. Find out if mobs are coming."

"All right. I'll see if anyone knows."

But Will was unable to find William Clayton. Everyone seemed to know something, and at the same time, certain information contradicted what others were saying. Willard Richards had written to Emma, and the content of the letter was being quoted widely. Brother Richards seemed to think a band of men from Missouri had attacked the jail and might be heading for Nauvoo next. But so far there was no sign of mobs moving toward the city.

Everywhere around him, Will found a kind of grief that he had never witnessed before. Everyone looked the same—overcome with sadness and clearly turning inward to ask themselves what would come next. Time and again, he heard people say, "The Prophet. They've taken the Prophet." He saw burly men say the words and break down in tears; he saw women embrace other sisters, cling to one another, and sob. And he knew what they were feeling. No matter how dangerous the situation had become lately, it always had seemed that Joseph would be protected by heavenly power.

Word came after a time that the bodies of Joseph and Hyrum were being brought back to Nauvoo and would arrive early in the afternoon. Will walked home, and then he and Liz walked to Mulholland to wait—with hundreds and gradually thousands of others. It was after three o'clock before the sad procession moved down the street toward the temple. An escort of eight state militia soldiers preceded a pair of white horses. The horses were pulling a wagon covered over with limbs and greenery, which Will understood was to shade the coffin. The rough wood of the pine box became visible under the brush as the wagon neared. Will assumed that Joseph was in the first wagon. It was driven by a man Will recognized: Mr. Hamilton, the proprietor of the Hamilton Hotel where Joseph and Hyrum had stayed in Carthage.

Just as the wagon passed, the reality of it all struck Will. His friend Joseph was in that box. Joseph was not just a Church leader, he was a man Will had laughed with, offered to pull sticks with. Joseph had believed in Will, had called him on a mission, and Will had looked into his blue eyes and had known that he was a prophet of God. He thought of Joseph's big hand clamping down on his shoulder, pulling him back when Will had wanted to go after the enemy. And now his body was lying in a pine box, all that life simply gone.

Will had been holding on since that morning, trying to be strong for Liz and the boys. But something broke in him now. He tried to hide it all, to gulp down the sobs, but he choked, and then he couldn't hold back. He was holding little Jacob, and he pulled him tight against his face and cried into the little boy's chest. Jacob kept patting Will on his head, his cheek, as though to console him.

Will only cried harder. And when Liz wrapped one arm around the two of them, still holding Daniel in the other, they all cried together.

Will glanced up to see the other wagon with the same covering, the same kind of coffin. This one was driven by William Smith, Joseph and Hyrum's brother, who looked broken himself. Will thought of Hyrum, who had consoled Will when Mary Ann had died. He thought of Hyrum's wife and children, thought how much pain was compounding itself today.

But Will had to get control. He knew he couldn't worry Jacob this way. "Daddy's all right," he said. "Everything's all right."

He turned and watched the procession as it continued down Mulholland. People stood quietly, their hats off, watching and then bowing their heads after the wagons passed. Some joined the procession and followed the wagons. A man turned to Will and said, "Apostle Richards will speak at the Mansion House as soon as the coffins arrive." The man's eyes looked vacant, but they were red from crying. He was someone Will had seen before, but he didn't know his name. Still, he felt a kinship, as he did with everyone he saw.

"I don't know what Brother Richards can tell us that will make any difference," Will said.

"It doesn't matter what he says. It never should have happened. I don't know why God has abandoned us. I don't understand anything anymore."

"We'll be all right. We'll . . . move forward."

"I can't do it. I can't start over again," the brother said, and tears spilled onto his cheeks. He walked away.

Will turned to Liz. "Do you want to follow the wagons down to the Mansion House?" he asked.

But that was a mile and a half, or more. "No, Will," she said. "I need to get the boys out of this heat—and me, too. You shouldn't walk that far either."

"I can walk well enough. And I do want to hear what our leaders have to say."

"Then go. I know you want to be there. Are you all right? I know what Joseph meant to you. You were—"

"Let's not think about that. We have to . . . make the best of things."

But the look on Liz's face worried Will. She looked as hopeless as the man he had just talked to—as hopeless as Will felt inside.

Will didn't follow the procession. He walked back along Rich Street and carried Jacob, who fell asleep in his arms. Leaving Liz and the little boys at home, he walked through the woods to the flats, arriving before the wagons did.

He watched from a distance as the wagons reached the Mansion House and the coffins were carried inside. Willard Richards struggled to heft his weight up the ladder onto the platform where others had spoken lately. Once the members had gathered close, he spoke in measured, careful language, like the physician he was. He told the people that he had promised Governor Ford that the Saints would not seek retribution. He asked everyone to think carefully before they acted, and then he asked for their sustaining voice to promise to preserve the peace. No one seemed to disagree with his sentiment, but Will found that there was nothing consoling in what he said. Will wanted the Spirit to speak peace to his soul, but he felt no solace.

What Will had heard by now was that while the Saints were grieving, word had spread through the county that the Nauvoo Legion was on the march. Panic had spread through all the towns, but especially Warsaw. Thomas Sharp had put out a sheet that in a hasty paragraph urged the citizens of Warsaw to prepare for attack, and he invited men from other towns to hasten to help them. He had also explained what had happened at the jail: Mormons had

attacked the jail, he claimed, and the guards had been forced to protect themselves. Will was almost certain that Sharp was behind the
attack on Joseph, and his claims were unbearable to read. It was one
thing to claim the murder of Joseph and Hyrum as somehow justifi-
able, but it was quite another to invent such an egregious lie.

On Saturday the Saints gathered again at the Mansion House.
A long line extended well up Main Street. All day the people waited
patiently to walk through the house and view Joseph and Hyrum,
lying in repose. The two had been placed in caskets with glass windows on top, hinged but kept closed, and those who walked by
could look down through the glass and see the faces of the men
they loved. Joseph looked pale but natural; Hyrum's face had been
mutilated by a ball that had penetrated just to the side of his nose.
Something was burning in the room, certainly to mask the smell,
but the odor of death was still what Will would always remember.
He carried Jacob, but he didn't let him look, and he only glanced
at the faces himself. He remembered instead the good men he had
ridden with at the beginning of the week. That was the memory he
wanted to keep.

As Will and Liz were leaving, Will glanced into the parlor of the
house to see Lucy Smith, her face pale, her eyes fixed, and Emma
bent over her, saying something in a soft voice. Will had never seen
such a picture of grief. But it was young Frederick who touched
Will's heart. The boy was only eight—old enough to understand
what death meant, and yet too young to grasp why his father had
been taken. He was standing near his grandmother, staring straight
ahead, as much confusion as sorrow in his eyes. Will had seen the
boy with his father the previous winter, both of them out sliding on
the ice on the frozen river. It was that sort of thing that he was surely
missing already, that kind of father.

Thousands passed through the house. The procession continued all day until an end had to be called, and a funeral was held in the old grove west of the temple. W. W. Phelps gave a fine tribute to the Prophet and the Patriarch, and he said that the Church would go forward. The work of the Restoration had not ended. The words were easy to assert—and just as easy to doubt—but Will was comforted by the calm confidence that he heard.

As the funeral was still in session, horse-drawn wagons passed the assembled congregation. Everyone watched as the coffins were hauled up the hill and past the temple. They were heading in the direction of the cemetery east of town. It was a moment of final grief, and Will could feel the pain in the air, hear people crying. But even though the worst had happened, Will's breath came a little easier as he realized that the Saints were not in a panic, not being attacked, not running for their lives. Maybe Zion wasn't lost.

CHAPTER 22

President Crowe opened the door to his office, looked out, and spotted Jeff. "Come on in, Brother Lewis," he said. "Thanks for waiting."

Jeff shook the stake president's hand and stepped into his office. It was April now and a perfect day outside. Jeff had helped Abby get William strapped into his car seat and then had told her to drive home and he would walk. As he'd waited in the hall, he had become increasingly curious to know why the president had asked to see him.

"So what's your situation now, Brother Lewis?" President Crowe asked. "Are you going to be here a while yet, or will you be leaving?"

"We might be here quite a while, President. My job's working out quite well."

President Crowe smiled and nodded. "The Lord's been listening to your bishop's prayers," he said. "I know he's really hoping that you and Abby will stay here forever. I feel the same way."

"Well, it's been great for us to be here. We've enjoyed teaching together."

344 · DEAN HUGHES

President Crowe let his eyes slip upwards as he smiled. Jeff knew immediately that everything was about to change. But the president only said, "My daughter keeps telling me how much she and the other young people in your class love the two of you. She told me that her dream in life is to find a husband like you—and have a marriage like you and Abby have."

That touched Jeff more than he wanted to let on. He looked down at his hands and said, "I'm not sure Abby would recommend me quite so highly. Those kids in the class only see me at my best."

"Well . . . that's true for all of us. But you've been a blessing to them."

Jeff didn't really know President Crowe all that well. He knew his family somewhat better. The president always seemed a pleasant, thoughtful man. He had dark hair that was graying a little, quiet eyes, and a calm way of speaking. One thing Will loved about him was that he seemed to remember everyone—or at least he had always called Jeff by name since the first time they had met.

"Your baby is looking great," President Crowe said. "I think the whole ward has adopted him. Melanie comes home from your Sunday School class talking about little William every week—and how she got a chance to hold him."

"I don't know how we could have received more help or support—from the entire ward. That's one of the reasons we want to stay." And that was certainly true. Jeff did want to stay in Nauvoo. It was only his job that he still had reservations about.

President Crowe sat back and folded his arms. "I know you like teaching with your wife," he said, "but we've decided it's time to reorganize the elders quorum. Yesterday, we called Malcolm McCord to serve as president. Malcolm talked things over with Bishop Harrison, and this morning the bishop submitted your name to serve as Malcolm's first counselor. Would you be willing to serve in that position?"

"Sure. But would I have to give up the Sunday School class?"

The president laughed. "I talked to your bishop about that. He thinks it might be good to have Abby teach by herself—and step out from under your shadow just a little."

"I think she's done that already. The kids in the class absolutely love her. But I do talk too much. It probably would be good for her to know that she had the whole lesson to herself. Would it hurt anything if I still went to class with her, though? I'll miss those kids."

"I think I'd let her be on her own for a few weeks. Just let her establish herself as the teacher, and then, if you wanted to go in sometimes, that might be good. I still want our young people to have couples like you as their role models."

"Actually, that's better. I can take William during that time, and then she won't have that distraction. That'll help her more than anything."

"I think that's right." But the president still had his arms folded, was still watching Jeff. "What about serving under Malcolm? Are you all right with that?"

"Of course. He's my best buddy."

"That's what I understand. But Malcolm told your bishop that *you* should be the president. He thinks you're more of a leader than he is. He says you're a teacher and speaker, and he's just a working man."

"That sounds like Malcolm. But he's got it wrong. Malc's the best guy I know. He's perfect for the job. All the guys in our quorum respect him—and the truth is, they consider me a bag of hot air. I spend most of my time in quorum meetings telling myself to shut up."

"So you don't have any trouble playing second fiddle to a guy who isn't nearly so well educated as you are?"

"Here's what you need to know, President. Malc's actually smarter than I am, and he knows the ward a lot better. He's really reliable, too. He'll be better than I could ever be."

President Crowe leaned forward. He looked more relaxed now. "You're too humble, Jeff," he said. "I think, at first, your bishop wasn't quite sure how to take you. But he tells me that you're a solid man. He said that when you spoke in sacrament meeting, you bore a strong testimony and at the same time you raised questions that made people think. We need that."

"Well, I hope so. But I won't try to dominate Malcolm, if that's what you're worried about."

"Malcolm's the one who thought you might have some doubts about him."

"I'll tell you what Malcolm is, President. He's good. He'll always be ahead of me in that department."

"He is good, Brother Lewis. But don't underrate yourself." He nodded, seemed to think for a time. "Here's the other thing I'm wondering. Bishop Harrison told me about all the work you two are doing on your homes. Will you be able to find time for a busy calling like this?"

"We'll just have to put first things first. But our projects are winding down a little, so we should be all right. Besides, I know how much time Bishop Harrison puts into his calling. If we elders do our job right, we can take some of the pressure off him."

"I'm glad you said that, Jeff. Like most bishops, Bishop Harrison has a tendency to take care of too many things himself—family problems and all those kinds of things—but his first priority is always supposed to be to the youth of the ward. Your presidency can take care of a lot of things he's doing now and give him more time with the youth."

"To tell you the truth, President, that sounds exciting. I need to feel like I'm serving others—the way I did on my mission—and not thinking quite so much about myself all the time."

President Crowe was nodding again, looking pleased. "I've been worried about this call, Brother Lewis, but now I see the inspiration in it. We have another counselor to call today, and then we will make this change next Sunday in your elders quorum meeting."

Jeff saw inspiration in the call too. He had thought for a long time that a ward should be a little section of Zion, and this was the best opportunity he could imagine to help that happen.

Jeff walked home, up Mulholland past all the little stores and businesses, most of which were closed on Sunday. He loved the small-town feel of Nauvoo. Everyone he saw along the street—even passing in cars—waved at him, whether they knew him or not. He turned south on Warsaw and walked past the Methodist church and down through a little valley with a creek at the bottom. The woods had turned all shades of green in the last few weeks. In people's yards, fruit trees were blossoming, pink and white, and birds were setting up a noisy chatter. He really did love this place, and he was pleased that the stake president would put this new trust in him.

Of course, Jeff did find himself wondering how he was going to get everything done. Abby needed his help with William, and the house wasn't quite so close to finished as he had implied. Still, he liked to think about all the good he and Malcolm could do.

• • •

On the following Sunday the new presidency was sustained and set apart, and then on Tuesday Malcolm called a presidency meeting. Larry Garner, a man at least twenty years older than Jeff and

Malcolm, would serve as second counselor. He was a quiet man, rather insecure about being a leader, and Jeff guessed that part of Malcolm's reason for calling him was to give him some experience. That meant, even more, that Jeff would have to watch himself and not do all the talking. But the meeting went well. Malcolm came in with an agenda and some thoughts about what they needed to do, and Jeff and Larry agreed with his priorities.

They also agreed that they would all three go out together the following evening and visit some families that Bishop Harrison was worried about. Jeff knew that he and Malcolm probably would have spent that time working on some final touches in Jeff's—or actually Harv Robertson's—kitchen, but at least the place was no longer torn up. Abby had a kitchen to work in, and she loved what Jeff and Malcolm had done. When Jeff had told her that he wouldn't have as much time to work on the house, she had told him, "Just finish the kitchen when you can. The Robertsons will be thrilled when they see this place." But Jeff still had work he wanted to do in the bathroom, and he also hoped to start changing out the single-paned windows for double panes.

Malcolm took his truck on Wednesday evening, and Larry and Jeff crowded into the seat with him. They rode to Niota, a little town up the river from Nauvoo. The men didn't know the family they were about to visit, nor did the bishop, but their records had been sent to the ward. The family was named Doherty, and the husband, Garret, was thirty-eight and an elder. He and his wife, Eva, had five children, but two of them were named Talbot, apparently from an earlier marriage.

When the presidency located the address they were looking for, the place seemed much too small for a family of seven. It was a frame house with white paint peeling off, revealing gray, weathered siding. A picket fence was in the same condition, and one section had fallen over. The lawn was in bad need of cutting. "Wow," Malcolm said. "Do you think this is the right place?"

"All we can do is ask," Jeff said, but he hated to think what kind of family they were about to meet.

The three walked to the door, and Malcolm tried the doorbell. When there was no sound and no response, he knocked. The door came open after a few seconds. A little boy, maybe four, was standing behind a tattered screen door, staring up at the men. "Is your dad here, or your mom?" Malcolm asked.

The boy was wearing only a shirt and oversized underwear that hung to his knees. He nodded, but he didn't say anything, didn't go off to find anyone. Before long a woman appeared at the door. She didn't look nearly so ragged as everything else, but Jeff thought she looked tired. She had blondish hair that was a little scattered, and she had gentle eyes, sort of blue, maybe sad. She looked out at the presidency curiously, as though she couldn't imagine why a white-shirted, tie-wearing threesome would be at her door.

"Sister Doherty?" Malcolm asked.

Her eyes took on a little more life. "Yes," she said, and nodded.

"We're the elders quorum presidency, from Nauvoo. We just received your records. Did you move in recently?"

"Not really. We've been here a while. We haven't . . . made it to church yet." She pushed the hair back from her eyes. "I'm sorry. If I'd known you were coming I'd have . . ."

But she didn't finish her sentence and Malcolm was quick to say, "No. It's our fault. We didn't have a phone number for you, so we just drove up to see if we could meet you. Is Brother Doherty home?"

"No." Her little son was leaning against her now, and she put her hand on his messy hair. "I guess you could say we're separated. Or . . ." She shrugged. "Or at least he's gone—*somewhere*."

"Can we help you?" Malcolm asked.

She took a long look at Malcolm, and then tears spilled onto her cheeks. "I don't know," she said. "I don't know what to do."

That night the presidency learned a lot about Sister Eva. She had been raised in the Chicago area and had married very young. Not long after, she had had a baby and then another. But her husband had never really been able to provide for his family, and he had used all the money he could get his hands on to buy drugs. Eva had done some of that herself in her younger years, but she had tried to be a decent mom. She had finally divorced that first husband, worked as a secretary, and gotten by without any child support. It was at her job that she had met a man named Doherty who was entirely different from men she had known before. He had a good job, dressed well, took care of himself, and he treated her beautifully. He told her he was a Mormon and had been a missionary. She had never taken much interest in religion, but she took the missionary lessons and joined the Church, and the two had married. Some good years had followed. Her husband had been transferred to Burlington, Iowa, and their family had kept growing. Then one day he had told her he no longer believed in God, didn't love her, and didn't want to be married. He had packed up and left that night. She didn't know where he was, and he had never sent her a penny.

Eva had found a minimum-wage job and managed to sell the house Doherty had left her with. But the house hadn't moved quickly, and by the time she got it sold, she was way behind on payments. What equity was left in the house had mostly been lost. She had found this house in Niota, which cost very little to rent, and she was working across the bridge in Fort Madison at a grocery store, but she barely made enough to pay her rent and buy groceries. Her car was dying, she feared, and gasoline cost so much that she could afford little more than to make it to work each day—and pay the $2.00 fee to cross the bridge.

It was Jeff who finally asked, "Would you like to come to Church, if someone could give you a ride?"

She took a long look at him. "I don't think so," she said. But she didn't explain.

"What can we do to help you?" Malcolm asked.

"Nothing, I guess. I just can't come to church—at least for now."

"But we can't abandon you now that we know your situation. I know this house is rented, but would the landlord mind if we made it more livable?"

Eva had some fairly nice furniture—from her previous life, Jeff assumed—but the interior of the house was a mess, with gouges in the sheet rock, curtain rods bent and broken, a door on the kitchen cabinets missing. "The landlord told me that if I wanted to fix it up, he would give me credit on my rent. But I don't have any tools, and I've never—"

"All right. Don't worry. That's what we're good at. We'll get things looking better, so you'll all feel better. But what about food?"

"We get by. Pretty much."

"Eva, we won't let you go hungry. There's no need for that. Would you mind if the Relief Society president came up? I think the sisters would like to help too."

"No, I don't mind. But . . ."

"What about clothes for your kids? Is that a problem?"

"Well . . . yes."

"Is that why you don't feel you can come to church?"

She hesitated, as though ashamed, and then she nodded, and tears rolled down her cheeks again.

"Would it bother you if we worked on that, too?" Malcolm

asked. "I know we could get some things for your kids—even if it's just hand-me-downs."

Eva didn't answer; she leaned over and cupped her hands over her face, and she sobbed. By then, Jeff was shedding tears himself. Part of it was having the chance to do something for this family, and part of it was watching Malcolm, who knew exactly what to say and do.

Over the next month Malcolm and Jeff and Larry—or more often, just Malcolm and Jeff—spent several evenings with the Dohertys. They repaired cabinets and plumbing and splintered woodwork; they patched walls; they caulked around windows and fixed doors that wouldn't shut right. And then on a Saturday they brought a big crew from the ward, both men and women, and they painted the house, inside and out. The Relief Society got involved and collected nice outgrown clothes from families in the ward—not only for the kids but for Eva. Young men and women from the ward came on another Saturday and worked on the yard, and a brother got Eva's car running better, but even after that, members of the ward took turns driving to Niota, nine miles, to bring the family to church on Sundays.

There were other families that needed help, and Malcolm and Jeff found themselves putting their own home projects mostly on hold, but they were still working together, more than ever, and all of it felt good to Jeff. "I love to imagine Zion," Jeff told Malcolm as they were heading home from visiting one of the less-active elders, a young man named Dave Quarry. "But this is the first time I feel as though I'm part of making it happen."

"I know. I was thinking the same thing tonight," Malcolm said. "It's really frustrating that we can't do anything for some people—like Dave. But we've made a difference in a few cases. We really have."

That night Dave had come to the door, taken a look at the men, and said, "I know who you are. I grew up in the Church, and it's a good thing if you're into that kind of stuff. But I have . . . other interests." He laughed, and then he shut the door. Inside, there had been a burst of laughter as several people—all young, it seemed from the sound of their voices—enjoyed the moment.

Jeff understood. The guy had a right to go his own way. He knew that was always a problem—that some people received the chance to glimpse Zion but never embraced it. Still, it felt so good to try, to work at it, and not just talk about the concept. Jeff had found himself speaking less and less in Church discussions and doing more and more during the week. He knew he would always be sort of annoying to a lot of people, but he felt better about himself than he had in a long time.

• • •

Abby didn't complain about Jeff being gone in the evenings. She knew he was doing good things, and he came home full of stories about the elders quorum presidency and the things they were doing. Some nights the men still worked at Malcolm and Kayla's house, since that kitchen still needed more work. When Jeff went there, Abby usually went along and spent time with Kayla.

One thing Abby had certainly learned was that a baby was demanding—no matter how thankful she was for him. Little William didn't supply a lot of two-way conversation, and his lungs hadn't been damaged by his heart defect. The boy knew how to cry—and he didn't let up when he felt himself wronged.

The hardest thing was that he wasn't sleeping through the night. But he was only three months old, and he had started small, so she knew she had nothing to complain about. Still, she longed, more than anything, for a full night's sleep, and that never happened.

Kayla kept saying, "Just wait until you have some rug rats around. At least now, you can catch a nap when he naps during the day. Once you have more babies, there's *never* a chance to sleep." Abby assumed that was true, but right now everything seemed hard enough without imagining bigger challenges.

What Abby had learned was that she really didn't know how to do the things that so many "mothers in Zion" had learned to do. She loved to read, and she tried to find time for novels when she got a chance. She was working from a list of "great books" she had been given by a college English professor, but she was missing so many days between reading sessions that she usually couldn't remember what she had read the last time.

And she wished she had more household skills. Her mother had always had someone come in and clean once a week, and she had never sewn at all. She was a good cook—Italian style—but she hadn't taught her daughters. Instead, she had kept pressure on them to do their homework and practice their piano lessons. So Abby had left home without much domestic training, and she hadn't improved any at Stanford. Her interest in home decor had been inspired more by her love of art and architecture—all learned from books—than by practical application. She was finally starting to decorate the house; she had done some painting with Jeff and had bought new carpets and drapes and curtains—with Brother Robertson's money. She liked seeing the house take shape now that the dirty work had been done. But she didn't know how to repair Jeff's church pants when a seam split.

That was the great thing about Kayla. She had cooked and sewn all her life and knew how to alter clothes, replace zippers—almost anything. What Abby was starting to learn was that some of those things weren't really so difficult. It was just a matter of being shown—and practicing. But it was also amazing how much better she felt about herself as she found she could take care of herself and her family—and save some money in the process. Jeff was making a decent salary now, but not so much that they had money to throw around. She was learning that they didn't need all that much when they handled their money carefully.

One afternoon, when Jeff came home from work, he told Abby that he was actually going to be home all evening. "Honest," he said, "I'm home to stay. I like Malcolm and all that, but a night home sounds great. Maybe we can put Will down early and get to bed early ourselves."

"That would be great. I really need the sleep."

"Well, yeah. Me too. But you know—that wasn't entirely what I was thinking about."

Abby laughed. She had known that, of course.

Abby had made a stab at an Italian dinner: ravioli with marinara sauce, garlic bread, and a green salad. Of course, the ravioli was from a package she had bought in the frozen food section of the grocery store, and the sauce was out of a bottle. All the same, she knew Jeff loved ravioli, and she was pleased when she saw him dish out a second helping.

"I've noticed something about you lately, Jeff," Abby said.

"What's that?"

"You seem happy."

Jeff looked up from his food. "What?"

"You've seemed happier than usual lately."

He shrugged. "Yeah. I guess I am."

"What's going on?"

"I don't know." He sat for a time, not eating, and seemed to think about the question. "I do love spring. I hear those cardinals singing outside in the morning and I don't mind getting up. And then—I don't know—I've had some good stuff happen lately."

"You mean the things your presidency is doing?"

"Well, yeah. We've been a little too busy, but the work we're doing is satisfying. What I was thinking about, though, was the way work has been going the last little while."

"Work? Really?"

"Yeah. Yesterday, Linda, the boss's administrative assistant, called me. She was trying to get a project finished and she was really frustrated with her computer. She was trying to cut and paste some data into a spreadsheet, and the program had jumbled everything up. She couldn't get the columns to line up, and . . . well, anyway, she was coming apart, actually crying."

"Did you know what to do?"

"Not immediately. But I told her to take a break, and I sat down at her computer. She came back about fifteen minutes later and I had everything working. It was just unbelievable how thrilled she was. She brought a plate of cookies to me today."

"So that's why you're happy? Cookies? Where are they?"

"I couldn't get them away from the place. All the guys decided it would be nice for me to share."

"Oh—thanks a lot. Great guys!"

"Actually, they are good guys. It's taken them a while to get used to me, but I like most of them now, and they seem to like me."

"So this job's working out okay. Is that what you're telling me?"

Jeff took some time again before he said, "No. The job's about the same—and not very exciting. But Linda *really* appreciated what I did for her."

"Is she in love with you?"

Jeff shook his head in mock disgust. "She's old enough to be my mom," he said.

"Maybe so. But I'll bet she's in love with you. Every woman in the world is. That doesn't matter. I got you."

"No wonder I'm happy."

"Really, though, are you happy? Because, for a long time, I didn't feel like you were."

"I guess that's all it takes for me, a few cardinals singing in the morning and a plate of cookies."

"Be serious for a minute. Tell me what's changing."

Jeff wiped his mouth with a paper napkin, and he seemed to consider for a time. "I have everything I need, Ab. You and Will. Good friends. Good ward. But I think I've told myself all my life, I have to be *somebody*. I have to leave my mark on the world. Maybe I'm just growing up, but I don't think much about that lately. We had a chance to do something for Sister Doherty, and in a way, we saved her life. If I hadn't been involved, Malcolm still would have gotten it done. But I got to be there. And Linda, at work, she needed a guy to solve a little problem for her, and a lot of people could have done it—but I got the chance. That *is* sort of making your mark on the world. You know what I mean?"

"It's being a nice person."

"Yeah, I guess. But I never knew that was what I wanted to do when I grew up. When people tell you to *dream big*, they never mention 'becoming a nice guy' as a particularly lofty achievement."

"They should. It's what I want to teach William."

"Yeah. Me too, actually. It's funny you say that, because I've thought a lot about that lately. I don't want to be one of those dads who pushes his kids to feel like they have to win everything. I don't want them to feel like life's a contest and they have to compare themselves to everyone else all the time."

Abby liked that. She had worked hard in school, but sometimes her mother had made her feel that nothing she did was quite good enough. She wanted to believe that life could be simpler than that, less pressured. She wanted William to do good things with his life, but she didn't want him to feel that he had to be the best at *everything*.

"Jeff," Abby said, "this weekend, could we look around and see what houses are for sale in Nauvoo?"

"Sure." Jeff smiled, as though he understood the logical connection Abby was making. "I've been thinking a lot about that, too. But I don't know how we can come up with a down payment."

"I think my parents would help us."

"Yeah, they probably would. But I don't want to ask them."

"Well, let's at least see what's available."

"Okay."

Abby liked all of that. But later, when she had a little time to think, she wondered whether she wasn't asking too much of Jeff. He did have things he wanted to do in life, and there was nothing wrong with that. All winter, during her worries about William, and then caring for him once he was home, she had centered her life on herself and her baby, and Jeff had done everything to support her. She had to think more what he needed now.

And there was something more she wanted to do. She wanted to do something for someone other than herself. It was time for her to give back to some of the people who had kept her going all these months.

CHAPTER 23

A week had passed since the murders in Carthage. Will kept telling himself to move forward, but he found no joy in his work—or in anything else. Will's wound was healing and he wanted more than anything to work, to feel normal. But Jesse had made the long walk into town to get his horse back from Will, and he had told Will there was not much to do at the moment, with the corn crop still young and rather sparse. Will certainly shouldn't show himself out at the farm, where the danger would be much worse.

Will had hoped for a better harvest this year, but that was unlikely. For that matter, nothing looked promising right now. The Saints were worried that they would be at war at any time, so no one would hire him to open new fields, and he certainly couldn't ride over to Carthage to bid on county roadwork. He had not heard a word from George Samples, but every day he wondered when Harmon Wilson might show up to arrest him.

Most of the Apostles had been traveling across the nation campaigning for Joseph Smith for president, and they had not yet returned. Those still in Nauvoo—Willard Richards and William

Marks, the stake president—kept advising the Saints to go on with life. Peace could still be established. But Will had a hard time imagining that that could happen. As soon as people in the county had realized that the Mormons were not attacking, they had returned to their homes and begun their threats again. Will had seen another of Thomas Sharp's diatribes in his newspaper. Sharp claimed all sorts of righteous reasons why the men who had killed Joseph were only carrying out the will of the people. He had dropped his claim that the jail had been attacked by Mormons, but he expressed no regret for what had happened. In fact, he had begun once again to call for the expulsion of all the Saints from the county.

With the danger of attack still hanging over Nauvoo, it was hard for Church members to believe that the hope of a Zion in Illinois was still reasonable. Much of the talk around town was about migrating west. But Will still didn't want to leave. He could only think that this was the first land he had ever owned, and he had put so much work into it. He still wanted to stay, somehow, and still wanted to build a fine house for Liz. He was a different man from the one who had arrived in Nauvoo, and his ultimate purposes in life had certainly adjusted, but the dream of land and a comfortable house for his family had pushed him for a long time, and he was not ready to give it up. This, however, would probably be another year merely to survive. If the Saints somehow avoided expulsion and remained in Nauvoo, and if he managed not to be arrested—or attacked by George Samples and his friends—he wasn't sure that any brighter hope was ahead. And yet, in spite of all of that, he knew that he must carry on—for Liz and his boys.

The trouble was, all day every day, a presence in Will's head kept saying, "The Prophet is gone." At first he had felt overwhelming sadness at the loss of both Joseph and Hyrum, but what he hated more was a sort of despair that seemed to be settling into his mind as part of who he now would be. He felt it not only in himself but in everyone he talked to.

Something else was bothering Will, even though he tried to push the thoughts from his head. He had read the complaints published in the *Nauvoo Expositor* by the dissidents, and some of their arguments were hard to dismiss. He really didn't doubt that Joseph had been a prophet, but he wondered why God hadn't directed His people somewhat better. Gathering to one place in such great numbers really did present a problem, just as William Law and the others argued. Such a mass of people, most of them voting the same way, and building up a large army, did threaten neighboring communities and create some of the hatred that had erupted.

Joseph had also taught principles that were always going to create difficulties. Will knew by now that there were some in the community who had not only accepted the doctrine of plurality of wives but were living it. No one openly admitted to such arrangements, but so many people in town reported that it was happening that Will knew it had to be. William Clayton had more or less admitted that it was so. Will understood why the dissidents would resist the practice. When he tried to imagine such a life, it seemed adulterous, and he knew he could never embrace it.

Will knew that the *Expositor* had been a nuisance—designed to entice people of the county to attack the Saints—and he understood the legal arguments that Joseph and the city council had used to justify its destruction. But how could Joseph not have known what wrath those actions would bring upon him and all the Saints? It seemed as though God should have warned Joseph not to do something that would seem so un-American to most people. It just seemed to Will that Joseph could have denounced the lies in the paper without destroying property and interfering with the dissidents' rights to express their own opinions.

Maybe Joseph and Hyrum did need to seal their testimonies with their blood, as many were saying, and surely Joseph had accepted the Lord's will in those final days. But that didn't change the way Will felt, the way everyone felt: that everything would be more difficult now that the voice of inspiration they loved so much had been taken from them.

In spite of everything, however, Will was trying to move ahead. He didn't go to the farm, but he had begun to put in some full days around his own place. He built a better fence around his corral, finished the cistern he had dug but had never bricked up all the way, finally plastered the outside of the house, and started work on a smokehouse. Work had always been the one thing he turned to in times of difficulty—to give his all, all day, sunup to sundown. The last thing he wanted to do was wait and worry. So he prayed with Liz each morning, tried to trust in the Lord, and they both kept themselves busy.

One morning, not long after sunup, Will was outside feeding his animals when he heard a wagon approach. His first reaction, as always, was that he was about to be arrested. He waited and watched to see who was driving the wagon. It took him a moment to remember the man and realize that he was looking at Oscar Clarkston, Jacob's father. There was a young woman sitting in the wagon with him.

"Hello, Will," Oscar said, and Will heard a nervousness in the man's voice that frightened him. He knew immediately what this was about.

"How are you, Brother Clarkston?"

"I'm aw right, Will. This is my wife, Amanda. We've been married two months now. I said before I would na' marry again, but time can change a man's mind 'bout such things."

Will glanced at Amanda, noticing that she was very young. She wouldn't look at Will. "I suppose that's true," Will said, but he was trying to think how he should react, what he should do to head this off. He would not let this man carry Jacob away. The boy was Will's son, not Oscar's.

"How's little Jacob doing?" Clarkston asked.

"He's fine. He's happy. We've raised him as our own, and that's how we think of him."

"I 'preciate that. I heerd you have another son now. Is that so?"

"Yes, we do. It's good for Jacob to have a little brother." For a moment Oscar looked directly at Will—which he had been avoiding—and Will let him know with his eyes that he was resolute.

"Could we na' see 'im?"

"Of course you can. But it's very early. I don't think he's awake yet."

"It is early, but we needed a good start. We're a-goin' back to St. Louis today."

Will hoped that the man only wanted a glimpse of the boy, and then he would travel on. But he didn't believe that. "I'll see if he's awake," Will said, and he walked into the house. Liz was actually dressing Jacob, kneeling in front of him. "Oscar Clarkston is here," he said.

"I know. What does he want?"

"He says he wants to see Jacob. I don't know what else he's thinking. He's got a wife now."

"I saw her." Liz had pulled on her housedress quickly, and her hair was still loose and disheveled. Will noticed that the color had gone from her face. She hardly had breath enough to speak.

"Do you mind if he sees the boy?"

"No. Of course not." She picked Jacob up and carried him outside, but Will noticed how tightly she was gripping him. And outside, she didn't put him down.

Brother Clarkston had gotten down from his wagon. His wife was seated as she had been, but she still wouldn't look at Will, didn't even look at Jacob.

"Hello, Sister Lewis," Oscar said. "My goodness, he's a fine, good boy. You ha' taken good care of 'im." And then, in a softer voice, "His eyes is like his mum's, same color zactly."

"People say he looks like Liz," Will said. "He has the same coloring."

Liz didn't speak. And she didn't hand him over.

"Hello, Son. I'm yer dad."

Surely those words made no sense to little Jacob. He didn't seem troubled, or even very curious about this man who was speaking to him. But he did twist a little, struggling to get down. Liz set him on his feet, but Will could see how tightly she was holding his hand, even when he wanted to wander off.

"After I lef' him here," Brother Clarkston said, "I went down to St. Louis. I got mysel' some good land down there, so I hope ta stay. I 'spected to be a bachelor aw my life, but I met Amanda at church." He gestured toward her. "We ha' plenty o' good members down there."

He was trying to sound cordial, but Will still heard his nervousness. And he thought Amanda looked ashamed. She was neat and clean, simple in appearance, and quite plain. What struck Will was that Oscar had been lonely, and he understood all that—even understood what he wanted—but Jacob was Will's son. That was the whole of it.

"When we heerd about Joseph and Hyrum, we come to be with the Saints, but we're a-goin' back now. My thought is, anythin' could happen. The Saints could be scattered ever'where before long."

"It looks more all the time like we'll manage to stay."

"I've been thinking 'bout everythin'," Clarkston said, and now he stared past Will, past Liz. "I know I axt ye ta keep Jacob, but now, with everythin' a-goin' on, and me with a wife . . . it's better if he come with me now. I do 'preciate what you ha' done and everythin', but now it's time for 'im ta be with his real dad."

Will took a step toward Oscar. "He is with his real dad," he said, and there was no hiding the anger in his voice. "I asked you two years ago whether something exactly like this wouldn't happen, and you stood right there in our house and told us no, that you would *never* come back for him."

"I do na' recall that I used zactly them words. I—"

"That *is* what you said. I questioned you on it because I knew what it would do to my wife if you went back on what you were telling us."

Brother Clarkston took a glance at Will, obviously having heard the anger, but then he looked down at Jacob. "Will, my wife had on'y just died back then. I could na' think right. I on'y knowed that Jacob could na' stay alive more'n a few days if he did na' have a woman ta feed 'im. But he is my son, and I ha' longed for 'im since the day I let you take 'im. And now I got me a wife, and I do na' want to be cut off from 'im all my life. It's na' right to split apart a man an' his son, no matter what we said back then."

Will felt the man's pain. He really did. But he couldn't let him walk away with Jacob. He looked at Liz, who reached down and picked up the boy again. He didn't know if she was defending him or getting ready to hand him over. What he did know was that this was wrong—wrong for Jacob more than anyone, and deeply wrong for Liz.

"What you don't understand, Oscar, is that Liz is the boy's mother. She's the only mum he's ever known, and he won't understand if you try to carry him off. It can't be good, what that would do to him."

"I've thought 'bout that, Will. I know what ye be sayin'. But he's young enough, he will na' remember in a while. And he'll think of Amanda that way—as his mum."

Will heard a little sob break from Liz, and he understood how deeply the thought cut into her—that Jacob would forget her, never remember the two years they'd had together. Jacob was surely understanding some of this now, and he had wrapped his arms around Liz and was clinging tight.

"You can't have him," Will said. He took another step closer to Brother Clarkston, let his greater size dominate the man. "You'll have to fight me first, and you won't win. You gave this boy to us, and we've done everything for him. How can you just come back and act like that won't matter to us?" But Will's voice had begun to break. He ducked his head and stopped.

"I understan' aw that, Brother Lewis. I do. But I look at my son an' I see Rosemary. I thank you for what you ha' done, but how can I walk away from him one more time? He's mine for aw eternity, no matter what you ha' done for him. He's *my son*." He dropped his head down, and a little sob broke from him.

Will didn't back away, but he was moved by the man's pain. He and Oscar were facing the same agony; one of them had to give way. But this young girl in the wagon, she didn't know the boy. She had nothing to lose in this, and Liz would never be the same, with one more loss of this kind.

Will felt Liz's hand on his arm. She was pulling him back gently. "Brother Clarkston is right," she said. "Jacob is his son."

Will spun around. "By what right? He's been *our* child his entire life."

"It was our gift to Jacob," she said. "But we can't be selfish. He's not property to fight over." She looked back at Oscar. "He has some other clothes. And some little toys that Will made for him. Let me put his things together before you take him." She seemed under control, but Will could hear how her voice was shaking. She turned and walked back to the house.

Will turned back to Oscar. "Do you know what she's doing? She wants to hold him one last time—say good-bye to him. How can you do this to her?"

"I know how hard it be. I did it once mysel'. But aw will be right this way. I know't, Will."

Suddenly Will's hands shot out and grabbed Oscar by the shirt. He pulled the man up to him and shouted into his face, "You're a liar and a thief! You're going to kill my wife. Don't you understand that?"

And then he heard a voice. Joseph's. That deep, soft voice. "No." That was all it said. "No."

It took Will another few seconds to let go, but he did. And then he said, "I'm sorry. I shouldn't . . ."

He spun away, bit down on his lip, bent forward, and strained with all his muscles not to cry. But this—this on top of all the rest—it was just too much.

• • •

"Jacob, Mummy loves you. Do you know that? Mum will always love you—and never forget you." Liz was trying not to cry, but she could feel tears running down her face. Jacob was staring at her, obviously confused and frightened. "Do you love Mummy?"

Jacob nodded, and then he reached for her again. She had set him down while she had gathered a few things to put in a flour sack that she planned to send away with him. She picked him up and wrapped her arms around him, held him close. He was still a baby in her mind, the only hold on life she had clung to for such a long time after Mary Ann had died. She had always known that this could happen—had feared it—but she also knew she couldn't fight for him the way Will had wanted to do. It just wasn't right. Brother Clarkston had his claim, and she couldn't deny it.

What Liz couldn't accept was the idea that Jacob would forget her, as Oscar claimed he would. All the days they had spent together, the words she had taught him, the hurts she had kissed and hugged away—how could Jacob grow old never remembering, maybe never even knowing all that? If he went to St. Louis now, she might never see him again.

"You're going with your daddy, Jacob. He loves you. And you'll have a new mum. She'll love you too. You'll be happy, Jakey. Everything will be just fine. Do you understand that?"

He gripped her tighter. She didn't know how much he was understanding. The words he knew weren't adequate for what he must be feeling—fearing.

"I'll love you forever, and I'll try to find you someday—so you can remember me. And in heaven we'll be friends. I know we will. Then you'll know me, I'm sure of that." She was losing control, feeling as though she could never walk out the door with him. And yet, she was already moving that direction, and now Jacob was crying, tightening his grip.

• • •

Outside, Will was standing with his head down, not saying anything. When he finally glanced up, he saw that Brother Clarkston was also looking at the ground. Amanda was still sitting stiff, still not looking at anyone. Everything was silent outside, except that a cardinal repeated its pretty song at intervals. Liz had taught Jacob to look for the pretty red birds in the trees, to know their song. Would he remember that song someday? Would he know why he recognized it?

Liz walked to Clarkston and handed him the flour sack. She embraced Jacob with both arms again, and then she tried to hand him to Will. "I can't," he said. "I'll run away with him before I'll hand him over."

"Just hug him."

So Will took him in his arms. "I love you, Jake," he said, but tears were coming now, and Liz knew that that was humiliating to him. He handed the boy back to Liz quickly and walked toward the house.

Jacob grasped Liz tight again, so she hugged him one more time, and then she said, "It's all right, Jacob. Go to your new daddy now. It will be all right."

But he wouldn't let go, and as she tried to pull him loose, he screamed. She pulled one of his arms free and Brother Clarkston grasped him around the middle and tugged him away. Jacob was going wild by then, kicking, reaching for his mother, wailing.

"I am sorry for this," Brother Clarkston said. "I tell ye now, I will allus take good care of 'im, and I will allus tell 'im what you done for 'im."

Liz thought her legs were going to go out from under her, but Will had come back and was there now, holding her, keeping her up.

Brother Clarkston walked around his wagon, stepped up, and took his seat next to his wife, still holding Jacob, who was fighting to break free. Amanda untied the lines and took them up as though she had driven plenty of wagons in her life. She gave the lines a flip and said, "Giddup." The horses plodded forward and made a wide turn, then headed out to Rich Street.

The last time Liz saw Jacob, he was still reaching and screaming, "Mummy! Mummy! Mummy!"

She turned to Will and he held her for a moment, and then they walked back to the house. Daniel was awake now and crying. She was glad for that. She hurried to him, picked him up, and pressed her face against him.

"We have Daniel," she told Will. "We'll be all right." But she didn't believe it. She only wanted Will to be comforted. It seemed even harder for him than for her.

"This isn't right," Will said. "He's riding off with *our* son. What makes him the father any more than I am?"

"We'll be all right. We'll go on. It's what we have to do."

She told herself that she had survived before, after Mary Ann, and she would survive again. But it didn't feel as though she could. All the gloom of losses seemed to be piling up on her. The Prophet was gone. Her father was gone. Her mother and sister were lost to her.

"Why do things keep happening?" Will said. "When is God ever going to look out for His people?" And then with anger in his voice, he declared, "I wish we'd stayed in England!"

"Will, don't do that to me," Liz said. "I don't need that now. I need you to be strong."

He wrapped his arms around her again, her and the baby. "Liz, I can't do any more of this. I'm *angry.* I want to strike back at the men who killed Joseph. I want to *bludgeon* George Samples again for the fear he's caused you. And I want to chase down Oscar Clarkston and do the same to him. All God ever tells me is to accept His will—and I say, why should I? When are things ever going to be made right?"

"We'll be all right, Will. We have Daniel. We have each other." She didn't say it, but she knew somehow that God *was* with them. All the pain and disappointment had made better people of them. There were blessings with the pain. But she couldn't get that many words out, couldn't even remember what she was thankful for; she just knew that they couldn't fall apart, that they had to accept one more hardship and move ahead once again.

"I'm sorry," Will said. "I'll fight this off. I will. I won't let you down. But Liz, I need something to go right. I need to know that everything won't always go wrong for us. How much can God ask of us?"

She didn't know the answer to that. And she was somehow glad that Will was angry, not just willing to hand over their son without caring. She knew he would fight for her, too; she had always known that. She couldn't live without his strength.

And then she heard Jacob, screaming. Had the wagon stopped out on the road somewhere? Why weren't the Clarkstons just moving on as quickly as they could?

But the sound was coming closer. Will had heard it too. He let go of Liz and strode to the door. When he threw it open, Liz heard Oscar outside, heard that he was saying something to Will over the screams of her son. Just as she got to the door, she saw him hand Jacob to Will. Jacob grabbed his daddy, but then he saw Liz in the doorway and screamed again, reached for her. She ran to him and grabbed him into her arms.

She held him tight as he clung to her, still crying. And then she looked at Brother Clarkston, who was saying, "I am sorry for this, Sister Lewis. Sorry I did this to you."

What was he saying?

"I did na' understan' 'til we drove away. 'Twas Amanda stopped the wagon and tol' me, 'This is wrong. You can na' do this ta this child.'"

So it was true. Brother Clarkston was bringing him home.

"You won't ever leave the Church, will you?" Oscar asked.

"No," Will said. "We'll raise him in the gospel."

"Could I stop to see 'im fro' time to time?"

"Yes, yes," Liz said. "Oh, Brother Clarkston, we'll cherish him forever, and I'll tell him what a good father he has. He'll know."

"If you get pushed out, you might think 'bout St. Louis. There's work there—and land for sale."

"We'll go with the Church," Will said. "We'll do what the Brethren want us to do."

"Well, that's right, I guess. But if you move on, let me know where you go—aw right?"

"I promise you, we will," Will said. He reached out and shook hands with Brother Clarkston.

"Good-bye, Jacob. Please do na' forget me." But he didn't step closer, clearly understanding how much he had already frightened the boy.

He walked away, but as he did, Liz saw that the man's body was shaking. She knew that he was crying. And now she could only think of *his* pain.

CHAPTER 24

Nauvoo was quiet, solemn. Something like peace had descended upon Hancock County. Even though Thomas Sharp and a few others continued to advocate expulsion of the Saints, most of the old citizens seemed to take for granted that the Mormon church would now die on its own and mob action would not be necessary. The *Times and Seasons* called for justice, demanded that the murderers be tried and punished, but Church members admitted to one another that no one would ever be convicted by a jury of local citizens. Still, the nervous calm—unlikely to last forever—was better than war, and both Mormons and old settlers began to go about their lives. Most were farmers, and they had crops to look after. They hoped to harvest enough from a thin crop to feed their families for another winter.

In Nauvoo, as a few weeks passed, there were those who decided to leave, or who sided with the dissenters in their opposition to Joseph's latest teachings, but the majority of the members went back to their work, whatever it was. Life would go on, they told each other, and they had to commit themselves to carrying on the work of the kingdom established by their Prophet.

Will had a chance to talk to Jacob Backenstos again one day, and he learned that Blake Samples was slowly recovering. "He may not ever be quite right, the doc says," Backenstos told him. He smiled. "I said that if he wasn't, it would be hard to tell any difference." Will didn't laugh. He was relieved to know that he hadn't killed the man.

"I can tell you right now that those boys won't bring any charges against you. I made it very clear to George that I didn't believe a word he was telling me, and I promised him that I'd look very closely at his part in the whole thing if he pushed the matter. He might come after me sometime, and he'll probably look for a way to get at you sooner or later, but I told him if he did that, he would spend the rest of his life in jail. I don't know if that scared him or not. I know one thing: He still looks like he's suffering with some bad headaches. And that's just what he had coming."

Will still couldn't laugh. He thought of what he had done to those men—had to do to them, he told himself—but the vision of it was terrible to him. He had gone back a good deal lately to reading the scriptures, and he could find very little that consoled him. He wondered what Jesus would have done in such a situation, and he knew that he could never picture the Savior attacking men that way. Will had wanted so badly to be a better person, and now he had blood on his hands. Liz told him that she was thankful he had defended himself—for the sake of her and the boys—and Will liked to think of it that way. But the memory was in his hands and arms, the feel of those blows he had delivered, and it was in his vision, the blood running between George's fingers.

Another concern for Will and for everyone else was that the Church felt leaderless. No one knew who could bring direction to the membership again. Some believed that Sidney Rigdon carried the highest authority, since he was the only survivor from the First Presidency, but he had moved to Pittsburgh just days before Joseph and Hyrum's death, partly to establish residency for his run as vice president to Joseph Smith. Most people knew that Joseph had asked for Brother Rigdon to be removed as First Counselor the year before, and only after an impassioned speech had Sidney received support from other leaders. Beyond that, he had been unstable in recent years, never really the same man since his months in Liberty Jail. For many members, he didn't appear to be the man who could lead as Joseph had led.

Over the years, various leaders had served as Assistant President, and different methods of succession had been in place. Some argued that young Joseph Smith III, only eleven years old, had been ordained to succeed his father and carry on the work when he was of age to do so. Others held that Joseph had passed his authority to the Twelve Apostles. From that perspective, the Apostles were the only ones who possessed the priesthood keys to perform temple ordinances and to lead the Church.

Will spoke with William Clayton as often as he could, and he heard a great deal about all the discussions going on among the leaders. Brother Clayton had told Will that a secret council Joseph had called that spring—known to insiders as the "Council of Fifty" or the "Kingdom of God"—had been established to deal with secular matters such as locating new places where the Saints could live. A few of that group were now claiming that it was the only body that could carry on in Joseph's absence. But that, to Brother Clayton, made no sense, since it was a secular council; some members were not even Latter-day Saints.

According to Clayton, President Marks felt that something needed to be done quickly so that a chosen leader had authority to handle financial matters for the Church. A trustee was needed to settle issues of land ownership—and debt. Many property holdings in Nauvoo were in Joseph's name, and it was not clear what had belonged to him personally and what belonged to the Church. The great problem for Emma Smith was that there were more debts than assets, and she was worried about providing for her family. President Marks and his wife were close to Emma, worried about her, and wanted to hold a meeting to settle on a trustee. John Taylor and Willard Richards had been the only Apostles not serving missions at the time of Joseph's death. They were joined after a couple of weeks by Parley P. Pratt and George A. Smith. These four Apostles were adamant that they must hold off any major decisions until the return of Brigham Young, President of the Quorum of the Twelve, along with all the other Apostles.

So everything remained in stasis for a time, and Will felt the strain on the people. When troubles had come before, always there had been Joseph to stand before the members and provide perspective and faith. Even in those dark days when he had been locked up in the Liberty Jail in Missouri, or when he had been hiding from lawmen more recently, Joseph had written his revelations and sent them to the Church, and the hope of his return had galvanized the membership. Now, however, there seemed no one to step forward and offer direction.

On August 3, more than five weeks after the murders—now called "the martyrdom" by most members—Sidney Rigdon arrived on a riverboat from Pittsburgh, and the following morning, Sunday, he spoke at the east grove. Will and Liz, like most people, were eager to hear what he might propose about the future of the Church. Will had always found President Rigdon a little too zealous and oratorical for his taste. Since his days in the United Brethren, Will had not liked preachers who carried on too much, who ranted and shouted, and Sidney Rigdon had a little too much of that in him. Joseph had presented his ideas in straightforward explanations and had never minded using simple comparisons, even humor, to make himself clear. Will really felt the Church needed someone like that again. Still, Brother Rigdon had long served next to Joseph, and perhaps now the mantle of leadership had fallen upon him.

The congregation that morning was not as massive as the ones that had heard Joseph at the end of his life, but still, there were thousands of people. Will thought they had all come for the same reason he had—to see whether they felt the power of authority in Brother Rigdon.

But Sidney Rigdon was never one to get to his main point quickly. He spoke for a long time and developed his thoughts slowly. Gradually, however, it was clear what he thought to be true: Joseph was the Prophet of this dispensation, and he was gone. No one could "replace" him. Brother Rigdon, however, had received a revelation while still in Pittsburgh. God, he said, had told him that he should lead the Church himself, as a "guardian." He would be president and trustee, and he would build the Church up to Joseph and take care of the organization until Joseph III was old enough to assume the role. But even though he called himself a guardian, Will noticed that he expected Joseph Smith to inspire his words and actions—from the other side of the veil—and Brother Rigdon himself would be "a god to this generation . . . as Moses was to the children of Israel."

Something in this didn't sound right to Will. The man claimed to be inadequate to replace Joseph, but at the same time, his grandiose descriptions of himself sounded anything but humble. And then, as he continued on and on in his frail voice, he seemed to become carried away with his own words. Instead of offering the membership a vision of how the Church could move forward, he spoke of the great winding-up scene, the apocalyptic battles that would end the world. He saw himself as the military leader who would defeat the evil nations of Babylon. Will was especially surprised, even alarmed, when Brother Rigdon said that he would walk into the palace of Queen Victoria and demand a portion of her riches and dominions, and if she turned him down he would "take the little woman by the nose and lead her out." Will couldn't imagine what that had to do with being a follower of Jesus Christ.

In the end, President Rigdon claimed that he had no personal desire to lead the Church; he was only offering his revelation for the people to accept if they believed it. He implied that he wanted a response very soon, but no motion was presented to the leadership. When the Saints returned for an afternoon session, Charles C. Rich spoke. But President Marks actually interrupted him, at President Rigdon's request, to announce that another meeting would be convened that week, on Thursday, and the members would have a chance to vote their will.

Will had been uneasy during President Rigdon's sermon, and he became more troubled as the day continued. He didn't want the members to act too quickly, especially not until the other Apostles returned. As he and Liz walked back to their house with their boys, Will asked Liz what she thought. "I don't know, Will. If Brother Rigdon's vision is from God, I want to be obedient, but I didn't like the spirit I felt."

"You mean, he shouldn't be promising to lead the queen around by the nose?"

Liz had been letting Jacob walk, and the boy had stopped now to watch a squirrel that had dashed across the road and was sitting up on its haunches under the canopy of trees nearby. Will, who was carrying Daniel, had continued to walk, but now he looked back at Liz. "Why would he say that?" she asked. "And what was all that about fighting a war in Jerusalem? Does he really think the end is so close—and that *he* is the one to lead the final battle?"

"He seems to. But Joseph never made any claims like that."

"Oh, Will, we need Joseph. Sometimes I wonder what will happen to us, without him."

Will came back and picked up Jacob, held his boys, one in each arm, and then tramped on up the hill toward their house. Liz's reaction had only reinforced his own. But during the following week, he talked with members who agreed with Brother Rigdon that Joseph could not be replaced and that, in time, Joseph III should be the one to lead. What Will sensed, however, was that the majority of Saints were nervous about President Rigdon taking over. Some hinted, and others admitted openly, that they thought Brother Rigdon wanted too much power for himself.

On Thursday morning, August 8, Sidney Rigdon spoke in the east grove again, repeating many of the same ideas he had expressed on Sunday. It was a windy day, however, and blowing toward the stand. Brother Rigdon began his talk, but it became obvious that his thin voice was not being heard. He had a wagon brought in and placed down the hill, more under the wind, and the congregation was asked to turn around. He walked down the hill, mounted the wagon, and spoke from there. Behind the congregation, on the wooden stand, sat eight of the Apostles. Brigham Young, Wilford Woodruff, Heber Kimball, and Orson Pratt had all arrived from the East since Sunday.

Sidney Rigdon spoke for an hour and a half, and he once again made the case for his guardianship of the Church. He was not quite so zealous in his rhetoric this time, but he asserted again his claim as the rightful spokesman for the Church, ordained to that purpose. Will watched some of the people around him and saw that they were growing weary as the midday heat mounted.

What Will realized was that Brother Rigdon was preparing the Saints for a sustaining vote. But as he began to formulate the words

380 · DEAN HUGHES

for that request, suddenly a booming voice from the congregation rang out, and everyone turned around.

It was Brigham Young who had stood up. "I will manage this voting for Elder Rigdon. He does not preside here," he stated, his big voice penetrating the wind. His long, reddish hair was blowing across his face, and he pushed it aside. "This child will manage this flock for a season." But he didn't call for a vote. He announced that the meeting would be adjourned until two o'clock that afternoon.

By the time everyone returned, the heat was worse, but there seemed more anticipation among the congregants. For one thing, the quorums had been asked to sit in their proper order, and that meant that the afternoon meeting would serve as a solemn assembly. Will was hesitant to sit with the elders and not with his wife, who liked to have help with the little boys, but he assumed that a vote would be taken, and he didn't want to miss the chance to express his opinion, so he sat at the back of his quorum, where he could see Liz. Daniel was asleep, and another sister was helping to watch Jacob. What worried Will was that no leader had stepped forward as an alternative to Sidney Rigdon. He hoped that would happen this afternoon.

Brigham Young conducted the meeting and also gave the first speech. He offered his opinion about the succession. What he believed, and explained, was that President Rigdon's authority had been lost when Joseph had died, since the Quorum of the First Presidency had been dissolved. The body that now held authority was the Quorum of the Twelve Apostles. Joseph had ordained them all and had given them the keys of leadership and the sealing power to perform ordinances in the temple when it was completed. No one else held those keys. He felt that no one person should try to fulfill the role that Joseph Smith had played in directing the formation and development of the Church from its outset. Only God could choose such a man to lead again, but when He did, only the Twelve would have the power to ordain him because they held all the keys that Joseph had held.

"We have a head," he said, "and that head is the Apostleship." He added, "Brother Rigdon was at his side—not above. No man has a right to counsel the Twelve of Joseph Smith. Think of these things. You cannot appoint a prophet; but if you let the Twelve remain and act in their place, the keys of the kingdom are with them and they can manage the affairs of the Church and direct all things aright."

This made sense to Will. This was the way Joseph would have talked, how he would have laid out the line of authority. He wouldn't have shouted about himself taking on the armies of Satan; he would guide the people forward without making so much of himself. Brother Clayton had told Will about a meeting the previous spring when Joseph had conferred all his authority upon the Apostles. He'd even talked of the need there would be for men to carry on when he was gone. Joseph had taken relief in rolling the responsibility of leading the Church off his own shoulders onto theirs. So, to Will, Brigham Young wasn't pushing himself forward; he was merely describing the proper order of authority in the Church.

Brigham didn't speak so long as Sidney Rigdon had—even though he was a man who could go on for a long time himself. His voice had carried much better than Rigdon's and seemed to possess more power. More than anything, he seemed more like Joseph in his manner, his logic, his way of setting things out so everyone could understand. In Will's mind, it was as though Joseph himself had come before the people, and with that realization, a kind of thrill had gone through his mind and body, a verification that there was someone to direct the affairs of the Church on a daily basis, someone who had the spirit to hear the promptings of the Lord and the intelligence to interpret what he understood so the people could comprehend.

When Brigham ended his talk, he invited Amasa Lyman and W. W. Phelps to give their opinions. Both supported President Young's position. Brother Phelps said, "If you want to do right, uphold the Twelve. Do your duty and you will be endowed. I will sustain the Twelve as long as I have breath."

Will felt something powerful in those words; he felt the Spirit resonate within him. He had worked so hard on the temple all winter, and he had felt good about doing it because he wanted to receive the endowment that Joseph had often spoken of. It was the Twelve who possessed the power to carry out temple work. Sidney Rigdon had never said a word about that.

Brigham Young stood again, and he summarized the positions that the people had heard that day. He called upon *everyone* to vote, not just the quorums. He asked people not only to vote but to carry out the commitment they were making with their choice. Church members needed to be unified in their purpose and supportive of their chosen leaders. Will understood that. When the members walked away that day, they needed to know that the Church had not been thrown into chaos.

Brigham first proposed that the members vote on Sidney's revelation—and his offer to serve as a guardian leader. But Sidney interrupted Brigham. Will couldn't hear what Brother Rigdon said, but Brigham addressed the congregation again and stated that Brother Rigdon had suggested that the membership vote first on Brigham's proposal that the Twelve lead the Church. Will thought he understood that. He had seen what was happening to people during the time that Brigham had spoken. He had seen many in the congregation nodding, men around him whispering to one another, clearly agreeing. Will had felt a spirit pervade the grove, and he knew how the vote would go. Sidney must have known it too, and Will hoped this was his way of bringing unity by letting the people approve Brigham's proposal and then moving forward.

So Brigham called for a vote of everyone—both men and women—on his own proposal for the Twelve to lead the Church, and in that great sea of people every hand seemed to go up. Will was overcome. He turned to look back at Liz, who was holding her hand high. Her lips were quivering with emotion. She obviously felt, as he did, that Joseph's work would not end after all. So many times in Will's life he had wished that he could receive clearer promptings, greater manifestations of truth, but at this moment he was moved as never before, his chest filled with the vibrations of affirmation.

· · ·

Liz felt a powerful spiritual manifestation. She looked around and saw the satisfaction and joy in all the eyes. When Brigham called for those opposed to the proposal, she supposed that someone surely must have voted no, but she saw no hands in the air. As she walked home with Will, she felt that the world had been righted again. Joseph's death hadn't been the complete tragedy it had seemed at first. It now served as a motivation for the Saints to push forward.

What Liz learned as the next few days passed, however, was that attitudes among members were not quite so unified as she had believed. Will came home one day after conversing with Willard Richards and said, "I fear a split is coming in the Church."

"A split?" Liz asked. "How can that be? Everyone voted for the Twelve. How could they—"

"Not everyone. There were many who didn't even bother to attend the meeting. Some left the city weeks ago. Some raised their hands at the time but have changed their minds since. Even some of the leaders agree with the dissidents more than they do with Brigham Young."

"About what?" Liz was nursing Daniel, sitting in her rocking chair by the fireplace. Will was standing in front of her. She could see how disheartened he was, and she knew what he was feeling. They had come home from the grove after the vote feeling confident for the first time in such a long time.

"They aren't people who would fight against the Church the way the Law brothers and Fosters and Higbees did, but they don't believe the doctrines that Joseph taught here in Nauvoo. They think those ideas should not be considered revelations."

"What ideas?"

Will grabbed a wooden chair away from the table and sat down in front of Liz. "They don't believe that a man can become a god, or that there can be more than one God."

"He said there was only one 'God the Father' for our world," Liz pointed out. "And the Bible teaches that Jesus is His Son, and is also a God."

"I know that," Will said. "It was such an exciting idea when Joseph taught it."

"I was so moved by it. It was as though I understood the meaning of life for the first time. We go on forever, and we keep learning and advancing and—"

"I know, Liz. I agree. But it's one of those things that angers people. They say it was mere speculation on Joseph's part, and it doesn't need to be part of our 'creed.'"

"Joseph always said that we have no creed. We simply keep searching for every truth."

"That's right. And he tried to open our eyes to bigger things. He wasn't demeaning God. He was saying that the universe is vast, and there are other planets with people, and a God for those people, too."

"He made heaven sound exciting," Liz said.

"The important thing to me is, it's a place where I'll still be married to you. That means everything to me. But some people don't like that, either. They say he was a fallen prophet at the end, espousing things that aren't taught by other Christians."

"It's all this talk about plural marriage that's bothering people, isn't it?"

Will nodded.

Liz could tell that Will didn't want to talk about that, and that worried her. "Do you think Joseph Smith had other wives besides Emma?"

Will rubbed his hand across his cheek. He sat back. "He has taught that doctrine, Liz. Last year he had a revelation read to some of the Church leaders. It explained about marriage lasting into the eternities—and about plural wives, in some cases. It wasn't announced to everyone, but a lot of people in town know about it."

The truth was, Liz wasn't surprised. For a long time now she had been telling herself to ignore the talk she heard, but her friend Sarah Kimball had suggested that Female Relief Society meetings had stopped because Emma was "struggling" with certain doctrines she had heard from Joseph. Sarah hadn't said what those doctrines were, but she had hinted that there were bad feelings between Emma and Eliza Snow. Liz had felt something strange in Sarah's reticence, and she had wondered whether there were not a connection to the rumors she had heard. All of it had worried Liz, even frightened her. "Do you think President Young and the Twelve will teach these things?" she asked.

"Yes, I think they will. I think some of the Brethren already have more than one wife. But maybe it will only be leaders who will be asked to live that way."

"What if you were called to do so?"

"I'm sure I wouldn't be."

But it bothered her that Will didn't want to look at her. "Still, you could be, if what you say is right. So what will you do?"

"What would *you* do? Would you approve of such a thing?"

"Do you have to ask?"

"You wouldn't. And I would never enter into such a life. I couldn't."

"You might quite like it, I would think. There are pretty girls out there to chase after—and I'm not so pretty as I once was."

Liz knew she was pushing Will for the response she wanted, but she was surprised by how strong his reaction was. He dropped on his knees in front of her. "Liz, there's no woman as beautiful as you, but that's not the point. I loved you when I thought I had no chance at all to have you—and the Lord finally opened the way for us. I would never share what we have with anyone else. I couldn't. I absolutely couldn't. I love the Church, but I would go to hell if I had to, to avoid living a doctrine of that kind."

Daniel had stopped nursing and had fallen asleep, but Liz didn't move to put him down. She merely stared into Will's eyes. She had always known how much he loved her, and she didn't doubt it now. She loved him just as much, but she doubted he understood that. He had always treated her as his gift, as precious, and she couldn't imagine him sharing his love with another woman. But what was Will saying? "Do you have doubts about Joseph, then, the same as the dissenters?"

"No. Not at all. The Lord spoke to me more than once and told me Joseph was a prophet. But that doesn't change how I feel. I simply cannot take another wife. God asked Abraham to kill Isaac, and he was willing—but if God asked me to slay one of *my* sons—I would say no. I'd fail the test. I'm sorry, but I know I would. And I'll fail the test if the Lord—or anyone else—asks me to split my love with another woman. I've thought and thought about this, and I swear, I'll accept damnation rather than marry someone else."

"Then let's not think about it again. Let's just know that it's nothing we'll ever be part of."

"Aye. It's nothing we have to consider, ever."

"Who are the ones who might leave the Church?"

"Sidney Rigdon. He raised his hand for Brigham in the meeting, but he doesn't believe some of Joseph's teachings. And William Marks feels the same way. They'll fight to keep those doctrines out, but if Brigham and the Apostles continue to teach such things—even that marriage can be eternal—I don't know what they'll do."

"What about Emma?"

Will sat back in his chair. "Oh, Liz, I feel so sorry for Emma. She's trying to figure out what to do to take care of her family, and she's frightened. Brother Brigham came into town and didn't even go by to see her at first. She has to resolve all the money issues, and yet some of the property probably should belong to her. William Clayton says that Brigham never has gotten along well with Emma, and he's not reassuring her in any way. She only needs to know that all the debt of the Church isn't hers, and that some of the property will be available to give her a livelihood."

"And what if Brigham teaches plural marriage?"

"I don't think she'll ever accept it. She's close to William and Rosannah Marks, and I think, if they reject Brigham's leadership, she might side with them."

"We were all so unified in the meeting on Thursday. How can this happen?"

"It's how life always is, Liz. We try to create a perfect society and help one another to live as perfectly as Jesus. We just always fall far, far short."

Liz had seen that too. But she had Will, and she had her boys. And she had her sisters in the gospel. She couldn't solve all these problems, but she could cling to what she knew was true—and she could trust. The Twelve would lead the Church, and she would follow. "Even if we fall short, we have to keep trying," she said. "We need to create the best place we can."

"That's exactly right, Liz." He bent forward and kissed her, and then he kissed little Daniel. Jacob had been playing on the floor, but he came for a kiss too. And Liz thanked the Lord once again that they were all still together and that Jacob was still her child.

CHAPTER 25

Jeff had never been busier in his life, but he felt good about the things he was doing, especially in the elders quorum. A young man in the ward, Michael Sturdivant, was trying to work and go to college at the same time, and he was struggling with some of the papers he had to write. Malcolm decided Jeff was just the guy to tutor Michael, and as it turned out, he was right. Jeff liked the time he spent with Michael, working with his writing, but he learned also that the boy had lots of questions—and doubts—about his faith, and Jeff felt he was having a positive effect in the young man's life. At the same time, Malcolm was able to salvage a couple of used tires and put them on Michael's car—and then he ended up doing a brake job on the car while he had it in his shop. Sister Sturdivant, who was a single mom, cried when she told Malcolm and Jeff how much she appreciated what they were doing for her son. "He's starting to believe in himself," she told Jeff.

Jeff had experienced, as a missionary, what it was like to make a difference in someone's life, but he realized that after he returned to college, he had devoted almost all his time to himself. He had rarely looked about to see what others needed. He liked feeling "useful," and he realized how different his focus was becoming. Of course, part of that was also having little William in his life. Jeff found himself holding his son at times and trying to picture what the child's future would be. He thought of his own dad, who had always been steady and reliable. He had provided for his family and opened doors for Jeff and his sisters, making sure they could go to college and have experiences that enriched their lives. It was strange to think that just as his own career was beginning, it was already his son's future that had to matter more than his own. There were things he wanted out of life, but he couldn't pursue them if they compromised his family's future.

It was May now, over a year since Jeff had lost his job in California. It was strange to think that only one year had passed. He wasn't the same person who had come home with the news that he had been laid off. He knew he wouldn't want to pass through another year like this last one, and yet, he was thankful for the experience. He had always been taught that mortality was mainly an opportunity to learn and grow—and to pass the tests each person had to face—but all that had been made real now, and he felt grateful for what he had learned.

Jeff's great-aunt had sent him another little segment of his great-grandfather's life history. It told about the first year that Grandma and Grandpa Lewis had lived in Nauvoo. "I thought you would want to see this," his aunt had said. "Great-Grandpa Lewis mentions his house near Rich Street. Your father tells me that you live on the same street. I think you might also recognize some of the other landmarks he mentions."

Jeff certainly did recognize the landmarks: the riverboat landing close to Joseph and Emma's log house, now usually called the Homestead; the hillside west of the temple where meetings had been held; Joseph's store, now called the Red Brick Store. What interested Jeff most, however, was the hard struggle William and Elizabeth had faced. They had lived in a broken-down shack at first, and then they had had to settle for a two-room log cabin that some other men had helped Grandpa build while he was sick with cholera. Grandpa had promised his wife something better, but the two of them had been happy at least to have a house that was warm and cozy that first winter. As Grandpa Lewis described the house, the sheds and corrals, the animals he had raised, Jeff tried to picture it all. He wondered how his grandpa had dealt with his new life. He had dreamed of escaping poverty in England, dreamed of owning land, of prospering, but he had traded one kind of poverty for another—and he had worked from sunup until sundown every day, just as he had done in England.

Jeff had imagined Grandpa Lewis as stoic and single-minded, but he had written in his life history: "I had promised Liz's father that I would build her a fine house, and I suppose I thought that would be a simple matter once I landed in America, but we soon learned we had to make the best of things, just as all the other Saints were doing. Liz liked to tell me that our cabin was her castle, but it weighed heavily on my mind that I wasn't providing something better for her."

Somehow, Jeff had always assumed that once his grandpa had joined the Church he had marched forward, never looking back. It was good to know that the man had had his dreams and his disappointments, and that he had had to deal with his own inner struggles. Jeff had known that Grandma and Grandpa Lewis had lost their first little daughter, Mary Ann, after only a couple of weeks of life. He had seen that on the family group sheet. What he hadn't known was how devastated they had been. What didn't show up on the records was the little boy they had adopted and raised. Jacob.

Grandpa said in his account that he always thought of Jacob as his natural son and loved him as much as any of their children.

Jeff, of course, thought of his little Will. Modern science had kept him alive, and he and Abby hadn't had to give up the baby they loved. He was thankful for that, but he felt connected to old William and Elizabeth Lewis all the same, knowing that they had shared some of the same fears and worries.

One Saturday morning when the blue jays were screeching, Jeff walked back to his grandfather's lot. It seemed a different place now as he stood and thought about this little plot of land where Grandma had given birth to her first child—only to lose her—and then, where she started a family all the same, with little adopted Jacob. Jeff knew from the family records that another son had come the next year, and his name had been Daniel. It was through Daniel that Jeff's line of ancestry had come.

Jeff stood in the woods and tried to picture those two little boys learning to walk and then to run, and surely, even as toddlers, making first explorations into these woods. Little Daniel couldn't have imagined as a boy that generations would follow, and each one would look back to him for what he passed down to them.

"Daniel, thanks," Jeff said out loud. "This is where you started. I hope you know that I've come back to this spot."

Jeff thought of cycles. His own little William was one more life beginning, one more link in the chain. He had always known about generations, about genetic traits being passed along—even mannerisms and attitudes—but now he saw circle after circle, and he finally thought he was glimpsing the understanding that Joseph Smith had gained here. Joseph saw heaven, saw the connectedness of families, received the doctrines and the ordinances that could tie everything together. Christianity had lost this understanding, but Joseph Smith had heard the voice of God in Nauvoo, and he'd begun the process of sealing the generations one to another. Jeff loved the temple that Joseph had envisioned on the crest of the bluffs, and he understood why Joseph had worked so hard to see it finished—and why the Saints had kept building it even when they knew they would have to leave. This was holy land. Here William and Elizabeth Lewis had struggled just as he and Abby had struggled this last year, and life had rolled forward for the better part of two centuries, all joined in circles.

Jeff had read that sometimes Grandpa walked down a trail through the woods to get to the flat area by the river. So Jeff decided to make his own way through the trees in the same direction. He wanted to feel what the place might have been like back in those days. He was glad that the woods were still there, now part of Nauvoo State Park, with a lake in the center, and tall white oaks, some of them perhaps the "offspring" of the ones that existed back at the time that his grandpa had passed through. So Jeff avoided the nature trail and cut through a thicket of trees, and he tried to imagine those days when the Saints had lived in Nauvoo. At times he felt as though his great-grandfather William Lewis was actually walking with him.

• • •

Abby was glad that Jeff had taken a walk. He hadn't had much time to relax lately, and she worried about him. He did seem happy, as she had told him before, but she wondered all the same whether he weren't shaping his life to her needs and giving up on the things he'd always wanted.

Abby had been getting more sleep lately, as William sometimes slept most of the night. But he was staying awake much more in the daytime, and she knew she was much too indulgent about holding him, which he clearly loved. She told herself she was going to have to learn a little more "tough love" and not spoil him, but she also knew he had come into the world the hard way, with an intrusion into his body in his earliest days. She wanted his little spirit to forget all that and remember only a wonderful sense of being loved and cared for. She hated to think of him ever falling down and skinning his knee, or falling out of a tree—or any of the things that kids did to themselves. Jeff kept telling her not to think of him that way—that he was an ordinary boy now and had a right to experience the little knocks and bruises that came with that.

Maybe. But not yet. So she held him too much—and she knew within herself that she did it for herself as much as for him.

Abby did use William's nap times to study for her Sunday School class, putting in many more hours a week preparing than she probably needed to. The young people she taught didn't ask nearly so many questions as she had feared they might. But she couldn't help posing questions for them. She knew all the things she had been trying to grasp since joining the Church, and she wanted them to comprehend what they had inherited, not just wander through life the way some people did, "active" members, but not very committed. She loved the young men and women in her class, and she was glad that she had them to herself most of the time now. Jeff hadn't meant to dominate, but he sometimes had, and what she liked now was not so much "teaching" but building a spiritual connection with her students. They seemed to like her, and they even sought her out at times outside class, not necessarily to ask her questions, but to continue their friendship.

One young woman, Kristen Beaucamp, liked to talk about college. The girl was clearly very bright. She told Abby one day after church, "I've always been a good student. I've just wondered whether I could afford to go to college. My parents probably can't send me away to school, but I'm thinking I can manage if I can get a decent scholarship." And then she said something that Abby hadn't expected. "I want to be like you, Sister Lewis."

It was a simple statement, but it had changed Abby. She knew that she was doing more than preparing lessons for these kids—she was someone they looked to for direction in life.

But Kristen had also said something that *didn't* surprise Abby. "Part of why I want to be like you is so I can find someone like Brother Lewis." She laughed and turned red, but Abby understood—completely.

Abby was in the middle of changing a very nasty diaper when Jeff returned from his walk. "Hey, come with me. There's something I need to show you," he said.

"Just tell me where it is and I'll go look—while you clean up this son of yours."

"Oh, wow. That's a bad one. Isn't it time we toilet train that kid?

"Yeah, right. At four months."

"I will change his diaper, though. I don't take my turn very often."

But the face he was making made it obvious he was hoping she would turn him down. And she did. "I'll take care of him, if you get rid of this thing." She handed him the diaper, which he took with two fingers and carried outside to the garbage.

And then, once little William was wearing a new diaper, Abby pulled his Onesie into place and snapped it between his legs. "Okay. What is it you want me to see?" she asked Jeff.

"Wrap him up, and I'll carry him. It's in the woods."

Abby had to change her shoes and get a hoodie to wear, and the truth was, she didn't really want to wander into the woods, where the ground was probably still muddy, but she didn't say any of that. She was glad to have Jeff around this morning, and she did need to get outside more than she had lately.

So they walked into the woods, passed through the little clearing that Jeff liked to assume was his grandfather's lot, and then worked their way through some rather dense growth. Jeff was carrying William with both arms, protecting him from the limbs he bent back by turning sideways and pushing his shoulder through.

"Jeff, do we have to go through all this—"

"It's not very far." He kept making his way on through until they broke into another clearing. "Look up there," he said. "Do you know what that is?"

Abby looked up into a clump of tall trees. Toward the top was a cluster of large sticks, all interlaced and stacked like a bird's nest—but much too big for that. "I have no idea," Abby said. "It looks like a basket—big enough for a bear to sleep in."

"That's a pretty good guess—except that it's entirely wrong. That, my New Jersey city-girl wife, is an eagles' nest. I'll have to admit, I've never seen one before either, but I've seen pictures and I know that's what it is."

Abby had learned in the last few years that this was a time to pretend that she was *fascinated*. Jeff lived in a world where a discovery of this kind was exhilarating, and he had never really comprehended that most people weren't quite so amazed. "Wow," Abby said. "Why do they build such *huge* nests?"

"Well, they're big birds, for one thing. But eagles get married. They stick together in pairs. When chicks hatch out, they need a pretty big place. It's exactly the same reason Mormons build big houses."

Liz laughed, but she said, "The nest doesn't look very comfy."

"Yeah, I don't know if they line their nests with something soft or not. I can't tell from here."

"*Don't* climb up. Okay?"

Jeff laughed. "What makes you think I'd ever try a stunt like that?"

"I know you."

"Well, I did think about it."

He was smiling at her now, and little William was squirming in his blanket, trying to see out. Abby was struck in an instant by how much she loved these two. "Please don't teach William to be *quite* so curious as you are, okay?"

Jeff looked down at the baby. "Come on, Will, let's climb that tree right now. It's about time you learned how."

Abby shook her head, but she was smiling, too. Life with these boys would always be an adventure, she suspected. She looked back up at the eagles' nest. It *was* impressive, and she was glad that Jeff knew what it was—knew so many things. She decided she was even glad that so many things excited him. "So where are the eagles?" she asked.

"I don't know. The ones that come down here in the winter— from up in Wisconsin and northern Illinois—don't nest here. They go back home to have their babies. But the ones in this nest must live here year-round. Or they've moved out. I watched for a while, and no eagles were around."

The woods were full of sounds this morning: songbirds and creatures moving in the brush, even a bit of a breeze. Everything had come back to life these last couple of months. Abby liked to see it all, smell it. She was glad now that Jeff had dragged her down here.

"I'm thinking we should make like a pair of eagles and get our own nest," Jeff said.

"But what about the down payment?" They had actually looked at some houses in the last month, but prices were fairly high, and getting a loan sounded impossible.

Jeff stepped closer to Liz. He turned William so he was upright, sitting on Jeff's forearm. "I heard about a possibility this week—something that might work out for us."

"What kind of possibility?"

"The Poulsens have had their house up for sale for a year, but everyone is in the same shape we are these days. Prospective buyers like the house, but they can't get a loan. So Brother Poulsen was telling me he could rent it to us, with an option to buy, and part of our payment would go toward a down payment—you know, until we could save enough to qualify for our own loan."

"I'm not even sure what house you're talking about."

"It's an old house—nineteenth century—that they've done a lot of work on. But I guess it still needs a new kitchen." Jeff laughed. "That's what got Brother Poulsen thinking I might want to take it on. He said the work I would do could pay our rent at first. That would help us save, but also, if we decided not to stay, he would have a better property to sell."

"What about the Robertsons' place?"

"I still need to finish the windows, but I've done most of what he wanted. I talked to him the other day, and he said that anything I wanted to do was fine, but he was too busy to think about it. We can have free rent as long as we want. But I don't know. I feel kind of funny about that."

Abby was a lot more interested in the Poulsen proposal than she wanted to admit. But it was the idea of buying that she had liked—as a way of saying, "We're here. We're going to stay." Jeff had been hedging a little on that. Still, she decided not to have that conversation again. She only asked, "Have you seen the Poulsen place inside?"

"No. But Malcolm said it's not bad. It's not a dream house, but it's pretty nice, and it's right on Knight Street, close enough to walk to church."

Abby didn't feel excitement coming from Jeff—not that same pleasure he had taken in showing her the eagles' nest.

"Do you really want to stay here, Jeff? Or are you still thinking you want to go back to school?"

"I love Nauvoo. You know that. And I like what's happened to us here. Mostly, though, it just seems like it's time to build a nest and to hatch out some more chicks."

"Right away?"

"What? The house or—"

"No. The chicks."

"Your mother would come after me with an axe if you had another baby right away!"

"But you told her she's not going to make that decision for us."

"I know. But she had a point about—"

"I want another baby quite soon, Jeff."

"Really?"

"Don't you think we should have our kids close together and not spread them out over too many years?"

"Well . . . yeah. Whatever you want, I'd be glad to help."

"I'm serious. It's not what I *think* is best. It's what I've been *feeling* lately—and I don't exactly know why."

"Well, okay. It doesn't feel wrong to me."

"But, Jeff, you've got to be honest with me. Do you want to stay here?"

"Well . . . a daddy eagle picks a spot, builds a nest, and then he goes out and gathers up fish—and roadkill—and he brings the meat back and stuffs it in the mouths of his babies. That's probably what I ought to be doing. Unless you'd prefer bread and milk and Hamburger Helper—stuff like that."

She ignored his facetiousness and said, "But what about going back for your doctorate?"

"I don't know, Abby. Maybe a chance will come along, and we'll make a decision then. But it seems like we ought to move forward as a family—not always feel like we're waiting to get started."

She liked hearing that, but she still felt a certain hesitancy in Jeff, and she wondered how much of a compromise he was making in his own mind. "Last winter," she said, "when we'd drive along the river, we'd see all those eagles out soaring, hunting for something to snatch up and take home. But I always noticed, they would ride the wind, lean this way and that way, almost like they were skiing on the air. I'd always get the impression that it may be the eagle's job—you know, to fish and to 'feed the family'—but that he was also enjoying every minute of it."

"I don't know, Abby. It probably gets pretty routine to them. They—"

"Maybe so, Jeff. But I can't take all the soaring out of you. There has to come a time when you feed the family but feed yourself, too. Feed your soul."

Jeff nodded. "Maybe it's myself I need to change more than my job."

"You're doing that, honey. But I don't think you can be happy if you're not learning. That's just who you are."

"But there are all kinds of things to learn. Most of them don't come from college classes."

"You're a gifted man, Jeff. It's not right to ignore that and never find out what you could do with your life."

It was what Jeff wondered about so often, but he also knew he had to measure what the cost would be to Abby and to his children. He looked up at the nest and the blue sky above it. He wondered whether he could have both, whether there really was a place for him to soar. For now, though, he was happy he had a nest, and happy that Abby understood his need for sky.

CHAPTER 26

As autumn of 1844 came on, a little optimism had begun to return to the people of Nauvoo. The Saints did what they had always done best: they worked hard. They took up the work on the temple with new zeal and even harvested a fairly decent crop in spite of all the spring rain and the harassment they had experienced at planting time. Will began to work at his farm, but he didn't wander beyond it. He had heard the Samples brothers were home now, both up and around, and he wondered every day whether they were planning anything, but he saw no sign of them and, so far, heard no report that they were spreading accusations about him.

Ague came again in late summer, as always. Will experienced some recurrences of his own fevers and chills, but he was able to obtain quinine powder again, and that helped greatly. With the resurgence of work on the temple, he and his oxen were needed again. He devoted much of his time to the quarry, and to hauling stone, but he worked with Jesse and Daniel as often as he could, and all three harvested enough corn for their own winter needs and turned enough into cash to make payments on their land or to trade for other commodities.

Liz had become quite competent at curing pork and storing produce from her garden. Will was amazed at the strength she had developed. She was as beautiful as ever, as far as he was concerned, but her mother would have been shocked to see how tanned her skin was, how rough her hands had become, and what strong muscles she had developed in her arms. She had learned to pack her baby around on her hip the way other farm women did, and she could be firm with Jacob when she needed to. Will had even seen her give him a swat on his backside more than once, and somehow he had never expected to see that.

It hadn't taken long for Will to recognize that the Church was not leaderless. Brigham Young had spoken of the Twelve holding the authority, but Brother Brigham was the president of the quorum, and he was clearly directing the affairs of the Church. He was not a polished speaker but a powerful one, and he was not afraid to call the members to repentance. He offended some people with his bluntness, but Will liked his practical, no-nonsense way of doing things. When Will thought of Brother Joseph—and good Brother Hyrum—he felt their absence and knew that no one could replace such men. But Brigham wasn't going to allow the Saints to look backward. He was going to march the membership forward and chastise the stragglers along the way. Joseph had brought spiritual enlightenment to the world; Brigham was going to turn Joseph's doctrines into realities.

One October evening, after the nights had become cool and the days glorious, Will came into the house after doing his afternoon chores. "Walk out with me a little, Liz," he said. "There never was a finer evening."

"I've been wanting to do that," Liz said, and she took off her apron. "Come on, Jake," she said. "Should we walk outside?"

Will picked up Daniel and, once outside, swung him up on his shoulders. He was almost eight months old now, and a burly little boy. There seemed no question that he was going to be bigger than Jacob, and probably more of a handful. He laughed now to have this ride, and Will laughed to hear him.

They walked along the trail that they often used to cut through the woods to the lower part of the city. They came to a place where they could look down on Nauvoo and on the great bend in the river. Close to the river, the willow trees were a bright yellow, and among the houses and cabins were scattered maples, brilliant red. Chimneys were emitting smoke in gray columns that bent to the south and then diffused into a layer of haze, down the valley. But west, out over the river, the air was remarkably clear. The sun had gone behind some torn clouds just above the horizon, and everything—sky and clouds and river—was tinted in tones of amber. As they watched, the color gradually brightened, turned golden, and then began to take on shades of orange. Two great birds—blue herons, Will thought—swooped through all that golden light and skidded to a landing on the river, close to the shore.

"All this beauty—and the sunset—makes me think of Wellington Heath," Will said, his voice quiet.

"It's not very like it, though, is it?"

"Not really. But the light was like this sometimes in the fall, and the colors in the trees. There's not the pastures and hedges and sheep and all—but there's peace. Finally."

Jacob had found a stick to play with, and Daniel was squirming to get down. Will pulled him down from his shoulders but knew that Liz wouldn't want him crawling in the grass. When Daniel reached for his mum, she took him in her arms.

"Do you sometimes still wish you were home in England?" Liz asked.

"I wish I could see it again, and see my mum and dad and all the family, but I wouldn't want to work for another man ever again."

"Not even the Crawfords?"

"That wasn't so bad. But I still hold out hope that we'll someday have a better life than we could have had in England. After everything we've gone through these last two years, I still feel blessed that we're here."

"Well, we do have a good life," Liz said.

Will looked at her. She had given up almost everything, and she had to work very hard, and yet, she did seem satisfied.

"Do you still wish your sister would immigrate to Nauvoo?"

"I do wish she could come, but I don't think she should just now. No one's coming, and I understand why."

"But if things calm down, and people around here decide they can live with us, maybe there won't be so many problems. I keep thinking, maybe we can work things out so that we can have our temple and our life the way we like it, and no more bloodshed."

"But you always say that some of us will have to leave."

"Aye. It's the one thing that will take the threat away, so other folks don't worry so much about us."

"What if our leaders ask *us* to leave?"

"I don't know how that will be organized. Maybe some will be called to leave—or maybe enough will choose to leave that we won't have to. But if we're given our choice, I'd rather stay. Jesse and Dan and I have invested too much sweat out there in those fields just to let the work go for nothing. And I hate to think of Jake and Faith Winthrop, just arriving and already facing such hard things."

"Faith told me she's not sorry they came."

"I know. And maybe they'll be able to build something here.

I know I still see that brick house on our lot one day." He smiled at Liz. "And fine rugs on the floor and a pianoforte in our living room."

"Brother Benbow told you houses aren't so important, and you told me you believed him."

"I know all the things that are more important, but I still think I'd like to have something nicer for you and the children."

"Won't farming always be the same? As many bad years as good ones, and no way to get any savings put away?"

"Aye. That's the way of things. But Jesse and I talk about opening a business of some sort—along with our farming. During the winter, when the riverboats are stopped by the ice, a man could make a pretty penny on overland transport. We could add more oxen to our herd and keep busy all the months when the river is closed off. Certain goods still have to be carried north, even in cold weather."

"And I'd worry every minute you were gone. If boats unloaded below the rapids, in Warsaw, how would you dare go there?"

"That's the worry, all right. But who knows? I've thought of going to ol' George Samples and saying, 'How about the two of us becoming business partners?' If he thought he could make some money, you never know; he might say, 'These Mormon fellers ain't so bad after all.'"

Liz laughed at Will speaking like a backwoods American, but she said, seriously, "Will, you broke his head. You almost killed him *and* his brother. You always think you can change people's minds, but you will never change the Samples brothers."

"But it's going to take more of that sort of thing to change how people feel about us. It's not good to separate ourselves from others so completely. Zion is a fine idea, but we live in this county, and we need to trade with the people, do business, even compare beliefs and find out we're not so different as they think we are."

"You think you can make friends with *anyone.* But sometimes that's not possible."

"I know. One thing for sure, if we all start putting in crops again next spring, Tom Sharp will be getting people riled up to come after us."

"And what will we do? Will we fight back?"

"No. I doubt it."

"What about you? What if George Samples comes after you one day? Are you going to try to reason with him then?"

Will had never told her about everything he had experienced in Carthage. The details, at the time, would have been too frightening to her. But now he said, "That first night when I arrived in Carthage with the Prophet, George Samples was there. He was shouting and threatening, and he tried to get to Joseph. I took hold of him, and I was about to throw him down on the ground, but Joseph grabbed my shoulder and pulled me back. He said, 'It's no use to fight them. It's what we have to learn.' He knew how quick I've been to take on a fight—and he was always that way, too—but he said he was putting his life in God's hands. It's what I'm trying to remember now."

"But we had the Legion, and Joseph talked about defending ourselves."

"I know. He unsheathed his sword. He told us to be ready to spill our blood if that was what it came to. But I think, when he saw all that hatred, he must have envisioned what would come if he kept the fight going. On the way over there, he seemed to know he was going to his death, and he accepted that. I think he did it so the rest of us wouldn't be destroyed. But his advice to me, personally, was not to fight. And that's what I'm trying to remember."

"What else could you have done? Two men were standing over you with guns pointed at you."

"They told me that if I'd promise to leave, they would let me live."

"You didn't believe that."

"No. I guess I still don't. But sometimes I wonder whether I shouldn't have accepted their promise and then moved away—the way I told them I would. I actually meant it at the time. I find myself thinking that I've broken my promise by staying."

"Will, that makes no sense. It's not a true promise when a man threatens to kill you—and has a gun pointed at your head."

"But I wanted them to believe me and let me go. So maybe we still need to leave."

"No. That's what the mob wanted in Carthage. They're willing to kill some of us in order to drive the rest of us away. And that's not right. We own our land. They can't force us to leave."

"That's true. But I don't ever want to strike a man like that again. I've used my muscles way too much already in my life. I want to be better than that."

· · ·

Liz was moved by Will's sweet desire to be a better man. She hoped he was right—that he never would have to fight again. But there was too much evil around them. She hoped he would always be willing to defend her and her children.

The sun was sliding deeper behind the horizon, and the clouds were red-orange now. The river was glowing. But Daniel was losing his interest in standing around. He wanted to be down on the ground with Jacob. "Put Danny back on your shoulders," Liz said, "and come with me. Jake and I found something back in the woods, didn't we, Jakey? Let's show Papa what we found."

She took Jacob by the hand and led Will off the trail into the woods. The underbrush was dense enough that the going wasn't easy. Liz was also not sure she knew exactly where they had been before. She had to pick up Jacob to get him through the bushes, but they finally broke into the little clearing they had found a few days earlier. High in a cluster of black walnut trees was a great nest, but she was startled by what she spotted there. An eagle, its white head taking on the orange light of the sunset, was standing atop the nest, looking out toward the river as though it were enjoying the sunset.

"Oh, look," she whispered.

But Will had already seen it, and even little Daniel was looking up, as though he understood that he was seeing something glorious. The four stood and watched the eagle for quite some time, but Jacob was a little too noisy, and suddenly the great bird lifted and flew off toward the river.

"Does it have chicks in the nest?" Will asked.

"I don't know. We only saw the nest before. I didn't even know for sure that it was an eagles' nest."

"Maybe by now the chicks have left the nest for this year," Will said. "But there must be a pair. That's how they live."

"Don't the males ever run off and look for a different mate?"

"No. I think they stay together all their lives."

That seemed right to Liz, but it brought up the issue that had been troubling her. She wasn't sure she wanted to say what she had been thinking, but she felt she had to, and this might be as good a time as any. "Will, we shouldn't have said those things we said— about men having more than one wife."

Will's head popped around. "What do you mean?"

"You said that the doctrine might be from God, but you would go to hell before you lived it."

"That's how I feel. I can't help it."

"I guess I do too. But we can't ask so much of God as we've asked, and then say we'll choose what doctrines we'll live and which ones we won't. I keep thinking of you telling God no—that you would never sacrifice your son—but that means giving up on being like Abraham. Is that what you want?"

Liz watched Will wrestle with her question, looking intently into her eyes the whole time. "Maybe God can ask too much, Liz. Maybe I just know what I can do and can't do—and I have to hope that a test like that will never come my way. Maybe some of us could never be like Abraham, however much we tried."

"But we did give Jacob to Brother Clarkston when he came back and asked for him."

"No. You did. I was ready to fight."

"But you let me do it. You accepted when you had to. And then we got our son back. That's how it works with the Lord sometimes, don't you think?"

"Aye. But some things, I hope the Lord will never ask."

"Will, I feel the same way. But let's not vow to defy God. We've come too far for that."

"All right. I won't vow. But I still know what I can do—and cannot—and I expect I won't change."

Liz was satisfied with that. The last thing she wanted to hear was that he was ready to take another wife. She thought again of the eagles, paired for life. She liked that two animals could comprehend that it was best to stay together and bless one another's lives. She nestled closer to Will. "Tell me this," Liz said. "Does the male eagle do all the fishing and hunting?"

"I don't know. I think males and females both do that. But here's what's interesting. The females are actually bigger than the males. So maybe they're better hunters. I think they do trade back and forth."

"How do you know such things?"

"What things?"

"That female eagles are bigger than males."

"I don't know. Things interest me. I read it, or heard it somewhere, and it stuck in my head."

Liz was still holding Jacob, and Will had Daniel. Liz took Will's arm, so the four of them were all locked together. "You're my eagle," she said. "Did you see how that one stood there, so magnificent, like he knew he was just about the finest-looking bird in the land?"

"Is that what you think I am? Too impressed with myself?"

"No. I think you're magnificent—and you look the part, too."

"That might have been the female, for all we know."

"I think that's how things should be," Liz said. "The two of them look out for one another, work together, raise a family. I'm afraid we make life too complicated most of the time. Sticks seem to make a pretty good home."

"Aye. It's true. Maybe I worry too much about that."

Liz felt a surge of spirit, telling her that life was good. The truth was, she didn't feel safe—never did anymore—but Will would look after her, and she would look after Will, no matter what dark times might lie ahead.

AUTHOR'S NOTE

Through Cloud and Sunshine is my 100th published book. Some people write one blockbuster and then retire. That hasn't worked out for me. I've been "at it" for thirty-four years. There will be one more book in this series, and then who knows? I might look around for a nice rocking chair.

Actually, I'm not ready to retire just yet, but lately I've thought about it. I think this has been the most difficult book of all 100. The challenge of writing about Nauvoo is not that information is hard to find, but that too much is available. It was hard to know where to stop the research and even harder to know how much historical information to include. I drafted and redrafted the book ten or eleven times, and much of my effort was devoted to cutting, trying to create a good novel, not a historical textbook. Still, I hope you learned something about the city that was called the "center place of Zion" and at the same time came to care about the characters.

In the preface to this book I described the challenge of trying to see through the filter of one's own time to comprehend another era. But that's not easy. I suspect that if Joseph Smith or one of the

412 · AUTHOR'S NOTE

Apostles from his time were to preach in a worship service today, he might shock a modern congregation. For one thing, he would probably look unkempt. Men often owned one suit of clothes, cut and sewn with rough fabrics, and instead of sending those clothes to a dry cleaner, they brushed them off and kept wearing them. They surely looked rumpled, and they didn't bathe or shave as often as men do now. Their teeth were often bad, and as people grew older, they usually had spaces where teeth had been pulled. But more than anything, their sermons probably would have sounded strange to us. Not only did they speak for hours, but they often speculated, starting with an idea and developing it right on the spot. Joseph Smith was not as flamboyant as some, but he was full of surprises. Many of his speeches offered a new "take" on the doctrine, and he liked homey analogies, humor, and sometimes a challenge to enemies of the Church.

Because I had the notes from many meetings held in Nauvoo, it was tempting to put them in the book, complete with some of the procedures and the interesting and sometimes quirky content of the talks. I'm sure it's a good thing that my trusted editors helped me extract some of that, but if you're as strange as I am, and find such stuff interesting, I'll offer you some sources in this Author's Note.

The point I'm making is that we can probably never fully know Nauvoo and its people. What I have tried to show, however, is that human beings, inside, don't change very much from one era to another. The loss of a baby hurt just as much then as it does now, even though so many more were lost in the nineteenth century.

The last thing I want to do is to "tell you what I've told you," but I do want to say that to a large degree, we have "made up" the early Saints. We've inherited stories of faith and passed them along, but we've tended to discard the less comfortable accounts. We've used our filter to make the people quite different from what they probably were. That's the nature of history, especially the oral history that has come down to us. I keep saying this in various ways, but we do need to get over the idea that the pioneers were made of better stuff than we are. Certainly many of them were strong and stalwart, just as some in our time are, but their pains were the same, and so were their fears, their flaws, and their self-doubts.

What I hope is that you've come away from this book wanting to learn much more about Nauvoo. There are more resources than I can offer you here, but let me recommend some of the best books that I've used in my research.

I said in my Author's Note to volume 1 of this series that the best general history of Nauvoo is Glen M. Leonard's *Nauvoo: A Place of Peace, A People of Promise* (Deseret Book, 2002). It's organized by topics and contains a great treasure of information on the Mormon years in Nauvoo.

In Old Nauvoo: Everyday Life in the City of Joseph, by George W. Givens, provides lots of insights into the way people lived. And *500 Little-Known Facts about Nauvoo,* also by George W. Givens (Bonneville Books, 2010) is replete with interesting, sometimes surprising Nauvoo trivia. Samuel W. Taylor's *Nightfall at Nauvoo* (Avon, 1974) has remained controversial for its novelistic style and its lack of documentation, but it's provocative and fun to read.

Joseph Smith's *History of the Church* (Deseret Book, 1978), usually referred to as the "Documentary History," along with B. H. Roberts's *A Comprehensive History of the Church of Jesus Christ of Latter-day Saints* (BYU Press, 1965), is always a good starting place for LDS history. What has added greatly to these two sources is the Joseph Smith Papers Project. All Joseph Smith's known papers are being published (Church Historian's Press and Deseret Book) and made available online (josephsmithpapers.org). So far two volumes of his journals, two volumes of his revelations and translations, and two volumes of his histories have been printed, and in 2013 two volumes of documents will be in print.

Biographies have been written of most of the early Church leaders who lived in Mormon Nauvoo. There are far too many to list here, but one resource to mine first is your own family heritage if you had family that lived there. Two books that will help you understand important figures in Nauvoo's history and tie these individuals to the events of the time are *Joseph Smith: Rough Stone Rolling* by Richard Lyman Bushman (Knopf, 2005), and *Brigham Young: American Moses* by Leonard J. Arrington (University of Illinois Press, 1986). *Women of Faith in the Latter Days, Volume 1, 1775–1820,* and *Volume 2, 1821–1845,* edited by Richard E. Turley and Brittany A. Chapman (Deseret Book, 2011–12), along with *In Their Own Words: Women and the Story of Nauvoo* by Carol Cornwall Madsen (Deseret Book, 1994) help fill a void by providing histories of many women who lived in Nauvoo.

If you should travel to Nauvoo and wish to locate historical sites and buildings, two good resources are *Sacred Places, Ohio and Illinois* by LaMar C. Berrett (Deseret Book, 2002), and *Old Mormon Nauvoo and Southeastern Iowa* by Richard Neitzel Holzapfel and T. Jeffery Cottle (Fieldbrook Productions, 1990). A remarkable new source contains an exhaustive set of maps, photos, and information on Mormon history and includes an excellent section on Nauvoo: *Mapping Mormonism: An Atlas of Latter-day Saint History,* edited by Brandon S. Plewe, S. Kent Brown, Donald Q. Cannon, and Richard H. Jackson (Brigham Young University Press, 2012). A beautiful photographic portrayal of Nauvoo is *Nauvoo* by John Telford, Susan Easton Black, and Kim C. Averett (Deseret Book, 1997).

Some books on specialty topics, such as *The Nauvoo Legion: A History of the Mormon Militia, 1841–1846,* by Richard E. Bennett, Susan Easton Black, and Donald Q. Cannon (University of

Oklahoma Press, 2010), and *Nauvoo Temple: A Story of Faith* by Don F. Colvin (Covenant, 2002) add detailed information on subjects of particular interest.

Not all my information came from books. I "Google" a great deal these days. When I want to know about farming with oxen, coins and currency in the nineteenth-century, clothing, food—and dozens of other things—I can often find websites that are of great help. Many of the issues of the *Times and Seasons,* the *Wasp,* and the *Nauvoo Neighbor* can now be found online, and they offer very interesting "real time" historical records.

I often emailed or called my friend Lachlan Mackay, who manages the Community of Christ historical sites. He lives in Nauvoo and knows it well. He could almost always answer my questions or guide me to the right sources. He also recommended *The Memoirs of President Joseph Smith III (1832–1914),* edited by Richard P. Howard (Herald Publishing House, 1979), which contained wonderful memories from Joseph III's childhood in Nauvoo.

Kathy and I served our mission in Nauvoo under the leadership of President Robert Ludwig. Julie Roper, daughter of Bob and Martha Ludwig, gave birth during that time to a baby with a serious heart defect. All the missionaries in Nauvoo prayed and waited for news of little Adam, out in Denver. As it turns out, Adam is doing very well, and he served as inspiration for my story about little William. The heart defects I describe were not exactly the same as Adam's, but some long telephone calls to Julie helped me understand the experience of having a child in a neonatal intensive care unit. Abby's reactions were not modeled on Julie's. My story is certainly not Julie's. But I learned much that helped me to write about the experience parents go through when heart surgery is required immediately after a baby is born. So I appreciate her help.

What taught us most about Nauvoo was living there for two

years as we served a public affairs mission. We shared the experience with hundreds of senior missionary couples, sister missionaries, and performing missionaries, but we also became friends with hundreds of local people, not only in Nauvoo but in many communities in Illinois, Iowa, and Missouri. We know every street, every outlying settlement, every nuance of weather, and every historic site, but above all, we know the good people of all faiths who continue to love and look after this sacred land. We never became tired of looking up the hill toward the temple, now restored, or just knowing that we were walking the streets that so many of our honored early Saints also walked. If you want to know Nauvoo, be sure to go there sometime in your life.

Something remarkable happened when we arrived in Nauvoo. We moved into a house on Warsaw Street (which had been known as Rich Street in the 1840s). We soon visited the Lands and Records Office in the historic area to learn where our own forebears had lived. As it turned out, Robert Harris Jr. and his wife, Hannah Maria, my third great-grandparents, owned a piece of land that is now part of Nauvoo State Park and is directly across the street from the house we lived in. I often walked over there and stood on my grandparents' land, and I tried to imagine them and their children living there. Is any of this sounding familiar? Well, the fact is, they probably didn't live there. They owned two other pieces of land, and all indications are that they decided to live east of Nauvoo, where most of the English Saints chose to settle. But you can see where ideas come from. And you can see why Kathy and I feel so connected to this sacred place. Living in Nauvoo changed us forever. We love the city and the people—all the people, of every faith—and I hope a sense of that love came through to you in this book.

Once again I have Emily Watts and Cory Maxwell to thank for their editorial guidance. I know this book is better than it would have been without their insights and patience. As to my wife, Kathy, what do I say? She read the book one last time, just before I submitted the final version, and she said she liked it—*really* liked it. That was the most important endorsement I could have received. Time and again, she helped me cut the things I didn't need and enhance the emotions and intensify the actions that go into creating a novel. I'm glad she's a tough critic, but even more, I appreciate her trust that I would eventually get it right. I hope I did.